PROMISE ME NOVEMBER

A NOVEL

L. B. JOYCE

Promise Me November ~ 1st edition
Print ISBN: 978-0-9600311-0-8
Ebook ISBN: 9781393930211

ALSO BY L. B. JOYCE

This book is the fourth in the series,
Twelve Months, Twelve Love Stories:
A Million Decembers
For the Love of July
February's Angel
Promise Me November
An Unexpected June
A January to Remember
September's Moonlight Serenade
Goodbye Heartbreak, Hello May

Holidays in White Oaks Valley:
A Grand Slam Kind of Christmas

I can't believe this is already the fourth book of the series! I've had so much fun writing each one, getting to know the characters and watching them grow. It's been said a romance novel is a story of two people who fall in love, with always an optimistic and satisfying ending. I can only hope, as you turn each page, you'll find this to be true.

Nobody said it would be easy.
They just promised it would be worth it.
~ Anonymous

CHAPTER 1

When two people are meant for each other,
no time is too long, no distance too far.
~ Anonymous

Why don't we take a trip back in time ... let's say about eight months ago ...

Carrie Mazzori looked up from her computer to see she had a visitor.

She smiled.

It was Sam. He had a bakery bag in one hand and a container of coffee in the other.

After she hit save for the interior design proposal she was working on, she leaned back in her chair, waving him towards the chair in front of her desk.

Still smiling, she studied him.

Sam Bridges restored homes for a living. But not ordinary homes. No, he had chosen to specialize in homes that not only claimed the age of one hundred and fifty years or older, but also those housing a wealth of historical secrets and information. With his flair for design, he had an eye for knowing what was needed to bring, what could be a house doomed for destruction, back to its former glory days. Each job he accepted received his complete attention, down to even the smallest detail.

Let's just say he was very good at his job.

Five years older than Carrie, he had the rugged good looks of a football player, having earned the title of all-star quarterback during his high school years. He then went on to surprise everyone by giving up the sport entirely when he went to college to major in architecture. Once he earned his degree, he made the decision to specialize only in the restoration of historical properties.

He had come into Carrie's life about year ago when they'd worked together on the same project, a restoration of a mansion in Shaker Heights. They'd immediately hit it off, at least as far as their interest in design was concerned. And since then, they'd collaborated on a few other projects.

He was witty, always in a good mood and quick with a smile.

He was also very single.

Over the past month or so, he'd been showing up more often at her office, sometimes only just to talk. Or he would bring her a coffee and scone from the coffee shop they met at occasionally.

This made Carrie wonder if he was looking for something more than just a business partnership. She was flattered by this, but as much as she liked him and the fact they had so much in common, he wasn't the man for her.

She valued his friendship, but she knew this is what he would always only be … a great friend.

She watched as he set the cup and bag on the desk. He followed this with a big sigh of relief as he plopped down into the chair.

After she took a sip of coffee, she peeked into the bakery bag. She was smiling when she looked over at him. "Blueberry?"

He nodded. "Yep, I got the last one. The lady next in line tried to wheel and deal it out of me, but I stood firm, knowing how much you like them."

He chuckled, shaking his head. "The things I do for you."

She laughed before she peeked in the bag again, giving a big sigh of pleasure. "Oh my gosh, Sam … you don't know how much I appreciate this. Because the way things are going, it looks like I won't even be able to take time for lunch. So, this is absolutely perfect."

When he merely nodded, she studied him more closely.

A big smile on his face, he looked like he was about ready to burst, eager to share some exciting news.

Caught up in his enthusiasm, she grinned at him. "So, what's up? You look like a cat who's swallowed a canary. I take it you've got some news you'd like to share?"

Typical of Sam, a teasing glint came into his eyes. "*Hmm* … a cat who swallowed a canary?" He shook his head. "You and your little phrases. I don't know where you get them from."

She was too busy eyeing the bag to comment on this. Something he understood. After all, it was her favorite. He chuckled. "Go ahead, I know you want to dig in. You can eat and listen at the same time."

He watched her remove the scone, knife and packet of butter out of the bag as he spoke. "And you're right. I do have good news. Along with a proposition for you, a big one. So, keep those lips sealed and hear me out until the end."

After she nodded, he spoke, his excitement coming through in his voice. "I've just received a job offer, this one of all places, coming out of Quebec."

Observing her raised eyebrows, he nodded "Yes, Quebec. The very Quebec we know as being all the way over in Canada. This particular project involves the restoration of an early nineteenth century mansion once owned by one of the up-standing and wealthier families in the area. From the photos I've seen, even though the structural part of the estate seems to be in good shape, the interior is in dire need of a complete overhaul. And this is now going to be possible with the huge grant the city's historical society finally received. I guess they've been lobbying for this grant for quite a long time."

Here he had flashed that boyish grin of his at her. "I was told after going through a long list of possible candidates and viewing every-one's work, the society board members have come to the unanimous decision I'm the man for the job."

When she opened her mouth to comment, he held up his hand, his grin becoming even bigger. "Hold your applause, lady. Remember, lips sealed. Let me finish."

After she rolled her eyes, he watched as she buttered another piece of the scone before he continued. "But you can imagine the complexity of this project. If I decide to take it on, I'm going to need help. A lot of help. With a time-line of less than six months, this is far too big for me to tackle on my own."

He leaned forward in his seat. "And this is where you come in, Carrie. I want you to be my partner for this job. With my knowledge of restoration and your flair for design I know, together, we'll make this mansion shine as it had in the height of its glory days."

An earnest expression came over his face. "Carrie, this is such a great opportunity. For the both of us. Just think, we'll be able to show everyone the work we're capable of, not only here in the states, but maybe even in other parts of the world as well. Why, the possibilities are endless."

He sat back in his seat, an expectant expression on his face. "So, what do you think?"

Completely overwhelmed by his proposal, at first Carrie had no idea what to say. Which was ridiculous. An opportunity like this didn't come along very often, if ever. Especially to someone as young as she was and so new to the business.

Come on, you know you'd be crazy to pass up a chance like this. Tell him yes.

But at the same time, a part of her wasn't willing to make this move. She'd be out of the country for six months, probably even longer. She knew how these projects always tended to run longer than planned. Delays were inevitable. And then there was Chris …

Chris?

Yes, Chris Gardner... the man who knocked you off your feet and sent you into a place you now have no idea of how to deal with. A man who also said he was going to call. Over two weeks ago, he promised this.

Yeah, but he hasn't. At least not yet, he hasn't.

But she was refusing to give up hope.

Because, again … he promised. And she was pretty sure he wasn't the type of guy who would break his promise.

A girl could dream, couldn't she?

"Carrie?"

She blinked to find Sam waving his hand at her, a curious expression on his face. "Are you still with me?"

Embarrassed, she shook her head. "I'm sorry. I was thinking … well, I guess …. *Wow.*"

She sent him a bright smile. "I feel so honored you thought of me. It sounds like a wonderful opportunity and I know it would be amazing to work with you on such an interesting project."

"Can I have a little time to think this over? I need to check my calendar, too. I have to make sure taking on such a big project won't mess up any of the other jobs I've got going on right now."

She hesitated before she went on to add. "And there's something else I have to work out. A personal thing. I'm sorry to leave you hanging, but this is the best I can give you right now."

He stood, a disappointed smile on his face. "Sure, but don't take too long. If we do this, we'll need to start making plans."

Then he smiled his usual smile. "How about dinner tonight? I promise not to utter a single word about business." Here he hesitated, his eyes searching her face intently before he spoke. "No, this will be all pleasure. Two close friends sharing a glass of wine and a great meal."

At the hopeful expression on his face, she was tempted. But she shook her head. "Oh Sam, I'm sorry. I'm afraid I can't. I have this client consultation later this afternoon and I have a feeling it will probably go into the evening hours. This woman can't make up her mind for the life of her. Even a simple decision about doorknobs sends her into a tizzy."

She checked her calendar. "Maybe later on this week? Thursday?"

"Sure, I'm going to hold you to that. By then, I hope you'll have your answer on Quebec, oui?"

He chuckled. "And that, my dear, is about the extent of my grasp of anything French."

He suddenly looked worried. "I hope this won't be a problem. We will be working with people who also speak English, right?"

She laughed as she walked him to the door. "I'm sure it will be fine. In the meantime, it couldn't hurt to brush up on your French. You can't rely on 'oui' as your answer for everything. This could very easily get you into trouble."

She patted him on that arm as she reached up to give him a kiss on his cheek. "I'll call you soon. Very soon, I promise. And thanks again for the coffee and scone."

After giving her a thumbs-up, he left.

She made it back to her desk just as her phone rang. It was a call she'd been waiting for all morning and demanded her complete attention. Tucking Sam's proposal in the back of her mind, she made a vow to herself she'd make her decision by the end of the day.

Maybe, just maybe, something would happen by then.

Like a long-awaited phone call, perhaps?

Carrie made the turn out of her office parking lot.

She was exhausted.

It had been a day filled with a million and one problems. Problems you can't seem to fix. One after another, they just keep coming right at you.

All day long.

Almost eight hours had passed since Sam had stopped by her office. And now it was already dark.outside. It was also pouring. As she drove, she could barely see, her windshield wipers going at full speed against the heavy rain.

When she finally turned into her driveway, she gave a big sigh of relief. Never before had her little house looked more welcoming.

On her longer than usual commute due to the weather, she'd had plenty of time to think about how she was going to spend her evening. First things first, she would change into her pajamas. Then she'd definitely have a glass of wine with dinner. Only after this would she go over her notes of today's meetings and enter all of the data into her computer. Hopefully, then it would all come together.

By the time she sprinted from the garage to the house, she was soaked. After she flipped a switch, flooding the kitchen with light, she dropped her computer case and purse on the island countertop. She shrugged out of her coat and hung it, dripping wet, on the hook by the door.

Once she'd turned on the lamps in the main living area and started up a fire in the fireplace, she wrapped her arms around herself, rubbing her arms to get warm.

She slowly gazed around the room, giving a long, contented sigh.

She loved her little house.

She liked to think she'd adopted it, saving it from it from destruction to bring it back to happier times. And now it was almost impossible to remember back to when she first saw it, abandoned and almost swallowed up from view in the waist-high weeds.

When she'd first contemplated making an offer on the house, everyone had warned she was making a huge mistake. It would be crazy to tackle such a huge project by herself, they told her. Why not buy something new and ready to move right in?

Vacant for at least a dozen years, or maybe more, everything had needed to be replaced or redone. The roof was leaking and most of the windows were either broken or completely non-existent and boarded up. Both the kitchen and the one teeny, tiny bathroom were unsalvageable.

They also discovered a very active and rapidly expanding family of mice living in the basement. Along with a pair of very unfriendly raccoons camping out in the rafters of the attic.

But, trusting her intuition, she had decided to go for it. Her offer was accepted and just like that, she was a home owner.

And now?

She had what she believed was the perfect house.

It wasn't a large space, but more than big enough for her. Because of the limited space, she'd kept the décor very simple. The kitchen had white shaker style cabinets, the butcher block counters and hardwood floors were a natural maple. The walls were a cheerful, but subtle yellow. Early Sunshine was the name of the paint color.

She had chosen this shade for a reason. With how the kitchen was situated, it was the first room the sun made its debut every morning

For the rest of the first floor, she went all out.

She knocked down walls to give the area an open look, making the fireplace, with the original, hand carved oak and marble mantel, the focal point of main room. She painted this white to match the woodwork and crown molding and the shade she chose for the walls was a light blue-green color called Ocean Breeze. She had decided on the same natural maple hardwood floors that were in the kitchen, these continuing up the stairs and throughout the second floor.

She was happy with her decision to add the floor-to-ceiling arched windows, one on each side of the fireplace. Before the room had been so dark, the screened-in porch blocking the incoming light. But after removing the porch, adding new windows and refreshing the color of the walls, room was now bright and filled with light.

The sofa and side chairs arranged in front of the fireplace were upholstered in a white chenille-like fabric. While a collection of throw pillows picked up the vibrant splash of colors of the area rug.

And the finishing touch, what she considered her one big extravagance?

This was a large arrangement of fresh flowers on the glass coffee table. The random blooms, in all the colors of the rainbow, were something she faithfully replaced every week.

If you ever get married, something that's looking like a long shot right now, this is the kind of bouquet you want to have for the wedding.

But back to her house …

There was one last thing she needed to do. This was to find something to put over the mantel. She was having a hard time with this. Whatever she finally chose, she wanted it to be perfect.

Oh … and let's not forget the front door.

Original to the house, she had spent hours removing the many layers of paint applied over the years. Now all sanded and prepped, it was waiting for a fresh coat of paint. Her plan was to have this done before the holidays.

If only she could decide on a color. Right now, she was leaning towards a warm red.

With a loud purr, Jingles began weaving her way around Carrie's feet, her tail wrapping around her legs.

After she picked up the snow white long-haired cat and, hugging her close, carried her across the room where she pressed a small pad on the wall.

Josh Groban's voice flowed through the room.

She had splurged on this option to have music piped throughout the house. That she was able to change the music to fit her mood with just a simple touch of a button felt like such a luxury to her. She had even talked her brother Chester into installing the same feature when she did the interior decorating for his condo.

A long meow erupted from Jingles, a sign she was getting impatient and more than ready for her dinner.

This prompted Carrie to start up the stairs, the cat in her arms. Pressing a kiss to the top of her head, she smiled down at her. "Jingles, I know you're hungry. Let me change and then we'll have dinner. I don't know about you, but, it's been a long day. And just like you, I'm starving."

After the last of her dinner dishes were loaded in the dishwasher, Carrie sat down at the island and turned on her computer.

She glanced over to see Jingles had curled up on one of the chairs by the fireplace. Her hunger appeased and her grooming completed, she was now keeping watch over Carrie with hooded eyes.

While she waited for the client page she needed to come up on the screen, Carrie sat back in her seat, her thoughts going to Sam and the conversation they had.

She knew she was being foolish. She should call him right this very minute and tell him yes, she was in. The fact she hadn't already done this was absolutely insane.

You're basing your decision on a man, for all you know, may have already forgotten you even exist.

And once again, here she was, getting caught up in her memories of Chris. But, for the life of her, she couldn't talk herself into forgetting him.

This was because when she and Chris first met, even though it started out with him dumping his entire drink down the front of her dress, something out of the ordinary had happened.

Or as she liked to think, someone or something had suddenly come out of the blue to wave a magic wand over them.

And with that one simple action, everything had changed. Almost as though the universe had slowed down just enough for both of them to come together in the same place and at the same time.

Just like that …

Maybe a match made in heaven?

You'd like to think so.

That he was a complete stranger and she knew so little about him, none of this mattered in the least.

It was just so, so right.

After he'd gone back to New York, she hadn't been able to stop thinking about him. He'd become a permanent fixture in her mind, all of the feelings he'd stirred up inside of her, still there and going strong.

And this frightens you … because, come on, how could one unexpected and totally random meeting, with a complete stranger, make you feel this way?

Giving a frustrated sigh, she glanced over at the calendar hanging next to the refrigerator.

It had now been two weeks and four days since she and Chris met at Abby and Kevin's wedding.

And yes … she'd been counting the days.

During this time, the only contact she had from him were the three texts he had sent. These were in the two days after the wedding.

The texts had been very casual texts. The kind of text a friend would send. They were to let her know he'd made it back safely to

New York, he would always remember how they first met and he would be calling her.

But maybe when she'd responded to the last text, the one informing her he'd be calling her, she should've asked him to be more specific?

Like, exactly when was he planning to call? Would this be soon? In a few days? Weeks? Or maybe just sometime in their lifetime?

Yes, this would've been nice to know. Since, as of that last text, she hadn't heard another peep from him.

Nope.

No text.

No call.

No email.

Absolutely nothing.

Which is a good indication it's over and you won't be hearing from him at all.

So, the smart thing for her to do would be to forget about him.

But she couldn't.

She wanted one more chance. She wanted this so badly, it was all she could think about. She wanted to find out if she still felt the same heart-stopping-breathless-this-is-it-feeling she experienced during the time they spent together, as short as it was.

She was pretty sure he had also been rocked by the instant chemistry that flared up between them. Leaving them to stutter their way through their first few minutes together.

Yep, she'd bet the whole carton of rocky road ice cream she had in the freezer on this.

So, why do you think he never called?

And therein lies the real problem. Because as much as she didn't want to admit this, she always came to the same conclusion.

It was really very simple ... he'd merely changed his mind.

Chris had swooped into her life as her hero, in what was to become their own little fairy tale.

At least this is what you'd like to think happened.

Now granted, spilling his drink on her wasn't a prince-like thing to do. Nor was it the best of beginnings. And she didn't even want to even think about what happened after that, when he showed up just in time to rescue her from the unwanted advances of Doug, her poor choice of date for the evening. Because after that, the evening had only gone on to get better with every passing second.

Yes, their time together had been magical—a Cinderella-goes-to-the-ball kind of night.

A night every woman should be so lucky to experience at least once in her lifetime.

She and Chris had gone on to dance every dance until the band played their last song. After taking the shuttle to the hotel where he'd reserved a room for the wedding, they'd settled on the sofa in front of the fireplace in the lobby. It was there they shared their thoughts, their dreams and even a few secrets until the early light of dawn began to filter in through the skylights of the lobby. And the fire in the fireplace had been reduced to a pile of faintly glowing embers

He'd insisted on sharing her taxi ride home, to make sure she arrived safely. The good-bye kiss he gave her was touched with a hint of uncertainty about what was to come next. Yet at the same time, it was a kiss that held the promise of so much more.

She liked to think, for him, it was a kiss telling her he'd give anything to stay. While for her, it was a kiss letting him know she didn't want him to leave.

She closed her eyes, the vision of how he sprinted to the waiting taxi, so clear her mind. She could still see the crooked smile he gave her, the words he called out engraved in her memory.

"I'll call you ... honest, I promise."

And, now here she was, still waiting for his call.

She blinked.

She was a fool.

Now, sitting here in her kitchen, she came to the decision this was the only explanation. What she'd believed was a beginning, in reality, it had been the end.

She shook her head. *Yeah, you believed it was real. Even more pathetically, you believed him.*

She gave a frustrated groan and slapped the cover of her computer shut, the loud snapping noise slicing through the stillness of the room.

This brought an incensed meow from Jingles as she came flying off the chair. After she stopped for a moment to glare over at Carrie, she gave an irritated jerk of her head and went shooting up the stairs. Carrie knew she would later find her, all curled up on her bed and sound asleep.

Crossing her arms tightly across her chest, she stared angrily into the flames flickering in the fireplace.

I'll call you ... honest, I promise.

She blinked away the beginning of angry tears.

What in the world had she been thinking? If anyone should know not to believe any promise coming from a man, it would be her. Why, judging from just about every kind of behavior she'd experienced in the past, it was obvious the word promise shouldn't even be a part of a man's vocabulary.

With an irritated sigh, she picked up her wineglass and after tossing what wine remained in the sink, she put the glass in the dishwasher. She plugged her phone into the charger, turned off the gas flame in the fireplace and turned out the lights.

She was going to bed.

Again, it had been a really long day.

The bright morning sunshine, coming across the bed and shining in her face, was what woke Carrie the next morning. She squinted over at her alarm clock to see she'd overslept.

Sitting on the edge of the bed, she groggily ran her hands through her hair. In a perfect world, she'd already be in her car and driving to her office right now.

She hadn't slept well.

She'd gone from one dream to the next and in each dream, she was always chasing that elusive man. You know the one, not ready to settle down, let alone take the time to even listen to what you had to say.

Dragging herself out of bed, she showered and dressed before she headed down to the kitchen. Her first order of business, to call her assistant Marion and let her know she would be later than usual, she picked up her phone from where it was charging on the counter.

Her heart almost coming to a standstill, she briefly closed her eyes. She looked at the phone again. She must be hallucinating.

Nope, there it was, staring her right in the face. The message there was a call from Chris.

He'd finally called?

According to what showed on her phone, he'd called last night at 9:31 p.m.

Puzzled, she glanced up from the phone and staring into space, she tried to think back to the events of last night.

How did you miss this?

This had to have happened when she was upstairs getting ready for bed.

So ... after she'd almost convinced herself it was over, he wasn't to be trusted, he was just like every other man out there and the best thing she could do was forget all about him ...

Then he calls?

And you missed it? Didn't this figure.

She checked again to see if he'd left a voice mail.

He had.

Her heart beating a mile a minute, she hit voicemail and turned on the speaker. As his voice filled the room, she sank down on one of the stools at the kitchen island.

> *"Carrie, it's Chris. I'm so sorry I*
> *haven't called you. I can't even begin*
> *to tell you sorry I am about this. I've*
> *been out of town and it's been non-stop*
> *hectic. Crazy. Yes, I know. I have no*

*excuse. I should've called like I
promised. But to tell you the truth, I
didn't want to call and then have to
hang up because of another call.
Again, I know this sounds like I'm
once I hear your voice again, I won't
want to hang up at all."*

There was a silence, bringing Carrie to lean even closer to the phone. She closed her eyes, giving a sigh of relief when his voice once again traveled throughout the silent room.

*"Carrie, I want to see you again. I've
been thinking about you. No, this is
an understatement. It's more like I
can't get you out of my mind. There
was something between us, something
I think we really need to pursue. If
this works for you, I could come to
Cleveland this coming weekend. I'll
book a hotel room for myself and we'll
just take things as they come. Maybe
you can show me the sites or whatever
you'd like to do. I don't care. As long
as I'm with you, I know I'll be happy.
So, call me when you can. Call me
anytime. Night... day, I don't care.
Just call me."*

There was another pause. As she began to wonder if this time he was finally gone for good, he spoke.

*"Promise you'll save all of your kisses
for me. Umm... okay, then. After that
I think I better hang up. God knows*

> *what I might say next. Again, call*
> *me ... soon."*

She stared down at the phone, a huge smile on her face.

She listened to the message again.

And then, she played it again.

She checked the time. It was 9:44 a.m. Not too early to call him back. She took a deep breath, picked up her phone and hit call.

She waited.

A woman answered. "Hello?"

Uh oh ... this is not at all what you were expecting.

Her mouth suddenly dry, she tried to speak, but nothing came out.

The woman spoke again, an irritated tone creeping into her voice. "Hello? Who Is this? Hello?"

Carrie cleared her throat, her voice finally coming out in a husky whisper. "Hi. I'm calling for Chris."

"Chris is not here. Who is this calling?" The woman's reply was sharp. She had the kind of voice demanding an immediate answer.

"I ... it's Carrie. I mean ..." She cleared her throat again. "I met Chris a few weeks ago, at a wedding in Cleveland. He called me last night and left a message, so I'm returning his call."

Do you really need to give this woman all of this information? Who is she? And why is she answering Chris's phone? Did she work with him?

But she couldn't seem to shut up. For some reason she was filled with this sudden need to defend her reason for calling. Taking a deep breath, she spoke in what she felt was a more confident tone of voice. "He ... Chris, that is, wanted to let me know he was planning on coming to Cleveland this weekend. And well, I wanted to let him know this would be fine. It would be great, actually. Yes, I'd really like this."

She realized she was smiling, more like grinning, as she waited for a response, but there was only silence.

This prompted her to say more. "I'm sorry. I don't even know who I'm speaking with. Do you work with Chris? Or can you tell me the best time to reach him?"

There was another long silence, this finally followed by an answer that had Carrie almost dropping the phone.

"This is Lauren Fisher. And, no … I don't work with him. I'm his fiancée."

Carrie closed her eyes as she tightened her grip on her phone, her heart plummeting down to the pit of her stomach.

She felt like she was going to be sick.

His fiancée?

Oh my god … what's one supposed to say in a situation such as this? Should you just hang up?

Fortunately, Lauren took this decision right out of her hands. "I don't know who you are, or what Chris told you. Or maybe it's highly possible you may have misunderstood him? Because, as far as I know, he's not planning on making a trip to Cleveland this weekend. Or for that matter, even in the near future. As you can imagine, since we've been engaged, our weekends are completely booked. So, whoever you are, it would be best if you didn't call again."

After a brief silence, she delivered her final words. "I'm sure you understand. Goodbye." This was followed by a dead silence.

Carrie didn't know how long she remained where she was, the phone pressed to her ear and in a state of disbelief. She finally blinked, and almost in slow motion, set the phone down on the counter.

She gazed around the kitchen, trying to calm the confusion swirling inside of her. She was surprised to see the bright sunshine coming in through the windows, casting a cheerful glow over the room.

How could this be, when inside she felt like everything she had been daring to hope had now gone up in smoke?

I'm sure you understand.

Her gaze went to her phone.

Yes, you do. You understand completely.

Almost in a trance, she picked up the phone. She found the number she needed and hit send

After two rings, Sam's deep and familiar voice came in her ear. "Hey Carrie, good morning. What's up? I hope you have good news?"

She didn't even realize she had begun to cry.

Frantically wiping the tears from her face with the back of her hand, she took a deep, gulping breath. Even so, she was barely able to answer him. "Hi Sam, good morning to you, too."

She took in another deep breath. "I'm calling to see if your offer still stands. If it does, I accept."

"Yes, of course the offer still stands." She could hear the smile in his voice. "Carrie, this is fantastic news. You've made my day. I promise this will be something you won't regret."

The tone of his voice changed, becoming serious. "But what about you? Are you okay? Because you don't sound like you are. You had mentioned there was a personal issue you needed to deal with?"

She closed her eyes, shaking her head.

No, it's nothing personal. At least not anymore. Turns out what you've been dreaming about, has turned out to be just that ... a silly dream.

She swallowed. "I think I might have a cold coming on. But don't worry, Everything is fine. I'll be ready to go as soon as you need me."

"That's good to hear. Again, I can't tell you how thrilled I am about this. I happen to be on the computer right now, going through some of the details I've received from the historical society. I'm thinking, what we need to do first, is ..."

As he began talking, she tried to keep up with what he said, but between the tears that refused to stop and the dull ache that had settled deep in her heart, she found it hard to concentrate.

After they ended the call, she deleted all of the texts from Chris.

But she couldn't bring herself to delete his voice mail.

The dark and threatening morning sky couldn't even begin to compare with how Lauren Fisher was feeling about what just happened.

After she ended the call from this ... this ... Carrie, or whoever this woman was, she slapped Chris's phone down on the countertop.

You never should have answered it.

But, for some strange reason, the caller i.d. had sent a warning flashing in her head. Carrie Mazzori … with a Cleveland area code. Who could that be?

For a few moments she glared down at the phone.Then she sent a furtive glance towards the steps leading downstairs to where Chris was still getting ready for work. At the sound of the hairdryer, she picked up the phone again. After deleting the call, she threw it down, watching as it went sliding across the counter.

She didn't want it anywhere near her.

Yes, when it came to Chris's phone, the further away it was, the better. She was already walking on thin ice as far as this was concerned.

Only yesterday he'd found her going through his emails. She could still see the skeptical look he gave her when she'd mumbled some lame excuse about how she was only checking to see if he'd received an email she'd sent him.

Which she hadn't … sent him an email, that is.

No, she was only checking to see if her intuition, telling her he'd met someone else, could actually be valid.

And then this phone call happens. So, now she was beyond furious.

Closing her eyes, she gripped the edge of the counter, fighting the urge to grab his phone and throw it in the trash. She needed to calm down. She certainly didn't want to give him any reason to think she may have done something wrong.

She picked up her cup of coffee and walked over to the French doors leading to the backyard. The cup cradled in her hands, she gazed out at the enclosed patio area. It looked like it was going to be one of those typical early spring days in the city, the rain coming down in a heavy drizzle.

For a few moments she stared at absolutely nothing, still trying to deal with what just happened.

There was only one good thing about all this. At least she now had an explanation for the sudden change in Chris's behavior. Her suspicion had been right all along. This was why he gave her the 'this just isn't working out' and 'I think it's best we start seeing other people' speech the night he returned from the wedding in Cleveland.

All because of this Carrie, or whatever her name was.

Her name wasn't important.

She gave a frustrated sigh. As much as she didn't want to come right out and admit this, things had begun to get a little rocky between her and Chris before that weekend. And yes, she'd grudgingly acknowledge their relationship had begun to cool a bit even weeks before that.

What she was having a hard time dealing with, was how Chris had called this woman, already making plans to visit her this coming weekend.

It hadn't taken him much time to move on, had it?

If only you could've persuaded him to take you to that wedding. This would be happening right now.

She closed her eyes, her short conversation with this woman still playing in her head. She knew this was silly, but the sound of her voice alone set her nerves on edge.

With that husky and seductive voice of hers, she sounded like some kind of sex kitten. Or one of those scantily clad women on late night TV advertising a good time. She could only imagine what kind of promises this woman had made to lure Chris back to Cleveland.

She gave a frustrated sigh.

Chris belongs with you. The two of you are perfect together.

Hadn't all of their friends agreed with her on this? They'd also been quick to assure her this latest uncertainty in their relationship was only a temporary blip. With a little more time and effort from both of them, they'd be able to make it work.

This was why she'd come up with the brilliant idea to ask him if she could stay at his place while the floors were being refinished in her apartment. And up until now, she'd cautiously begun to hope they were falling back into the same camaraderie they shared before he'd gone to Cleveland for the wedding.

But now?

Her confidence had been shattered, leaving her unsure.

She wasn't blind to how most women reacted to Chris. He was a charmer, she had to give him that. If you added up his engaging smile, his outgoing personality, along with the subtle sexiness brought on by his confident demeanor, you had a man who was a real catch.

Then add in the fact he was a successful New York real estate developer, and you've hit the jackpot. So, she could easily imagine what went on in this Carrie's little head when she met Chris at the wedding. No doubt she saw him as her ticket out of Cleveland.

Well, the fairy tale happy ending this woman was dreaming about wasn't going to be happening with Chris. She was going to make sure of this.

She was going to win this one, hands down.

Chris was taking much longer than usual to get ready for work. His hope was, when he finally went up to grab a quick breakfast, Lauren would already be gone. The theater group she worked for had a zero-tolerance policy for late arrivals, so she always made it a point to be on time.

After all, there were hundreds of girls just waiting for a chance to take her place as a dancer in the highly rated show she was in. Wasn't she always quick to remind him of this?

For a few moments he stared into the mirror. He shook his head, giving a big sigh before he adjusted his tie. After he pulled the knot firmly up to his collar, he studied the finished look.

Not bad ... you'll do.

He was feeling very optimistic this morning. This was even though Carrie still hadn't returned his call of last night.

But he certainly couldn't blame her for not getting back to him right away. After all, when you promise someone you're going to call, but then let two weeks pass by before you finally follow through? Even he knew this was not acceptable.

And this is exactly what he'd done.

If anything, you shouldn't be surprised if she doesn't call you at all.

But he wasn't even going to go there. Nope, as far as he was concerned, this was going to happen.

They were meant to be. It was fate. Or whatever the hell you wanted to call it. It didn't matter how long it took, or what he had to do.

He was going to convince her of the same.

So, it was a chipper and whistling Chris who came bounding up the steps and into the room.

Still standing by the French doors, gazing out onto the patio, Lauren made a desperate attempt to push her anger aside before she turned to him. The last thing she wanted, was say something she'd regret.

You mean something like, who is this Carrie? And why is she calling you?

Immediately noting the tenseness in her posture and the stiff smile on her face, Chris's whistling came to an abrupt halt.

Damn ... you know that look. Something's up ...

Cautiously making his way over to the counter, he popped two slices of bread in the toaster. It was only after he poured out a cup of coffee and had taken a big gulp, a foolish move that almost had him burning his mouth, he glanced over at her again.

She didn't say a word. But her expression pretty much said it all. She was mad about something. And it probably had to do with him.

And this is proof of why you decided to end it. The more time you've spent together, the more everything about you, seems to make her mad.

But this morning? He'd be damned if he was going to let her drag him into whatever scenario she had brewing in her mind.

He took a more cautious drink of this coffee before he finally spoke, one eyebrow raised. "Well ... good morning. I thought you'd be gone by now. Late rehearsal today?"

She merely shrugged. She was studying him very intently, as if there was something she wanted to say. This brought on that familiar feeling of anxiety to settle over him, one she always managed to stir up inside him as of late. The feeling he wasn't doing enough.

And you'd be the first to admit you probably aren't. But it's all you're able to give her right now. Since you've already made your feelings known, what more can you do?

She remained silent as she walked over to the island and with a deliberate slowness, set her coffee cup on the counter She then began, just as slowly, loading items into her purse.

It was only when she saw he was watching her, she gave a sharp nod to where his phone was on the counter. "Your phone is right there in case you were looking for it. It didn't ring or anything. So, if you were expecting a call?"

She shrugged. "Not to worry."

After she said this, she looked over at him, the searching expression still on her face.

He gave her a puzzled look. Since when was she so worried about him missing calls? If anything, she was more apt to complain he was always on his phone in order to avoid talking to her.

When she starts acting like this, maybe you are.

The sudden ping of the toast popping up out of the toaster made him jump. Relieved at the distraction, he quickly moved to get the butter out of the refrigerator. At this point, he'd come to the decision it would be best if he acted as though nothing was amiss.

The last thing he wanted this morning was a confrontation of any kind.

No, he wanted to hang on to this good mood he had going on.

Busily spreading butter on his toast, he glanced over at her, sending her a smile. "That's good to hear … I guess? Speaking of calls, have you heard from the contractors on when you can move back into your apartment? I'd think the floors would be done by now."

He didn't want to be mean, but he felt it would be best if she went back to her own apartment. She'd already been here much longer than she'd originally told him she would be.

She shook her head, avoiding his gaze. This was because she wasn't being completely truthful. Only yesterday she'd received a call to let her know the work on her the floors was finished and she could move back in at any time.

She'd been staying in Chris's apartment for over a week. Since they weren't considered a couple anymore, she knew he'd been very reluctant to let her do this.

She, on the other hand, had hoped to use this opportunity to change his mind about them.

But this hadn't happened. And now you know why.

She closed her eyes in an attempt to fight the anger bubbling inside of her. Again, she needed to stay calm. Only then would she be able to think clearly about how she was going to handle this. If she made even one wrong move, it could finally be the end of them.

Something you don't even want to think about.

She picked up her cup to load in the dishwasher, the perfect excuse to keep her back to him as she answered. For some reason, he could always sense when she wasn't being truthful. "There was some kind of problem with the final coat not setting properly because of all the rain we've been getting. I was told I would need to keep the windows open for ventilation. Because of the strong fumes."

She paused, turning to give him a somewhat provocative look. "And you know how I hate to be cold."

When he merely nodded before taking a bite of toast, she began to feel desperate. "But hey, it shouldn't be much longer. In the meantime, I'd like to show my gratitude to you for letting me stay here. And giving up your bed for me."

She frowned over at the rumpled blanket and pillow on the sofa. This is where Chris had been spending his nights while she was here. Even more of a reminder their relationship was far from perfect.

Another thing you've been refusing to think about.

She moved closer to him, giving him a coy smile. "I thought maybe we could do dinner and a show this weekend? It will be my treat. It's my first weekend off in a long time."

He hesitated slightly, before slowly shaking his head. "Gee, I'm afraid I can't. There's a possibility I may be going out of town. To visit a friend in Cleveland."

For a few moments she studied him. She didn't know what made her angrier, his answer or the look of what she read as pity on his face.

Any attempt at remaining calm no longer possible, she lost it. To his complete surprise, she spun on her heel and after snatching her purse from the counter, she went marching over to grab her coat from the closet. After she struggled to put it on, she turned to him, her expression bordering between anger and despair. "Fine. Go to Cleveland. Just don't come crying to me when nothing works out for you."

She turned to leave, but then swung around to face him again. "Just remember, things aren't always what they seem."

With this, she went storming out the door, slamming it hard behind her.

Leaving him with a mouthful of toast.

And, as usual, in a total state of confusion.

What you've just finished reading is a flashback to the series of events that brought this story to life.

Since that time, Carrie has completely ignored the other four calls Chris made to her in the weeks following her conversation with Lauren. But she is still hanging on to his voicemail, unable to bring herself to erase it.

Promise you'll save all of your kisses for me.

She tells herself she's only keeping it as a reminder not to be so trusting in the future. But deep down in her heart, she knows it's because she isn't ready to let him go.

And Chris? Even though he knows its way more than a long shot, he's still hoping Carrie will eventually return his calls.

So, as promised, here comes November.

CHAPTER 2

On this cold and rainy Saturday morning, Carrie pulled up her hood to shield her face from the freezing rain.

Was it her imagination, or had it now turned to sleet?

She held out her hand and, sure enough, she watched the frozen pellets bounce off her mittens.

Hello, November.

Huddling even deeper into her coat, she sighed. She couldn't believe the year was almost over. This was also a sad reminder she would be turning twenty-seven in just a few weeks.

Yes, she would be turning twenty-seven on the twenty-seventh of November. A day she should be celebrating with the one she loved.

Don't even start thinking about this ... it's not going to happen.

Thank goodness this wasn't a hundred years ago. During that time, a woman her age and not married would've been considered an old maid. Pressured into marrying whoever asked her. Whether or not she loved them, or even if she didn't want to get married at all.

Or, in her case, with her brother Chester and his wife Sophie about to have their first child at the end of this month, she'd take on the role as the spinster aunt.

Well, it could be a lot worse. If anything, she should be counting her lucky stars this was the twenty-first century. And with the good news she was finally able to share, she had proof she was more than capable of taking care of herself.

With your record of failed relationships at an all-time high, this is probably a good thing. Seriously ...

She shivered as a drop of rain rolled down the back of her neck. Shaking her coat collar, which sent even more water trickling down her back, she glanced down at the little dog she was walking. His nose pressed intently to the ground, he appeared completely oblivious to the miserable weather conditions.

She shook the leash in an attempt to get his attention. "Come on, Mr. Pickles. Aren't you ready to go back inside where it's warm? And nice and dry? I bet there might even be a treat or two waiting for you."

It was only when a truck went flying by, sending a wave of water right at them, the little dog looked up. And with what she'd swear was an almost irritated look on his face, he gave a vigorous shake. Then he turned around and took off in a fast trot, pulling Carrie with him. As he appeared to know where he was going, she let him lead the way.

She gazed up at the sky, the clouds dark and threatening. She hoped this gloomy weather wasn't an indication of what was to come. As if in answer to this, it began to sleet harder. She sighed, quickening her pace.

A hot cup of tea was sounding really good to her right now.

Carrie was settled at her kitchen island, a blueberry muffin and a cup of tea in front of her.

She picked up her phone to see if she had any messages. She'd missed a text from Chester.

Just landed. Be home in about 20 min. Bring Mr. P back anytime.

He had been out of town for the past three days participating in a team sponsored golf outing in Arizona. All of the proceeds going to charity, it was an event he'd committed to over a year ago.

He'd asked her to take care of his dog Mr. Pickles while he was gone. He thought this would make things easier on Sophie since she was so far along with her pregnancy.

Carrie had also offered to take Sophie's two dogs, Snowball and Popcorn, but Sophie said no. Mr. Pickles was the problem, she said. He still hadn't quite accepted the other two dogs and lately, he seemed to be causing more trouble than usual.

Sophie and Chester had many an argument over him making this trip. He'd wanted to cancel, while she insisted he'd already committed to attend and certainly couldn't go back on his word. They finally compromised with him shortening his stay from five days to three.

This was only after Sophie assured him the doctor told her the birth wouldn't be happening anytime soon. At least not in the next two weeks.

Carrie shook her head.

She couldn't believe how Chester had just about lost it with this pregnancy. He was a nervous wreck. There was no doubt in her mind Sophie had to be relieved he'd be gone for a few days. He watched her like a hawk, concerned about every move she made or any discomfort she experienced. His eyes were clouded with a constant look of worry.

She sighed. How deeply in love her big brother had fallen. She could only hope one day she'd find a love like Sophie and he shared.

A few months ago, you thought maybe you had. But it certainly didn't work out that way, did it?

With another sigh, she pushed herself away from the counter to get more hot water for her tea After she was settled once again at the counter, she glanced over to where Mr. Pickles was curled up in his dog bed.

He was dreaming.

Resting her chin on her hand, she watched as his back feet began moving at a frantic pace, giving out little grunts and growls.

She wondered what he could possibly be dreaming about... chasing squirrels? Running with other dogs? Or maybe chasing Popcorn and Snowball, trying to show them he was the boss?

It was a dream, she was sure, a lot less complicated than any human would have.

Her gaze dropping back to her phone, she saw her mailbox was almost full. She began scrolling down through the voice mails, deleting those she knew were no longer important. This brought her right to the voicemail she'd saved from Chris.

She stared down at the phone, her finger hovering over the delete button.

Then she did what she knew she shouldn't. She tapped the phone to listen to his voicemail, waiting for the one sentence she couldn't forget, no matter how she tried.

Promise you'll save all of your kisses for me.

She stared off into space, wondering for what had to be about the millionth time, what kind of man would say this to a woman when he was already engaged to another

Who does this?

She smiled, thinking of what Sam's answer had been to this.

During the time they worked on the project in Quebec, she and Sam had become very close, spending almost all of their time together.

One night, following a long stressful day on the job and after two glasses of wine, an amount way over Carrie's usual limit, she was giggling about something he said.

His expression suddenly becoming serious, he leaned forward and after taking her hands in his, he cleared his throat. "Carrie, I have to say something. I don't know if this is the right time, or even the right place, but I have to get it out."

He glanced down at their hands for a moment before he looked up and into her eyes. "I've come to care for you. And the more time we spend together, I keep hoping you might be feeling the same."

He paused to take a deep breath. "Carrie, I guess what I'm trying to say is, I'd like to take our friendship to the next level."

The giggling-happy feeling she'd been filled with?

Well, it was gone, leaving her about as sober as she could possibly get. Her lips parted, she'd only been able to stare at him, while at the same time, she'd frantically searched her brain, trying to come up with the right answer.

She finally spoke. "Oh, Sam … I like you. I like you a lot. But …"

He'd abruptly pulled his hands from hers and leaned back in his chair. He pinched the bridge of his nose with his fingers, a deep groan coming from him. "*Damn* … Carrie, please stop right there. Because I'm pretty sure I know what's coming next. And it's not the answer a man wants to hear after he's poured his heart out to a woman."

She'd felt so awful, her eyes pleading with him. "Sam, listen to me. I wish I could say yes, but I can't."

For a few moments, he'd studied her. "Is there someone else?"

She'd shrugged, finding it hard to meet his gaze. "There is and then there isn't. I don't even know how to explain. If I try, I'm afraid you'll think I'm crazy."

"Try me." The look on his face was so sincere, she did exactly that.

She told him everything.

From the very first moment she and Chris met to when she'd returned his call, only to find he was engaged. After she finished, they sat in silence.

Then she'd given a long, wistful sigh. "*Oh god*, Sam, I can't even begin to explain how wonderful it was. It was so right, almost magical. Never before have I experienced such an instant connection with someone. And I know he felt the same way. I could tell this just by looking into his eyes. You hear all of these stories about love at first sight. The right chemistry. Fate. Or the feeling where everything in your life has fallen into place. Well, I felt all of those things. Times ten."

His response to this wasn't what she'd expected.

"Then call him. You said he called you numerous times after your phone call with his so-called fiancée. Do you think it's possible this woman may have lied to you?"

She knew the look on her face must have been a horrified one. "But why? Why would someone do something like that? I certainly can't call him and say, hey, what's the story here? Is there any chance this Lauren who answered your phone, might have been making this up about the two of you being engaged? So, I thought I'd call again and ask you just to be sure?"

She'd shaken her head. "Oh, Sam … I could never do that."

He chuckled. "Come on, Carrie. What's the worst thing that could happen? Let's say this fiancée of his answers the phone again. At least you'll have your answer and you hang up."

He nodded. "Yep, you need to make the call again, hoping this time he's the one who answers. So, you can hear directly from him what's really going on. And if he feels the same about you as you feel about him? Trust me, he'll be thrilled."

He shook his head. "He's a fool if he isn't."

And even though he'd muttered this last comment under his breath, she'd heard him.

After that evening, she and Sam never talked about what either of them shared that night. She'd catch him watching her at times, a pensive look on his face. But when she caught his eye, he'd only smile.

Never once did he ask her if she called Chris. Something she was thankful for.

Because if he did, she'd have to tell him no, she hadn't. This wasn't only because she was worried Lauren might be the one to answer the phone.

No, if anything, she was more afraid of what Chris would say if he were to answer.

Call her crazy, but she didn't want to let go of the heart racing and breathless burst of-anticipation that filled her with even just the thought of him. And those few magical hours they'd shared together? She wanted to hang on to the memories of those moments for as long as she could.

There really wasn't anything wrong with this, was there?

Again … a girl was allowed to dream, wasn't she?

A loud hissing sound filled the room. This was followed by a series of loud meows as Jingles came flying through the kitchen with Mr. Pickles in hot pursuit. Startled, her conversation with Sam completely forgotten, Carrie watched as both the cat and dog went racing around the room before they headed back up the stairs.

Her head in her hands and her eyes closed, she waited for the loud thuds and series of excited barking and yowling that were sure to follow.

This was when she decided there was no better time than now to take Mr. Pickles back to where he belonged.

With Chester and Sophie.

Hopefully, it stopped raining.

CHAPTER 3

Settled in his favorite place in front of the fireplace and sound asleep, Mr. Pickles was more than happy to be back home. From where they were curled up together on the sofa next to Sophie, both Popcorn and Snowball were keeping a wary eye on him.

Her feet propped up on pillows and wearing one of Chester's team jerseys that barely fit over her baby bump, Sophie was eating a donut.

On his way home from the airport, Chester had stopped at her favorite donut shop, bringing a whole box of donuts home with him.

Her eyes closed, there was a look of complete bliss on her face as she popped the last bite of donut in her mouth. Licking her fingers, she sent both Chester and Carrie a sheepish smile.

"*Ooooh ... that was so good. I love their donuts.*"

After pouring out a glass of wine for himself and Carrie, Chester held out the box to Sophie. He grinned. "Do you want another one? You might as well enjoy them while you can."

Sophie sent them a wistful look. "Only if you both have one with me." Then she grinned at Carrie. "A glass of wine and a donut, what more could a girl ask for?"

Carrie set her wine glass on the coffee table to choose a donut from the box Chester held out to her. After they had all made their choice, Chester returned the box to the counter before he gave Sophie a smile. "Enjoy, angel."

She stared down at the donut in her hand. Then she looked over at Chester and burst into tears. He was next to her in a flash, a completely bewildered look on his face.

He put his arm around her. "Sweetheart, what's wrong? Have you changed your mind?"

She waved the donut at him for emphasis, her voice muffled against his chest. "*Oh my god, Chester* ... what's wrong? I'll tell you what's wrong. *Everything.* Look at me ... I look terrible."

She gestured towards the shirt she was wearing. "Look at your shirt. It barely fits around me anymore. Which means the last thing I should be doing right now, is eating donuts."

She gave a frustrated sigh. "My ankles are swollen and I can't even walk like a normal person. Instead I waddle like a duck. How can you even stand to be around me?"

A horrified look came over her face. "And what if I don't lose the weight after these babies are born and I stay fat forever?"

She stopped crying long enough to gaze mournfully up into his face. "If this happens, you have my permission to leave. I won't expect you to stay with me. I'll understand, I really ..."

Framing her face in his hands, he stopped the rest of her words with a kiss before he went on to kiss away her tears.

"Angel, I have never loved you more than I love you right now. You aren't fat, you're beautiful. And you're not going to stay fat. You're just feeling this way because you've been pregnant for so long and you want it to be over with."

He gave her another kiss, bringing her to close her eyes as she sighed against him. "I love you, too."

Carrie watched all of this, while at the same time, she was trying to figure out if she'd heard right.

She cleared her throat, this bringing Chester and Sophie to glance over at her.

"Sophie, did I just hear what I think I did? Because I'd swear you just said babies, not baby. Are you and Chester keeping something from all of us?"

She watched as Sophie shot a quick glance at Chester, a guilty expression coming over her face. This was followed by a nervous giggle.

"*Ooops* … I guess I just gave it away, didn't I?" She sent Carrie an excited smile. "Yes, we're expecting twins. We decided not to tell anyone because we wanted it to be a surprise."

She reached up to stroke Chester's cheek with her fingertips. "And this crazy man of mine didn't want to tell anyone because he's been so worried … insanely worried … about everything. When he has no reason to be."

Chester shook his head, the anxious look she was referring to slowly filling his face. "Well, you can never be too careful. I just want all of you to be okay." He gave her a kiss, a sudden teasing gleam in his eyes. "After all, we still have eight more to go."

Sophie burst out laughing. "*Oh my god* … I never should have agreed to that. But you caught me when I was most vulnerable." She glanced over at Carrie, a blush creeping into her cheeks. "Your brother can be very persuasive at times."

After she gave them both a hug, Carrie grinned. "I can see this. But twins … my goodness. I'm really going to have to polish up on my 'aunting' skills. I'm so excited for the both of you. And I promise your secret will be safe with me."

She laughed. "It's going to be so much fun. I can't wait." As if she was offering a toast, she raised her donut to Sophie. "Now, go ahead and eat your donut. Consider you're eating one for each baby. It's only fair."

Sending her a grateful smile, Sophie proceeded to do just that.

After a few moments of silence, Carrie smiled over at Sophie and Chester. "I also have news to share. Not as momentous as yours, but it's good news. I have been nominated for an award, the New and Upcoming Interior Designer of the Year for the Midwest."

She grinned at Chester. "I know, it's a mouthful. I guess you could call it the rookie of the year award in the interior design world. I found out about this while I was in Quebec, but I wanted to wait until they finalized the list of nominees before I told anyone. The awards dinner is going to be held in New York at the Seasons Hotel in Manhattan. This is a week from this coming Monday, actually."

Sophie quickly handed Chester what was left of her donut so she could give Carrie a hug. "Carrie, how exciting for you. If anyone deserves this, it's you. You're going to the awards ceremony, aren't you? And I hope you're taking someone with you. Maybe Sam?"

Carrie shook her head, a rueful smile on her face. "He's in LA. He told me he would be more than happy to meet me in New York. But, I don't think it's a good idea. I … well, I just don't think I should ask him."

Chester's expression was thoughtful. "Wait a minute, whatever happened to the guy from Kev's wedding? His friend from Chicago? Chris, I believe his name was. Doesn't he live in New York?"

Don't think he didn't notice how Carrie reacted to this, the swift, almost nervous glance she shot over at him. He was pretty sure she was even starting to blush, something she didn't do that easily.

Hmm … it looks like you might be on to something here.

He watched as she composed her face into one of indifference. When she followed this with a casual shrug, he nodded. "Perhaps I'm wrong, but I got the distinct impression there was something between the two of you that night. But you never said anything about him afterwards, and then planning our wedding, I confess it slipped my mind."

He winked. "A wedding has a way of doing that to a man. Especially when he's the groom."

After he said this, he smiled at Sophie, who was listening to all of this with interest. There was nothing she liked more than the possibility of a love story in the making.

She returned his smile. "The best groom ever." And just as Chester expected, her attention veered right back to Carrie.

"I remember him. He was at our table for dinner. He and Chester really hit it off. He seemed so nice. And if I remember right, he was cute, really cute. He had such a nice smile." Her glance swiveled back to Chester. "Didn't you think so?"

Amused, Chester shrugged. "Cute? I guess you could say that? But I'll agree, he did seem like a decent guy."

Sophie was gazing curiously at Carrie. "So, what happened? Did the two of you ever get in touch with each other after that weekend?"

Carrie stood and picking up her wineglass, she went into the kitchen. After she put the glass in the dishwasher, she leaned back against the island. She tried to act nonchalant, as though what she was going to say was of no real importance.

"He did call, but I missed it. He left a message he wanted to come to Cleveland for the weekend so we could spend some time together. So, I called him back. Unfortunately, a woman answered his phone. A woman who informed me she was his fiancée. So ... you can imagine my surprise."

Her smile was bright. "I guess he turned out not to be who I thought he was. He did call me a few times after that, but I didn't answer his calls. Then everything got crazy with all of the last-minute details for the Quebec project."

She shrugged. "After that, I guess I forgot all about him."

Yeah, right. Who are you trying to kid?

Watching all the different emotions play across her face, Chester slowly nodded. He wasn't fooled one bit. "Ah, I see... I wondered why you took off for Quebec so quickly."

He paused, a thoughtful expression on his face. *"Hmm ... so he's engaged? I find this hard to believe after what he told me during dinner that night. I ..."*

Her gaze searching his face, Carrie interrupted him. "Why? What do you mean? What did he say?"

He shook his head. "Let's just say he gave me the impression you knocked his socks off. And this is all I'm going to say."

There was absolutely no way he was going to share what Chris had told him. That when he met Carrie, he knew he'd found the girl of his dreams and believed fate was what brought them together. Chester couldn't imagine any man would come out and admit something like this unless they were serious.

Nope, guys didn't do this. At least, not the guys he knew.

There also hadn't been any mention of another woman in his life. Or any sign he was engaged, or even thinking about getting engaged. And if he was engaged, why wasn't his fiancée with him?

Something wasn't making any sense.

Unless this Chris was a damn good liar ...

So, this was why, before he said anything more to Carrie, he was going to talk to Kevin. Since Kevin and Chris had been friends since they were kids, he'd be the one to know the real story on this supposed engagement.

But for now, he thought it best to change the subject. He smiled over at Carrie. "So ... are you going to call Livy to let her know you'll be in town?"

Carrie sighed. "I did call her. She said she'd ask me to stay with her, but this wasn't a good time. I asked her if everything was okay and typical Livy, she brushed me off."

She shrugged. "So, I asked if we could at least meet for dinner or lunch. She agreed, but didn't sound very excited."

Chester was frowning. "I bet it has something to do with that guy she's been with for, what is it, five years now? Zack?" He shook his head. "I don't trust him. He couldn't even take time off to come with Livy to our wedding. It's always the same story. He's in the middle of some big deal he's hoping to close. He also treats Livy like ... well, let's just say he doesn't treat her very good. I'd be willing to bet he cheats on her, too."

Sophie moved closer to him, a frown coming over her face. "I hope not. I like Livy. I can't wait to see her again."

After having met Chester and Carrie's sister Livy at their wedding,

Sophie wasn't exaggerating when she said this. She was dying to get her hands on Livy. Not in a bad way of course. Because if there was anyone in dire need of her expertise, it was Livy.

This would be in the form of a complete makeover. Hiding behind the big, unattractive glasses she wore, along with those bangs of hers, hanging like heavy drapery fringe and covering a good portion of her face, Sophie knew there was a lot of potential.

With contacts, a new haircut, highlights and a complete revamp of her makeup and wardrobe, she was confident Livy would be just as stunning, if not even more than, Carrie.

And she, of all people, should know, right?

Look at what a great job she did with Chester. Not that he needed all that much help, but like Livy, he'd been hiding one amazing man behind that unruly mop of hair and beard he had going on.

Yep, she knew her stuff.

She liked to think of herself as an artist of makeovers.

This reminded her of something. She struggled to get up from the sofa, but Chester put a stop to this, tightening his hold on her. "Angel, please, whatever you want, just let one of us know. We'll get it for you."

She gave an exaggerated sigh and settling back next to him, she gestured to Carrie. "The mail is on the counter behind you. Look through it and you'll find a postcard with a photo of a very colorful abstract painting. It's Julian's artwork, my friend from Paris. He's going to be showing his work at a gallery in New York. And if I remember correctly, there's a preview show, invitation only, this coming Saturday."

When Carrie held up the postcard, Sophie grinned. "Yes, that's it! If you plan is to arrive a few days early, you should try to talk Livy into going to this show with you. I'm sure I can get you an invite. And you'll be able to meet Julian. He is such a kind and amazing man."

She sighed. "He is also so sexy and charming."

She glanced up at Chester who was frowning at this, not happy about what she just said.

She laughed. "Oh Chester, I know if you met him, you'd like him, too. Everyone likes Julian. He's so sweet. And he has the kind of personality that draws people right to him."

She glanced over at Carrie, a mischievous smile on her face. "And that French accent of his... *ooh la la.*"

Carrie looked up from the postcard. "I would love to go. I love going to gallery openings. I've had a couple of clients who've actually requested I design their space around a favorite painting of theirs. So, who knows? Maybe I'll find something to put over my fireplace, since I still haven't found what I want. I'm waiting for something to jump out at me, I guess."

Sophie smiled at her. "I'll get in touch with him to let him know you'd like an invite. With a guest, in case Livy decides to go, too." Her eyes suddenly lit up. "And tomorrow we'll go to the boutique and pick out a dress for you... two dresses. One for the gallery opening and one for the awards dinner. We'll go there right after the baby shower. This will be perfect because the boutique is closed on Sundays and we'll have the place to ourselves."

Chester was shaking his head. "It always comes down to the dress, doesn't it? And of course, the shoes. I've learned how important shoes can be." He planted a kiss in Sophie's hair. "Most preferably, red."

Sophie laughed. "Yes, definitely red."

As Sophie and Carrie began discussing dresses, Chester once more made a mental note to call Kevin and ask him about Chris.

Something didn't add up.

CHAPTER 4

Carrie arranged the last tray of cookies on the table Abby had set up for the food they were serving at the shower.

Between the freshly baked aroma of the cookies and the fact she hadn't eaten since early morning, her stomach growled in response.

She sent a quick glance around the room to see if anyone was watching before she tentatively reached for a cookie. Her conscience taking over, she pulled her hand back.

A small voice came from beside her. It was Chloe. She grinned up at Carrie. "Are you going to eat a cookie? If you are, can I have one, too? I'm really hungry."

Chloe had come to the shower with her mom, Lisa. According to Lisa, Chloe was beyond excited about the baby and even though she was only eight years old, she was already talking about how she wanted to babysit. She'd been running around Abby and Kevin's condo ever since they had arrived, trying to help get everything ready.

Carrie smiled at her. "I bet you are, after all the work you've done since you got here. You deserve a cookie. But, I'm not sure. ... do you think we'll get into trouble if we take one?"

Abby's voice came from behind the both of them. "Go ahead. Take one. I won't tell anyone."

At the guilty look on Carrie's face, she laughed. "Seriously, take a cookie, both of you. There's plenty to go around." She shrugged, a big smile on her face. "You know you really want one."

Carrie didn't need to be asked twice. She quickly chose a cookie in the shape of a teddy bear. Chloe spent more time making her choice, finally making the difficult decision of taking a cookie shaped like a baby bottle.

After biting into the cookie, Carrie closed her eyes. She looked over at Abby, giving a moan of pleasure.

"Oh my gosh, Abby. These are so, so good. Someday, when I get the chance, I am going to come and watch you make them. Maybe I'll be able to learn a thing or two about baking. I also can't wait until the renovation is finished for your new baking space in that old warehouse we found. Kevin said to spare no expenses, so I know you'll love it."

Even though Abby was nodding in agreement, she was more interested in who had just entered the room.

Carrie glanced over to see two women searching the room. They looked like twins, both blonde and model perfect.

Abby turned to her, a concerned look on her face. "Uh oh, Sophie is not going to be happy about these two showing up here." She began scanning the room for Sophie.

Carrie watched as the one blonde made her way over to greet the group of women seated on the large sectional by the fireplace. Her loud and dramatic greeting rose above the chatter in the room.

Curious, Carrie turned to Abby. "Why wouldn't Sophie want them here?"

Abby nodded towards the blond by the fireplace. "That's Kelly. The other woman is her sister Mia who is married to Jordan, one of the guys on the team. Kelly is single and was hot for your brother from the very beginning. I still don't think she's accepted the fact he's married. I'm also sure this is the last place she wants to be, but Mia probably made her come. The two of them aren't very popular with the rest of the group. They may be beautiful, but their personalities leave a lot to be desired."

She groaned. "Oh no … and now here comes Sophie."

Sure enough, almost in a mad march, Sophie was bearing down on them. She had a what-the-heck-is-going-on kind of expression on her face.

Abby gave Sophie a big smile. "I know, I know. Or should I say, I didn't know. I'm just as surprised as you are that they're here. Or, at least that Kelly decided to come. Because we didn't want any hurt feelings, we left it as an open invitation to any of the wives or girl-friends of the guys on the team. Something that may have been a mistake on our part. I don't think you have anything to worry about."

Her eyes suddenly grew wide as she stared behind Sophie. "Again, maybe I'm wrong about that, too."

Sophie turned to find she was face to face with Kelly.

After a dramatic show of pressing her cheek to Sophie's, Kelly stepped back, her gaze slowly traveling over her, giving her a thorough once over.

She gave a dramatic frown. "Oh dear, are you having twins? Or triplets? How can you stand it? You must be so uncomfortable. And so worried about losing all of the weight after the baby comes. I know I certainly would be."

Now, Carrie wasn't one to cause a scene, but when she saw the crushed look on Sophie's face, she quickly moved to put her arm around her. There was no way she was going to let Kelly get away with what she said.

"Hi, I don't believe we've met. I'm Carrie, Chester's sister." She paused to smile. "It's funny you should say this because just yesterday, when I was over at Chester and Sophie's condo, he remarked about how Sophie keeps getting even more beautiful with each passing day."

She sighed, shaking her head. "I never thought I'd see my big brother so much in love. I can only hope someday to have a man love me as much as Chester loves Sophie."

Kelly's response to this was only a dazzling smile along with a vague nod. With her short attention span, it was questionable as to whether she had even listened to what Carrie said, her mind already moving on to something else.

Unfortunately, this would be Carrie.

Her finger going to her lips, Kelly gave her a long look. "Carrie, I know that name. My goodness, I never connected you with Chester. Aren't you also Doug Stone's ex-girlfriend? He told me about you."

Sophie felt Carrie stiffen against her. "I don't know what Doug told you, but just to clarify, I had the experience of being his date only one time. For me, this was a date that turned out to be one too many."

Kelly nodded, a smug look on her face. "Ah … he told me you'd probably say something like this. He said you were too serious and weren't in to having fun. This was why he broke it off with you." She gave a tinkling little laugh. "But this has worked out to my advantage, as we've now been spending a lot of time together."

Aware of what had transpired that night between Doug and Carrie, both Abby and Sophie instinctively moved closer to her, ready to protect her if need be.

Fortunately, Carrie decided not to respond to this. As far as she was concerned, Doug could say whatever he wanted, she didn't care.

And as it turned out, this wasn't even necessary. Chloe had an answer ready. "Since your sister made you come here and this is the last place you want to be, maybe you should have a cookie. It might make you feel better." She grinned up at Abby and Carrie. "Right, Abby?"

Before Abby had a chance to answer this, Chloe grabbed another cookie and went skipping away to join her mother in the kitchen.

Her brows furrowing, as though she was confused, Kelly watched Chloe leave. Then she shrugged, flashing another one of her megawatt smiles. "Well, she's just being silly, isn't she? I guess I should make the rounds. I'll talk to you later."

After she walked away, Abby and Carrie turned to Sophie, both speaking at the same time.

"Are you okay?"

When she nodded, Carrie shuddered. "What a horrible woman. I used to think I wouldn't wish Doug on anyone, but I think I've changed my mind. She deserves him just as much as he deserves her."

Sophie had a big smile on her face. "Well, I can see I have nothing to worry about when all of you are around." Then she started to laugh. "And Chloe … I keep forgetting she's like a little sponge. She repeats everything word for word, too. And she always nails it, right when it really matters."

Her attention was drawn to where her Aunt Louise and Carrie's Aunt Evelyn were dramatically waving for her to join them.

She frowned. "Oh dear, I hope this means it's time to open the gifts and not because of some shower game they've cooked up between them." She shook her head. "Those two are trouble when they get together. Wish me luck."

After she left, Abby laughed. "She's not going to be happy, because there is a game. Louise promised me it would be fast and fun, but I don't know…"

She hesitated, her hand going to Carrie's arm. "Don't worry about what Kelly said about you and Doug. No one believes anything he says." She shook her head. "And if he ever makes another move like he did at our wedding? The guys will be on him in a flash. Thank God Chris was there for you. He's seemed like such a nice guy." She gazed curiously at Carrie. "From what I heard, you two seemed to hit it off that night. Did you two talk after that?"

Carrie had quickly taken a bite out of her cookie as soon as Abby began to talk about Chris. This way, with her mouth full, she wouldn't be able to answer her. She didn't want to talk about Chris. Especially about how nice he was. She, of all people, knew exactly how nice he was, something she was trying so hard to forget.

Abby, sensing Carrie's reluctance, changed the subject. She laughed. "And now the plot thickens. Because look who just walked in … Chester. I'll bet you anything Sophie told him he had to come. I wonder how Kelly will deal with this?"

Carrie watched as Chester scanned the room for Sophie. When he spotted her, his eyes lit up as he made his way over to her.

She smiled.

The fact he'd come to the shower, brave enough to face a room full of women, told her one thing.

Sophie had nothing to worry about.

Nothing at all.

She grabbed another cookie before she trailed after Abby to the kitchen to see if they needed her help.

Carrie turned around one more time to study her reflection in the full-sized mirror at the Chic Boutique. She could hear Sophie and her Aunt Louise arguing again in the back room.

She smiled, thinking what an unusual relationship they had. So much alike, it was a clash of two creative minds, twenty-four-seven.

When Sophie came up behind her with more dresses draped over her arm, Carrie quickly turned to take the dresses from her.

"Sophie, please … no more. You have to be exhausted. This dress will be fine. And seriously? I don't really need another one. I can wear the same dress for both events."

Sophie shook her head. "No, you are going to pick out two dresses. After all, it's not every day someone we know is up for such a prestigious award, given out at a swanky dinner in New York City, of all places. This is big, Carrie. And I want you to look the part of the sophisticated designer that you are."

She grinned. "And hot. You need to look really hot. After all, you'll be representing the Midwest, so you need to do us proud."

She hung the dresses on the hook by the mirror before she plopped down on a nearby chair. "I especially want you to try on this red dress. We've already decided it's a yes for the one you have on, right? So, go try on the red one. Then I think we'll be done."

With a resigned sigh, Carrie headed for the dressing room. In only a short time, she returned in the red dress. After Louise came over to zip up the zipper, both she and Sophie studied Carrie from all angles.

Sophie finally smiled. "Yes, I believe this is the dress. Now all we need are shoes and jewelry. Do you have red heels?"

Carrie groaned. "Sophie, I'm sure I have shoes I can wear. No one will even notice my feet, so I can wear my black pumps. They're comfortable and stylish."

Both Sophie and her aunt both looked at her as if they thought she'd completely lost her mind before Sophie slowly shook her head.

"I take it this means you don't have red heels? Then we'll special order them. Because if we're going to do this, we're going to do it right."

The door to the shop opened. Chester came into the boutique, his gaze going directly to Sophie. "Angel, you have to be exhausted. Aren't you about done here?"

Carrie gave him a resigned look. "Chester, thank goodness you're here."

She gestured over at both Sophie and her aunt.

"These two are relentless. You need to take Sophie home and pamper her."

CHAPTER 5

I don't know where I stand with you.
And I don't even know what I mean to you.
All I know is every time I think of you,
I only want to be with you.
~ Anonymous

Ka-plink. Ka-plink. Ka-plink.

Chris Gardner was bouncing his pen on the desk, something he wasn't even aware he was doing. And this was only because he was pretty much in his own little world.

He felt like his mind was running all over the place as of late, unfortunately stuck on all these memories he should be trying to forget.

Memories about her.

Carrie ...

He gave a exasperated sigh.

It was always about her.

He let out a long breath and throwing down the pen, he pushed away from the desk. His hands in his pockets, he wandered over to the window, where he stared down at the drenched city. Was it just his imagination or had it been raining ever since he flipped his calendar over to the month of November?

The weather pretty much matches the way you've been feeling lately, doesn't it?

Reaching up to run his hand through his hair, he turned from the window to gaze around at the muted grey and tans that defined the mood of his office.

Pretty boring ... just like you.

He closed his eyes. God, is this what his life has become? Holed up in this cookie cutter office, working twenty-four-seven, like everyone else in this damn city?

For a moment, and this would be a very brief and fleeting moment, he was hit with the brilliant idea to call Carrie again. After all, she was an interior designer, wasn't she?

Yes, this is exactly what he would do. He would very casual-like, ask her if she'd be interested in the job of updating his office. You know, bring it up to par. Give it some zing. Make him look interesting.

And if she didn't answer, as had been the case with the numerous times he had called her up until now? Well, this time he would leave a message making it very clear this call was only about business. He wanted decorating advice, nothing more.

Yeah, what would be wrong with this?

He plopped down in his chair and throwing his head against the back of the seat, he gave a long groan.

Lame ... a really lame idea. And what makes you think this time will be different? The only reason she might even consider returning your call would be to leave you a return message to please stop calling.

He just didn't get it. No, he didn't understand any of what went on in a woman's mind, let alone Carrie's. If he did maybe he would be a hell of a lot happier right now.

Abruptly opening his eyes, he reached for his phone. Imagine his surprise when it rang as soon as he held it in his hand. Instantly filled with anticipation, he checked to see who was calling, only to be hit with the usual disappointment.

Again, why do you keep holding on to the hope it would be Carrie?

Because, as usual, it wasn't.

Nope, it was Lauren.

Damn ...

He very carefully put the phone back down on the desk, cautiously pushing it away from him. Almost as if, this way she wouldn't know he was refusing to take her call.

He should have expected this would happen when he agreed to meet up with her and their group of friends tomorrow night for a gallery exhibit of a new French painter. Something that was now beginning to seem like a very bad idea.

A really bad and stupid idea.

This had all come about because of his last-minute decision to attend the impromptu engagement party for one of his and Lauren's mutual friends last night. Even though he knew she'd probably be there, he was surprised when she made it a point to come over to talk to him. The last time they spoke was back in March, when they parted on very cool terms. This was after her short stay with him while her apartment floors were being refinished.

After that, along with the fact he had heard nothing from Carrie, he had immersed himself in his job. Working long hours and choosing his social activities very carefully, he was now pretty much of a hermit.

And now he knew why.

Last night, before he even knew what was happening, he had been swept up in Lauren's plans. Maybe it was because of the one too many drinks he had. Or the fact he was beginning to feel like a bit of a loser, now in the minority with another friend taking the plunge into marital bliss.

Whatever the reason, he'd obviously let his current mental state get the better of him. Why else would he have agreed to get together with her again?

He began bouncing his pen on the desk again.

Ka-plink. Ka-plink.

His hand stilled, a slow smile coming to his face. His thoughts were of the pact he and Carrie made that night in Cleveland. If neither of them got married within the next three years? They would marry each other, big wedding and all.

He stared off into space.

He could almost envision it in his mind. Carrie walking down the aisle, her beauty like none other. Their eyes would meet and they would know this marriage was what they had been waiting for all along.

But you don't want to wait three years. And come on, you're getting a little ahead of yourself, aren't you? And for this to even have a chance of happening, first you need to find her.

He wondered what had happened in her life since he last saw her? Hell, she may have forgotten all about him by now, already in a relationship with someone else. A few times he almost called Kevin to ask him about this.

He groaned, squeezing his eyes shut. He had no one to blame but himself for the way things turned out. Yep, he'd waited too long before calling her.

He'd left the most important phone call of his life get waylaid by something as stupid as his job.

Frustrated, he tossed the pen down on the desk. After wearily dragging his hands through his hair, he reached for his phone. He might as well to listen to Laura's voicemail.

Maybe, just maybe, he got lucky and the evening had been cancelled.

> *Hi Chris, just calling to let you know*
> *I had your name put on the list as my*
> *guest for the Gallery East artist*
> *preview tomorrow night. Everyone is*
> *planning to get there around seven*
> *-ish. You shouldn't have any trouble*
> *finding it. It's only a short distance*
> *from Gracie Ann's, the restaurant we*
> *went to a couple times after the show.*

> *I'm really looking forward to the*
> *w beginning for us. I've missed you,*
> *Chris.*
> *See you then.*

He stared down at the phone.

A new beginning? She certainly couldn't be serious. Or could she?

Here was proof, as with everything else in his life right now, luck was not on his side.

He leaned back in his chair and closed his eyes.

And this is how he remained.

For a long, long time.

Only a few blocks away, a total of four to be exact, Carrie was following the porter down the hall to her room at the Alexander Crown Hotel.

Once he showed her around the room, pointing out all of the amenities before he left, she leaned back against the door in relief.

After fighting her way through the crowded airport and having survived the erratic driving of the cab driver who spent more time watching her in his rearview mirror than he did the traffic, she welcomed the peace and quiet.

She walked over to the window to see the rain had now changed to sleet, swirling around the buildings in a frenzy. This, along with the heavy cloud cover, made it seem much later than the five o'clock hour it was.

Her eyes slowly scanning the buildings, she let her imagination run wild, wondering if she could actually be looking at the office Chris was in right now. And if he could possibly be gazing out of his window at the same time. Tentatively raising her hand, she waved.

Oh my god, what are you doing? Are you crazy? Like he would even be able to see you if he was out there.

She backed away from the window and after yanking the drapes shut, she gazed around at what would be her home away from home for the next four days. If it were any consolation, the room more than made up for the inclement weather.

Recommended to her by Sam, this hotel proudly boasted one hundred and forty-five years in the business. Their attention focused on preserving the details of their earlier years, Carrie could see why it was still one of the most popular places to stay when visiting the city.

Her room wasn't overly large in size, but the high ceiling made it feel bigger than it was. Both the woodwork and molding were all hand-carved mahogany, the floors of the same hardwood. The walls were covered in an ivy patterned wallpaper, the leaves highlighted with touches of gold, the drapes a rich ivory silk in a complimentary trellis pattern.

The ornate queen-sized bed almost dominated the room, the bedding also a rich ivory silk fabric with touches of decorative embroidery.

There was also an oversized armchair and matching ottoman, both upholstered in the same fabric as the window treatments, arranged in front of an ornate rod iron and gas fireplace.

And Carrie absolutely loved the bathroom. The floors and vanity were white marble, the walls painted a deep forest green. The ornate brass framed mirror matched the polished brass fixtures and lantern styled pendant lights.

But it was the large claw-footed tub that captured Carrie's attention, a stack of fluffy, white towels setting nearby. She'd swear it was calling out to her to indulge in a long, hot bubble bath.

She sighed. Unfortunately, she was due to meet Livy in less than forty-five minutes for dinner. And she needed to unpack the dresses Sophie had helped her choose for the gallery show and the awards dinner.

As she hung both dresses in the closet, she was still undecided about which dress she liked better. She was also beginning to wonder if she should've gone a more conservative route. Both dresses could definitely be considered quite sexy, certainly more than what she was used to wearing.

The dress for the gallery preview was a deep forest green, the fabric a very clingy knit that hugged all of her curves. The v-neckline was a bit lower than she was used to, but she'd been sold on the elaborate open and crisscrossed pattern of the back of the dress. Sophie had also talked her into the metallic pewter high heeled sandals, long dangling pewter earrings and what seemed like a whole armful of assorted pewter bangle bracelets.

The dress for the awards dinner was a rich, vibrant red. It also had an open back. And a v-neckline lower than she'd normally wear. But the fabric was what sold her on this dress. Consisting of layers and layers of chiffon, it flowed around her like water when she moved. Sophie had suggested simple gold jewelry to complete the look.

She'd also insisted on placing a special order for a pair of red high heels, insisting these were needed to complete the look. Every girl should have a pair of sexy red heels in her closet for luck, she had said.

So how could you refuse? If anyone could use an extra dose of luck, it's you.

So, between the shoes and the roll of Lifesavers Chester had tucked in her hand when he dropped her off at the airport, she should be pretty well set.

For dinner with Livy, she changed into a long metallic copper tunic and her go-to black leggings. She put her hair put up in a casual French twist, did a quick touch to her make-up and gave one final check in the mirror. Satisfied with the result, she gathered up her coat and purse, and was out the door.

Livy had texted her the name of the restaurant, adding it was one of her favorite restaurants and the food was to die for. Which was more than fine with Carrie.

She was starving.

"May I help you?"

This request came from the hostess at The Gilded Story, the restaurant Livy had chosen. As Carrie was about to answer her, someone called out her name. "Carrie, here... I'm over here."

She glanced over to see a woman was waving to her, a big smile on her face. Confused, she slowly made her way over to her, trying not to stare.

This couldn't be Livy. At least it wasn't the Livy she knew. This woman could pass as an older version of her... maybe? Her hair pulled back in a severe ponytail, her bangs nearly covered the glasses she wore. On top of this, she was dressed entirely in black. Together, all of these things gave off the impression she wanted to remain as inconspicuous as possible.

Carrie swallowed.

Oh, Livy ... what's happened to you?

She tried to compose her facial features, forcing out a bright smile. But when Livy remained stiff and unyielding as they hugged, she realized she hadn't done a very good job at hiding what she was thinking.

As they followed the hostess to their table, anger began to build in Carrie.

Oh my god, Chester must be right. What has this Zack done to her?

Once they were seated, she sent Livy a big smile. "So, here we are. It's been a long time, hasn't it? I'm so glad you agreed to meet me for dinner because I have a feeling we have a lot of catching up to do."

She knew she was talking a mile a minute, but she didn't know what else to do. She was afraid if she didn't keep the conversation going, she would come right out and demand Livy tell her what the hell was going on.

She picked up her napkin, making a big production of putting it on her lap, smoothing it with her hands before she glanced over at Livy again.

"So, how has everything been going with you? And how is Zack?"

Livy picked up her glass and after taking a small sip of water, she placed the glass slowly back on the table. Then she bowed her head, as if she was studying the unopened menu in front of her. She didn't move. Nor did she answer.

Seconds ticked by.

Carrie cleared her throat. "Livy?"

She was alarmed to see a tear plop on the Livy's menu, followed by another. Bewildered, she leaned closer, reaching out her hand. "*Oh my god*, Livy ... what's wrong? What's happened?"

Livy looked up at her, shaking her head. It was obvious she was trying to gather herself together enough to speak, so Carrie waited.

Finally taking a deep, shuddering breath, Livy's words came tumbling out. "Zack left me. I came home from work last Friday and he was throwing all of his stuff in one of those huge, black plastic garbage bags."

She stopped to stare into space before her gaze slowly came back to Carrie. "I knew something was horribly wrong because he has always been so particular about his clothes. They have to be folded a certain way. And hung according to colors and there are other things ..."

Here her gaze dropped back to her menu.

Carrie was about to say something when Livy looked up at her and shook her head. She was close to breaking down completely, her eyes pooling with tears, her bottom lip trembling.

"He told me his plan was to be gone before I got home. He was going to write a note, he said. But now he didn't have to ..."

She stopped to take a deep gulping breath. "Then he told me the reason he was leaving was because he met someone else, a woman he had been seeing for almost five months. All of the business trips he went on during that time? Most of those were not business trips at all. They were time he spent with her."

Here she began to cry in earnest, her words barely audible between the big, gulping sobs she had obviously been holding in for a long time.

"Then he left. Just like that. He walked out the door. And that was the last I've seen of him."

She looked at Carrie, her face crumpling in anguish. "Do you know what hurts the most? After being together for over five years, he hadn't even planned on saying good bye. He was only going to leave me a note. That's all ... just a stupid, crummy note."

This came out in aloud wail before she put her arms down on the table, where she rested her head as she cried.

Carrie quickly moved to sit next to her. After she put her arm around her and let her cry for a few minutes, she gave her a hug. "Oh, Livy … I'm so, so sorry. You should've called me. Or Chester. Or taken some vacation or personal time from work and came home. You know you always have a place to stay with either of us. Or even with Aunt Evelyn. She'd love if you came to stay with her. After all, you've always been her favorite."

She added this, hoping to make Livy laugh. And it did. It was a bit of a hysterical laugh, but at least it was a laugh.

Livy picked up her napkin from the table to wipe her eyes and blow her nose. "I'm sure Chester has his hands full now with the baby coming. And as far as taking personal time, I think I've already used more than I'm allowed. I'm surprised no one at work has said anything to me yet."

She took a shuddering breath. "I don't have the energy to get out of bed some days. And when I do, I end up going into work late. I haven't been what you would call a model employee."

Carrie smiled at her. "I find that hard to believe. You always give it your all. You couldn't be bad at something even if you tried."

When this brought another smile from her, a bigger one this time, Carrie gave a sigh of relief.

She slipped back into her seat and opened her menu. "For now, let's decide what we're going to order and get that out of the way. Then you can tell me everything. I don't know about you, but I'm really hungry. I think we both also need to order a glass of wine."

She smiled brightly at Livy.

"So, while we wait for our server, tell me what's good. What's your favorite thing to order?"

During dinner, they went over just about every single detail of Livy and Zack's break up, with Carrie trying to convince Livy she wasn't the one at fault.

It was while they shared a dessert, she was finally able to steer the conversation away from Zack. She talked about Chester and Sophie's upcoming baby. She told Livy about her experience working with Sam on the renovation in Quebec. And she showed her photos of the work she did on her house.

She filled her in on the reason she was in New York, about the award she was nominated for. How she was excited to be chosen, but certainly didn't expect to win.

It was when she started to describe her hotel, Livy groaned, a stricken look on her face. "Oh Carrie, I'm so sorry I wouldn't let you stay with me." She shook her head. "I'm such a horrible sister. But when you called, it was right after Zack left, and I was a mess. I actually had the crazy thought once he thought about what he did, he'd realize he made a mistake and beg me to take him back."

Carrie smiled. "Don't worry about it. I like my hotel room. There is something you can do for me, though. I want you to come to an art exhibit with me. Sophie became friends with the artist when she was in Paris, and she was able to get passes for the preview of his work. It's tomorrow night. She actually asked for two passes so you could go with me."

When Livy started to protest, Carrie shook her head. "If you don't go, neither will I. There's no way I would go alone. Come on, it will be fun. We can pretend we're wealthy members of high society for a night. If nothing else, we'll have fun people watching."

She smiled. "Remember how we used do that when we were kids? I'm sure it will turn out to be just as fun now."

She suddenly had an idea. "When I was reading the hotel brochure, I saw they have a spa. Tomorrow we can get a massage. And get our nails done. Sort of like a girl's day out. My treat. What do you think?"

Livy held up her hands and after studying the unkempt condition of her nails, she shook her head before giving Carrie an embarrassed look.

"As you can see, I still bite my nails. Especially when I'm stressed. I think a manicure might be a good idea. I'm not sure about the gallery show, though. I have no idea what I would wear."

Her eyes suddenly lit up. "Maybe we can go shopping, too?"

At Carrie's nod, she finally smiled, the most genuine smile Carrie had seen from her all evening. "It does sound like fun. I feel like I haven't done anything fun for a long time. Zack and I didn't do that much. He always said he'd rather stay in and get some work done on his computer."

A horrified look came over her face. "Oh my God, I bet all along he was messaging *her*. How could I have been so blind? Talk about not paying attention."

Carrie shrugged. "You trusted him. How were you to know?"

She raised her wine glass. "Let's toast to a fun night tomorrow, a new beginning for you and maybe, an award for me."

She laughed. "Remind me to give you the roll of Lifesavers I have in my coat pocket. Chester gave them to me at the airport. But since I already put a roll in my suitcase, I have a spare. For good luck and all. Aunt Evelyn would be thrilled to know you have one, too! You know how she believes they bring good luck."

Not too far away, in the theater district, Lauren was in her dressing room, applying her make up for the evening show.

She was humming as she worked.

She was happy. Happier than she'd been for a long time.

It looked like her patience had finally paid off. Well … this would be along with the little bit of investigating she did.

She'd be the first to admit she was pretty obsessed with how she'd kept track on Chris since they'd parted back in March. And from what she'd been able to find out, he wasn't seeing anyone else. Evidently this little fling with the woman from Cleveland had never materialized, thanks to yours truly.

Are you really surprised? After all, Chris is a smart guy. He wouldn't be fooled by some small-town girl from the Midwest. You'd be willing to bet it didn't take him very long to see right through her plans.

Did she feel guilty about telling this woman she and Chris were engaged? Maybe every once in a while, a small twinge of guilt flitted through her mind. But then she always managed to convince herself what she did was for the best. *For all of them.*

Chris was destined to be with someone who was sophisticated and knew the way in and around the complexities of big city life and high society. He needed a wife who would help him get to the top.

She frowned.

Carrie. Even her name was irritating. Who named their child Carrie?

She glanced over at her phone, wondering if Chris had received the message she left about the gallery show. She had hoped he might call her back. Or at least take the time to leave her a return message. But then it really didn't matter because she knew his word was always good. He told her he would meet her the gallery tomorrow night, so she could count on him being there.

She took a long, deep breath. She just needed to be patient.

She had big plans for the two of them. By this time next year, she hoped to be engaged. Or possibly, already the new Mrs. Gardner. She had been planning her wedding ever since she was a little girl, so with all of her wedding plans on file and ready to go in her mind, she didn't need a long engagement.

She put on her earrings, watching them sparkle in the mirror before she closed her make-up case with a decisive snap. After giving one more look in the mirror she gave a satisfied nod.

Fingers crossed, it looked like her plans were back on track.

CHAPTER 6

On this cold and miserable Saturday night, a mixture of snow and rain has already started to fall when Chris's ride finally pulled up to the curb. He got out of the taxi, glancing up at the sign on the building in front of him.

Gallery East

A large canvas was prominently displayed in the front display window. Abstract in design, the bold brushstrokes of rich and vibrant colors were eye-catching, bringing one to stop and study it even further. Even if you weren't a fan of contemporary art.

He also had a good view of the interior of the gallery. By the size of the crowd gathered there, it appeared contemporary art was more popular than he had thought. Running his hand through his hair, he groaned.

You don't have to stay long. Just go in, mingle for a while and then you can leave. No pressure ... no pressure at all.

Comforted by this promise he made to himself, he sprinted up the steps.

He gave his name to the girl by the door and after taking a glass of wine from the tray of a passing server, he gazed around the room.

He found it amusing that out of the dozens of people who were in the room, only a handful were even looking at the paintings on display. Yes, this was your typical New York social gathering, the possibility of social and business connections to be made always foremost in everyone's mind.

Well, he wasn't going to fall into that trap. Nope, he was going to be different. He slowly sauntered over to one of the paintings to read the description on the plaque beneath it.

Early Evening in Spring

He stepped back to study it, the first thought going through his mind, it wasn't all that bad. An opinion he knew the artist probably would be less than thrilled to hear.

As he studied the painting even further, he decided the longer he looked at it, he could almost, and this was a big almost, visualize what the artist was trying to portray. He could see the sun setting behind the trees, shining through the leaves and onto the flower covered ground below. In fact, he whole effect was one of exactly what the title of the painting implied.

An early evening in spring ... maybe not here in the city, but somewhere in someone's memory. A memory of a more peaceful time.

Hmm ... maybe you're more into contemporary art than you thought you were.

He felt a hand slip into the crook of his arm. He looked over to see it belonged to Lauren. She was gazing up at him, a bright smile on her face.

"Hi ... so you did come. You never returned my call, so I was unsure." She reached up to kiss his cheek. "I'm so glad you're here."

His gaze went back to the painting. The peaceful feeling inside of him only a few seconds ago?

It was gone.

You shouldn't be here.

Carrie was sitting on the sofa by the fireplace in the lobby of her hotel. Since the gallery was only two blocks away from the hotel, the plan was for Livy to meet her here.

According to the text she just received, Livy should be walking through the door in about fifteen minutes.

They'd spent a fun day together. After they met for lunch, they did some serious shopping. Returning to the hotel, they had a massage and finished up with a manicure and pedicure. Livy then left to go back to her apartment to get changed for the evening, giving Carrie enough time to indulge in a bubble bath before she also got ready.

She didn't know why she was felt so restless, but when she realized she was pacing aimlessly around her hotel room, she decided to wait in the lobby.

And now, still feeling unsettled, she pulled out her phone and began going through her emails.

"Carrie?"

At the sound of this familiar voice, she looked up from her phone. Her mouth falling open in surprise, she jumped up from the sofa.

"Oh my gosh ... Sam, what are you doing here?"

He laughed before giving her a quick hug and a kiss to her cheek. "Well, there are actually three reasons I'm here. I think I might have mentioned my cousin moved here last month. He wants me to meet his girlfriend, something that makes me believe he is finally serious about this one. So, I'm planning on spending the day with both of them tomorrow."

He ran his hand through his hair, giving her a smile. "Since I knew I was going to be here, I was able to set up a meeting on Monday with a potential client about a restoration job. It's a nineteenth century estate in upstate New York. Since it sounded really interesting, so I thought I'd check it out."

He shrugged. "You know how I am. After I saw the photos the client sent, I was hooked. And finally, since I knew you were staying at this hotel, I figured why not surprise you and be on hand to lend some moral support? Not that you need it, of course."

He grinned, gazing around at the lobby "So, what do you think of my recommendation?"

"I love it. I love my room." She smiled. "I love everything about it."

A worried look came over her face. "My sister and I are going to that art exhibit I told you about. The artist preview show. The artist Sophie met while she was in Paris. Maybe we can sneak you in?"

He smiled, shaking his head. "No need for that. I managed to get a call through to Sophie and I'm pretty sure she was able to get me on the list. If you don't mind me tagging along, that is."

She couldn't stop smiling. "I'd be mad if you didn't."

He picked up his bag. "Good. But first I need to take this bag up to my room and freshen up a bit."

The smile he gave her was genuine. "By the way, you look absolutely gorgeous. If your sister is anything like you, I am one lucky man to be hanging out with both of you tonight."

He winked before he turned to walk away, his words floating back to her. "Give me ten minutes and I'll be ready to go."

Livy had learned almost the entire life story of her taxi driver by the time he pulled up to the entrance of Carrie's hotel. When he was not driving a taxi, he informed her, he was trying to make his way as a stand-up comedian. This had a lot to do with why she was still laughing when she emerged from the taxi.

After waving goodbye, she slowly made her way to the entrance of the hotel, a smile still on her face. She was starting to feel really good about this evening out with Carrie.

The rain had turned to sleet, which had now turned to snow. So, if she wasn't careful, there was a really, *really* good chance she could wipe out with these new shoes she was wearing. Carrie had talked her into buying them when they were shopping earlier and even though she absolutely loved them, she wasn't used to wearing such a high heel.

Once she was in the lobby and saw Carrie sitting by the fireplace, her confidence high, she began to make her way over to her.

And, of course, you know what came next.

With the combination of new shoes, the soles still shiny and new, and a slick marble floor, it was bound to happen.

Her feet going out from under her, she landed on her back with a far from graceful sprawl of arms and legs. Her purse went flying from her hands and hit the floor. Where it flew open, everything inside, shooting in all directions.

Her eyes closed, she didn't move. Her first thought was to stay right where she was and pretend nothing happened. Her second thought? Why had she ever thought she'd be able to pull off these shoes? And her third and final thought? She hoped Carrie was the only one to have witnessed her fall.

But, of course, this was not to be.

A very deep and masculine voice came from above, a hand gently taking hold of her arm.

"My god ... are you okay?"

She froze.

Oh, no, no, no ...

Slowly, and very cautiously, she opened her eyes to find she was gazing into the eyes of a man who was leaning over her. The expression on his face was very concerned. It was also a face she found to be very, *very* attractive. In fact, everything about him was what she'd consider to be perfect.

He was, hands down, the most handsome man she'd ever set eyes on, even more so at such close range.

He had the kind of face that would stop you in your tracks. Well, at least for her, this was the case. With his tousled auburn hair, so thick and lustrous and the mesmerizing deep, almost navy, blue of his eyes, he was the kind of man any woman would love to get to know better.

But certainly, not under circumstances such as this.

My god, you've just about ruined any chance you have of making a good impression with this man, haven't you?

"Here, let me help you."

She immediately came to life. Part of her wanted to let him take over. Another part of her was telling her she needed to get hold of these feelings he brought on in her before she did something stupid. But the biggest part of her suddenly became very irritated. And this would be with him. Why? Maybe because she was embarrassed? She hadn't a clue.

Unfortunately, she went with the latter

She batted his hand away and struggled into a sitting position. This was when she realized with the close fit of her dress, actually getting back on her feet was going to be a major production.

Another thing you can thank Carrie for. Along with the shoes, she'd also persuaded you to buy this dress. Remember? She told you it was supposed to fit close. And you could carry it off, so why not go for it?

Evidently Carrie was way off with the you-can-carry-it-off comment. Here was all the proof needed to show she couldn't.

And now she was in big trouble.

She looked up to see her handsome new friend no longer looked concerned. No, now he was frowning. He reached down again to take her arm.

"You didn't break anything, did you?"

Then he shot a quick glance at her feet, slowly shaking his head. "But seriously, are these shoes really a wise choice? I mean… just look at you."

He shook his head again.

What?

Exactly what does he mean? Is he implying you don't look sophisticated enough to carry them off? Of all the nerve… never mind you just admitted the exact same thing to yourself.

Pushing her glasses more firmly against her nose and shaking her bangs out of her face, she pulled her arm from his hand with a jerk.

She glared at him. "I believe what I wear is of no concern of yours. Now if you excuse me, I believe I need to get up off of this floor."

Undeterred by her rejection, he extended his hand to her once again. And as before, she refused his offer, shaking her head even more vigorously this time.

"Just go … I'll manage on my own."

But how?

It was obvious she had no choice but to wait until he left. But after a few moments of silence, she glanced up to see he was still there, his arms now crossed over his chest as he gazed down at her. She gave a huge sigh and mumbled something.

Now Sam was pretty sure she was asking for his help, but he didn't want to give in to her quite yet. He wasn't quite sure why, but he was enjoying this exchange between them, finding her stubbornness intriguing. Leaning closer, he tried not to smile. "What was it you just said? I didn't quite hear you."

She got the distinct impression he was finding this all very amusing. But knowing she had no other option, she held out her hands to him. "Please, can you help me?"

He took her hands. "*Ah ... now that's much better.*"

In one quick move, he had her back on her feet. When he put his hands on her waist to steady her, a deep shiver ran through her. Confused, she abruptly pulled away. But not before she noticed the smile flash across his face.

A knowing smile, she'd have to say. No doubt this was the reaction he was used to getting from a woman.

In an attempt to ignore him, she began tugging at the skirt of her dress, trying to pull it back down to where it was supposed to be. Since it was already shorter than what she normally wore, she was now showing much more of her legs than she should be.

She glanced over at him, to become completely rattled when she saw he was watching this with interest, a bigger smile now on his face.

Determined not to let him see how he affected her, she quickly began gathering up the items from her purse, still scattered across the floor. But again, with her tight skirt, this was not the easiest thing to do. He quickly picked up on this and scrambled to help.

She took the comb and lipstick he handed to her and stuffed them in the purse, fumbling to close the clasp. Still refusing to look at him, she spoke. "Thank you, but I'm sure you need to go. You must have someone you're meeting up with. Your date for the evening. Or a girlfriend. Or your wife… or whatever."

Without thinking, her gaze drifted to his left hand. When she saw there was no ring, she glanced up at him, hoping he hadn't noticed her interest.

But he had. He nodded, following this with a bright smile.

"Nope. Not married. No girlfriend, either."

Why he bothered to tell her this, he had no idea. But for some odd reason, he suddenly found it very important she know he was available. He was also flattered she'd even checked this out.

Becoming even more undone, she immediately went right back into her tirade.

"Well, no doubt there's someone … or whatever. I just hope for your sake, it's a woman who's a lot more coordinated than I am. Or at least one who knows her limits as to what she can wear."

He stepped back with a groan, running his hand through his hair. "Geeez … that's not at all what I meant to say. What I wanted to say, with the snow and rain, maybe you made a mistake wearing the shoes you have on."

He knew he should probably stop right there, but instead he kept on talking, nodding towards her feet. "It's great to be fashionable, but come on … you need to be able to carry it off."

And … *bingo.* As soon as these words came out of his mouth, he regretted them.

What the hell is wrong with you? And why do you keep insulting this woman? You don't even know her. The last thing you want to do, is make her any angrier than she already is.

But he was quick to realize if he tried to apologize for his poor choice of words, the look on her face indicated this wouldn't be enough. The damage was complete and he had a very, *very* irate woman on his hands.

Livy was beyond angry. She was furious.

Who was this man?

He was acting as though she'd purposely thrown herself down on the floor. What did he think? She did this on purpose to get his attention? It was an accident, for God's sake.

She didn't need his help. Nor did she need his comments. In fact, if she were to stop and think about it, handsome face and all, she didn't need him.

Period.

And you're certainly going to let him know this.

She wrapped her coat tightly around her and began to back away from him, her fury making her all but spit out the words. "I don't know what your problem is and why you feel the need to insult me, but I've had enough. Just because you're so attractive, well... this doesn't give you the right to be rude. Why, even if you got down on your knees right now and begged me, I still wouldn't go out with you."

At the little twitch of his lips in a smile, she realized she may have gone a bit too far with her last words. Fighting the urge to cry and her and her chin raised high, she gave him as scornful of a look as she could. "So again, thanks for your help. And again, for a final time, goodbye."

With these final words, she swung around and headed for Carrie.

Carrie hadn't moved from where she was on the sofa. As she had watched this exchange between Livy and Sam, to say she was shocked, would be an understatement.

She was also very confused.

In all the time she'd known Sam, she had never once seen him act in the manner he had now. Certainly not over something so incredibly stupid.

Yeah, she'd seen him get worked up about some setback because of work, but certainly not to this extreme. Even when they were in Quebec and a contractor showed up late or the wrong materials were delivered. He'd always kept his cool. Not one to yell or scream, he always managed to remain calm and in control to swiftly resolve the problem.

And when it came to women? He had to be the most polite and kindest man she'd ever known. This was besides Chester, of course.

But Chester is your brother, so he doesn't count.

And what was up with Livy? She'd always been very shy, especially around men. The Livy she knew would've been so embarrassed by what happened, she barely would've managed to whisper out a thank-you before scurrying off without another word.

Instead, the two of them were acting like they had been thrown into the ring, the bell had rung and they were ready to fight it out.

Hmm ... or maybe come together in a kiss?
She smiled.
Well, well, well ... this was certainly very interesting.
She stood and after smiling tentatively at both of them, she cleared her throat. "My goodness ... this isn't at all how I expected this evening to start out. But now, after watching you both share whatever madness just went on between you, I believe introductions are in order."
She shrugged, holding out her hands to both of them. "Livy, meet my colleague and good friend Sam. And Sam, meet my sister Livy."

Carrie's announcement was met with dead silence.
It appeared neither Livy or Sam had anything to say.
Livy had gone completely still, as though she was paralyzed. Only her eyes showed any movement, her gaze darting from Carrie to Sam and then back to Carrie again, before she closed them.
She was mortified. What had she done?
Oh my God, could you feel like any more of a fool?
A totally bewildered expression on his face, a look that had been with him since Livy first tore into him while she was still on the floor, Sam let out a long groan.
Carrie knew it was safe to bet he had no idea of what just happened.
He swiftly moved to her side. "Carrie, I'm sorry. I don't know what the hell… well, let's just say, for some reason I lost it." He looked over at Livy, who quickly averted her eyes. "I'm sorry, Livy. I didn't know you were Carrie's sister."
This brought her head up, an even angrier expression flooding her face. So, he was quick to continue. "Not that it would've made a difference if you weren't. No, that's not at all what I meant."
He gave Carrie a desperate look. "Carrie, help me out here. Tell her I'm not the bad person she seems to think I am."
Carrie smiled, shaking her head. "You're not. I know that. And I'm pretty sure Livy does, too."

She studied the two of them. They were both trying so desperately to even avoid looking at each other. She watched as Livy reached up to push her glasses up more firmly on her nose, something Carrie knew she did when she was feeling threatened or uncomfortable.

She gave them both a big smile. "Okay... I think we need to start over. Let's forget about what happened and go to the art gallery as planned. We'll view some great art, share a glass of wine or two and then afterwards, go out to dinner."

Avoiding eye contact with Sam and her words aimed directly to Carrie, Livy finally spoke. "Why don't the two of you go on ahead? You don't need me tagging along. After all, I live here so I can go see the..."

Sam cut her off. "No, I'm the one who came barging in, causing all of this trouble. So, it would be better if the two of you go without me. I'll be perfectly happy going back to the hotel, ordering up room service and making it an early night."

Carrie reached over to pick up her coat. When she turned back to them, both the expression on her face and the tone of her voice held a warning. Whatever she was about to say, they were both going to agree.

"No. We're going to this show as planned. Together. And we're all going to have a good time. You're both very special to me and I want you to like each other. So, you'll just have to work it out."

She reached for her coat. With a smile, Sam swiftly reached over to help her. "Here, beautiful, let me."

"She has a name. It's Carrie."

Livy could feel the blush begin to rise in her cheeks as both Carrie and Sam turned to look at her, totally surprised by her comment.

She'd swear, on a stack of bibles if need be, she had absolutely no idea why she blurted that out.

Okay, maybe she did. And this was because it was so hard having a sister like Carrie. Men were attracted to her like a moth to a flame.

Take tonight for instance. Here she was feeling really good about how she looked and then she comes up against Carrie. And just like that, she's back to the same plain old Livy.

But this didn't end with Carrie. Look at what happened with Zack. It turned out she wasn't good enough for him either. No, he had to go out and find someone else. Probably someone prettier, smarter and a lot more fun than she was.

And now, for some insane reason, she'd been hit with this sudden and almost overwhelming attraction to Sam. It had come on so fast, she couldn't even think straight. This was more than obvious by the way she was acting like such an idiot.

She knew this was the Sam Carrie had worked with this past summer on a renovation project in Quebec. From what Carrie had told her, it was obvious she didn't think of him as a potential boyfriend.

But Livy could tell Sam felt differently.

The fact he was even here in New York confirmed this.

So, once again, she didn't have a chance.

It just wasn't fair.

Carrie was giving Livy the look … the what-the-heck-are-you-doing-and-you-better-get-it-together look that demanded an answer.

This brought on even more of a reason for Livy to be upset. She was the older sister, for heaven's sake. This would be by two years and seven months. But instead here she was, feeling like she was right back to where she used to be when they were kids, the sister who was always left out and invariably in the wrong.

Both Sam and Carrie were still looking at her, waiting for an explanation.

She gave a frustrated sigh. "I mean… well, what I meant to say is most women like to be called by their name. Not some flattering or cute little nickname. Or whatever."

She gave them a tentative smile.

When neither Carrie or Sam had anything to say to this, she rambled on. "At least I find this holds true for me. Unless…" Her words trailed off. If she kept talking, she'd no doubt go on to say something even more stupid.

Like possibly asking Sam if he thought she was beautiful, too.

She sent a desperate glance over to Carrie.

It was Sam who responded. "Even though I disagree, I'll try to remember your take on this."

He shrugged, a sheepish grin on his face. "I'm sorry. I find all women beautiful. I can't say I've ever met one I didn't like."

An uncertain expression suddenly appeared on his face after he said this. Which made Livy hope to God he wasn't thinking there was always a first time for everything and this was happening now. Adjusting her glasses and nervously swiping at her bangs, she glanced over at Carrie, a bright smile on her face.

"So, are we ready to go, then?"

When Sam and Livy both turned to her, waiting for her answer, Carrie felt like she'd been dropped into the middle of something she didn't understand. Sort of like a play she didn't know her lines. Or a test she'd studied the wrong information.

Seriously, it was as though the two of them were teetering on the edge, their emotions swinging wildly between love and hate. And there was no way she could help them.

Nope, they're going to have to work this out for themselves.

She gave Livy a reassuring smile. "Yes, and since the gallery is only two blocks away, we don't really need a taxi. We can walk."

At this, all attention veered to Livy's feet. She immediately bristled. "Don't worry, I'm more than capable of walking there."

At the stubborn look on her face, Sam immediately checked what he planned to say and gave a slow nod instead. "Ah… yes. I guess we shall see, won't we?" He held out his arms to both of them. "So, ladies, are you ready?"

His grin was huge. "How can one man be so lucky? A night on the town with a woman on each arm."

Here he paused to wink at Livy. "And might I add, two very beautiful women at that."

He watched as Livy actually smiled, a blush spreading over her cheeks before she quickly glanced away.

This was when he decided his goal of the evening would be to see more of her smile. Because, for some reason and there was no way he could even begin to explain this, when she did smile, he felt it tug at his heart.

It wasn't a big tug, but it was enough to get him thinking.

Their walk to the gallery was made without a single mishap, though Livy wondered if maybe Sam was holding on to her a little tighter than was necessary. But this could very well have been her imagination. A more logical explanation for his firm grip would be the two times she almost lost her footing on the slippery sidewalk.

Whatever the reason, and as much as he had this way of irritating her, she wanted to savor the feeling of having someone so strong to lean on. She actually felt a pang of disappointment when they finally arrived at the gallery and he released his hold on her.

Now in the packed gallery, Carrie and Livy were wandering from one painting to the next as they waited for Sam.

He had left, promising to return with a plate of appetizers for them to share.

Carrie took a sip of her wine as she studied Livy, who was reading a description under one of the paintings. Looking over her shoulder to see Sam was still nowhere in sight, she leaned in closer to her.

"Do you want to tell me exactly what was going on back there in the hotel lobby? Between you and Sam? What got you so riled up?"

Livy's attention suddenly zoomed in on the painting as though it was the most fascinating work of art she'd ever laid eyes on. She gave a nonchalant shrug. "I have no idea what you're talking about."

With Carrie trailing behind, she quickly moved on to the next painting, glancing down at the name plate beneath it. "So, what do you think of this one? Do you see the bird they're talking about? Because, I don't. Maybe I'm..."

Carrie rolled her eyes, interrupting her. "Livy, stop it. I don't care about the painting. And I know you don't either." She paused to point at the painting. "Though I have to say, I think that's the bird right there. That blue blob of paint. See the wings?"

As Livy leaned in closer to look, Carrie sighed. "Livy, *come on*. I want you to tell me what made you and Sam act like a couple of five-year-olds."

Her focus still on the painting, at first Livy didn't answer. Then she sighed. "I don't know what happened. I only know he made me mad. He's seems so arrogant. And I didn't need his help."

She frowned. "Nor did I want his help."

"Sam? Arrogant?" Carrie shook her head. "Oh Livy, if anything, he's more like a big, cuddly teddy bear. And he was only trying to help. I've known Sam for a long time and he is one of the nicest guys around. And you're wrong, you definitely needed his help. There was no way you were going to get up off that floor by yourself."

She nodded toward Livy's dress. "Not with that dress. Which by the way, looks even better on you now than it did in the dressing room. You look stunning."

Livy smiled. "Thanks. And you look amazing as always."

They both smiled at each other.

Carrie sighed. "Getting back to you and Sam… if it makes you feel any better, it wasn't just you. Sam was just as crazy. I've never seen him act like that before."

Livy groaned, closing her eyes. "Oh God, I made such a fool of myself, didn't I? What's wrong with me? I thought I'd gone off men completely after the whole fiasco with Zack. But then along comes Sam and… well, you've got to admit, he's just so darn attractive."

She stared down at her wine glass, to then look back at Carrie, her eyes bright. "It's not right. Here he came all the way to New York because you're here and you don't even like him. As a boyfriend, that is."

Carrie shook her head. "He didn't come to New York just because of me. He came here to meet up with his brother his new girlfriend. He also has a meeting set up on Monday with a possible client. And he knows how I feel about him. I told you that."

She smiled. "We're friends, good friends."

Livy abruptly turned to her, her expression fierce. "But he's hoping you'll change your mind. Can't you see this?" Blinking furiously, she turned back to the stare at the painting, her vision blurred. She had no idea what was wrong with her, why she suddenly had this urge to rest her forehead against the wall and cry. She knew she was acting totally irrational, but she couldn't help it.

My God... you just met the guy. And you, of all people, should know that no guy is worth crying about.

She took a deep breath. "Do us both a favor and forget about what happened in that hotel lobby, okay?"

Alarmed to see Livy's eyes pooling with tears, Carrie was silent for a few seconds. Then it all became so completely clear to her.

"*Oh my god,* you're attracted to him, aren't you? The two of you have some kind of chemistry going on, don't you? That's why you both reacted so strongly."

She stared intently into Livy's face. "You know there's a fine line between love and hate, don't you? In the beginning it can be easy to confuse the two."

Livy closed her eyes, vigorously shaking her head. "No, no... of course not. That's not what's happening. Certainly not on Sam's part." Her laugh was sharp. "And who believes in any of that love at first sight nonsense? I know for certain I don't." Turning away, she moved to the next painting.

Carrie followed her and raising her glass to her lips, she was surprised to find it was empty.

For her, this was certainly something out of the norm. She wasn't one to gulp down a glass of wine. She was more of the take-a-little-sip-at-a-time-here-and-there type of drinker. But, with the way the evening was progressing, why was she even surprised?

She glanced in the direction Sam had gone. What was taking him so long? Maybe she should go search for him?

She smiled. Knowing Sam, he was probably talking to someone. He was the type of person who managed to make friends wherever he went.

Arrogant? Sam?

She shook her head. Livy was way off with that assessment.

But she really wished he'd come back with those appetizers he'd promised. Lunch with Livy now felt like it was a long, long time ago. This probably also explained why the glass of wine she'd just polished off was starting to get to her, making her feel a little lightheaded

So, you'd think this would be enough to stop her from trading her empty glass for a full glass, off the tray the server was holding in front of her.

Unfortunately, it wasn't.

Instead, she enjoyed another sip of wine before she finally responded to Livy's comment.

"I do." She sighed. "Believe in love at first sight, that is."

Surprised, Livy turned to her. "You do?"

Carrie nodded. "Yes, not that it's done me any good. Unfortunately, everything I thought he was, he wasn't. Instead, after he called and left a message he wanted to see me again, when I called him back, his fiancée answered the phone."

Her laugh was bitter. "As you can imagine, this was certainly not at all what I expected."

Livy slowly shook her head. "Oh no … and now?"

A trace of despair was in Carrie's voice. "Oh Livy, I'd give anything to see him again. I can't get him out of my mind for the life of me. So, yes… I'm a believer."

"Oh, Carrie … I'm so sorry." Livy reached over to give her a hug. "Maybe there's something you …"

Carrie shook her head. "No, there's nothing to be done. He's engaged. Which, as far as I'm concerned, means it's a done deal. Even if he did break off the engagement, how could I ever trust him? What kind of man makes a woman all kinds of promises when he's already engaged to another? As far as I'm concerned, this is cheating. Big time. And if he's doing this to her, the chances are very high he'd turn around to eventually do the same to me."

"So, girls … here's the most I could rustle up. This crowd hasn't eaten in weeks, it appears. It was a fight to even get this."

At the sound of Sam's voice, they both turned to find him standing behind them, holding a plate with a meager display of a few crackers, what looked like a blob of bright orange cheese spread and three olives and a pickle. He has a look of such disappointment on his face, both Carrie and Livy burst out laughing.

He shook his head. "I think they ran out of appetizers and this is what they were able to scrounge up here in their kitchen. A very sad assortment, I'm sorry to say."

He held the plate out to Livy. "Here, you first. Go ahead, dig in."

She tentatively took a cracker, shaking her head when he kept holding the plate out to her. "I'm not going to chance the cheese … or whatever it is. Fake cheese, maybe?"

Instead of stopping right there, she went on to completely ruin the moment. "After all, we both know what could happen with someone like me … I could very well drop it right down the front of my dress."

Oh, for heaven's sake. Why in the world did you have to go and say that? It's him … he brings out the nasty side of you?

He gave her a long look before she saw a smile touch the corner of his mouth. He cleared his throat. "Touché. But I'm going to counter that remark of yours and say it wouldn't matter. Because nothing, not even fake cheese, could take away from how good that dress looks on you." He followed this with a wink.

Completely flustered, Livy did the only thing she could think of… she stuffed the whole cracker in her mouth, hoping to God, she didn't choke on it.

This man was definitely out of her league. It didn't matter what she said to him, he was always going to come right back to put her in her place. And she had absolutely no idea of how she was supposed to deal with this.

And Sam? He wasn't quite sure what to think.

The only thing he did know?

He'd been completely honest when he gave her the compliment about her dress.

CHAPTER 7

"Chris? How does the weekend of November twenty-seventh sound? Are you in?"

Chris was daydreaming, wishing he were anywhere else. This is why Lauren's voice came as almost a shock, bringing him crashing right down to where he didn't want to be.

The twenty-seventh of November?

A faint smile on his face, he was immediately whisked right back to a happier time and place. Back to the night following Kevin and Abby's wedding in Cleveland. Remembering how he and Carrie had been curled up together on the sofa in the lobby of his hotel. Where they had talked through the night and into the early morning hours, about everything and anything, with never a loss of words between them.

This was also when he learned the twenty-seventh of November was Carrie's birthday.

After they checked the date to see the twenty-seventh fell on a

Saturday, he convinced her she should come to New York for that long weekend. They would spend her birthday in style, he told her. Dinner, a show, shopping, the works… whatever she wanted. He could still see the excitement on her face, when she'd confessed it had always been a dream of hers to come to New York during the Christmas season.

If this is what she wanted, well, he was going to make it happen.

Yeah, you promised her you'd make her dream come true. Even going as far as to seal this with a kiss if you recall.

After all, a person only had one chance to experience their twenty-seventh birthday on the same numbered day of the month, he'd told her.

An event that definitely called for a celebration.

Lauren's sharp laugh, along with her not so gentle tug to his arm cut right into these pleasant thoughts.

He stared at her, almost in a daze.

This prompted her to squeeze his arm.

Hard.

"Chris, what in the world are you thinking about? Did you even hear any of what I just said?"

Damn … yes, you heard her. The twenty-seventh. And no, you're not in.

He glanced around to be met by the awkward silence and uncomfortable glances of their friends. Flashing a bright smile, he finished off his wine and placing the empty glass on the tray of the nearest server, shaking his head at the suggestion of a refill. He was beginning to see, more than anything, he needed to keep a clear head.

He glanced down at Lauren, who was still hanging onto his arm. Funny, he didn't remember her as being this clingy.

She was gazing up at him, a hopeful look on her face. Her smile was too forced, too desperate. As if she was trying to draw something out of him he wasn't able to give her.

The tone of her voice was overly bright. "It will be so much fun. If only to get out of the city during the Thanksgiving weekend." Her glance going around the group, she scrunched up her face in disgust. "All of those crazy tourists descending on the city is enough to turn anyone off the holidays."

Chris shook his head, a wry smile on his face. "You better be careful about what you say. After all, it's those crazy tourists who come to see your show and keep you employed."

She waved her hand at him. "Oh, pooh, pooh… you know what I mean. But back to this trip, think about it. The peace and quiet of the snow-covered mountains, a picturesque lodge, a fire burning in the fireplace, wine …"

She moved closer, her voice lowered. "You … me."

Briefly closing his eyes, he shook his head.

No … you can't do this. You should've never agreed to come here tonight. You need to leave. Now, before things get out of control.

Removing his arm from her hold and giving everyone an apologetic smile, he pulled her away from the group.

His voice was gentle. "Lauren, I'm sorry, but I think it's best I leave. I shouldn't have come here tonight. It was a stupid move on my part. It's obvious you want what I can't give you. I'm sorry."

When she turned her head, refusing to look at him, he put his finger under her chin and raised her face to his. His smile was bittersweet.

"Come on, you need someone to love you so much more than I ever will. Deep down, I think you know this."

Her eyes searched his, not finding what she wanted to see. She jerked his chin from his hold.

She shrugged. "Well, I think you're wrong, but now is probably not the time to discuss this. We can talk later."

Then she took him completely by surprise. Reaching up to clasp her hands behind his head, she sought his mouth in a kiss. She was desperately trying to draw him into the kiss, when he suddenly pulled away, giving a sharp intake of breath. This was followed by his harsh whisper.

"My god…"

Her eyes flying open, she knew right away his reaction wasn't in response to her kiss. He was gazing over her shoulder, a look of complete disbelief on his face. It was when he slowly began to smile, she turned to see a woman staring right at them. Even across the room, Lauren could see the shocked expression on her face.

Then she disappeared into the crowd.

A deep groan came from Chris right before he abruptly moved Lauren aside. He began pushing his way through the crowd, the sound of his voice rising above the chatter in the room.

"Carrie, no … *Please stop.*"

Blinking frantically in an attempt to halt the angry tears that were beginning to flood her eyes, Lauren could only watch him go.

Carrie?

The woman from Cleveland?

What the hell was she doing in New York?

When Carrie glanced across the room and saw Chris, she thought she had to be imagining what she wanted so badly wanted to happen. How was it even possible, in the sea of people that made up Manhattan, the two of them would wind up in the same place and at the same time? It had to be at least a million to one, right? Or maybe even more like a billion...

Unable to tear her gaze away, she watched as the woman he was with put her arms around his neck and they kissed. A woman who was blonde, beautiful and from what she could see, close to perfect.

This had to be Lauren. His fiancée.

And just like that, reality came crashing down on her, putting everything in perspective.

Why shouldn't they be kissing? He's engaged, remember?

She panicked, her heart pounding in her chest, her breath coming hard. She couldn't let him see her. She began looking wildly around the room for the nearest means of escape.

Then knowing she shouldn't, but unable to stop herself, she looked once more in his direction.

At that exact same moment, Chris lifted his head and their eyes met. Frozen in place, she could only watch as the shock in his eyes turned to a burning intensity, sending a tremor through her from all the way across the room.

It was when his mouth curved into a smile, she finally ducked behind the person standing next to her, spilling the rest of her wine down the front of her dress in the process. Horrified, she stared down at the rapidly spreading stain.

Oh my god, look at you. Is this some kind of sign?

She grabbed Livy by the arm and shoving her empty glass in her hand, her words poured out. "Livy, here … take this. I need to leave. I can't stay. Chris… he's here. And he's seen me and I can't …I just can't … I'm sorry."

Before Sam and Livy even realized what was happening, she turned and disappeared into the crowd.

As she made her way to the entrance of the gallery, she could hear Chris calling out her name. Moving faster, she became even more determined to get as far away from him as she could.

Because, all of that nonsense she told Livy just minutes ago? About how, for her, it was over?

Well, it was now very obvious she'd been wrong.

Very wrong.

Chris pushed his way through the packed gallery to finally arrive at the front entrance. Stopping to catch his breath, he scanned the area for Carrie. But there was no sign of her.

Bewildered, he ran his hand through his hair. Did he imagine what happened?

He shook his head. No. It was her. He'd know her anywhere. And he wasn't going to give up until he found her.

There is no way in hell you're going to let her get away. If only to find out why she never returned your call.

No, whatever her reason, he wanted to hear it.

This was the only way he'd be able to stop thinking about her and get back in control of his life.

On the chance she'd gone outside, he pushed open the door, a groan coming from him when he saw a wet snow had started to fall, coating everything with a fresh layer of the white stuff.

But this was all forgotten when he saw Carrie. Just now reaching the bottom of the steps, she was about to start down the sidewalk.

He took off after her.

It was when Carrie arrived at the bottom of the steps, she realized she'd left without her coat. And now it had started to snow.

If you think back, you'll remember the back of her dress was pretty much non-existent.

So, between that, and what happened in the gallery, she was shaking. But, since it would be too risky to go back for her coat, she started walking, thankful her hotel was only a few blocks away.

"Carrie, for god's sake, stop."

At the sound of Chris's voice, she came to an abrupt halt, almost losing her footing. He sounded like he was right behind her. Close enough to touch her if he wanted.

Well, this wasn't going to happen.

Shaking her head, she wrapped her arms more tightly around herself and began walking faster. She was almost thankful for the slick surface of the sidewalk. Since it was taking all of her concentration to keep from falling, she had no time to think about how he was right behind her.

After a few seconds of silence, he spoke again.

"Carrie, come on. It's me, Chris. At least slow down so you can hold on to my arm. I'm afraid you're going to slip and fall."

When she continued to ignore him, he gave a frustrated sigh and slipping out of his jacket, he moved closer to drape it over her shoulders.

He wanted to reach out and turn her around to face him. If only so he could look into her eyes and possibly get a clue as to why she was so determined to ignore him.

But, unsure as to how she'd react to this, he held back.

Carrie's steps faltered when he put his jacket around her. Still warm from the heat of his body, the familiar scent of his cologne clinging to the fabric, it was an instant attack on her senses.

The memories of everything about that night in February, hit her all at once. And it took every ounce of control she had, to not turn and go right into his arms.

Because you can't ... remember? He's engaged.

She wrapped his coat more tightly around her and putting her head down, she began to walk even faster. It was when she slipped on an icy patch, almost falling, he finally reached out to grab her arm.

He groaned. "Carrie, *come on ...*"

She twisted away from him, refusing to meet his gaze. "You need to go back to your friends. My hotel is not far from here, so I'll be fine. Please, just go."

At the husky and seductive tone of her voice, his whole body reacted, memories of when he was last with her, flooding his senses. His eyes scanning her face, he desperately searched for even the smallest sign of the Carrie he'd been with that night. But he saw only a deep sadness.

This is when he knew there was absolutely no way in hell he was going to turn around and leave her. Nope, this wasn't going to happen. He was going to take her somewhere so they could talk. And straighten this out.

Still holding on to her arm, he swiftly moved them to the curb where he began signaling for a taxi. Miraculously, she didn't fight him on this. Even more amazing, a taxi pulled up within seconds.

But when he opened the door to the back seat, motioning for her to get in, she hesitated, sending a nervous glance at him and taking a step back.

She shook head. "I don't think this is a good idea."

He smiled, the sexy, crooked smile she remembered so well. The same smile that had haunted all of her dreams over the past months.

It was also the same smile that took hold of another little piece of her heart, each and every time he gave it to her.

"Don't worry. It's not like I'm kidnapping you. I only want to take you somewhere where we can be alone."

When she took another step back, he was quick to add. "So, we can talk. This is all I want. I promise. I only want to talk to you."

His hand extended to her, he waited. Finally, and very slowly, she put her hand in his.

Once they were in the taxi and Chris had given the driver an address, he sank back in the seat, breathing a silent prayer of thanks.

He couldn't believe how relieved he was. Completely baffled by her behavior, he had no idea what he would've done had she fought him on this.

He didn't understand. It was almost as if she was afraid of him. Or furious with him. Or maybe it was a combination of both. Whatever it was, it wasn't making the least bit of sense. Thank God she'd agreed to get in the taxi with him. This was at least a sign she trusted him.

Yeah, either that, or she only went along with you because she's afraid of the crazy way you're acting.

As the taxi began to move, he glanced over to see she'd wrapped his jacket even more tightly around her and was gazing out the window.

She was shaking.

He wasn't quite sure if this was because she was cold or it was from whatever she had going on in her mind.

He cleared his throat. "Are you warm enough? Do you want me to ask the driver to turn up the heat?"

She slowly turned her head to study him, her eyes huge in her face. He watched as she went to open her mouth, only to close it again before she shook her head. Then she turned her face back to the window.

He closed his eyes, giving a frustrated groan. He wanted to take her into his arms. She wouldn't have to talk. He'd just hold her, maybe whisper something soothing. He'd do anything.

God, anything ...

And this was when he knew, with a certainty, nothing had changed.

It was still there, the same pull, the same chemistry between them. It was as though they'd never been apart.

And what was going on in Carrie's mind?

She knew she should say something. But she couldn't bring herself to say what she didn't want to admit. This was she shouldn't be with him. It was wrong. Watching him kiss his fiancée in the gallery should have been enough to convince her of this.

She closed her eyes. Nothing about this was right.

"Carrie?"

When she turned to face him, the desperation in her eyes was like a blow to his heart.

"Come here …" In one swift move he pulled her into his arms to hold her against him. And as if he knew what she was thinking, his mouth moved in a continuous whisper through her hair. "Everything is going to be fine. We're together, so it's all good."

Having observed all of this in his rearview mirror, the taxi driver smiled. He eased his foot off the gas pedal and began to drive at a more leisurely speed.

When it came to his passengers, he prided himself on being a good judge of character. After all, in his twenty years of driving a cab, he'd about seen it all.

And from what he could see with these two, the look of longing in the man's eyes told him these two could use this time alone.

He gave a long, satisfied sigh.

This is when he really loved his job.

CHAPTER 8

Sam and Livy watched Carrie disappear into the crowd.

Her intention to go after her, Livy set the wine glasses on the floor, shoving them against the wall. She started to leave, but Sam grabbed her arm.

"No, let her go."

Bewildered, she glanced up at him. "But why? And who is Chris? Do you know him?" Comprehension dawning in her eyes, she nodded. "Oh, I think I understand. But she can't just take off like this. She doesn't have her coat and she shouldn't be out there alone."

He slowly shook his head, his smile resigned. "I have the feeling she won't be alone."

He had seen the look on this Chris's face as he went tearing after Carrie. The fact he didn't care who saw, or heard him call out her name, was a pretty good indication he was going after the woman he loved.

And there you have it ... what was it they said? If you love them, let them go? This pretty much sums it all up when it comes to you and Carrie, doesn't it?

He gave a big sigh. "Well, it looks like it will be just you and me for the rest of the evening."

Still gazing off in the direction Carrie had disappeared, Livy gave a loud gasp before she whirled around to face him. She glared up at him. "Let me assure you, I certainly don't expect you to spend any more time with me than you want. You're more than free to go. Right now, if you'd like."

She waved her hand at him. "So, go …"

He stepped back, and holding up his hands, there was an expression of mock fear on his face. "*Whoa*, take it easy. I have no intentions of going anywhere. And even if I did, I'd make sure you were taken care of first."

Ooops … and again, this certainly wasn't how you meant for that to come out.

Just as he expected, this comment irritated her even further, her response flying out fast and furiously. "I think I've already made it more than clear I'm perfectly capable of taking care of myself."

And she wasn't finished. Evidently, everything she'd told him up until now hadn't sunk in like it should have. This meant she needed to tell him again.

Hands on her hips, she blew out a big breath, sending her bangs flying up in the air. "For your information, I've lived here for almost seven years. And if I'm not mistaken, you haven't. So, don't think you can start pulling your knight in shining armor act on me. I …"

Her words came to a quick halt. A stricken expression coming over her face, she closed her eyes.

Sam watched as she then began to count to five, very slowly and softly whispering each number aloud.

Again, he was intrigued. This woman was by far the most confusing woman he'd ever met. One moment she was yelling at him, finding fault with whatever came out of his mouth. The next moment, it was as if she was afraid to even look at him. And if at any time they did by chance make eye contact, she became completely flustered, her cheeks immediately flushing a rosy shade of pink.

He didn't understand. How was it even possible she and Carrie were sisters? From what he'd been able to observe so far, the only thing they had in common, was their voice. Low and seductive, it was a voice any man would find difficult to forget.

It spoke of stolen kisses in the moonlight. Or of long romantic evenings carrying into the dawn.

Yep, definitely a voice to make you take notice. Every single inch of you.

But other than this, any similarity between the two women came to an end.

For some reason and beyond his comprehension, Livy had taken an instant dislike of him from the moment they met, leaving him the recipient of her anger more times than he'd like to count.

Where he and Carrie never had that problem. They'd hit it off from the very beginning, their friendship only growing stronger over time.

And now it looked like he was destined to spend the rest of the evening with Livy. Hot tempered and unpredictable Livy. An evening she'd be sure to have him defending every move he made.

But this was through no fault but his own. After all, he'd taken a big risk showing up here in New York to surprise Carrie.

He glanced over at Livy again, to see her eyes were still closed. His gaze traveling over the unflattering glasses and heavy bangs she had going on, he wondered what the real story was with these.

Obviously, she was hiding from something. Or maybe someone. Or, was it that she was just very insecure?

And suddenly, for some odd reason, he found he was interested in what the answer was to this.

Yes, he wanted to know what made Livy Mazzori tick.

You're completely out of your mind. You don't need to take on a woman with problems. You already have enough going on as it is.

There was also the fact she was Carrie's sister. This could make things very difficult, if not a little crazy. Certainly not the best scenario to work with.

Wait a minute here... where are you going with this? You have no interest in Livy. Certainly not from a romantic perspective.

No. Absolutely not.

He was merely curious.

He only wanted to get to know her a little better. That's all, nothing more.

And yes … he honestly believed this.

Libby opened her eyes to find Sam gazing over at her, a perplexed look on his face.

She tried to remain completely aloof as he continued to study her, absentmindedly twirling the stem of the glass between his fingers.

She nervously cleared her throat.

Abruptly coming to life, he finished off his wine in one gulp.

He blinked. "Sorry, just doing a little thinking. But, in response to what you said, I'd have to say I've never been referred to as a knight in shining armor before." Here he paused, his mouth turning up in a slight smile. "But I sort of like it. Makes one feel sort of powerful. Ready to jump right up on that horse and go charging out to rescue a damsel in distress."

When she opened her mouth to say something in response, he held up his hand. "*Ah* … trust me, there's no need for you to say anything. I know very well what your opinion would be on this. I assure you, I wouldn't even think of coming to your rescue."

He gave her a long look, before he winked. "Unless, of course, you got down on your knees and begged me."

With this a reference to what she'd said to him earlier, a blush crept into her cheeks. Her gaze darting around, anywhere but at him, she zeroed in on her wineglass, still on the floor. She reached down to pick it up and lifting it to her lips, she gulped down what was left in the glass.

Amused at this, he quickly looked down at his watch to hide his smile.

While at the same time, Livy wanted to kick herself.

What did you just do? You don't do things like that. You're not even that fond of wine. But now he's going to think you're an alcoholic … or just plain crazy.

He gestured over to one of the servers before he reached over to take her empty glass. After he put their wine glasses on the server's tray, he picked up the glass still on the floor and added it to the tray.

He turned to see Livy was smiling at this. He shrugged. "Just another of my nice guy acts. Contrary to what you may think, I enjoy helping out when needed. Even if I'm not appreciated." He shrugged "I like the good feeling it gives me."

When she only continued to smile, he began to feel embarrassed. But at the same time, he was feeling pretty proud of himself to have brought a smile out of her.

Yeah, it looks like you've got this.

He glanced around the room to see it was getting more crowded by the minute. He wondered if this might be a good time for them to make their exit.

He turned to Livy. "I don't know about you, but I've seen more than enough paintings for now. How about you?" At her nod, he grinned, rubbing his hands together. "And I'm starving. Since you live here, close to seven years as you've pointed out, what's your suggestion for a good restaurant? One that isn't loud and crazy."

She wanted to suggest Gracie Ann's, but hesitated. She'd gone there many times with Zack, even once going on to suggest the restaurant should be their special place, since it was where they went on their first date. Funny, now that she thought about this, Zack hadn't agreed with her. He told her she was being ridiculous, making too much out of nothing.

No doubt, this was another one of those signs she failed to pick up on when it came to where their relationship was headed.

But Gracie Ann's really was a great place to go. It fit all of Sam's requirements. It wasn't loud or crazy. And the food was always good.

She glanced up at him to see he was staring at her again, something he seemed to be doing more frequently as the evening progressed. She was beginning to find it quite unnerving, wondering what this meant.

Seriously, you have no chance with this guy. So, don't get your hopes up.

He raised an eyebrow. "Well?"

She pushed her glasses up on her nose and gave him a tentative smile. "I think you'd like Gracie Ann's. The food's great. And it's quiet and cozy, definitely not crazy. Plus, it's only about a block from here."

He smiled. "Okay, Gracie Ann's it is." He took her arm. "Come on, let's grab our coats and get out of here. Stay close to me so I don't lose you in this crowd."

"Wait a minute." This came from her almost in a squeak.

He raised an eyebrow. "Yes?"

She was clearly confused. "You want me to go with you?"

For a moment he looked surprised. Then he began to chuckle. "Of course, I do. I'll admit it's a big gamble on my part, because I'm sure you'll discover a whole other slew of things wrong with me before the night is over."

He grinned. "But, from what little I know about this new knightly status you've bestowed on me, I believe this is the way we knights roll. Taking chances, and all. And as I just said, I'm starving. Which means I'm also pretty desperate."

A sharp look coming from her at his comment about being desperate, the expression on her face hinted she was about to let loose a stinging retort. But when she saw the teasing glint in his eyes, she quickly snapped her mouth shut.

And darn if she wasn't blushing again.

CHAPTER 9

The taxi slowed to a stop in front a turn-of-the-century brownstone townhouse. Without even thinking, Chris pressed a kiss in Carrie's hair.

"Hey… we're here."

Her eyes closed, she barely even stirred. She really didn't want to open them, let alone move from the comfort of his arms. During the drive she'd settled into this dream-like haze and this is where she wanted to stay. Where she could keep up the pretense this was the way it should be. The two of them together with nothing to spoil it, no unanswered questions or fiancée lurking in the background.

Yes, she would be perfectly happy to stay in this taxi and in his arms forever.

Chris hadn't uttered a single word during their journey. God no, if anything, he was still having such a hard time believing she was actually with him.

From the very first instant he'd spotted Carrie across the room, he had ceased to think of ordinary things. She was all that occupied his mind. There were a few times he almost spoke but then he quickly changed his mind, afraid if he did say something, he'd wake up to find it was all a dream.

So, like Carrie, he wanted to savor the moment, a moment up until now he'd only been able to imagine.

Watching them in the rear-view mirror, the driver smiled. His eyes meeting Chris's, he gave him a thumbs-up before he got out of the taxi and scooted around to open their door.

Chris pressed another kiss to the top of Carrie's head. "Come on, princess … this is where we get out."

She turned to give him a searching look.

Princess? How you wish you were. Like you'd dreamed about.

She slid across the seat and out of the taxi. He quickly followed, immediately taking hold of her hand. Not that he thought she'd run off on him, but he certainly wasn't going to take any chances. He led her up the steps to the building and after he unlocked the front door, he ushered her inside.

Quickly taking back possession of her hand, he took her up another set of steps. When they came to the top of the steps, he flicked a switch. The recessed lights scattered across the ceiling came on with a welcoming blink, softly illuminating the room.

Carrie was instantly wide awake. She handed Chris his jacket as she slowly gazed around the room. When she finally turned back to him, there was an expression of awe on her face. "Oh my gosh, this is absolutely beautiful. Where are we?"

He had thrown his jacket over one of the chairs and had now come to stand next to her. But not too close. No, even with this slight change in her and the sense that maybe, just maybe, she was softening towards him, he certainly wasn't going to push it.

Again, this could be his imagination.

Or more like what he wanted to believe.

He smiled, the words coming straight from his heart. "We're home." Embarrassed at what he'd implied, he cleared his throat. "I mean, this is my home, where I live." He waved his hand around at the room. "The living, dining room and kitchen are on this floor. There is a bedroom, office and bathroom on the first floor. It's not a large apartment, about fifteen-hundred square feet of space. But considered quite sufficient when compared to other apartments available in the city."

Here he stopped to shake his head, sending her an apologetic look. "I'm sorry. I don't mean to sound like a realtor. Or that I'm bragging. I guess I tend to get carried away. Then there's the fact I still can't believe it's actually mine."

Uh, yeah ... just what the hell are you doing? Trying to impress her? Because this is exactly what it sounds like.

"That's okay. I understand." She smiled at him after she said this. It was a small smile, but it was a smile. Giving him even more reason to hope.

He sensed she wanted to give everything a closer inspection, so he stepped back to give her space. He more than understood. The attention to detail throughout the entire space was what drew him to the apartment in the first place. And she was an interior designer.

His hands shoved casually in his pockets, he adopted an air of nonchalance while he watched her take it all in. Though, truth be told, he was nervous. It was suddenly very important to him she liked what she saw.

As she gazed around at the open space, Carrie was in awe, the architectural details alone demanding her attention. The twelve-foot ceilings were bordered by what appeared to be the original hand carved cherry wood molding, this a perfect match to the gleaming cherry hardwood floors. The decorative and ornate fireplace mantle also appeared to be original. The walls were painted a very light leaf green and the overstuffed sofa and chairs, grouped in front of the fireplace, were upholstered in a soft ivory leather. These were anchored by a large oriental rug in shades of muted reds, blues and greens.

When she noticed the large flat screen TV over the fireplace, she glanced over at Chris, an accusing expression on her face. He shrugged, that crooked smile of his flashing across his face. "I'm sorry.

What can I say? I'm a man and you know how we love our high-tech toys. And come on, you haven't lived until you've watched a game on this TV. You'd swear you're at the actual event."

At first, she could only stare at him, his smile sending her back to when they first met. Then she gave a slight shake of her head. He, in turn, thought this was in response to his comment about the TV.

Well, he'd get rid of it then. Right now. He'd gladly put whatever she suggested up on that wall if it meant she'd turn back to the woman he remembered.

You'd do this in a heartbeat.

She'd made her way over to the kitchen where, of course, everything was all high-end, no expense spared. Stainless steel appliances, marble countertops and solid dark cherry cabinets. It was a kitchen that gave the promise it could turn anyone into a chef.

She wondered if Lauren was a good cook.

Probably a lot better than you are ...

Chris came over to stand next to her. When he saw a touch of uncertainty on her face at this, he gave her a casual smile.

"Would you like some wine?"

Say no ... you need to tell him no, you should leave.

But she'd already started to nod.

This earned another smile from him before he retrieved two wine glasses from the cupboard. After he selected a bottle of wine from the wine cooler, he looked over to see she was watching him.

She nervously averted her gaze.

He sighed. He was beginning to feel like he was dealing with a wild animal, ready to bolt at even his slightest move.

He cleared his throat. "So, what do you think?"

This, she realized, was the problem. She wasn't thinking. Nothing felt real. But this was probably because deep down, she knew it never could be.

She kept her gaze riveted to the bottle of wine he'd set on the counter. "If you're asking about the apartment, it's amazing. If you're asking about the wine, whatever you've chosen will be fine."

And what if, just perhaps, he was asking about them?

Well, this is your chance ... ask him why he brought you here.

Her courage failing her, she gazed around the kitchen. A photo pinned on the message board next to the refrigerator caught her eye.

She moved closer to see it was a group photo taken on what appeared to be New Year's Eve, everyone in evening wear. Chris was in the photo, standing next to the same woman she saw him with in the gallery. The woman he'd kissed. Arm and arm in the photo, she was leaning against him as they both smiled into the camera.

She turned to him. "Is this a photo of you and all of your friends?"

He was searching through a drawer. He shot a quick glance over at the photo. After giving her a nod, he resumed his search, to finally pull out a corkscrew. "Yes, I went to college with three of the guys in the photo and since we now live in different parts of the country, we made a pact to get together every New Year's Eve. This past year it worked out great for me because everyone wanted to come to New York."

After studying the photo more closely, she turned to watch as he became completely caught up in his struggle to remove the cork from the wine bottle. She couldn't stop the next words that came out of her mouth. "The woman ... the one next to you in the photo, she's very beautiful."

His concentration on the task at hand, he didn't notice the hesitation in her voice. After glancing more closely over at the photo, he shrugged. "Yeah, she is. *Damn ... I hope I haven't botched this. Ah, hah ... here we go.*"

He looked over at her, a jubilant smile on his face as he waved the cork at her.

At the same time, he was a little puzzled about her interest in the photo. And more so, her interest in Lauren. He tried to think back, had he talked about Lauren the night he and Carrie were together?

He gave a slight shake of his head.

No, you're pretty sure you hadn't. Lauren had been the last thing on your mind that night.

So, his answer was a little hesitant, if not quite brief. "That's Lauren. She's actually a dancer in one of the shows on Broadway."

As you can imagine, this was the last thing Carrie wanted to hear.

Oh, no ... not only is she beautiful, but she's a dancer as well? And you didn't think it could get any worse.

He filled the glasses with wine before he smiled over at her.

"I think you'd like everyone. Two of the couples are married and another recently got engaged. Just the other day, in fact." He smiled. "So, out of my group of friends, it looks like everyone is engaged now."

Carrie suddenly felt very cold. And this wasn't because of the open back of her dress. Or because she no longer had Chris's jacket to keep her warm. No, this chill coming over her was because of what he just said.

Why are you still here? You're a fool What more proof do you need?

She shivered and wrapping her arms around herself, she glanced over at Chris.

He was gazing at her with concern. "You're cold. Come on, I'll get a fire going in the fireplace."

He picked up the two glasses of wine and motioned for her to follow him over to the sofa. Once he put the glasses on the coffee table and turned on the gas fire, he sent her another smile. "Make yourself comfortable. I'll be right back."

She watched as he went running down the steps, to return in what seemed like only seconds, holding one of his sweaters. "Here, put this on. We need to get you warmed up."

He'd seriously considered forgoing the sweater, to instead settle her close to him on the sofa, something he wouldn't have hesitated to do the first time they'd been together. But then she certainly wasn't giving him any kind of sign she'd welcome this.

It was killing him the connection between them had somehow been broken. My God, this alone was what kept him going over the past months.

She pulled the sweater on over her dress and perched on the edge of the sofa. When she reached for her wine glass, he leaned in closer to tip his glass against hers. "To a great night. A reunion of sorts, shall we say?"

She sent a quick glance over at him, her lips parted. Thinking she was about to say something, he leaned closer, waiting. Instead, she merely nodded before she took a sip of wine.

Hiding his disappointment, he cleared his throat. "So, what brought you to New York?"

She appeared startled, almost spilling her wine. He could see her hands were shaking as she put the glass down on the coffee table.

"I'm here for the annual awards dinner put on by the American Board of Realtors. It's on Monday night." Then she dipped her head, giving him a shy smile. "I was nominated for an award. New and Upcoming Designer for the Midwest." She shrugged. "It's not really all that big of a deal. I'm certainly not expecting to win."

He gave her a genuine smile. "Carrie, this is wonderful! And it *is* a big deal. You have every right to be proud. I know how hard it is to get nominated for one of these awards. The competition is huge."

This was followed by a short silence before they both began to speak at the same time. She smiled. "Go ahead, you first."

Instead, he gently took her glass from her and set it on the coffee table. He reached for her hand, smiling at her surprised look. "Your hands are shaking. I thought you might still be cold."

They both looked down at their hands before he cleared his throat. "But, back to what I was going to say ... how did you come to be at the Gallery East tonight?" He tilted his head at her, his expression thoughtful. "Are you a friend of the artist? Because for some reason, I can't see you as a fan of such a contemporary style of art."

He'd linked her fingers with his. He knew he was taking a huge chance doing this, but damnit, the urge to touch her was so strong he was to the point he almost couldn't think of anything else.

And miraculously, she didn't pull her hand away. If anything, she seemed to relax, leaning back more comfortably into the sofa.

He smiled.

We're making progress here ... this is good.

Carrie knew she should probably pull her hand away, but it felt so right. It brought back the memory of how he'd held her hand almost the entire time that night in February.

Then she frowned. This was different. They shouldn't be holding hands. Even though he was right … her hands *were* cold.

So, maybe it wasn't all that wrong?

She only knew she didn't want him to let go.

She finally answered him. "My brother, Chester … do you remember him from the wedding? His wife Sophie knows the artist from when she was in Paris. He sent her a notice about the show and since I was going to be here, she was able to get an invite for both me and my sister Livy. She lives here in New York."

She smiled. "And you're right. Even though I found his style of art to be very eye-catching and colorful, it really isn't my style at all."

She glanced over at him. "And you? A fan of the artist? Or is this just an ordinary Saturday night out on the town with friends or …"

Her words fading, she averted her gaze, staring into the fire.

Or was he only there because his fiancée wanted him there?

She was really beginning to dislike the word fiancée. If she were to ever become engaged, she was doing to make it perfectly clear she wasn't to be referred to as someone's fiancée. Whatever they wanted to call her would be fine.

As long as it wasn't fiancée.

At her long silence, Chris abruptly stood and retrieving the bottle of wine from the kitchen counter, he poured more wine into their glasses.

Though he didn't want to feel this way, he was becoming extremely impatient with the way their conversation was going. He didn't want to talk about art. Or engage in any other small talk. My God, what was going to happen next? Were they going to start discussing the weather?

He managed to check his groan.

Please, why couldn't they talk about them?

He gazed at her for a few moments, hesitating almost as if this was exactly what he was going to do. Instead, he put the wine bottle on the coffee table and sat on the sofa, settling much closer to her this time

"This evening was just a chance to get together with friends. And, no, the artwork wasn't really my style either. Though, I did like one painting. It was probably the least modern of the collection. Early Evening in Spring, I believe it was titled."

He gazed around the room before he turned to give her one of those crooked smiles of his. "And now that I look around, I think it might even be a good fit for this room. Maybe to take the place of the eyesore you pointed out above my fireplace?"

Don't think Carrie didn't notice how he had moved closer, her whole body responding to his nearness. Nervously fingering her wine glass, she managed to smile at his comment. "I'd definitely say this would be an improvement. But please remember this is only from a decorator's point of view."

Her training and experience kicking in, she ran with this. Probably a bit more passionately than was necessary. "After all, you have to go with what is most comfortable for you. Your home is your sanctuary, your place to escape the pressures of the outside world. I always tell my clients they need to pick one thing they love and build around that." Here she actually gave him a teasing look. "A big screen TV isn't usually something I'd suggest they choose."

Her expression suddenly turning serious, her eyes held his.

"And one of the biggest rules... you don't want to complicate things any more than necessary. This goes for every aspect of your life. Work, friends, family... *everything*."

He nodded, his look puzzled. "Uh huh, okay then ..." He wasn't quite sure ... was she trying to tell him something? Because he really wasn't the type of guy who led a complicated life. Nope, he had no desire to take on more than he thought he could handle. At least he didn't think he did.

Unless it was her. He'd drop everything in a flash for her.

Evidently you just don't get it. But don't worry about it... just keep talking. About anything. How about her brother? She said he got married? Go with that.

He chuckled. "So, your brother got married. I must say, this doesn't come as a surprise to me."

Her eye lit up, a big smile coming over her face. "Yes, only a couple of weeks after Kevin and Abby's wedding, Chester surprised Sophie with the wedding." When Chris raised an eyebrow at this, she nodded. "Sophie had told him she didn't want a big wedding. So, he did all of the planning and it was beautiful. And now they're expecting twins at the end of this month."

She clamped her hand over her mouth, a look of dismay on her face. "No one is supposed to know. About the twins, that is. Not even me. I found out by accident."

He laughed at her expression. "Don't worry, your secret is safe with me. And you'll love being an aunt. My sister has a little boy who is four, his name is Connor James."

He grinned, shaking his head. "He's a real character. I had no idea how much I would enjoy being an uncle."

When she gave him such a genuine smile, he felt as though he was finally beginning to see the Carrie he thought he knew.

And this was when he decided he couldn't wait any longer. He was going to say something.

Rubbing his hands together, he took a deep breath and looked right into her eyes. "Carrie, I have to ask … why didn't you return my calls? God, I feel like all I've done over the past months is wonder what happened. Was it something I did? Or something I said?"

She gave a faint shake of her head, her gaze dropping to her wine glass. She knew he was waiting for her to give him an answer, but she couldn't. She wanted to hear what he had to say.

She *needed* this.

If only to find out the truth.

So, she waited.

At her silence, he had no choice but to stumble on.

"When I saw you tonight at the gallery, I honestly thought I was imagining things. That maybe I'd finally lost my mind. I can't even begin to tell you how many times I've imagined something like this would happen. That I'd look up to find you standing right in front of me. Or, my phone would ring and the call would be from you."

He stopped to shake his head, a wistful smile on his face. "And then tonight … I looked across the room and there you were. It was unreal. In fact, it still feels unreal."

She still hadn't moved.

He gave a frustrated sigh. "I don't know, maybe I was wrong, but I thought we had something special. And now? I don't know what to think. I only know I'd give anything to get back to where we were, to what we had."

His voice became gruff with emotion. "I want that feeling back. The feeling where everything is the way it should be."

She abruptly came to her feet, almost knocking her glass over when she shoved it on the table. Completely bewildered, he scrambled to his feet, watching as she tugged at his sweater, yanking it over her head and throwing it on the sofa.

She backed away from him, her words spilling out. "I shouldn't have let you bring me here. I need to leave. Now."

Confused, he watched as she frantically began patting her dress. "But I don't have any money. Or my credit card. It's in the pocket of the coat I left at the gallery. So, if you can lend me the fare for the taxi, I'll pay you back once I get to the hotel. Or I can send it to you. Whatever you want."

He saw her eyes were beginning to fill with tears. "Carrie, I …"

When he made a move towards her, she stumbled back in a panic. "No, please don't touch me. Because If you do, I seriously don't know what I'll do."

She suddenly became deathly calm. Wrapping her arms around herself, her eyes pleaded with him. "Please, just let me leave. Because this is so wrong. She deserves more than this. I can't even imagine what she's thinking right now, wondering where you went." A look of alarm filled her face. "What if she comes back to find I'm here with you?"

When she threw this at him, the reason for her behavior so totally unexpected, it took him a few moments for her words to sink in. He ran his hand slowly through his hair.

He didn't understand. Who the hell was she talking about? Who was this she? No one lived here with him. He lived here alone. There was no roommate. No woman. No dog. No cat. Not even fish.

It was … take a deep breath and then look at me. *Please.*"

He waited until she did as he'd asked before he took a step closer. "Who are you talking about? Who is this she?"

"Your fiancée." When he didn't respond, his expression still puzzled, she whispered. "Lauren."

"Lauren?" He shook his head. Very slowly he did this. "You think Lauren is my fiancée? And we're engaged?" He knew he was repeating everything, but he was trying so desperately to make sense of it all.

When she nodded, her eyes fixed on his face, he slowly shook his head again. "Carrie, I'm not engaged. And even if I was, which I assure you I'm not and never have been, it certainly wouldn't be to Lauren. I don't understand, why would you think this?"

She searched his face, looking for a sign he wasn't telling the truth. But the only thing she saw in his eyes was confusion.

Afraid to acknowledge the glimmer of hope building inside of her, she held his gaze. "I want you to know I did call you back. At least after the first time you called, I did. It was the morning after you left the message you wanted to come to Cleveland for the weekend."

A faint smile touched her lips. "I was so excited. I had begun to think I wasn't going to hear from you." She shrugged. "But a woman answered your phone, I figured you were at your office and it was someone you worked with. But after I explained why I was calling, she told me her name was Lauren and she was your fiancée. I … I didn't know what to think. And she sounded … well, she sounded so sure."

She waited, so much depending on his answer.

A slow anger had begun to build inside of him. Not only because of Lauren and what she'd done, but also because of all the time he and Carrie had lost because of this misunderstanding.

He closed his eyes, his mind searching back to that morning. He vaguely recalled Lauren's strange behavior, her anger towards him while they were in the kitchen and leading up to her dramatic exit.

He must have come into the kitchen right after Lauren had answered his phone. This also had to be when she decided to delete the call. Because he sure as hell knew he never got a message indicating Carrie had called.

He shook his head. He was trying, he really was, but he was having a really difficult time trying to understand all of this.

"God, Carrie, I don't know what to say. Lauren and I dated, but this was only for about two months. I'd already planned on breaking it off with her even before I met you. I told her the truth, that it wasn't working for us. This was right after the wedding."

He massaged the back of his neck. "I remember that morning. The only reason Lauren was even here was because I agreed to let her stay while the floors in her place were being re-finished. At the time, we were no longer seeing each other and I was under the assumption it was over and we were friends, nothing more. Since that time, we've never once been together. Until this last week. But both times this was just hanging with friends."

He began to move towards her, very slowly he went about this. His eyes never leaving her face, his next words were a husky whisper. "Carrie, if it were Lauren or any other woman, it wouldn't matter. I wouldn't have wanted to be with any of them. Because after I met you, well … meeting you changed everything."

She had, just as slowly, begun to back away from him and was now pressed up against the railing of the steps. She was trying so hard to believe him, yet at the same time, she couldn't forget what she had witnessed only a short time ago.

"But tonight, at the gallery, I saw you kiss her." She gestured over to the photo in the kitchen. "The woman in the photo … Lauren."

He nodded, still ever so cautiously moving closer. "I didn't kiss her. She kissed me."

At the look of disbelief she gave him, he groaned, a pained look on his face. "God, how do I explain this without coming off sounding like a complete jerk. Tonight was a mistake. A really stupid mistake on my part. Last week I went to an impromptu get together for the couple I told you just got engaged. Lauren was there and we started talking. She told me how all of our friends were planning to go to this gallery preview tonight and she convinced me to join them."

Mesmerized by the look in his eyes, his earnest expression pulling her in, Carrie could only watch as he continued to inch even closer.

"That night I had a couple of drinks and I'm embarrassed to admit I started feeling a little sorry for myself. Out of all of my friends, I was about the only one who was still single. And it was finally starting to sink in I was probably never going to see you again. It had been too long and even though I knew how I felt, you had changed your mind."

He shrugged. "So, I tried to tell myself it was time to move on. But this was the last thing I wanted to do."

He was now close enough to put his one hand on the railing next to her. "When I saw Lauren again tonight, I knew I had made a mistake. I never should have agreed to meet up with her. She was already making plans for us. Plans I could never be a part of, certainly not with her. So, I told her I was sorry, but I needed to leave."

His other hand had moved to the railing on the other side of her. But she had no intention of leaving. She was waiting, hoping what he was about to say, would be what she so desperately wanted to hear.

And it was.

"And the kiss you saw? She initiated the kiss. It meant absolutely nothing to me. It couldn't have. Because you had already spoiled me."

She closed her eyes, the words coming from her in a whisper.

"Promise you'll save all of your kisses for me..."

He smiled, slowly moving his hands to rest them at her waist. "*Ah, I did say that, didn't I?* And, I meant every word. I still do."

Her body slowly relaxing into him, she gave a long trembling sigh as she rested her head on his shoulder.

He tightened his hold, a wistful smile on his face. "Tonight, I found out everyone is planning to spend the long Thanksgiving weekend at a ski lodge in upstate New York. The weekend of November twenty-seventh."

Her head jerked up.

Their eyes meeting, he nodded. "Yes ... and do you know what? The only thing I could think about, was the twenty-seventh is your birthday. And you and I had decided turning twenty-seven on the twenty-seventh day of the month called for a special celebration."

He tilted his head, a question in his eyes. "There was also the promise I made to you. A promise you gave right back to me. That we would spend this day together. Do you remember this?"

She nodded, her gaze fixed on his face. The tenderness she remembered was shining in his eyes. His promise reaching deep to take yet another little piece of her heart.

He smiled, that crooked smile of his. "Carrie … tonight when I glanced across the room, falling right into your eyes, from that moment on, you were all I could see. I vowed I wasn't going to let you disappear without at least talking to me. Even if this meant I would have to search the entire city to find you."

He reached out to gently brush his fingertips over the soft curve of her cheek. "So, what do you think? Can I go ahead and set up the plans to celebrate your birthday like we talked about? Together?"

She nodded again.

Right before she started to cry.

When he gathered her against him, she began to cry even harder.

He let her cry.

His eyes closed and his lips pressed in her hair, his whispers flowed through her.

"It's all okay. It's all good."

CHAPTER 10

*S*o far so good.

This is what Sam was thinking as he gazed around the restaurant where he and Livy had been seated. A booth in the back corner, it was quiet and quite cozy compared to all of the activity going on in the front of the restaurant where the bar was located. The plush padded seating, low hum of conversation and the soft background music was a welcome treat after the crowded gallery.

Yes, this is more like it.

The server set their drinks on the table, a scotch and soda for him and coffee for Livy. A shiver running through her, she immediately cradled her cup in her hands and after taking a sip, she closed her eyes. For some reason, she couldn't seem to get warm.

Sam leaned towards her. "Hey, are you cold?"

Startled he'd asked her this, while she was thinking the exact same thing, her lashes flew open. When she saw the concerned look in his eyes, she abruptly removed her hands from the cup, knocking it over. This sent a river of coffee across the table and right into his lap.

Horrified, she grabbed her napkin. This sent the silverware, tucked inside, to go shooting under the table.

"I'm sorry. Oh my God, I'm so sorry. I should've warned you. I'm such a klutz. I always do something like this. I'm so, so sorry."

She kept repeating this over and over as, half kneeling on her seat, she frantically tried to soak up the spilled coffee on the table with the napkin. After he used his napkin to wipe as much coffee from his jeans as he could, Sam reached over to take the napkin from her hands.

When she finally got up the nerve to look at him, he smiled. "Hey, take it easy. It's okay. It was an accident."

She slowly sank back down into her seat, closing her eyes.

Oh my God, why are you even here? Tell him you aren't feeling well. Or you just remembered there's somewhere else you need to be. Anything to give him an easy out.

She finally opened her eyes to find he was studying her, an amused look on his face. He rested his forearms on the table and leaning towards her, he shook his head.

"Tell me, are you this nervous with everyone? Or is it just me? And if it is me, why?"

As she tried to think of something to say to this, he let out a low groan. He leaned back in his seat and crossed his arms over his chest. "Wait a minute, what the hell has Carrie been telling you about me?"

How in the world was she supposed to answer this? If she told him Carrie described him as a really nice guy and a good friend, with no chance of any romantic feelings ever blossoming between them, she had a feeling this wouldn't be what he wanted to hear.

Nope, this certainly wouldn't be a boost to his ego. If he liked Carrie as much as she suspected he did, this might just kill him. Well, maybe the outcome wouldn't be quite that drastic, but he certainly wouldn't be very happy.

Even though he'd taken it pretty well when Carrie went running out of the gallery with another man in hot pursuit.

She frowned.

She knew, as well as anyone, love was blind. A person could become totally focused on seeing only what they wanted to believe. Something, she suddenly realized, that was exactly what she'd been doing with Zack. Even though all of those signs of their imminent break-up were right in front of her nose, she'd blithely let everything go right over her head.

She glanced over to see Sam was still studying her. He started to say something, but stopped when the server came to place another cup of coffee, napkins and silverware in front of them.

Carrie went to pick up the cup, but then quickly drew her hands back and put them in her lap.

Sam chuckled, shaking his head. And for some reason, this sent a warmth through her she knew the coffee couldn't even begin to match.

Then she watched as he slid out of his seat and after removing his jacket, he came over to drape it around her shoulders.

She seriously wanted to cry.

Because, come on ... why did he have to do this? Now you're definitely starting to fall in love with the guy.

She knew it was absolutely insane for her to feel this way, but she couldn't help it. She pulled his jacket even more securely around her and without even thinking, she burrowed her face in the collar.

She closed her eyes, the spicy scent of his cologne filling her senses.

When she realized what she was doing, she quickly patted the lapel of the jacket with her fingers before she casually picked up her cup. She took a sip of coffee, holding on to the cup as though her life depended on it.

Once the cup was safely back on the table, she smiled at him. "Thank you."

When he nodded, a smile his only response, she quickly began to talk. "Getting back to your question, Carrie speaks very highly of you. She said you are one of the nicest guys she knows."

Tapping his fingers on the table, he gave her a wry smile. "Yep. That's me, always the nice guy."

She tilted her head to study him, an almost irritated look coming over her face. And as what seemed to be the norm with her tonight, the words came, uncensored, and flying right out of her mouth.

"What would you rather she said? You're all good looks and charm? A man who gives off this trustworthy and good guy image? But deep, down inside, beneath this barrier you've built around you, you're really this bad boy, just waiting to make your move. So, you can show the right woman what real passion is all about."

Her mouth snapped shut.

Oh dear ... you certainly hadn't intended to say all of that.

No, she'd certainly never planned to go into such detail. A simple maybe-you're-not-what-you-seem would've been more than enough.

But after all of this came tumbling out of her mouth, she realized she was actually talking about herself. She wouldn't mind being that woman, the one to break down this image he had going on. She wasn't sure how she knew this, but she had a feeling when this happened, to be with him would be amazing.

Completely embarrassed by her outburst and even more by what she was thinking, she stared down into her cup.

You're out of control. You've absolutely no reason to be thinking like this.

And what was Sam thinking?

Well, as a matter of fact, he rather liked what he just heard. If anything, he'd like to think there was some truth in what she'd said.

He was also thinking about how she kept on surprising him. Every single time she opened her mouth. She kept him on his toes, wondering what she was going to come up with next. To have him scrambling to defend himself. Or apologizing for something he hadn't even known he'd done.

She had him guessing, all right. But at the same time, he found he looked forward to what was going to come next.

Yeah ... sort of like Christmas, the anticipation keeps building. With the expectation each present you open will be better than the last.

It was her glasses that threw him. Not that he had anything against a woman who wore glasses. Oh no, if anything, glasses could be very sexy. It was only hers were so stern looking, the rims so heavy and dark. Fitting right in with the heavy bangs she had going on.

He had a feeling, hiding behind these, was a beautiful and sensuous woman just waiting for the right moment to show the world who she really was.

Hmm ... maybe you're two of a kind, huh?

He held out his hand. "Here, give me your glasses."

She hesitated, giving him a puzzled look. But when he kept holding out his hand, she took off the glasses and handed them to him. He set them on the table and leaned back in his seat, where he leisurely began to study her.

She squirmed uncomfortably in her seat. And yes, there was no denying this, she was starting to blush again.

Just as she was about to ask him what the heck he was doing, he nodded. "*Ah* ... just as I thought. You have beautiful eyes. Sort of a cross between blue and violet."

He picked up her glasses and waved them at her. "It's a real shame you're hiding them behind these."

He peered more closely at her. "Have you ever thought of wearing contacts?"

When he saw her start to frown at this, he held up his hand. "Hey, I'm not criticizing, just curious."

Without her glasses, he was pretty much of a blur to her right now. Probably to her advantage with how closely he was studying her.

She gave a nervous laugh. "Yes, I actually do have contacts, but rarely wear them. Carrie lectures me about this all of the time." She shrugged. "I don't know, I guess I've worn glasses for so long, I'm used to them. It's easier."

He smiled. "*Ah...* but by doing this, you're shortchanging the rest of us."

This was when she decided if she could, she'd run home right now and put in her contacts.

Yes, if this is what would make him happy, you'd do this in an instant.

He handed the glasses to her. After she put them on, with him watching her the entire time, she nervously glanced around the room.

Where was their server and why was it taking him so long to bring their appetizers? At least if she was stuffing food in her mouth, there would be less of a chance she'd embarrass herself any further by blurting out something stupid. Or insulting. And, as it had been the case so far, something she really didn't mean to say.

With no server in sight, she busied herself with placing her napkin in her lap before she shot a quick glance over at him.

"So, what exactly is it you do?"

She saw, by the quick smile that crossed his lips, she probably wasn't going to get a straight answer.

Sure enough, he raised an eyebrow before he answered. "You mean when I'm not going around rescuing women from everyday disasters? Shining my armor? Or out in the barn, grooming my horse?"

She narrowed her eyes at him. At the same time, she was trying not to smile. "Yes, that's exactly what I meant."

Sam was sidetracked when the server stopped at their table with their appetizer order. Immediately popping one of the stuffed mushrooms in his mouth, he followed this with a swallow of wine before he reached for another mushroom.

This was when he glanced over at Livy to see she was watching this, an amused expression on her face.

He had the grace to look totally embarrassed.

"God, I'm sorry. But I'm so damn hungry. Airline food just doesn't do it for me. Or the snacks in the hotel mini bar."

He held the plate out to her. "Here, you better take some before I eat all of them. You do eat, don't you? You're not a nibbler, are you?"

"A nibbler?"

Worry lines crossed her forehead. Was she?

"Yes, you know what I mean. One of these women who hardly eats anything when on a date, just a dainty little bite of everything. And then just like that, she's full, stuffed … can't even think of eating another morsel. Men aren't all that stupid, you know."

He grinned. "At least not about this. We know it's all for show."

Livy had picked up on only one thing he had said.

A date? He considers this a date?

She slowly shook her head. If it was necessary, she was going to eat everything put in front of her. If he didn't like 'nibblers' well, then…

she was going to eat like a woman who enjoyed her food. No fake show for this girl.

She reached for a mushroom. "No, let me assure you, I do more than my fair share of eating. "She frowned. "I sometimes think it's one of the few things I do well. "

A thoughtful came over her face. "If I had more time, I would love to start cooking more. And then, you know … have dinner parties and all of that kind of thing."

She sighed, pausing to think about this after she put the mushroom on her plate. When he cleared his throat, still holding the plate out to her, she quickly grabbed two more.

She picked up her knife and fork. After she managed to completely mutilate one of the mushrooms on her plate, she set her fork and knife back on the table.

She gave him a bright smile. "So, how about you? Do you cook. Are you a man who knows his way around the kitchen?"

He shrugged before he nodded at her plate. "You might find it easier to just pick it up and eat it. I won't tell anyone you used your fingers. I promise. Go ahead, just dig in."

Only after she did this, he answered her question. "As far as spending time in the kitchen, I've found it's not all that enjoyable when you're flying solo. It's a much easier to get take out or order in. But if I have someone to cook with, I have to admit I do enjoy puttering around the kitchen."

Her imagination running away with what he just said, wondering what it would be like to be that someone, she stared into space.

When she realized what she was doing, she started, vigorously shaking her head.

Again, it's not going to happen, so just eat your mushrooms.

She popped one in her mouth, slowly chewing and swallowing before she nodded. "I know, I watch the food channel on TV where the co-hosts are cooking together, it looks like so much fun."

She picked up the last mushroom from the serving plate and after staring at it for a few seconds, she shrugged. "Oh well, maybe someday."

She popped the mushroom in her mouth.

A big grin on his face, Sam gave her a thumbs-up. Then he held up his glass in a toast. "Here's to all those nibblers out there. If they only knew what they're missing."

The server had removed their empty plates and re-filled Livy's cup with coffee. Sam had tried to persuade her to order an after-dinner coffee, but she'd refused.

Absentmindedly stirring his scotch and soda, he gave a satisfied sigh before he smiled over at her. "This restaurant was an excellent choice, Livy. The food, the atmosphere and, I'm happy to say, even the company has made for a very pleasant evening."

He winked after he said this, happy to see an actual smile from her.

He realized, against all odds, they were cautiously beginning to fulfill Carrie's wish of becoming friends. In fact, unbeknownst to either of them, neither was ready for the evening to end.

She smiled. "I'm glad you liked it. Now you have a new restaurant to come to when you come back to New York." She paused to smile at him. "If you plan on coming back, that is."

Oh boy ... now he's going to think you're fishing for some kind of commitment with a comment like that. Again, you're reading more into this than you should.

She sighed and picking up her cup, she was about to bring it to her mouth when a horrified look came over her face. She dropped the cup back on the table, coffee sloshing over the rim and spilling on the table. Her gaze fixed towards the front of the restaurant, she frantically began swiping at the coffee spill with her napkin, almost sending both the cup and napkin flying right at Sam.

"Oh my god ... oh no, no, no ..."

Startled, Sam craned his neck to see the hostess was leading a man and woman over to the same area of the restaurant he and Livy were seated.

Were they the cause for Livy's distress? Did she know them?

He swiftly turned back to her. "What's wrong, sweetheart?"

For about a millisecond, the fact he called her sweetheart pleasantly registered in her mind before she leaned towards him, a look of complete panic on her face. "Please, you need to do me a favor. Act as if you're madly in love with me. Or pretend like you really like me. I can't believe this is happening."

Sam was totally confused. The only thing registering with him, was Livy looked like she was about to burst into tears. And, if there was one thing he couldn't handle, it was a woman when she cried. For some reason, he completely fell apart at even the slightest sign of tears. His sister had won every argument they had while they were growing up, only because she was able to cry at the drop of a hat.

Just as he reached across the table to take her hands, someone loudly cleared their throat. He turned to see the hostess had seated the woman in a booth across the room, but the man was now standing next to their table.

A frown on his face, he looked at Livy.

"Livy, this is a surprise."

She pushed her glasses firmly against her nose and shook her bangs out of her eyes before she answered him.

"Zack … yes, it is. How are you?" She glanced wildly over at Sam, her look desperate.

One hand keeping a firm grasp on Livy's, Sam held his other hand out to Zack. "Hey, Sam Bridges here. Are you a colleague of Livy's? If you are, I must say you're damn lucky to work with such an amazing woman."

He glanced over at Livy and gave her a slight wink only she could see. "The server is coming this way. Did you want him to bring more coffee, sweetheart?"

There it was again … sweetheart. But remember, this is all an act …

She shook her head, more vigorously than was necessary.

Zack turned to Sam, his expression puzzled. "So, are you an old friend of Livy's? Funny, I don't remember her ever mentioning you."

Sam chuckled before he slowly shook his head. "You know, I feel like we're old friends." Here he stopped to bring Livy's hand to his lips for a kiss before he continued. "Let's just say, from the moment we met, there was this instant connection and both of us are still reeling, trying to take it all in. I keep trying to convince her we're proof there really is such a thing as love at first sight. Right baby?"

Livy was blushing like a house on fire. After sending a shy glance over at Sam, she nodded. This appeared to make Zack angry, his gaze darting from Livy to Sam, before finally coming to settle on Livy.

"I've been meaning to call you. Did you happen to find my red sweater? You know the one I'm talking about. You got it for me when we went on that weekend trip to Vermont? I think I may have left it, ah… with you."

Sam watched as Livy slowly came to life, the anger he'd become more than familiar with, spreading across her face. He hid his smile, composing his face into one of complete indifference as he watched her.

Livy sent Zack a long look before she finally nodded. "Yes, you did. I gave it away. Along with all of the other things you didn't take with you. I assumed *everything* you left behind, was what you no longer wanted. Or no longer cared about." She shrugged, a completely innocent look on her face. "I hope this is okay?"

Then, in typical Livy fashion, a sudden fury flashed in her eyes. "Like you told me, it's time to make a clean start. So, that's exactly what I did."

She turned to Sam and gave him a brilliant smile. "Sam is my clean start. Right, Sam?"

When he gave her a funny look at this comment, she wondered if maybe she wasn't being flirty enough. But come on, to be thrown into a situation like this was completely out of her comfort zone.

She swiftly reached over to run her fingers lightly up his forearm. "I'm about ready to leave. Are you?"

Sam was staring down at her fingers. Again, if she hadn't known this was all an act they were putting on, she'd swear he seemed to be fascinated by what she was doing. Then, confusing her even further, he glanced up at her, a slow smile coming to his face before he brought her hand to his mouth again. Only after he brushed his lips across her knuckles, leisurely taking his time with this, did he finally respond. "Sure, I'll do whatever you want, baby. You know you call the shots."

Their eyes meeting, the brief thought flittered through Livy's mind she'd never cared for the endearment of baby. But somehow, this coming from Sam? Well, it now sounded quite appealing.

Baby?

Yes, she could very easily get used to being called this. As long as it came from him. In fact, either would work. Sweetheart or baby. She didn't care.

Stop it. This isn't real, remember?

Zack cleared his throat. Loudly, he did this. "Well, I better get back to my date. I guess I'll be seeing you around, Livy. And if you happen to find any more of my stuff, don't throw it away. Call me and I'll stop by to pick it up."

Livy gave a jerky nod. She was now gripping Sam's hand so tightly, he was seriously beginning to fear she was going to injure him. He tried to ignore the pain as he addressed Zack.

"We'll be sure to do this. Though I'm sure I'd know if I mistakenly put on something of yours." He gave Zack a quick once over before he shook his head. "I'm pretty sure you're shorter than I am."

Indignation bubbled in Zack's eyes as he drew himself up to appear even taller. "I'll have you know I'm five-eleven." Then realizing how petty he sounded, he gave a short laugh, this coming out more as an angry bark. "So, I'll see you around."

Sam grinned. "Yeah, sure. It was nice meeting you."

After Zack had gone in a rather brisk march over to his table, Sam tried to gently disengage his hand from Livy's crushing grip. She started, jerking her hand away. "I'm sorry, I didn't mean to keep holding on to your hand. It's just … I can't still believe … he …"

Her bottom lip beginning to quiver, she shook her head, a single tear making its way down her cheek.

He groaned. Remember? He wasn't good with tears. He leaned back in his seat, his hand going up to rub the back of his neck.

Damn ... now what do you do?

"Livy, *please* ... don't start crying on me."

Instantly taking this as a sign he was irritated with her, she became angry. And now she wanted to be anywhere else but in the restaurant. Or even with him.

She sent him an accusing glance "I certainly don't want to bother you with my tears. So, maybe I should leave."

She began sliding out of the booth, while at the same time, she tried to shake off his jacket. Unfortunately, it had become caught up in the hook on the back of her dress. Frustrated, she gave it one good yank. When this resulted in a loud tearing noise, she checked the inside of the jacket, horrified to see she'd ripped the lining.

Oh my god, could things get any worse?

She shot a guilty look over at Sam before she began searching through her purse, her words coming out in an almost incoherent babble. "I want to give you money to pay for my dinner and to cover the cost of getting your jacket repaired. Or, if you'd rather I take care of it, I will. Then I'll send it to you."

Sam could see her hands were shaking so hard she could barely hold on to anything as she began pulling one item after another out of her purse and tossing them on the table. She suddenly stilled and her shoulders hunched, she stared down at the almost empty purse.

"I think I forgot my wallet." The tears started coming faster. "I'm sorry. I'll pay you somehow."

He slid his hand across the table to cover hers. "Livy, look at me." When she finally did as he asked, he sighed. "Stop it. You're not going to pay for your dinner. Or for my jacket. Now sit."

She was so surprised by this command, she plopped down on the seat. She closed her eyes, her breath coming in quick bursts.

A long silence fell between them before he finally cleared his throat. "Since I don't know your history with this Zack, it's not my place to tell you what to do. But, take it from someone who knows, sometimes it's best to just let it go." He shrugged. "What is it they say, you can't force love?"

He glanced over at Zack and his date, to then look at her. "And, hey, you don't want the amazing show we just put on to go to waste, do you? If you go storming out, waving my ripped jacket through the air as you go, this could very well happen."

When he saw the small smile flit across her face at the reference to his jacket, he forged on. "Do you want to talk about it? If you do, I'm here to listen." He checked his watch. "Hell, I've got all night if this is what it's going to take."

At first, she remained silent, her eyes intently searching his face. Then once she started to talk, she realized she wouldn't have been able to stop even if she tried. It was as if a dam burst, the genuine interest on Sam's face encouraging her to let it all spill out.

Well, not everything. Certainly not as much as she had confided to Carrie, but enough for him to get the picture.

When she finished, her voice fading into silence, he shook his head. "Ah, Livy … it sounds like you got a raw deal. No one deserves to have this happen to them. But seriously, would you really want to go back with him after what he did? He's completely betrayed your trust and I truly believe once this happens between two people, it becomes impossible to forgive and forget."

"Have you ever been in love?" She blurted this out before she realized this probably wasn't something she should be asking him right now. Not with Carrie and all.

He fingered his drink stirrer, hesitating slightly before he answered her. "Yes … or maybe I should say, at least I thought I was. But I've learned very quickly it's hard to be in love when the other person doesn't feel the same way." He shrugged. "I'm sure it's something you eventually get over." He sighed. "At least, this is what I've been told."

Their eyes met, his telling her what she already knew and the words flew right out of her mouth. "Well, she's a fool. Any woman would be lucky to have your love."

As soon as she said this, she wanted to grab the words right back so they could pretend she'd never said them. But since this wasn't possible, she could only hope she didn't look as embarrassed as she felt.

He leaned back in his seat, a slow smile coming over his face. This, along with the teasing glint in his eyes, was a warning of what was to come. And he didn't disappoint. "My, my, my … could it be possible you've finally come to accept that I'm not all that bad? Goodness, who would've ever thought?"

He was grinning. It was a huge grin. "Does this mean we're now friends?"

Friends?

After what he just said, about how it would be hard to be in love with someone when that person didn't feel the same? Well, she'd have to say no. She didn't think she could be his friend.

It would be too hard.

This was because somewhere over the course of the evening she'd realized, with him, she wanted to be more than friends.

She wanted to be that woman.

You know … the woman lucky enough to see the bad boy version of him.

So, he could show her what passion was all about.

Sam was trying to get Livy's attention.

"Hey … so what do you think? You said you've always wanted to try their chocolate brownie soufflé. Maybe this would be the time?"

A dazed expression on her face, she blinked.

He smiled. "I'm game if you are."

She smiled.

Right before she nodded.

If nothing else, he'd never be able to accuse her of being a nibbler.

CHAPTER 11

If there is anything better than to be loved, it is loving.
~ Anonymous

Still chuckling from the conversation he'd shared with Kevin, Chester checked his phone for the time.

He was surprised to see it was already close to midnight.

He wondered, was it too late to call Carrie, or should he wait until the morning? After all, it was Saturday night and she was in New York, Which meant, for her, the night was still young.

They hadn't nicknamed it the city that never sleeps just for the hell of it.

For a few moments, he thought about this. Then he tossed his phone back on his desk.

Nah … he'd wait until the morning.

He wondered how the gallery show had gone. If Carrie had met the ever-so-hot and-charming Julian.

Or as he secretly referred to him, *Mr. Not Forever.*

He frowned. He was curious as to what Carrie thought of him. Or if he'd asked about Sophie.

As he was mulling this over, Sophie padded into the room. She had her hair pulled back in a ponytail and having just washed her face, it was all clean and shiny.

He smiled as he studied her.

If she wasn't so obviously pregnant, she could easily pass for a teenager. A very young teenager. She was wearing one of his jerseys, which came down to her knees. This was something she'd started to do right after they got married. She claimed she slept so much better when she wore one, even more so when he was on the road.

Her hands going to press against her lower back, she looked over at him, her face scrunched up in a frown.

Immediately concerned, he rose from his chair to go to her side. He took her arm to lead her over to one of the chairs arranged in front of his desk. "Angel, is everything okay? Here, sit down. More importantly, why are you even still up?"

She made a face at him. "Oh Chester, besides feeling like I've been pregnant for what feels like forever, and I'm carrying twins, I'm fine."

She turned away from him, twisting her hands together. He was immediately on alert.

Uh oh ... this isn't good.

He didn't need to be a genius to know something was very wrong. At least as far as Sophie was concerned. She was definitely one to wear her emotions on her sleeve. Always. And even more so since she'd become pregnant.

He tilted his head, his voice soft with concern. "Angel? What's wrong?"

She finally looked over at him, a look of such despair on her face, he almost smiled. Which, of course, he didn't, knowing how she'd react.

She averted her gaze. "I think we've made a big mistake. I'm beginning to rethink this whole pregnancy thing."

He chuckled and before she even knew what he was planning to do, he scooped her up into his arms and began carrying her down the hall.

She let out a small shriek. "You shouldn't be carrying me. I'm too heavy."

He merely smiled at this as he carried her into their bedroom and set her gently on the bed. Kicking off his shoes, he joined her. After he scooted on his side next to her and propped his head on his hand, he gazed down at her.

"Have I told you lately how beautiful you are? And how much I love you?" He leaned in to give her a kiss. "Sometimes I still find it hard to believe you're my wife. How did I ever get so lucky?"

She laughed, patting her stomach. "Chester, seriously? Look at me. If being in this condition isn't enough to convince you we're married, I don't know what would be."

She gave a huge yawn. "I'm so tired. But I wanted to get all of the baby gifts from the shower sorted and put away." She frowned. "It seems like there's a lot of stuff, but with twins? I'm beginning to wonder if it will be enough."

He smoothed the hair back from her face. "I'm sure we'll be fine. And if not? We'll just order more of whatever we need."

She nodded before she yawned again, closing her eyes. "*Mmm …* this bed is just so comfortable, isn't it?"

He nodded at this before he leaned in to give her another kiss. "Yes, it is. It's also late. Which means you should go to sleep. But before you do, I thought you'd like to know I finally talked to Kevin about Chris."

Her lashes flew open, an eager look on her face. "What did he say?"

"He said, as far as he knew, Chris isn't engaged. Never has been. He dated a woman for about a month or so around the holidays, but he broke it off about the time of the wedding."

She grinned. "Wow … this is so exciting. Do you think this was because he met Carrie?"

When he shrugged, she made a face at him. "I bet it is. So now you need to call Carrie and tell her this. So, she can call him." She gazed earnestly at him. "I think you should do this right away. Like now."

He frowned at this. "I was going to call her in the morning."

She shook her head. "No, no … you need to call her now. Then you make her promise to call him as soon as she gets off the phone with you. Because this is something that can't wait. Especially after what

Chris told you about Carrie being the woman of his dreams. And how he believed it was fate they met."

She gave a long sigh. "It's so romantic. I love it when a man isn't afraid to let everyone know how he feels about a woman."

He frowned again. "Hey, I believe I'm very romantic, too. It doesn't matter who's around to see this."

She pulled his face to hers, giving him a lingering kiss. "You are by far the most romantic man in the world and I love you to pieces. And if you want to prove just how romantic you are, before you call Carrie, maybe you can bring me some of that chocolate chip cookie dough ice cream?"

She patted her stomach again. "I am eating for three, you know."

He chuckled before he leaned over to press a kiss to her stomach. "Okay, I'll be right back. I want all three of you stay right here and relax."

"Unfortunately, they never seem to want to settle down when I do." She gave another long sigh as she watched him get off the bed. When he began whistling as he left the room, she smiled, closing her eyes.

By the time Chester returned, bowl of ice cream in hand, she was sound asleep. He tucked the quilt around her before he pressed a kiss to her forehead.

"Love you, angel. Sweet dreams. I'll be back to join you after I call Carrie."

After he'd returned the ice cream to the freezer and he was back in his office, he leaned back in his chair, propping his feet up on the desk.

He gazed around at the photos on the walls, zeroing in on one taken when he was in little league. His team had finished at the top of their division and this photo showed him holding a trophy just like every one of his other teammates had received. Standing next to his father, both of them had huge grins on their faces. This had taken place the last year he played with this group of friends. It was also the last year his father had been alive. It was right after this he and his sisters moved to Cleveland to live with his Aunt Evelyn.

It was his father's love of the game that made him pursue a career as a baseball player. And to this day, he still felt his father's presence on the field with him during a game. It was always an encouraging and comforting feeling.

Now his grandfather … he was a whole other story. But he wasn't going to start thinking about him.

He had more important things to think about now. Like how he was soon to become a father, something he was still finding so hard to believe.

A father to not only one baby, but two.

Even though he and Sophie had both decided to keep the sex of the babies a surprise, Sophie kept asking him what he wanted. Did he want boys or girls? Or one of each?

Hell, he didn't care. He just wanted them to be healthy. And he wanted nothing to happen to Sophie. He knew he was probably worrying needlessly, because after all, women had babies every day. But Sophie was so small and the fact she was carrying two babies was almost too mind boggling for him to even think about. And even though she shrugged off his concerns, he knew she had to be worried, too.

How could she not? Her comment, minutes ago, about changing her mind confirmed this.

At the sound of the wind whipping around the corner of the building, he glanced over at the window. He sighed. Since they were on the top floor of the building, the wind could be quite fierce sometimes.

Lately, he had been doing a lot of thinking about the possibility of moving. Because as much as he liked the changes Carrie had made to the décor of the condo, it really wasn't the ideal place to raise a family.

He hadn't told Sophie this, but only a few days ago he'd asked Carrie to keep an eye out for a house they might like, preferably a house located somewhere along the shores of Lake Erie.

He smiled again. Heaven forbid it be a big house. Sophie had already made it quite clear to him and everyone who'd listen, she was not going to live in a humongous and pretentious mansion. This wasn't her style. She wanted a house with character, she said. An old farmhouse would be ideal.

He shook his head. All this money, and she wouldn't let him spend it on her.

He chuckled. Most people would say he was crazy to be upset about this. After all, what man, at least one in his right mind, wouldn't welcome such a problem?

This was a reminder he needed to call the jeweler to find out if the two interlocking eternity rings he ordered for Sophie were ready yet. He wanted to give them to her when the babies came.

And yes, they would be real diamonds and everything. Because no matter what she said, buying her diamonds was one thing he was never going to stop doing.

He picked up his phone and set up a reminder to call the jewelers.

He sat in the silence, lost in his thoughts before he finally searched for the number he needed and hit call.

Sophie would never let him hear the end of it if he didn't call Carrie.

CHAPTER 12

Chris stared into the fire.

He truly had no idea how long Carrie had been curled up next to him. Or how they even came to be on the sofa after she first began to cry. If anything, he was still finding it hard to believe she was even here. In New York, and in his condo. Or, even more amazingly, in his arms.

He was pretty sure she'd finally cried herself out. At least he hoped so. She was now completely silent, her head resting against his chest and her hand holding his. She was holding on to him so tight, almost as if she was afraid if she didn't, he'd leave.

Like there's even a chance this would happen.

He planted a kiss to the top of her head.

"Hey … are you okay? All cried out?"

Yes, she was. And no, she wasn't. The bottom line? She felt so, so incredibly stupid. She'd handled everything all so wrong, foolishly jumping to a conclusion before she even gave Chris the chance to give his side of the story.

And what was even worse? Both Chester and Sam had tried to tell her this.

Chester will never let you live this one down, this is for sure.

She gave a long, shaky sigh, her words muffled against him. "I'm so sorry. I'm such a fool. I should've trusted you."

He placed another kiss in her hair. "Carrie, look at me."

When she gazed up at him, her expression one of such distress, he smiled. "Hey … it's okay. You're here and we're together. Maybe a little later than we'd planned, but I'll take it. Gladly."

He framed the side of her face in his hand. "But there's one thing I want you to do for me from now on. You need to trust me."

When she nodded, he gave her a slow smile. "Good. Because if I make you a promise, I won't go back on my word."

She leaned into his hand, closing her eyes. "I know you won't. And I should've listened to Chester. And Sam. They both told me I needed to talk to you. So, I could hear the real story."

"Well, they were right. Think of all the time we've lost." He hugged her close. "But I'm going to make it up to you." Then he tilted his head, his eyes studying her. "And who is Sam? I don't remember you talking about a Sam?"

"Sam is a friend and colleague of mine, His restores historical properties, so I've done a few design projects with him, the latest in Quebec this past summer. He's actually here in New York this weekend. He went to the gallery show with me and Livy".

Her eyes wide, her hand went to her mouth. "*Oh, no* … I left him and Livy at the gallery. The only thing I told them was I needed to leave."

She started to giggle. "They met for the first time tonight and it was like a defective fireworks display went off, the way they went at each other. No matter what Sam said, Livy was offended."

She shook her head. "Poor Sam, I don't think he had any idea what hit him."

She smiled. "I think, even though I'm sure they'd both be so quick to deny this, there was a whole lot of chemistry going on between them."

Then she completely surprised him by reaching up and clasping her hands behind his neck. She gazed up into his face, her words coming out in a whisper. "When are you going to kiss me? I really need you to kiss me. I've been waiting for this for what seems like such a long, long time."

He was tempted. Don't get the wrong idea, he really was. More than anything. But if he did kiss her, he knew it wouldn't to be enough. No, that one kiss would escalate into so much more. And he didn't want this to happen.

Not yet. Not with their reunion so new.

There was also the fact she was sort of, if not more than, a little bit drunk. When he kissed her, he didn't want it to be a kiss she'd look back and remember only in a haze.

He tucked her hair behind her ear. "Carrie, how much wine have you had?"

She shook her head. "I don't know? Two glasses? Three?" She scrunched up her face. "Maybe four?"

Her fingers were now gently combing through the curls at the back of his neck, making it almost impossible for him to think. It was when she shifted against him to get even closer, pressing a soft kiss to his jaw, he finally untangled her fingers from his hair, holding her hands captive in his He smiled at her, shaking his head.

"I see. And when is the last time you had something to eat?"

Again, she shook her head. Then her eyes lit up. "Wait, At the gallery I had a cracker. And a pickle."

She shuddered, wrinkling her nose. "The pickle was so sour. I don't like sour pickles. Do you?"

He chuckled. *"Hmm...* no, I'd have to say they're not one of my favorites. But, a cracker and a pickle aren't what I'd call very fortifying. Especially when you've had, as you said, possibly four glasses of wine. I seem to remember you telling me you don't drink very much. One glass is your limit, you said. This leads me to believe you're a little drunk right now."

He slowly rose to his feet, pulling her up with him. "Come on, you're going to come over and sit at the counter. Where you can watch as I make you something to eat."

At the look of disappointment on her face, he lifted her chin with his finger until their eyes met. His voice was a husky whisper. "Don't think I don't want to kiss you right now. Because even though I do, more than anything, I'm not. Because when I finally do kiss you, I'm going to want all of you to feel the kiss… and remember what it was like."

She remained completely still, her lips parted and her gaze locked with his. If she only knew how much control it was taking him to keep from picking her up and whisking her downstairs to his bedroom, no matter how many glasses of wine had been consumed. After all, this was something he'd been dreaming of ever since they first met.

But, no.

For now, he was going to feed her.

After he'd settled her at the counter, he opened the refrigerator, his gaze roaming over the contents. He turned to her, one eyebrow raised. "Scrambled eggs? Toast? And I'm pretty sure there's bacon in here, too. Sound good?"

The crooked smile coming right at her, she nodded. She was gazing at him with so much trust in her eyes, he actually felt his heart stutter in his chest.

And then, honestly? He couldn't help what he did next. He caved, this the only explanation. He leaned across the counter and cupping her chin in his hand, he kissed her.

It was a hello, I'm back, kind of kiss. Or maybe more like a testing the waters kind of kiss. One might even argue it couldn't be considered a kiss at all.

But for Chris, the kiss confirmed what he'd believed all along. His mouth still hovering over hers, he gave a contented sigh. "Yep, it's still there." He traced her bottom lip with his thumb. "God, I can't even begin to tell you how glad I am you're here."

He abruptly turned back to the refrigerator and began pulling out the items he needed. This was mostly in an effort to ignore the way she was gazing at him, her elbow on the counter and her chin propped in her hand. A dreamy expression on her face, her eyes had gone even a darker shade of violet and were pulling at him like a magnet.

Yep, the way he saw it, they were sending him an invitation to take everything he just set on the counter and toss it back into the refrigerator. Then he'd give her a real kiss.

Instead, he took a deep breath, running his hand through his hair.

"Okay, then." He cleared his throat. "I hope you're ready to watch a real chef in action. Scrambled eggs might be one of the few things I can make, but I know how to do them up right."

He sent her a wink and a smile. "So, be prepared to be wowed, princess."

Carrie gave the plate one last wipe with the towel. She handed it to Chris, who put it in the cupboard. After he took the towel and tossed it on the counter, he took her hand to lead her back to the sofa.

Once they were settled, his arm around her and her head resting on his shoulder, he glanced at his watch. It was just past midnight.

He was torn.

He knew he should offer to take her back to her hotel. But he didn't want to let her go.

God, no ...

He wanted her to stay. If only so he could spend the night holding her in his arms. Like he had on that cold and snowy February night.

There was also the fear if he did let her go, she would somehow disappear again. He didn't want to take the chance of this happening. There was already too much time lost between them.

What he felt for her was different from anything he had ever experienced. But as crazy as this may sound, he wanted to wait before they took the next step. He didn't want to jeopardize this second chance they had been given.

When they did finally make the ultimate commitment to each other, he wanted it to be one of the defining moments between them, one they would remember for the rest of their lives. A turning point in the whole crazy story they had already started to write together. It would be a story to share with their children, their grandchildren, and all the generations to follow.

Children? Grandchildren? Where the hell did that come from? Are you really serious about this? Because once you take that leap, this is it.

Yes, he was in. He had always been in.

From the very start.

For real.

Carrie snuggled closer to Chris, giving a contented sigh.

One of her biggest fears had been, when they did meet up again, the chemistry between them would no longer exist. But now she knew this was never going to happen. It had been waiting for the right moment to burn even brighter.

Unlike Chris, she didn't want to go slow. She wanted the doubt she had carried around with her for the past months to be gone. She was all in, ready to commit to him fully. She would stay right where she was and in his arms for as long as he would let her.

Forever, if she could.

She had gathered up the courage to tell him this when, deep in the hidden pocket of her dress, her phone began to vibrate. You can imagine Chris's surprise when she suddenly pulled away from him, her hands frantically patting her dress.

He started to laugh. "What the ..."

She stood, her hands still searching her dress. "I have a call. My phone is in the pocket of my dress and I am trying to get to it." She grinned up at him. "The best feature of this dress is the pockets. And as you can see, they provide a very secure hiding place."

As far as he was concerned, the best feature of her dress was definitely not the pockets. No, absolutely not. It was how the dress fit so perfectly, showing off every beautiful curve, leaving so much to his imagination. But before he could tell her this, she pulled out her phone, a triumphant expression on her face.

"Voila!"

She laughed. "I'm sorry. I don't want you to think I'm crazy when it comes to answering my phone. Because, honest, I'm not. But with the babies coming any day now, I have to make sure it's not Chester."

Peering at the now silent phone, she sank down on the sofa, turning to Chris with an excited smile. "It was Chester! Oh my gosh, I need to call him back."

He reached for the phone, a mischievous grin lighting up his face. "May I?"

She handed him the phone and watched as he hit the call button. Then after he put the phone on speaker, he grinned at her.

Chester's voice filled the room. "Hey Kitten, how's it going?"

Chris grinned at Carrie, holding his finger to his lips. "This isn't Kitten. But hey, not to worry. Everything is going great. Fantastic, in fact."

There was a long silence.

Just as Carrie was about to break down and say something, Chester responded. "*Ummm…* whoever you are, what have you done with my sister? And should I be worried?"

"Chester, this is Chris. We met at Kevin and Abby's wedding. I'm Kevin's friend from Chicago and your sister is sitting right next to me, safe and sound. If you think back, you might remember what I said to you that night. This being Carrie would always be safe with me."

He sent Carrie a teasing glance. "And hey … thanks for having some faith in me, something she failed to do."

Chester chuckled. "You have to realize it's hard for her to accept I'm always right."

Carrie groaned. "Chez, I'll give you this one. And, okay, maybe a few others."

She sighed. "It's just so hard for me when you gloat like you do. But enough of that. Why are you calling? Is it time? Are the babies coming?"

He chucked again. "No, unfortunately for our sanity, no babies yet. I was calling to give you some information you seem to already have. You have to remember, you'll always be my little sister. Which means I'll always be looking out for you, kitten."

In fact, leaning back in his chair, Chester was feeling not only happy, but extremely relieved with this turn of events. He wasn't blind. He'd seen the expression on Carrie's face at even just the mention of Chris's name. Hell, Chris had even more of an infatuated look on his face when they'd been together at the wedding.

You're turning into one of these sappy, love-struck guys, wanting everyone to have a love like yours. You can blame Sophie for this.

He cleared his throat. "I'll let you go. I'm glad to see things are working out for the both of you. And Carrie, if you need me to pick you up from the airport when you get back into Cleveland, let me know."

Carrie gazed over at Chris, shaking her head, her eyes bright. "I'm fine, Chez … more than fine. And thanks, I will. Love you."

"Love you, too, kitten. And Chris, I'm counting on you to keep taking good care of her."

After Chris put the phone on the coffee table, he pulled Carrie close. "I should take you back to your hotel, but I don't want to give you up yet. I want you to talk to me. I want to know everything I've missed. What's been going on in your life since I saw you last. For, what has it been, almost nine months?"

"It's actually been eight months, three weeks and two days."

He drew back, a slow smile coming over his face when he saw the blush start to rise in her cheeks at her revelation. "You actually kept track? *Oh Carrie...*"

He brought her hand up to his mouth for a kiss. "Have I told you yet how glad I am to finally have you with me again?"

At her nod, he pulled her even closer. "So, tell me. I want to hear it all. Everything that's happened in those eight months, three weeks and two days of your life."

He smiled. "So, I can pretend I was there with you all along."

They talked for hours.

About everything.

She told him about Chester and Sophie. How they almost broke up when Chester's ex-wife showed up, claiming he was the father of the little boy she had in tow. How Sophie had gone back to Paris, unaware Chester had found out his ex-wife had lied. And it was only when Chester got injured during spring training and Sophie came back home, Chester asked her to marry him.

She gave him all of the details about Chester and Sophie's wedding and how it was exactly what Sophie wanted, on a beach, at sunset and with only their closest friends and family there to help them celebrate.

She told him how only a few weeks after the wedding, Sam asked her to join him on a project involving the renovation of a historic mansion in Quebec. It was a project they worked on, almost twenty-four-seven, for close to six months.

She didn't tell him about Sam's suggestion they take their friendship to the next level. She didn't feel there was any reason to share this information, because nothing had happened.

She valued Sam's friendship and she wanted him and Chris to be friends. She also had a hunch Sam's attention may have already taken off in a whole new direction.

And this would be with Livy.

She smiled.

Who would have thought?

CHAPTER 13

We come to love not by finding a perfect person,
but by learning to see an imperfect person perfectly.
~ Anonymous

Midnight had already come and gone when Livy and Sam found themselves standing on the front steps of Gracie Ann's.They were huddled under the small and, according to Sam, sorry excuse for what was supposed to be a covering over the door.

This grumbling and irate opinion of his came right after a deluge of snow and water came sliding down over the top of the awning, almost slamming into them in the process.

It hadn't been their choice to leave the warmth and coziness of the restaurant. It was only when they noticed they were the last customers still seated in the dining section of the restaurant, they decided to leave.

Livy was still thinking about the scene they had witnessed between Zack and his date. Shortly after they'd been seated, Zack's date had gone storming out of the restaurant, with him following a few minutes later.

And what was Sam's take on this? He'd shrugged, a wry smile on his face. "It looks like your ex's new life isn't working out at all like he thought it would." He had then gone on to change the subject.

Livy told Sam about her dream of becoming an author. This was why she took the job at the publishing company she now worked for as an editor. But after a full day of editing, she found the last thing she wanted to do in her free-time was write. Or even look at a book.

So, now she was re-thinking her choice of career. She still wanted to write, but wondered if she needed to make a fresh start.

Easier said than done.

While Sam had been more than happy to share stories about the different renovations he'd worked on, even bringing up photos on his phone. This was something he normally wouldn't do on a date, but she seemed genuinely interested.

It had been a long time since a woman had shown so much interest, or had been so impressed, with the work he was so passionate about.

If he stopped to think about it, the women he'd dated over the past few years were more interested in how successful he was. Or how much money he made. Or worse yet, were hung up on his past athletic accomplishments. As far as he was concerned, that part of his life was no longer what he was all about.

In fact, Carrie had been the only woman he actually enjoyed spending time with. But after what happened tonight in the gallery, he was finally able to accept they would never be anything except friends. And he was fine with this. He only wanted her to be happy. Even if it wasn't with him.

And Livy? With her … he was confused.

Really confused.

And now an awkward silence had fallen between them.

Livy shivered, pulling up the collar of her coat. Sneaking a glance up at Sam, she was surprised to find he was studying her, a distracted look on his face.

She gave him a tentative smile. "Penny for your thoughts?"

For a few moments, he didn't say anything.

Then he gave an almost embarrassed laugh. "*Hmm ...* I guess I was thinking, even though you and Carrie are sisters and have a lot of the same characteristics, at the same time, you're so different."

She wasn't quite sure how to take this. If anything, it was a bit concerning. Just what did he mean by different? Was he implying she was the different one? In what way? And hopefully, this would be a good different?

She needed to know. "What do you find so different about us?"

A big sigh coming from him, he jammed his hands in his pockets. "Well, the way I see it, even though Carrie is very passionate about what she does, she tends to keep her feelings in check. She always puts up a reserved front."

Here he paused to study her again, his mouth turning up in a slight smile. "Where you ... you're also passionate. But no matter what the situation, you take it as a personal challenge."

He smiled. "Let's just say you're certainly not one to hold back what you're thinking."

He watched the frown come over her face, something he had expected. If anything, he was surprised she hadn't reacted more strongly. When she remained silent, he gave a hesitant chuckle. "It's not a bad thing. What I said about you, that is. If anything, I find it refreshing. It's a trait that definitely keeps a man on his toes. I know for me, this has been the case."

Another silence fell between them. And this was because Livy had no idea what to say.

Well, she did. But she certainly couldn't come out and ask him, if he had to make a choice between her and Carrie, who would he choose?

So, she merely nodded.

It had now begun to snow harder, big, wet, sloppy flakes. She glanced around to see the area around them was deserted. Evidently, they were the only people who weren't inside somewhere, seeking refuge from the miserable weather. Huddling deeper into her coat, she wondered if it was time to suggest they call it a night.

There was no doubt in her mind he would welcome this. If anything, she was surprised he had lasted this long.

She glanced up at him. "I can't believe it's so late. At least it's late for me." She shrugged. "I'm usually not one to be out at this hour. I'd much rather stay home and find a good movie to watch on TV. Or listen to music."

Well, this certainly doesn't make you sound like a very fun person to be around, does it? It also wasn't much of a compliment to Sam.

She quickly tried to explain. "I'm not saying I didn't have a good time with you. Because I did. It was all very nice. You've been nothing but nice."

Oh geeez ... this didn't come out sounding any better, did it?

He gave a short laugh. "You mean the good guy that I am, I take it."

Abruptly taking her arm to lead her over to the curb, his voice sounded almost irritated. "You look like you're cold. We should find a taxi and get you home."

He didn't know why he suddenly felt so angry. He had nothing to be mad about. She was absolutely right about what she said. It had been a nice evening and they had enjoyed a great dinner. All while getting along other after such a rocky start.

He was also pretty sure he'd convinced her he wasn't the jerk she thought he was. So, it all worked out.

Carrie should be happy.

After all, she did say she wanted them to be friends.

So, what's the problem? Why are you feeling so frustrated?

It was just that ... oh hell, he didn't know. There was this feeling of desperation inside of him.

A feeling he didn't know quite how to deal with.

What it all came down to, he needed more time. He wasn't quite sure for what, only that he was confused about these feelings Livy brought out in him. And once they parted tonight, he knew the chance of anything more developing between them could wind up fading into a memory instead.

At least this was the way he saw things turning out.

He also needed to take into consideration Livy was still struggling with a recent breakup. Certainly not the best time for him to make his move.

Make your move? Where the hell is this coming from? A few hours ago, the two of you hated each other. Well, at least she didn't like you. And now you're thinking of making a move? Exactly what kind of move would this be?

He stepped closer to the curb, now even more determined to flag down a taxi. With how his mind was operating right now, it would be best to get her home as quickly as possible. Who knew what could come out of his mouth next?

He was also beginning to think coming to New York hadn't been such a good idea after all.

Livy wasn't quite sure what was wrong with Sam, why he was so angry. It wasn't like she had, as he had so aptly put it, challenged him about his remark about her and Carrie. Even though she had been tempted, she'd kept her mouth shut.

But if he wanted a woman more like Carrie? She couldn't help him out with that. Nor could she change the way she was. And it wasn't her fault she fought him on everything. He encouraged this.

The snow now back to sleet, she inched closer to Sam to escape the stinging ice pellets coming at them. As if he sensed this, he slipped his arm around her, tucking her even closer against him as he attempted to flag down a taxi.

Instantly comforted by his solid strength, the heat from him surrounding her, she closed her eyes.

And then, even though she knew this was the worst possible thing she could do, she let her imagination take over.

She was floating in a whole new world. One she didn't want to leave.

A taxi came sweeping up to the curb, sending a spray of icy water right at them, with Sam bearing the brunt of the shower. After a sharp curse, he opened the door, gesturing for Livy to get in.

Once she was inside, she turned to thank him, surprised to see he'd slipped in right behind her and was now closing the door.

Her mouth dropped open.

"What are you doing?"

In the midst of wiping down his wet clothing he turned to her, an eyebrow raised.

She began sputtering. "There's no reason for you to come with me. Especially since you can walk to your hotel from here. I will be fine on my own. I've been ..."

After giving one last swipe at his jacket, he interrupted her. "I know, I know. We've gone through this before. What was it you said? Seven years, right? Which means you're completely capable of taking care of yourself."

He shook his head. "I'm sorry, but not seeing you home isn't something I feel comfortable doing. As far as I am concerned, you are my responsibility and I need to see this through. Getting you home, that is."

As you can imagine, this didn't go over very well with Livy.

His responsibility?

See this through?

Did this man ever think before he spoke?

At the same time, it felt good to have someone taking care of her. So, even though there was plenty she wanted to say, she kept her mouth shut.

She didn't want to spend the time they had left together arguing. Once he left her at her apartment, the evening would be over and there was a pretty good chance she'd never see him again.

This was bothering her a lot more than it should.

They were both silent during the short drive, a mix of tension and frustration swirling between them.

Twice, Sam glanced over at Livy to find she was watching him. And both times, when their eyes met, she quickly looked away.

The uncertainty was killing him.

When they pulled up to the curb in front of her apartment, Sam got out of the taxi and extended his hand to Livy. Of course, she refused, waving his hand away.

This took place a split second before she realized she should've taken advantage of his offer. If you remember, the dress she was wearing, besides being extremely flattering, wasn't ideal when it came to certain moves. A graceful exit from a vehicle being right there at the top of the list.

After a slight hesitation, she made a grab for the door and giving one good pull, she hoisted herself out of the taxi and onto her feet.

She sent Sam a smug grin.

Sam had watched this with interest. A smile twitched at the corner of his lips. "So, tell me, what are you going to do about your purse?"

Her purse?

She turned to see it was tucked way back in the far corner of the backseat. Where she had left it.

Oh, dear god ... now what are you going to do?

The tone of Sam's voice was amused. "Can you get it? Or will you be needing my help?"

She turned to him, suddenly irritated all over again, "If you were a gentleman, you wouldn't even have to ask."

Startled, he stepped back. Then he began to chuckle. "Ah ... I see. Now all of a sudden, I'm not enough of a gentleman for you? Correct me if I'm wrong, but I thought this was the kind of behavior going against everything you believed in."

Quickly noting her frustration and taking pity on her, he nodded. "But, you're right. A real gentleman wouldn't have asked. So, what do you think? Maybe this could possibly be some of that bad boy coming out in me?"

When she only shook her head, he reached in to grab her purse. He handed it to her with a smile. Then he nodded, his smile turning into a big grin. "Round one, I believe, is mine."

She clutched her purse and gave an exasperated sigh as she turned away from him. But what he said was like an echo in her mind.

Round one?

Did this mean there was going to be more?

When Sam took her arm to walk her to the entrance of her apartment building, Livy was silent. That she didn't refuse his support was a testament of how confused she was. Even when they were inside and he followed her up the steps to the second floor, taking her arm once again as they walked down the hall to her door, she still didn't fight him. Nor did she utter a single word.

She unlocked her door and turned to see he was watching her, an uncertain expression on his face.

Yes, Sam was wondering if he'd gone a little too far with what he said.

Round one? Where the hell had that come from? And what were you trying to say?

Again, the same feeling of desperation coming over him, he swallowed. "Livy ..."

Her head jerked up and for a moment they stared at each other. Then he gave a long sigh, shaking his head.

Interpreting this as his impatience to leave, these exact words came out of her mouth. "Don't worry. It's not like we were on a date or something. So, I'm certainly not expecting you to kiss me."

Oh, no, no, no ... now you've done it.

She watched as a startled expression came over his face. She had no idea this was because at that same exact moment, kissing her was what he was thinking about. If only to leave her with the memory he could be just as much of a bad boy as any other guy out there.

Yes, he wanted to, what was it they said? Rock it.

Exactly.

He wanted to shake up her world.

He had no idea where this was coming from. It certainly wasn't something he would normally think of doing. As he slowly shook his head he realized she was still talking, anger vibrating in her voice.

"What I meant is, now you're free of me. You can go back to your hotel and chalk this night up to a deed well done. I ..."

She never finished. This was because he swooped in and framing her face in his hands, he proceeded to give her a slow, mind clearing kiss. It was only when her purse slipped through her fingers to hit the floor, they jerked apart.

Her eyes closed, Livy was desperately trying to reign in everything this kiss had stirred up inside her. When she realized she was gripping his arms, she quickly dropped her hands to her sides.

Sam watched as her lashes slowly fluttered open, his lips curving into a smile when he saw the dazed look in her eyes.

Well, what do you know ... it appears you finally made an impression on her. And a good one, at that.

She was the first to move.

Searching for the doorknob, she finally opened the door. Her only goal to slip into her apartment so she could put an end to this agony. Or before she threw caution to the wind and launched herself right into his arms.

Or, here's an enticing thought, drag him with her right into her apartment.

The sound of him clearing his throat had her whirling around to face him.

He was still smiling. "Again, you seem to have forgotten something." At her startled look, he picked up her purse from the floor and handed it to her. "You seem to have trouble holding on to everything tonight. Got other things on your mind?"

This was followed by his big grin. She would have to say it was actually more of a smirk. A very satisfied and knowing smirk.

He nodded. "Thanks for the wonderful evening, Livy. I'll be in touch."

As he began backing away, his grin grew even bigger. "And, hey, correct me if I'm wrong, but I do believe I also just nailed round two. How about that? Two to nothing. All in my favor."

With a wink, he turned to casually stroll down the hall before he went running down the stairs.

Livy rested her forehead against the doorjamb and closed her eyes.

She didn't move, listening to the sound of his footsteps fading as went down the stairs. It was only after she heard the main door to the building close with the usual jarring bang, she entered her apartment and set her purse down on the kitchen table.

Her fingers going up to her lips, she was surprised they still felt the same. Because after Sam's kiss, everything else about her had changed.

Everything.

It was a whole new kind of different.

A good different.

She ran her hand through her hair, not in the least surprised to see it was shaking. Certainly not after what happened out there in the hall. If anything, she was surprised she was still standing.

She was so confused. Never in her wildest dreams had she expected the evening to end like it had. A kiss? And from, of all people, Sam?

Absolutely, not.

And we're not talking about your usual kiss. No, this one was a real eye-opener.

She suddenly found she was in the bathroom, rummaging through the drawers of the vanity. After she found what she was searching for, within minutes, the Livy smiling back at her in the mirror was minus the usual glasses. Somewhat surprised at how much better she could see with her contacts, she pulled her hair back from her face and gave a long hard look in the mirror.

She smiled.

When her doorbell rang, she quickly dropped her hands from her hair.

Maybe it was Sam? A big smile on her face, she went running out of the bathroom and over to open the door.

Her smile disappeared.

It was Zack.

A pitiful expression on his face, he had a black garbage bag slung over his shoulder. It was the same kind of garbage bag, he had carried out of her apartment over a week ago, packed with his belongings.

When she didn't say anything, he pushed past her and into the room. He threw the bag on the floor and turned to her.

"I've made a huge mistake. I've decided to come back."

Then he peered more closely at her, a puzzled expression on his face. "What happened to your glasses?"

Sam was still smiling when he slid into the backseat of the taxi. He gave the driver the name of his hotel and as they were about to pull out into traffic, he glanced over at Livy's apartment building.

Something caught his eye. Motioning for the driver to stop, he watched as a man walked up to the entrance of Livy's building, to then disappear inside. He'd been carrying a huge black garbage bag.

It was Zack.

With the driver watching him nervously in the rear-view mirror, Sam waited. For a good ten or fifteen minutes, he did this. When he thought about this later, he wished he hadn't. Because then he wouldn't have known Zack never came back out of the building.

Which could only mean Livy let him stay.

After he told the taxi driver it was okay to go, he leaned his head back against the seat and closed his eyes.

Well, it looks like, once again, you've struck out. Twice in one night, as a matter of fact.

Round two?

Dragging his hand back through his hair, he let out a long, frustrated sigh.

I guess that's pretty much your limit.

CHAPTER 14

Chris slowly extracted his arm from behind Carrie, trying not to wake her as he carefully slid off the sofa.

Her eyelashes fluttering, she gave a little moan before her hands reached out as though she was searching for him. Her fingers coming into contact with one of the sofa pillows, she pulled it to her with a soft little sigh.

He gave a soft chuckle before he leaned over and pressed a kiss to her cheek. "Go back to sleep, princess. I'll be right back. I'm going to get you a blanket."

He picked up his phone to check the time, a smile coming over his face. It was almost six o'clock in the morning. He shook his head. It looked like his plan to take her back to her hotel never materialized.

Once again, they'd talked into the early morning hours, with her finally nodding off against him. Almost to the point of total exhaustion, he had remained awake, his mind still struggling with everything that happened. Even now as he gazed down at her, it was hard to believe she was actually here.

He wondered what she would do if he picked her up and carried her downstairs to his bed?

He shook his head.

He didn't even want to start thinking about what he would want to happen next if he did.

But come on, look at her. She couldn't be comfortable in the dress she was wearing.

He sighed. Maybe instead of a blanket, he should try to dig up something of his for her to wear.

He rubbed the back of his neck, a wry smile on his face.

This is so damn hard. Maybe, but no, don't even go there. Remember? You want to take this slow.

This was when, as if to prove his point, Carrie gave a soft little moan as she tried to curl up even further into the corner of the sofa. He watched, almost in a trance, as the skirt of her dress rode up even higher above her knees. Then he frowned as she reached out in her sleep, trying to pull it down before she burrowed her face back in the pillow.

"*Dear god.*" He mumbled this, dragging his hand over his chin. He definitely needed to find something else for her to wear, something big and bulky.

And he needed to do this quickly.

Before he could change his mind, he went running down the stairs to his bedroom, where he rummaged through his dresser to come up with a pair of flannel pajama bottoms and a tee shirt. The smallest he could find, they weren't ideal, but should work. If anything, she'd be a hell of a lot more comfortable than she was now.

After he changed into his favorite jeans and a tee shirt, and grabbed a blanket from the closet on his way out, he went sprinting back up the stairs.

As soon as he reached the top step, he heard his phone vibrating from where he'd left it on the table by the sofa.

Who would be calling you at this hour?

He picked up the phone. It was his sister Emily. Concerned, he moved away from Carrie so he wouldn't wake her.

"Hey, Em … what's wrong?"

Her loud sigh came through the phone. A sigh almost long enough to travel all the way from Hoboken where she lived with her husband John and their little boy, Connor.

Okay, maybe not, but it was close.

This brought a long sigh from him in return. He had a feeling, whatever the reason for her call, her explanation would be longer and more detailed than he would like.

He loved his sister. Of course, he did. His only complaint was she always managed to turn everything into a major production. Two years younger than he was, he likened her to a miniature diva while they were growing up. And now? She hadn't changed a bit, a more grown up and sophisticated diva with how she went about getting her way.

Thank God, her husband John was now the one who had to deal with her dramatics. He liked John, he was a great guy. Calm and easy going, he was the one person who was always able to calm her down. And he and Emily did seem to have a great marriage.

As he wearily massaged his forehead with his fingers, another one of Emily's sighs came traveling through the phone. "I need your help. Well, not just me. We all need your help. We got the call, only about an hour ago, John's grandfather has passed away. This means we now have to make the trip to Connecticut for the funeral."

Before Chris he could even offer his condolences, Emily continued. Again, this was so typical. Caught up with this new drama in her life, she'd turn it around until it was all about her.

"As you can imagine, John's mother is not taking this very well. Of course, I can understand this. After all, it is her father. But she's being very unreasonable. She wants us there as soon as possible. She seems to think we can drop everything, just like that. Not even taking into consideration we're the only members of the family with a small child to care for."

Another sigh came floating through the phone. "I know, I know … you're probably shaking your head right now. It's not that I don't feel bad about all of this, I do. I really liked John's grandfather. But he hasn't been well for such a long time and at ninety-seven, he's lived a long life. The poor man hasn't been happy since his wife died five years ago. To make a long story short, we packed up everything as quickly as we could. But we've come to a disagreement about what to do with Connor. John thinks we should take him with us, but I don't feel he's mature enough to handle something like this. He is only four."

There was a long pause. "So, do you think Connor can stay with you? This would be only until Monday morning. Right after we got the call, I talked to Shelly, Connor's nanny. She's out of town, but promised she'd be available Monday morning as usual. She even offered to pick up Connor at your place if you have early meetings or something. And since today is Sunday, I figured you'd have nothing important going on."

Chris gazed over to where Carrie was curled up on the sofa.

No, that's not exactly true. You have something very important going on. More important than Emily could possibly imagine.

He gave a soft groan, pinching his forehead with his fingers. He could see Carrie had now flung her one arm over her head and her one leg had slipped over the edge of the sofa.

He shook his head, closing his eyes. He didn't dare look at what the state of her dress was in now.

His sister's voice came in his ear. "Chris? Are you there? Can you do this for us?"

His sigh was long. And, he realized, almost as dramatic as one he'd expect from her. "Yeah, sure. I'll watch him. When will you be dropping him off?"

Her voice immediately perked up. "Thank God. We'll be there in about fifteen minutes. We're actually in the car right now and on our way. I knew I was taking a chance on this, but I had a feeling you'd be around. Especially since you've turned into such a recluse lately, hiding away in your apartment most of the time."

Here she paused, her voice now adopting the bossy tone he knew so well. "We really need to find you a wife. I still don't understand why you broke it off with Lauren. The two of you made the perfect couple."

He scowled at this as he glanced over at Carrie.

Nope, never. You have what you want right here.

While he was trying to think up a less revealing response than this, he heard John say something in the background. This brought a laugh from Emily. "John doesn't seem to agree. He thinks you can do better."

Chris chuckled. "Well, I don't know exactly what he means by that, but tell him thanks for his support."

"Okay, I will. We'll be there in just a little bit. And Chris, thanks. John and I really appreciate you doing this for us. You always come through for us. Connor is so blessed to have you as an uncle."

"Yeah, yeah, yeah … I'll see you when you get here."

After he ended the call, he remained where he was, leaning against the counter. He smiled, wondering what Connor would think of Carrie. Even at only four years old, he already knew how to work the ladies. With his big blue eyes and curly mop of blonde hair, he was able to win over even the most standoffish member of the opposite sex.

He frowned.

Except Lauren.

She had made it quite clear children weren't something she was looking forward to, having mentioned many times she would be just as happy without them.

But he wasn't going to start thinking about her now. He glanced over to see Carrie had now curled into the couch as though she was cold, so he went over to cover her with the blanket. There was no doubt in his mind Connor would wake her up when he arrived, so why wake her now to change out of her dress?

He looked down at her. At the slight smile on her face, he wondered what she was thinking about. Maybe, just maybe it was about him?

He gazed around the room, hit with this unexpected feeling. There was something new in the air. Something that felt so right, so peaceful. As though everything had settled into place.

The space was no longer just another room, similar to what you'd expect to find in almost every other apartment here in the upcoming and trendy neighborhoods of Manhattan.

No ... this now felt like home. The way it was meant to be.

He gazed down at Carrie.

And it was official.

His heart was no longer his to keep.

Chris wandered into the kitchen, where he gazed absentmindedly around the room. He wasn't sure of what he had been planning to do next.

He smiled.

Oh boy, you're in deep, aren't you? Concentrate here...

Scratching his head, he gazed around the room.

Coffee ...

If he and Carrie were going to be taking on a four-year-old, they were going to need coffee. A hell of a lot of coffee.

Galvanized into action, he took a bag of coffee beans out of the refrigerator. As he began filling the coffee pot with water, his mind wandered to Carrie and what they had talked about through the night. He jumped back when the water flowed over the top of the pot, splashing into the sink and all over him.

Geeez ... come on, you need to pay attention.

He shook his head and muttering to himself, he mopped up the water with paper towels before he emptied the pot and started over.

His mind wandered off again.

Just as the coffee began to perk, he heard the knock on his door.

Connor had arrived.

After a long and very detailed set of instructions, Emily leaned down to give Connor another hug and a kiss.

"Now remember what I told you on the way over here. Uncle Chris is the boss and you need to listen to him. No whining and no late night tonight. You have play group tomorrow and you don't want to be the only crabby and tired little boy there. So, this means your usual bedtime."

This was accompanied by a warning glance at Chris, who shook his head in the affirmative.

You get it. The usual bedtime will be strictly enforced. You know how Emily is when it comes to routine.

Connor slowly shook his head as he glanced from Chris to his mom. "I don't need a lot of sleep now that I'm four."

Emily shook her head before she glanced over at Chris, rolling her eyes. "Let this be a warning of what you'll be up against. You'll find a lot of bargaining becomes necessary. Evidently, once you turn four, there's a whole new set of rules."

She gave Connor a stern look. "Just behave. This is all I ask."

He scrunched up his face, his look thoughtful. "I can only try. Isn't this what you always tell me to do?"

Trying to hide his smile, Chris watched as Emily gave Connor a big hug before she ran down the steps to where John was waiting.

As John navigated the car through the early morning traffic, Emily turned to him. "Something is going on with Chris. I feel like he's hiding something. He was guarding the doorway like there was something he didn't want me to see."

When John didn't answer, his look skeptical, she sighed. Then her eyes going wide, she looked over at him. "Do you think he has a woman friend staying with him?"

He glanced over at her, his grin turning into a laugh. "A woman-friend? And what exactly do you mean by this? Is there such a thing? I'm trying to think … do I have any woman friends that I know of?"

She gave him a sharp glance. "You better not. And you know exactly what I mean. I was trying to phrase it in a nice way. How else should I say it… his lover? After all, the sun hasn't even come up yet, so, whoever it is, they must have spent the night." She smiled. "Oh, I do hope it's Lauren."

Merging onto the busy road, it was a while before John was able to respond to this. He shook his head. "And I hope it's not."

Emily was puzzled. "Why not? She's beautiful, she comes from a well-established and extremely wealthy family and she'd be perfect for him. It's also a bonus her father is a big deal in real estate. He would be a great help to Chris's career."

He shook his head again. "Chris doesn't need any help with his career. He's doing just fine by himself. And Lauren? I don't trust her. I don't think she's as sweet and nice as she comes across. When she and Chris came to our Christmas party, I still remember her remark about how she always gets what she wants. Granted, she said this with a laugh, but I'm sure she meant it."

Emily gave an exasperated sigh. "Oh, you're just imagining things. I think you can't let go of the fact she didn't laugh at any of your jokes." She glanced over at him, shaking her head. "Not everyone appreciates your sense of humor, you know."

He gave a short laugh. "That's because Lauren doesn't have one. A sense of humor, that is. If you recall, she also said she wasn't a fan of kids."

For a while she remained silent. Then she looked over at him. "I think I might give her a call this week to see if she wants to meet for lunch, like we have in the past. Maybe I'll be able to get the scoop on why she and Chris aren't together anymore."

"No." At his abrupt and almost commanding response, Emily stared at him, her mouth open. "No?"

Again, he shook his head. "Yes. What I mean … no, I don't want you to go to lunch with her. Leave it alone. Since your mother died, I know you feel like you have to take her place when it comes to Chris, but he's old enough to know what he wants. And I assure you, he doesn't want Lauren. Like I said before, he can do better."

Emily had nothing to say to this. It was a rare day when John challenged her on something. So, when he did, she usually listened to him.

After a short silence, he reached over to take her hand.

When she looked over at him, he smiled at her. "One of the things I love most about you is how you always want to fix things. And you always have the best of intentions. But this time, I think you need to leave it alone. If Chris and Lauren are meant to be together, it will happen."

He brought her hand to his mouth for a kiss. "Just like it did with us. I knew from day one, you were the one for me. And we can only hope the same will happen to Chris."

He laughed. "Who knows? Maybe you're right, he did have someone staying with him. If so, I'm sure having Connor as a room-mate will put a damper on his plans."

Emily glanced over at him, a big grin coming over her face. "Oh my gosh, I didn't even think about that. Which means we have no reason to worry because Connor doesn't miss a thing."

He nodded. "Yep. If there's anything we need to know, Connor is our little Mr. Detective." He squeezed her hand. "Now, since it's only about an hour before we get to my parent's house, how about we stop at that little diner in town and get some breakfast? It may be the only time we'll have to ourselves over the next couple of days."

He grinned over at her. "Maybe once you've your morning coffee, you'll stop thinking about Chris and … what was it you called her? His woman friend?"

He shook his head as he started to laugh again. "Yeah, maybe they were having a pajama party, but minus…"

She swatted his arm. "Stop it. Again, you know what I meant." She rested her head against the back of the seat and closed her eyes. She was trying not to smile.

After all, she certainly didn't want to encourage him.

Someone was breathing directly into Carrie's face, the sound magnified in the silence.

She slowly opened one eye to look right into a pair of big blue eyes.

The eyes went wide, accompanied by an exaggerated intake of breath. This was followed by a very loud whisper. "Uncle Chris? Come here. I think she's waking up. She just opened one eye."

At this revelation, Carrie opened her other eye. This was rewarded with a big smile.

She blinked. Was she dreaming? The answer to this was another loud whisper. This time it was directed right into her ear.

"Are you awake? Are you Uncle Chris's new girlfriend? Are you going to live here now? Why are you sleeping here, instead of in the bedroom? Won't Uncle Chris let you sleep in his bed?"

This volley of questions was followed by silence. A very, very short silence. A loss of words didn't seem to be an issue with this small child who was now only inches away, his eyes wide and staring right at her. "You have really long hair. But Mommy said Uncle Chris's girlfriend has blonde hair like…"

This volley of questions was abruptly interrupted as the child was whisked out of her sight with Chris's voice taking over. "Connor, I think you've said enough for now. Let Carrie wake up a little bit more. Then maybe she can answer your questions."

Carrie slowly sat up, trying to shake the sleep from her mind. After she put her hands over her head in a long stretch, she glanced over to see Chris standing by the fireplace. He was holding a little boy in his arms, talking softly to him as he pointed to the fire.

When Chris turned to see Carrie was awake, he smiled at her before he looked at the child in his arms. "Connor, look … Carrie is awake. I bet she's probably wondering why you're here, don't you think?"

He lowered Connor to the floor. "So why don't you tell her."

A sudden shyness coming over him, Connor leaned into Chris's leg, shaking his head.

Carrie tilted her head, giving him a smile. "Did you come for a visit?"

When he nodded, darn if he didn't also give her a smile almost an exact replica of Chris's.

She glanced over at Chris. "Oh my gosh, he has your smile."

Chris nodded, flashing the same smile. "I guess. This is what I've been told."

Connor had cautiously moved closer. Leaning against the sofa, he slowly eased his way over to her. He gave her a shy smile, holding out one of the two small toy trucks he had in his hand. "Will you play with me?"

Before she could take the truck from him, Chris came over to them. "Connor, I'll tell you what, let's give Carrie a few minutes to get changed before she two of you start to play."

At Carrie's look of surprise, he reached for her hand to pull her up off the sofa. "I know you can't be all that comfortable, so I found something for you to change into. And to be honest, your dress is driving me crazy."

The look he gave her told her exactly what he meant as his gaze traveled down to the now tantalizing stretch of legs revealed below the scrunched-up skirt of her dress.

Blushing, she quickly tugged the dress back in place.

He sighed before handing her the pajama pants and tee shirt he'd picked out for her. "I know these may be a little big, but if you're going to be hanging out with a four-year-old, you need to be able to move."

He pointed to the stairs. "My bedroom is the first door on the right. Now go … I'll explain what's going on when you get back."

As she went running down the stairs, leaving him to gaze longingly after he and wishing he could go with her, there was a tug on his pant leg. He looked down to see Connor grinning up at him.

"I like her. She's pretty."

Chris grinned back at him.

No argument there.

He held up his hand, palm out.

"I agree with you, a hundred-and-fifty percent. Gimme five!"

Carrie fell back onto the sofa with a huge sigh of relief. When Chris plopped down next to her, she looked over at him, shaking her head.

He grinned as he put his arm around her. "So, what do you think? Any interest in having kids? What, maybe two, three, four? Or even maybe a half dozen or so?"

She laughed. "I didn't think we were ever going to get him to take a nap. My gosh, where does he get all his energy from? These past five hours felt like five days." She gazed curiously at him. "You'd really want to have that many kids?"

"With you, I'd have a dozen." As soon as he said this, he wanted to kick himself.

What the hell are you doing?

He cleared his throat. "What I meant is, you're very good with kids. I think you'd make a great mom."

This wasn't at all what he meant. He knew this and he was pretty sure she knew this, too.

After a short silence, she gazed up at him again. "I like children. And after watching you with Connor, I'd have to say you'd make a great dad, too. Even though I think I did a better job at pitching when we played baseball." She began to laugh. "Just tell me ... where were you throwing that ball?"

He shrugged. "Honestly? I have no idea. And give me a break... you had an advantage, growing up with a brother who's a professional baseball player. With all of these awards, no less."

He chuckled. "Now granted, I did play baseball with Kevin during high school, but I hugged the bench the majority of the time. I'll be the first to acknowledge, I was only there in case of an emergency. A very dire emergency, as you can imagine."

He suddenly reached over to cup her chin in his hand, his face coming dangerously close to hers. "And maybe I might've been trying to impress you? With my powerful throws? And show of agility?"

"*Hmm* ... it did enter my mind. But I thought it was Connor you were trying to impress, not me." She softened this comment with a smile, while at the same time, her gaze dropped to his mouth. With his face so close, the only thing she could think about was whether or not he was finally going to kiss her.

He knew exactly what she was thinking. Her eyes gave her away. This is why he moved even closer, his lips brushing over hers, his voice so deep and sexy. "So, do I at least deserve a kiss for trying?"

"Yes ... yes ... you do." She eagerly tilted her face towards his, her whisper caught up in his mouth in what he intended to be a sweet, lingering kiss. It was when she sighed in his mouth, he pulled her even closer to deepen the kiss.

"I can't sleep."

Startled, Carrie shoved Chris away from her to go diving off the sofa with him following right behind. They both gazed wildly around the room to finally locate the source of this announcement.

A big grin on his face, Connor was at the top of the stairs. His blanket in his hand, he was peering at them through the railing.

Carrie sank back down onto the sofa while Chris went striding over to Connor and picked him up. He held him in his arms, the tone of his voice quite stern.

At least this was his intention.

"Connor, what did we tell you? Don't you remember? Only if you take a nap, will we go out for dinner and ice cream. And if you're good, maybe we'll stop at the bookstore and pick out a new book. You've been down for, at the most, ten minutes? I don't think this constitutes a nap."

At Connor's puzzled look, Chris shook his head. "What I mean is, you haven't been in bed long enough. Come on, you must be tired. I know both Carrie and I certainly are."

Connor glanced over at Carrie. She nodded, keeping her expression as serious as she could.

Connor put his blanket up to his face and burrowed his head into Chris's shoulder.

His words were muffled. "I don't like being down there all by myself. It's too dark and I'm scared."

Even though Emily had forewarned him about this, Chris was finding it hard to believe they were about to bargain with a four-year-old. He and Carrie were the adults here? Shouldn't they be calling the shots?

He glanced over at Carrie, rolling his eyes. He mouthed the words, now what do we do?

Carrie smiled, patting the place next to her on the sofa. "Connor, come over here and I'll read you one more story. But this time, you have to keep your promise to take a nap. And you can't go back on this, either."

Connor studied her for a few moments. Then he smiled and nodded his head.

Chris swung him down to the floor, where he took off in a run to dive onto the sofa next to Carrie. He gazed up at her with a big grin on his face.

She laughed and gave him a hug. "Oh my, you're playing us, aren't you? You're a charmer just like your uncle."

She opened the book and began to read.

While Carrie was reading to Connor, Chris went to work cleaning up the mess they'd made in the kitchen with their lunch preparations.

When he was finished and not wanting to intrude, he leaned against the counter. Arms crossed, he watched as they both stopped to giggle over something Carrie was reading.

By the time Carrie finally closed the book, Connor's head had begun to droop, his eyes fighting a losing battle to stay open. She whispered something to him and with a small smile, he finally gave in and closed his eyes. She placed a kiss to the top of his head before she smiled over at Chris.

Chris was daydreaming, his imagination working overtime. He couldn't believe how much he'd like to change places with a four year-old right now.

He allowed himself a wry smile.

Who would've ever thought ...

CHAPTER 15

One day someone will walk into your life
and you'll understand why
it never worked out with anyone else.
~ Anonymous

After Chris carried a sleeping Connor downstairs to put him in bed, he came upstairs to find Carrie perched on the edge of the sofa waiting for him.

He sat next to her, smiling as he reached over to tuck her hair behind her ear. "What's up? You look like you have something on your mind."

She gestured to the pajama pants and tee shirt she was wearing. "Well, first of all, I need go back to my hotel and change into my own clothes. I can't wear these when we go out later. And with Connor asleep, this would be as good a time as any to do this."

He settled back on the sofa, pulling her next to him. "I have an idea. Why don't you bring your things back here? This way you can stay with me until you have to leave on Tuesday. I have to go into the office tomorrow morning, because there's a few things I need to do that can't be put off. But we can meet for lunch and I'll plan on taking the rest of the day off. This way we can spend some time together before you have to leave for your dinner."

He smiled. "This, of course, is all up for your approval."

Her smile, and the fact she didn't even hesitate before she nodded, was such a relief to him. He wanted to spend as much time as possible with her. He was trying not to think too much about how she would be out of his life again when Tuesday rolled around.

She spoke hesitantly. "There's something else I want to ask you, too. About the awards dinner. Will you go with me? I was given an extra dinner ticket and I'd planned to ask Livy, but never got a chance." She smiled "And now I'm glad I didn't ask her. Because I would rather go with you." She was quick to add. "If you want to, that is."

Now it was his turn to smile. "There is nothing I'd like more."

After she called for a taxi, she changed back into her dress, borrowing one of his jackets as a replacement for the coat she left at the gallery.

Chris watched as she ran out to the waiting taxi. Then he watched as it disappeared from view.

He tried to tell himself he had no reason to worry. She'd be back in no time. He could certainly find something to do while she was gone. He had emails to catch up on, a few calls he could make.

Yep, he had this.

Carrie hurried through the hotel lobby trying to act as inconspicuous as possible. As though it wasn't a big deal she was still wearing the same dress as when she passed through this lobby last night on her way to the gallery show.

I mean, come on ... this is New York. No one really cares what you're wearing. Or where you've been. And who could you possibly run into?

Well, there was Sam. She could very easily bump into Sam. Even thought she'd sent a text to both him and Livy she was okay, she was feeling a little guilty about running off and leaving them last night.

This was a reminder she also needed to call Livy.

"Ms. Mazzori?"

She closed her eyes

You've got to be kidding me ...

She turned to see the hotel associate manning the reservation desk was waving at her, with what looked like an envelope in his hand.

When she walked over to the desk, he handed it to her. "One of our guests, Mr. Bridges, asked we give this to you. I also believe he left one more thing for you. Let me go get it from our office." He returned with her coat. "Mr. Bridges also asked we give you this."

Clutching both the note and her coat against her, Carrie thanked him as she began backing away, to then turn and practically sprint over to the elevator. It was only her imagination he'd given her that look. You know, the look he was on to her and had a pretty good idea of what she'd been up to all night.

She leaned against the elevator wall, watching the numbers for the floors flash by.

She shook her head. If he only knew.

In the privacy of her room, she kicked off her shoes and sank down on the bed to open the envelope from Sam.

The note was handwritten. No texting or emailing for Sam. How many times had he told her how important it was to add a personal touch, especially when dealing with clients. He claimed this was something missing in today's business world.

She was smiling as she began to read.

> *Carrie, I've decided to return home*
> *earlier than planned. I was able to*
> *meet up with my cousin and his girl-*
> *friend this morning for brunch. And*
> *the client I was scheduled to meet*
> *tomorrow had to cancel.*
> *My fingers are crossed, the next time I*
> *see you, I'll be able to congratulate*
> *you on your new award. And even if*
> *this doesn't happen, you'll always be a*

> *winner in my eyes.*
> *I know, sounds corny, but at the same*
> *time, it's so true.*
> *You'll also be happy to know your*
> *sister and I managed to get through*
> *the evening without killing each other.*
> *Hopefully, we can catch up in a few*
> *days. Your friend, Sam*

Without killing each other? She was puzzled. What did he mean by this?

The fact he'd referred to Livy only as her sister and not even by her name, made it sound as though the evening hadn't gone well. But from what she'd witnessed, she'd swear there'd definitely been a whole lot of chemistry going on between them.

So, what could have happened?

She dug her phone out of her purse and hit Livy's number. As though she had been waiting for Carrie to call, Livy answered even before the second ring.

"Carrie, hi … it's nice to finally hear from you. If only to know you're still alive."

Her greeting was accusing, something Carrie knew she more than deserved. She dove right in. "I know. I'm sorry. I'll be happy to explain. But first, I don't understand. What happened with you and Sam?"

There was a long silence before Livy answered. "Carrie, hold on a minute."

After what seemed like much longer than a minute, Livy came back on the phone. "Sorry, I had to go in a different room. I'm in the bathroom right now. I … uh … well, Zack is here."

Carrie remained silent. Only because she didn't know how to respond. She also knew Livy probably wouldn't want to hear what she had to say.

Zack? Why was he there? Hadn't Livy vowed he was out of her life for good?

Livy's long sigh came all the way through the phone. As though she knew what Carrie was thinking. "He showed up right after Sam brought me home."

Her voice became agitated. "Which, by the way, I tried to tell Sam it wasn't necessary for him to see me not only to my apartment building, but all the way to my door." She gave a huffy sigh. "Is he always like this? Taking charge? *My god*, I'm not a child. I'm thirty years old and quite capable of ..."

Carrie put a stop to her rant. "I know how you feel about Sam and his terrible tendency to want to take care of people. But again, I know Sam and I'm sure he was only trying to be nice. It's the way he is and I hope he never changes. We need more men like Sam."

"Well, I think he should stop. It isn't a nice thing to do to a woman. It makes my ... I mean, a person's expectations too high."

This came out more passionately than she intended.

She groaned, closing her eyes.

My god, why does even just the mention of his name get you so riled up? So frustrated?

At the unhappiness in Livy's voice and no idea of how to help her, once again Carrie remained silent.

"Carrie?"

Carrie rubbed her forehead. Her head was starting to ache with all of this. Whatever was going on between Livy and Sam was too confusing. She wished she could give them both a good shake. If only to knock some sense into them.

She sighed. "Let's forget about Sam for now. I'm more concerned about what you said about Zack. Why did he come back? Why did you let him? And what's going to happen now?"

Once again there was a long silence before Livy gave another long sigh. "He ... Zack told me he realized he'd made a mistake. He wants to give it another try. So, I agreed."

She didn't tell Carrie she'd almost been relieved when Zack showed up at her door.

She knew him.

He was familiar.

After all, they'd been together for a long time. With him, she was comfortable.

Exactly. With Zack, you know where you stand. And this is a good thing, right?

But with Sam?

Though he'd made her feel so alive, he scared her. He brought out all of these new and crazy feelings she had no idea of how to deal with. She'd swear he knew exactly what she was going to say, or what she was thinking, before she even opened her mouth.

Carrie worried voice cut into her thoughts. "Oh Livy, I hope you're sure about this. I don't want to see you get hurt again. I was actually getting excited, thinking about you and Sam. I really think you would bring out the best in each other. You ..."

Livy cut her off, her anger obvious. "Well, you thought wrong. Because as we both know, I certainly wasn't Sam's choice of company for the evening."

She gave a sharp laugh. "And let's face it, there's no way he would ever want to be with someone like me. Which is fine with me. Since I'm not the least bit interested in him."

Here she grew quiet as she tried to convince herself what she just told Carrie was the truth.

But it isn't. And you know this. But hopefully with Zack coming back into your life, you'll eventually forget about him.

When Carrie had nothing to say to this, Livy spoke. "After all, you didn't give us much of a choice, did you? Running off with some man chasing after you. I was so worried."

Carrie sighed. "I know. And I'm sorry. But remember when I told you I believed in love in first sight? Well, this man you say was after me? He's the one I was talking about. It turned out to be a big misunderstanding. He was never engaged."

After she told Livy everything, starting from when she and Chris first met, she took a deep breath. "Livy, I love him. God help me, no matter what comes of this, he's the one I want to share the rest of my life with."

Livy sighed. "Oh Carrie, I can't even imagine."

Carrie opened her mouth to respond to this, but then changed her mind. Shouldn't Livy be feeling the same about Zack? Instead, she sounded resigned, as if she had already decided to settle.

Where, if she were to take a chance with Sam, Carrie had a feeling Livy would become the person she was meant to be.

For several seconds, neither of them had anything to say.

Livy spoke first. "Sam got your coat when we left the gallery. He told me he would make sure to get it to you".

Carrie closed her eyes.

Oh, Sam …

She swallowed. "I know. He left the coat and a note to let me know he was leaving today. He's probably already back in Cleveland as we speak."

Livy was sitting on the rim of the bathtub. She closed her eyes and bowing her head, she was filled with an overwhelming sadness.

So, he's gone. He came into your life, stirring up every possible feeling inside of you. And now, just as quickly, he's left.

She opened her eyes and looking in the mirror, she watched as a tear began to slide down her cheek, followed by another.

And suddenly she wanted nothing more than to throw a few things into a suitcase and leave. She would take only what she needed, leaving everything else behind.

Maybe even go home.

Then she'd take some time off to figure out what she really wanted in life. She'd make that fresh start she told Sam she was looking for.

But you can't. There's your job. You just renewed the lease on your apartment. And what about Zack? If you leave, you'll lose all of these.

She squeezed her eyes shut to avoid looking into the mirror before she took a deep, shaky breath. "I guess I should go. Zack is probably wondering where I am."

She doubted this was true, since when she left the room to talk to Carrie, he had been sound asleep on the sofa. "Since I won't be seeing you before you leave, I guess this is sort of a good bye. Maybe I'll plan a short trip home after Sophie has the baby."

Carrie could hear the sadness in Livy's voice, but knew there was nothing she could say to make things better. "Oh Livy, I wish you would. And I'm planning to come back here the last weekend of the month to celebrate my birthday with Chris. Then you can meet him, And I can meet Zack."

Even though Livy was shaking her head at this, she tried to sound as agreeable as she could.

Because, who knew? Maybe by that time, her life would be back to normal. With Sam only a hazy memory, pushed way into the back of her mind and out of her life.

She stood and gazing at her reflection in the mirror, she forced a smile on her face as she spoke. "Sure, that would be great. And thank you again for yesterday, the shopping, lunch, the spa and everything. And what turned out to be an interesting evening, Sam and all."

Carrie smiled. "Yeah, it was fun, wasn't it? And call me, okay?"

After she ended the call with Livy, Carrie sighed, running her hands through her hair. She didn't understand. This thing between Livy and Zack was so wrong.

But it wasn't her place to tell Livy what to do. She was the only one who could control what happened next.

She sighed again before she gazed around the room. She needed to pack everything up so she could get back to Chris and Connor.

After she changed into a pair of jeans and a sweater, and zipped up her suitcase, she headed back down to the lobby. As she was checking out, she was relieved to see a queue of taxis outside waiting for customers.

She was anxious to get back. She had a date with two special guys tonight for dinner, ice cream and a trip to the book store.

She couldn't wait.

For the longest time, Livy stayed where she was.

Then, slowly coming to life, she gazed around the bathroom. The case for her contacts was still on the vanity. After she woke up this morning, she had put on her glasses. Wearing her contacts didn't seem all that important. And Zack hadn't seemed to care one way or the other

She splashed her face with cold water and stared at herself in the mirror for a few moments. Why was it nothing felt right?

You should be happy.

From what Zack had told her, he was a changed man. When he saw her last night at the restaurant, he'd realized what a fool he had been to get involved with another woman.

He vowed he had never been more serious. He had learned his lesson and had no plans to leave ever again.

He had then gone on to suggest it was time for them to start thinking more seriously about the future. Possibly looking into buying a house together, somewhere outside the city. It only made sense they needed to find a more family friendly place id they intended to have kids.

You should be thrilled he even brought this up, since he's always skirted around these kind of issues in the past.

But when she opened her eyes this morning to find Zack next to her, sound asleep and his arm wrapped around her, why had it felt so wrong?

And when he made love to her last night, his whispered promises meant to reassure her, why hadn't she been able to clear her mind of the one thing she knew she shouldn't be thinking about?

Sam. Yes, it appeared Sam was still with her.

If only in your mind.

CHAPTER 16

The apartment felt empty without Carrie. So, Chris tried to keep busy.

He took a shower, did a quick scan of the Sunday newspaper and briefly considered checking his emails. He even hauled out the sweeper, to then just as quickly return it back to its place in the closet.

Not a good move, since Connor was still napping.

He finally decided to open a bottle of wine, the one thing that made sense to him. After he poured out a glass, he sank down onto the sofa and turned on the TV.

He stared at the screen for a few minutes before he began to smile. Reaching for his phone, he had an important call to make.

Ten minutes later, he was feeling very proud of himself. This is where he stayed, staring at the screen with no clue of what he was watching until he heard the front door open.

He met Carrie at the door, the kiss he gave her almost sending them soaring right into the next level of their relationship.

She stepped back, her hands gripping his arms and a dazed look on her face. "Oh my, your kisses just keep getting better and better."

He chuckled as he gazed down at her. "That's my plan. I want to make sure you keep coming back for more."

He dropped her suitcase at the bottom of the steps. "Connor is still asleep, so I'll put this right here. Come on, I've opened a bottle of wine. I want to enjoy your company, in the short time we have, until Connor wakes up."

An hour later they all set out for a small restaurant known for their hamburgers, following with a trip to Chris and Connor's favorite place for ice cream.

This turned out to be a very long and serious decision-making process on Connor's part. But, from what Chris told Carrie, this was pretty much the norm.

Then it was off to the bookstore to find the perfect book.

"Again! Do it again! Please, Uncle Chris?"

Chris half groaned, half laughed. Then he looked down at Connor's expectant face and gave a resigned sigh, "Okay, one more time. And I mean it this time. This is the last one. Got it? After this, we're done."

After Connor nodded, Chris grinned.

"Okay, at the count of three, One ...Two ... Three ..."

Holding Connor's hands, Carrie and Chris swung him high through the air between them.

Before he could ask again, Chris picked him up. "Your swinging time is over, buddy. Because, look where we are. Back at my place. Which means its time to go inside. A bath, a story from your new book, and then it's bedtime. Remember what your mom said, no late night for you."

He smiled over at Carrie. "It's bedtime for all of us, I think."

From his office, Chris could hear the soft murmur of Carrie's voice as she read to Connor.

He shook his head. Connor should've been in bed and asleep a long time ago. He had to be exhausted. He and Carrie had kept him busy from the moment he got up from his nap, through dinner and what turned out to be a very long stay in the bookstore, searching for that perfect book. He'd had his bath. His teeth had been brushed, and his Superman pajamas were on.

And now, Carrie was in charge.

She'd volunteered to read Connor his new book, giving Chris another chance to check his emails and make a few calls.

But, sitting here at his desk, his computer on and ready to go, once again, he wasn't accomplishing anything. He leaned back in his chair and closed his eyes

He smiled, thinking of the elderly couple they had met in the bookstore. The man had a walker, his wife hovering protectively beside him. After a short bout of coughing and throat clearing, the man had addressed Connor. "Young man, do you know how lucky you are to have a mom and dad who bring you to a book store and let you pick out a book? Why, they must love you very much."

His face scrunched up in confusion, Connor took time to think about this before he'd smiled up at the man. "She isn't my mom. And he isn't my dad. They're only keeping me for a little while. Then I have to go back." His mouth had then dipped into a very sad frown.

At the immediate look of concern the couple shared, Chris had jumped in to explain. "I'm afraid he's being a little dramatic. I'm his uncle. He's staying with me for a few days while his parents are out of town."

Seated on the floor with a pile of books in front of him, Connor had pointed at Carrie. "She stays with him, too. He used to have a girl-friend with blonde hair like mine, but now he has Carrie." A big grin lit up his face. "But I like her. She's nice."

Chris shook his head over at the elderly couple. "Like they say, out of the mouths of babes."

After giving Carrie and Chris a long, searching look, the man had smiled. "*Hmm ...* We had assumed you were a family, remarking earlier how much in love you seem to be."

His wife had agreed, nodding. "Make sure you enjoy every

moment. And with those words of wisdom, we'll leave you to your book search."

Connor had watched them leave before he gazed up at Carrie and Chris. "Are you in love? Does this mean you're going to get married? And have a baby?"

Chris checked his smile. "Well, I guess we'll just have to wait and see about that, won't we? But for now, let's find you a book. The store may be closing soon."

But Connor had more to say. "Mommy will be happy. She said you need to get married. And you need to do it soon. Or all the good ones will be taken." He had followed this with a huge grin.

And this time, Chris couldn't help it. He'd burst out laughing before he ruffled Connor's hair with his hand. "Connor, you're something else." Then he leaned down to whisper in his ear. "Not to worry. Because I'm pretty sure I got a good one."

He'd glanced over at Carrie, sending her one of those crooked smiles of his. "In fact, I believe I got the best there is."

With the sound of his neighbor's door slamming, Chris came to with a start. He glanced at his watch and surprised to see it was already past ten, he signed out of his computer. Surely, Connor was asleep by now. He turned out the light and headed for the bedroom.

He was greeted with silence. Curled up next to each other on the bed, both Carrie and Connor were sound asleep.

He eased onto the bed next to Carrie and wrapping his arms around her, he pulled her back against him. His lips moved in a whisper in her hair. "Hey, princess, have you decided to go to sleep on me?"

Slowly opening her eyes, she turned to give him a sleepy smile. "I'm sorry. I was waiting for Connor to fall asleep and I guess I did, too." She studied him in the darkness. "Did you get anything done?"

He shook his head. "No, not really. I spent almost the entire time thinking about you. But it's okay, nothing is so urgent it can't wait."

Carrie closed her eyes, caught up in the kisses he was slowly pressing along her jaw and down her neck, sending a riot of delicious sensations through her. So much so, she forgot all about Connor next to them on the bed.

She turned to face Chris and running her hands through his hair, her mouth searched for his.

He groaned, burying his face in her shoulder, his voice muffled. "I want this so badly with you. But I can't … we can't."

He brushed the hair back from her face, exhaling a long sigh. "You have to agree. This isn't going to work. Not with a four-year old in bed with us. Or not even on the sofa. This is the one time I'm wondering what the hell I was thinking when I converted the other bedroom into an office."

As if they needed proof of what Chris said, Connor suddenly let out a cry as he struggled to sit up. "Mommy?"

Carrie turned to him. "It's okay sweetie, go back to sleep. You'll see mommy soon." She waited until he pulled his blanket to his face and closed his eyes before she tucked the comforter more securely around him.

She gazed over at Chris, her expression serious. "I don't care where we spend the night. On the sofa or wherever. As long as I'm with you." She hesitated. And we have tomorrow night. We don't have to stay long, only until the awards presentations are over. I'd rather spend the time we have left with you."

His eyes caressing her face, he tucked her hair behind her ears. Then he gave her one last kiss. "I'm going to hold you to that promise."

Slowly and *very* reluctantly, he slid off the bed and held out his hand. "Come, let's go upstairs where we can talk louder than a whisper. We can set up our plans for tomorrow."

CHAPTER 17

Curled up under a blanket on Chris's sofa, Carrie opened her eyes to see the mid-morning sun was shining in through the windows.

The silence surrounding her told her she was alone.

She vaguely remembered a showered, shaved and immaculately dressed Chris dropping a kiss to her cheek before telling her he was leaving. This was shortly after she'd received a sleepy kiss and a hug from Connor before he went off with his nanny.

Again, she and Chris had almost talked the night away. How he'd been able to go to work was beyond her.

After a few stretches and just as many yawns, she pushed the blanket aside.

There was a note on the coffee table.

Hey, princess,
I don't think you have any idea

how hard it was for me to leave
you this morning. A taxi will pick
you up at noon.
If there's something you have
planned and want to change the
time, their number is at the bottom
of this note.
I remember you told me you like
blueberry scones so I got you one
from the bakery down the street.
Miss you already,
Chris

She smiled, and pressing the note to her lips, she wandered over to the kitchen.

After she was seated at the counter, her coffee and scone in front of her, she picked up her phone. She needed to call the taxi service to change the arrival time.

She had someplace she wanted to go before she met Chris for lunch.

Two hours later, Carrie's taxi pulled up in front of the Gallery East. She ran up the steps and inside.

A woman sorting through a stack of paintings looked up and smiled. "Good morning. I'm Sandy, one of the owners of the gallery. Is there something I can do for you?"

Carrie smiled. "Good morning. I hope you'll be able to help me. I was here Saturday night for the artist preview show and I'm interested in purchasing one of the paintings. I believe the name is Early Evening in Spring."

Carrie's heart sank when Sandy's smile disappeared, the look on her face certainly not what Carrie would consider a good sign. Sure enough, her next words confirmed this. "Oh no, I'm so sorry. That painting was sold yesterday."

She shot a quick look towards the back of the store. "But Julian, the artist, is here. Would you like to talk to him? Maybe he has a similar painting you'll find you like just as much."

Before Carrie could answer, Sandy hurried over to where a man was standing in front of one of the paintings, writing in the notebook he was holding. After she said a few words, he turned, a slow smile coming over his face when he saw Carrie.

And Carrie understood why Sophie had been attracted to him. Any woman would be. Julian Labarr looked like he had just stepped out of the pages of GQ. He had that mussed up, but at the same time, so put together look.

And for him it worked so well. So amazingly well.

He immediately came over to take her hand, his eyes roaming over her in a long. appraising look. After a dramatic sigh, he raised her hand to his mouth and brushed his lips lightly over her fingers. "*Ah... hello. So, so* beautiful. You are a welcome treat on this cold morning. A ray of sunshine to brighten our day."

He slowly let go of her hand, the expression on his face falling into one of despair. "But what is this I hear? You have come to buy one of my paintings, but it has already been sold?"

She nodded, thinking he was so dramatic, but so sweet. "Yes, Early Evening in Spring. I'd hoped to buy it for a friend. But this is okay. I'm certainly not going to begrudge you a sale."

She smiled. "I believe we have a mutual friend in common. I'm Carrie Mazzori. My brother Chester is married to Sophie. Or, as you knew her, Sophie Michaels. I, along with my sister and a friend, used the passes you gave her for your preview on Saturday night. I want to thank you for that."

He slowly nodded before he gave her a wry smile. "*Ah, yes* ... the infamous Chester. Once I saw the look on my *SO-pheee's* face when she began to talk about him, I knew she was lost to me forever. But this is okay. I only want her to be happy." A concerned look came over his face. "And she is happy, is she not? I believe she is almost ready to give birth? How wonderful for both her and Chester."

"Yes, they are both very excited." Carrie gave him an apologetic smile. "And very much in love. But you should know Sophie always talks highly of you. "

There was a moment of silence before he suddenly turned to her, his whole demeanor becoming very business-like "But, now I feel I've let you down, as the painting you wished to buy for your friend is no longer available. Unfortunately, it is my policy to never duplicate any of my paintings. This is because I know a lot of people prize the fact they own a one of a kind and original work of art. So, I will not be able to do another Early Evening in Spring for you."

He shook his head. "Not that I think of myself as famous. No, I would never consider putting myself in that category. But who knows? Maybe someday?"

Carrie was shaking her head. "Oh, Julian … I have a feeling you'll be quite famous. And I understand. As an interior designer, I know how people crave originality when it comes to design."

She shook her head. "No cookie cutter designs for me."

"Yes, yes! Exactly! No cookie cutters!" This brought a deep laugh from him before he peered more closely at her. "And this friend of yours? The one you wish to buy the painting for. Is he the someone special in your life?"

She nodded, a blush rising in her cheeks. "Yes, very special."

His disappointment was obvious. "I can't say I'm surprised. You are too beautiful to not be a special somebody in someone's life."

He suddenly laughed. "And this would be insane, no? If you and I were to, as you Americans say, hook up? I'm sure Chester wouldn't appreciate me coming into the mix." He shook his head. "*Ah, no, no, no. This wouldn't do. I will have to hope someday love will finally find me.*"

Carrie smiled. "Oh, I'm sure it will. You just have to be patient."

Again, you can see what Sophie saw in this man. Charming is definitely at the top of the list when it comes to describing him.

He shrugged. "*Ah* … I hope you are right about that. But for now, keep checking my work. Maybe another painting will catch your eye. Who knows? You may have inspired me to paint more of the same. Early Evening in Spring, that is."

He gave her a genuine smile. "And give *SO-pheee* my best. Make sure you tell her I wish both her and Chester a healthy and beautiful baby."

He glanced over at Sandy, who was patiently waiting to ask him a question. He took Carrie's hand, once again raising it to his lips. "I'm afraid I must go, as work is calling me. Thank you for all of your kind words and have a wonderful day"

With a wink, he turned to Sandy.

Even though she hadn't been able to get what she came for, Carrie was smiling as she ran back to her waiting taxi.

She couldn't even imagine what Chester would have to say if he met Julian.

She laughed.

Whatever it was, she was sure it would be a mouthful.

The taxi dropped Carrie off at the building were Chris's offices were located. After she sent him a text to let him know she had arrived, she wandered over to look at the huge waterfall taking up one corner of the lobby, water falling over the marbled glass stones and splashing into the lighted pool below.

She was engulfed from behind in a big hug, the familiar scent of Chris's cologne surrounding her. His breath tickling her neck, his voice was a deep rumble in her ear. "Hey there, gorgeous. Are you here to meet someone? How about you ditch him and spend the day with me instead? I'll be sure to show you a good time."

She'd been half asleep when he left earlier, so she hadn't been able to fully appreciate how amazing he looked.

But now? She wanted to take the time to slowly let it all sink in.

Between the perfect cut of his light grey suit, the warm look in his eyes and his killer smile, he was as close to perfection as you could get.

She gazed up at him. *"Hmm ...* I don't know. Can you be trusted? You look almost too perfect to be real."

His answer was to lean in, his lips just barely brushing over hers.

"*Ah, princess* … when I'm around you, I'm afraid I might not be accountable for my actions. And yes, what you see is all very real."

She didn't move, her eyes closed and her lips still parted.

"Carrie?"

She blinked, her lashes fluttering open.

With a smile, he reached for her hand. "Come on. Let's go up to my office. I still have a few things to wrap up. Once I finish with those, I'll be all yours."

All yours... she really liked the sound of this.

Once they were in the elevator, she watched as he hit the button for the thirty-sixth floor. When he glanced over to see her eyes were on him, he reached for her hand, bringing it up to his mouth for a kiss. She went weak at the knees, a deep shiver coursing through her.

And now, the only thing she could think about was how much she wanted him to kiss her.

Really kiss her …

Completely aware of this, he pulled her flush against him. "We have about twenty seconds before we reach my floor. And since we've been lucky enough to get this elevator to ourselves, we'd be foolish not to take advantage of the time."

His hand cupping the back of her head, his mouth claimed hers in a kiss that was definitely worth every single one of those twenty seconds. It was only when the bell rang to announce they had reached their floor, he slowly pulled away from her.

He cleared his throat. "To think, in the past, I've complained about this elevator being too slow. From now on, I'm sure I'll think differently." He then proceeded to press a quick kiss to her mouth right before the doors slid open. As he guided her out of the elevator ahead of him, he leaned in to whisper in her ear. "See? Perfect timing, perfect kiss."

From where she was seated at a desk facing the elevator, a woman looked up to nod at Chris before she gave Carrie a big smile.

Chris reached for Carrie's hand. "Iris, this is Carrie Mazzori." He turned to Carrie. "Without Iris, nothing would get done in this office. I'm afraid we all tend to take advantage of her more than we should."

Iris became almost completely undone, her cheeks turning a bright red as she stammered out a breathless thank you. "Oh, Mr. Gardner. You know that isn't true. You would never take advantage of any of us."

Chris shook his head. "I don't know if that's true, Iris. But for now, I want to let you know my plans for today. After I finish up a few things here, I'm going to take Carrie to lunch and I won't be back for the rest of the day. Carrie is from Cleveland and I promised to show her around the city."

Iris began to chat with Carrie about a trip she'd recently made to Cleveland. How much she enjoyed the play house district and the art museum. After patiently waiting until their conversation came to an end, Chris escorted Carrie to his office.

He spread out his arms, a wry smile on his face. "Well, here it is. My home away from home. A very dull and run-of -the-mill kind of space, I'm afraid."

Carrie gazed around the room, taking it all in before she looked at him. "It's not you."

He laughed, surprised by her seriousness. "No?"

She shook her head. "No, none of your personality is reflected in this room. You need color. More warmth. Excitement. Your apartment tells a much better story about you than this office does."

He leaned back against his desk, crossing his arms over his chest. He was trying not to smile. "And what story is that, may I ask?"

She peered more closely at him. Even though his expression was serious, at the same time he seemed amused.

Well, she could only blame herself. She was the one who took off running with this. It was bad enough she was still having a hard time taking in how incredibly hot he looked.

And now … with this casual pose he'd adopted, lounging against his desk, he was looking every part of the young and successful entrepreneur he was. Certainly, more than any man should be allowed.

He was definitely every woman's dream.

She frowned at this disturbing thought. She didn't want him to be every woman's dream. She wanted him all to herself.

"Carrie?"

She gave him a blank stare.

Yes? *Exactly what life changing advice had you planned to share with him?*

She tucked her hair behind her ears. "*Ah* … well, I guess what I'm trying to say, and remember this is only my opinion, even though you may think you're grounded and comfortable with your life, there's still something missing."

He raised an eyebrow at this, making her even more determined to make her point. "I know you're going to think I'm crazy, but this explains the TV over the mantel in your apartment. A painting would be your way of announcing to the world you've arrived. You're where you want to be in your life and ready to embrace what comes next. Where the presence of a TV, well, there's no reason to commit." She shrugged. "You can just keep changing the channels."

When he didn't seem to have anything to say, only giving a slow nod, she walked over to gaze out the window. She scanned the surrounding buildings, spotting the hotel she'd stayed at. She turned to point this out to him, only to find he'd come to stand right behind her.

She began talking a mile a minute "You have an amazing view from here. I can even see the hotel I stayed in." She glanced up at him, a faint smile on her face. "When I checked into my room on Friday, the first thing I did was check out the view from my window."

She hesitated. "I know this sounds crazy, but I wondered if I could actually be looking at one of the buildings your office was in. Or where you lived." She gave him an embarrassed smile. "I even waved."

Suddenly wondering why she'd chosen to share this with him, she gave a nonchalant shrug. "Of course, at the time I had no idea where your office was, or that it was so close. I think, well, I guess I was hoping for a miracle."

She gazed up at him, her words barely a whisper. "I know it

sounds silly, but I didn't want to let go of the belief we'd find each other again."

He wrapped his arms around her, resting his cheek against the top of her head. His voice was soft and reassuring. "I don't think it's silly at all, because I know I've been hanging on to the same belief."

She could hear the smile sneak into his voice.

"All eight months, three weeks and now, four days since you first came into my life."

CHAPTER 18

After a fun afternoon exploring the city, Chris and Carrie had returned to his apartment to get ready for the awards dinner.

Carrie was staring at her reflection in the bathroom mirror. She was becoming more frustrated by the minute.

For a good ten minutes or so, she'd been trying to arrange her hair into a presentable French twist. Or something that even slightly resembled one. But, as if it had a mind of its' own, one errant strand of hair kept springing out against the side of her face. This meant the sophisticated and sleek look she was going for probably wasn't going to happen.

She would give it one last try. If the same thing happened, she was going to call it quits.

And lo and behold, the same loose curl came bouncing out against her cheek.

Well, so be it then. Hopefully, her remaining efforts were enough. She wanted to look her best for this event.

Who are you trying to kid? This is all for Chris. You want to look perfect for him.

She put her brush on the counter and stepped back from the mirror for a better view. Errant curl aside, she was pretty happy with the final result. This was mostly because of the dress Sophie had chosen for her.

She loved, *loved* the dress. One, because it was red, her favorite color. Two, because it was so feminine with the layers of chiffon that flowed around her in an almost seductive swirl of fabric. It was the kind of dress that made you walk differently, giving a flirty sway of your hips, if only just to make it move.

She wondered if there would be dancing. She closed her eyes, her imagination taking her right on to the dance floor, slowly moving to the music. All while in Chris's arms.

She was suddenly both nervous and excited. It was almost too much, being nominated for the award and reconnecting with Chris.

It was almost all too perfect.

Striding purposefully into the bedroom, Chris was looking for Carrie. His attempt to tie his bow tie had fallen short and he needed help. When he saw Carrie was in the bathroom, he made his way over to check out his efforts in the mirror above the dresser.

He studied his reflection.

He sighed. Not good.

God, how he hated these damn things. He wanted to know, who was the person that looked at a man and decided a bow tie would be the perfect finishing touch to his formal attire?

It certainly wasn't another man. Of this, he was sure.

Nope, it had to have been a woman. A woman who had a grudge against a man for one reason or another. Maybe he forgot their anniversary or some other momentous occasion. So, she decided he needed to be punished.

Thus, the invention of the bow tie.

He took a moment to smile into the mirror, extremely proud of his take on this, before he went back to work on the tie. But the final result was worse than before.

Resigned, he gave the tie one last pat and reached for his jacket. As he was pulling it on, he caught sight of Carrie's shoes on the floor.

They were red.

He was smiling as he picked up one of the shoes. He'd have to say they were definitely red. A very sexy, high heeled and vibrant shade of red.

This sent a whole slew of thoughts racing through his mind, all of these involving Carrie. And most of them of her wearing these shoes and little else.

He cast a guiltily glance over at the closed bathroom door.

My God, get your mind out of the gutter. You need to cool it ... literally.

He already had a tentative plan in place. After they returned from the awards dinner tonight, he was finally going to make his move. As it now stood, knock on wood, there should be no reason he and Carrie wouldn't be alone.

He couldn't wait to take her into his arms and finally love her in a way, up until now, he had only been able to think about.

Still holding the shoe in his hands, he heard the bathroom door open. He turned just as Carrie walked into the room.

And at that very moment, with just this one look, he fell in love with her all over again.

Carrie had no idea Chris was in the room when she came out of the bathroom. She was too busy trying to fit her phone in her purse.

This finally accomplished, she snapped the purse shut. It was then she glanced up to find him standing almost in front of her, a bemused expression on his face.

Their eyes meeting, she came to an abrupt stop, a look of surprise spreading across her face.

For what seemed like the longest time, neither of them moved. Or spoke.

And this was because, honestly?

They couldn't.

Chris was completely blown away by how beautiful she looked, He could only stare, the corner of his mouth lifting in a slight smile at the stunned expression on her face.

But he could understand. Because he knew his reaction was the same. If anyone were to ask him, he would now be able to say he knew what it was like to let go and fall totally and passionately in love.

If the world came to an end tomorrow, he would be happy because of this love he had for her.

And Carrie?

She had thought it would be impossible to fall any deeper in love with him than she already was, but she now realized how wrong she had been. This connection between them was so strong, it was taking everything she had not to run to him and throw herself into his arms.

She watched almost in a daze as he slowly set her shoe back on the floor before he came to stand next her. He didn't need to touch her, the look in his eyes enough to hold her captive.

It was only when she moved closer, a low groan came from deep in his throat as he pulled her into his arms. The soft kiss he brushed across her brow, played havoc with her heart, sending it racing.

His lips trailed down to her mouth. "Carrie …" This came in a long husky sigh. "You're absolutely the most beautiful woman I've ever known. I…"

When his words trailed off, leaving a silence between them, she reached up to link her fingers behind his neck. She was riding high with the feel of him, filled with a desire to laugh out loud, yet at the same time, afraid she was going to burst into tears.

She gazed up at him, a smile touching her lips. "And you … you are just so incredibly handsome." She followed this with a long sigh. "No, I'd have to say you're hot. You look so darn, amazingly hot."

Her words traveled through every inch of him, the huskiness of her voice sent his heart thundering in his chest. He gazed down at her for a few moments before he grinned. "Hot? Wow, that's quite a compliment. But I'll take it."

He wound the wispy curl of her hair around his finger. The same curl she had spent so much time fighting. "I like this."

Doesn't that figure? And to think you spent all that time trying to fix the darn thing.

His next words surprised both of them, him even more than her.

That he even felt the need to say them was proof of the emotional state he was in.

"May I kiss you?"

But at the same time, she whispered almost the exact same words. Delivered in a low, husky whisper, he wouldn't have been able to resist even if he tried.

"Kiss me."

He bent his head, his lips brushing lightly against her cheek before his mouth found hers, taking it with a gentleness he hadn't known he possessed. It was only when she wrapped her arms around his neck to pull him closer, he deepened the kiss.

This kiss was so different from the other kisses they had shared. It was a kiss between two people who knew with a certainty what they had together was so right. And so breathtakingly real.

Somehow, what they had been so afraid they lost, had now been found. And everything they had believed from the very start, was now theirs to have.

The proof was in this moment. There was no sense of desperation. Or need for assurance. This didn't mean the kiss lacked the desire and passion so often found in a kiss. Of course, these were both present, but in a soft and unhurried way. With the gentle reminder they had all the time in the world waiting for them.

His eyes closed, he leaned his forehead against hers. "Can I ask you something else?"

Again, he couldn't believe he was asking for permission. But for some reason, it felt this was the right thing to do.

She nodded against him. How could she not? She would do whatever he asked, give him whatever he wanted. Something she had known from the first moment they met.

He smiled down at her. "Later tonight, promise me we'll meet right back here to continue from where we leave off now. Just the two of us."

A smile touched her lips as she tilted her head to study him. "Well… since you so kindly agreed to attend this dinner with me, I think this sounds fair."

He nodded. "Very fair, I would say. So, it's a promise?"

The hunger in his eyes sending a riot of sensations through her, she pulled his head down, her whisper coming against his mouth. "Yes, it's a promise." She was quick to confirm this with her kiss.

Reluctantly releasing his hold on her, he checked his watch. "Our taxi will be here any minute." He glanced over at her shoes. "Which means you need to slip into those sexy shoes of yours."

He smiled. "I like those, too."

He brushed his fingers over the curl on her cheek.

"I'm one lucky guy."

Chris reached for Carrie's hand.

When she turned to face him, her eyes wide and serious in the dim interior of the taxi, he gave her a reassuring smile. "Are you nervous? Because you know you have no reason to be. I'll be with you every step of the way."

She slowly shook her head. "No, I don't think I am. But then I'm not really expecting too much. If anything, I think it will be very interesting."

A frown creased her forehead. "Well, maybe I'm a little worried because I'm sure a lot of important people will be at this event. And I know they probably don't think all that highly of designers from the Midwest. Certainly not as competition in what is known as the interior design world. Which is so unfair."

She sighed. "I'm so glad you agreed to come with me."

He responded by pulling her even closer to place a kiss in her hair. "I'm more than happy to be here. But be warned, let anyone question your design ability and I'll be on them like a hawk. They'll wish they had kept their comments to themselves. Or wonder why they even opened their mouth."

She pulled away to look at him before she laughed. "Oh my, I hope it doesn't come to that. But it's nice to know you'll be there for me."

"Princess, I'll always be here for you. This is a promise."

As soon as he said this, he wondered if he had said too much, too soon. But after she studied him for a few moments her response, proved otherwise.

"I'd like that."

She smiled. "I really would. A lot."

Resting his cheek to the top of her head, he was smiling.

This was the kind of answer he had hoped to hear.

CHAPTER 19

Do you even realize how amazing you are to me?
Because you are.
~ Anonymously Yours

The main entrance to The Seasons Hotel was a hubbub of activity, an unending line of vehicles waiting to drop off their passengers.

The combination of horns blowing, shouts between the valet personnel and the flash of cameras, heightened the excitement, hinting something very special was about to happen.

Chris was watching Carrie as she took it all in. Abruptly, she looked down at her dress before she turned to him, an uncertain expression on her face. "Everyone looks so dressed up, so elegant. Maybe I'm underdressed?"

He chuckled before he shook his head. "Princess, you could wear pajamas and you would still look more elegant and beautiful than any of the women here tonight. I have a feeling I'm going to be the envy of every man attending this event when they catch sight of you on my arm."

"Oh Chris, thank you." She sighed. "You make me feel beautiful."

He pulled her to him. "*Ah ...* but you are. So much so."

When she smiled, leaning over to give him a kiss for this comment, he pulled her even closer to take over the kiss. It was at the sound of the taxi driver clearing his throat, they finally pulled apart to see they had reached the entrance.

Chris gently wound the curl, still hugging her cheek, around his finger. "So, are you ready?"

She smiled. "I'm ready."

The lobby of the hotel was a sea of people. And they were people who all seemed to know each other. Her hand in Chris's tight grip, Carrie was more than happy to let him take the lead, navigating them through the crowd.

He suddenly came to a stop, turning to her. "I see James Fisher is here. He is the owner of one of the firms I deal with on a regular basis. Come, I want to introduce you to him. He not only sells and buys real estate, he also has quite a few projects in the works. They're all over the country. I believe he has a few start-ups in Cleveland and Cincinnati, which could possibly be an opening for your design services. He is one of the most honest and down-to-earth guys I know. You'd never know he is as wealthy and successful as he is."

What Chris didn't tell Carrie was this man was also Lauren's father.

Yes, the same Lauren who so brazenly informed Carrie she was Chris's fiancée.

It wasn't because he was trying to hide this from her. He honestly didn't think anything of it. This is because it had never been an issue. In fact, he doubted Lauren's father even knew he and Lauren knew each other.

As far as he was concerned, what went on in his personal life had nothing to do with what happened in the business world. He had made it a point to keep his personal life as private as possible.

A thoughtful look crossed Carrie's face. For some reason, the last name of Fisher sounded very familiar to her. Then this completely slipped her mind as they approached the group and Chris began introducing her to everyone.

Slowly making her way across the room, her eyes taking in every detail she could, Amy Porter was on a mission.

As she eased her way into the group Carrie and Chris were a part of, she sent a casual smile to anyone who glanced in her direction. She was very proud of how easily she was able to accomplish this without anyone noticing she really didn't belong. After all, it was a very big and necessary part of her job to fit in. This was how she was able to gather all of the information she needed for her weekly posts.

She had started her blog, Who's Who in the Manhattan, about a year ago on a lark. An avid follower of the city's numerous social events, this beginning all the way back to when she attended NYU, she'd thought this would be a great way to meet people. Specifically, more like the *right* kind of people. And in all the *right* places.

She had no idea what she wrote would appeal to so many people and catch on so fast. Or open so many doors to her. Now she had invitations galore to all kinds of events.

Evidently there were a lot of people like her who craved information about what was going on in the high society world of New York. Or, the beautiful people, as she liked to call them. She also found the majority of these beautiful people loved nothing more than to see their name in print.

Of course, she was very careful to write only about the good things, something she credited to a big part of her success. She also made sure to always double check the information she provided, eliminating anything that could be construed as gossip. She certainly wasn't going to take the chance of a lawsuit or worse yet, ruin her own chances of eventually becoming a bigger part of the group of people she so admired

Tonight, her goal was to find out more about Chris Gardner. He had been mentioned in a recent article about the new and upcoming real estate entrepreneurs in Manhattan and the fact he was single, only in his early thirties and very easy on the eye, was garnering a lot of enquiries from her readers.

Unfortunately, one of these readers was Lauren Fisher.

She sighed.

Lauren wasn't really what she would call a friend. She was more of an on again, off again kind of acquaintance. Or if she were to be completely honest, she'd admit Lauren was someone she merely tolerated.

Lately Lauren started calling Amy almost weekly, just to chat, she said. This made Amy nervous, because it was obvious she was up to no good. Lauren Fisher wasn't one to chat. It also hadn't escaped Amy's notice every conversation seemed to center on Chris.

She sighed. The only reason she knew Lauren was because of her mother. Friends with Lauren's mother, going all the way back to their college days, she had insisted Amy call Lauren when she moved to New York.

So, she did.

Only to find out this had been a big mistake.

As silly as this may sound, Lauren scared her.

The first time they met up, she had come across as a very sincere and sweet person. But, Amy was quick to find out, she was neither.

No, Lauren was someone who would stop at nothing to get what she wanted. No matter who she stepped on in the process.

And she wanted Chris Gardner.

She had made this very obvious with the more than usual questions she asked about Chris in her phone calls. Was he dating anyone? And if he was, did Amy know who the woman was?

She also told Amy, a fact she told her not many people knew, she and Chris were destined to be together. She was only biding her time until he realized this.

Even though she had said this with a little laugh, Amy knew she was dead serious.

Yes, Lauren Fisher was obsessed with Chris Gardner. Definitely not a good omen for the woman who eventually did win his heart.

Amy shivered. She wouldn't wish that on anyone

And now, after having only spent a few minutes, closely observing both Chris and the woman he was with, she slowly made her way over to stand next to them.

Carrie smiled over at the woman who had suddenly appeared next to her.

This brought out her warm smile as she held out her hand. "Hi, I'm Amy Porter. I write a blog about the social events in Manhattan. Are you here as Chris's guest? Or as one of the nominees?"

Carrie smiled. "I'm Carrie Mazzori and I guess I'd have to say yes to both." She gave a nod towards Chris. "Chris is actually here as my guest, but since he seems to know a lot more people than I do, I'm more than happy to let him take the lead. And yes, I'm up for the Upcoming Designer of the Year for my region. I'm from Cleveland."

Amy was studying her so closely, Carrie felt uncomfortable. But it was what she had to say next, that she began to wonder if she should be worried.

"So, how long have you known Chris? I'm sure you're already aware he's a hot topic of conversation when it comes to who's who on the list of most desirable bachelors here in New York. It hasn't gone unnoticed, if he keeps up the pace he's at now, his future is looking very bright. He's smart enough to have already made the right moves by traveling in the right circles and with the right people. Which means you're in for a long, hard fight if you plan to hold on to him."

She nodded, intently searching Carrie's face before she gave her another smile. "So, I'd like you to take this as a friendly warning... just be careful."

Carrie had no idea how to respond to this.

Right circles? Right people? A friendly warning? Who was this woman and exactly what is she trying to tell you?

She moved closer to Chris, unconsciously seeking his protection.

Immediately sensing something was wrong, Chris quickly excused himself from the conversation he was in and turned to her. When he saw her worried expression, he rested his hand reassuringly on her back before he glanced over at Amy in an attempt to assess the situation.

His other hand shot out, grasping hers in a firm hold. "Chris Gardner. I don't believe we've met?"

As Amy shook his hand, she gave him a brilliant smile. "I'm Amy Porter. I write a blog, Who's Who in Manhattan. It's my small attempt to keep people informed on what's happening here in the city."

She nodded over at Carrie. "As I was just telling Carrie, you're very popular among my readers with your climb to the top in the real estate world. Let me be one of the first one to congratulate you on your success."

Before he could acknowledge this, she tilted her head, giving him a thoughtful look "I believe we have a mutual friend, Lauren Fisher?"

She nodded over at James Fisher, who was involved in a conversation with another couple in the group. "Mr. Fisher's daughter?"

She was watching to see if there was any reaction from Carrie.

And there was. Definitely. She tensed, a look of panic coming over her face before she glanced up at Chris.

She also noticed how Chris reacted, tightening his hold on Carrie before he leaned in to whisper in her ear. Unfortunately, this was something Amy wasn't able to hear.

But it really didn't matter. The information she had been seeking was now hers.

It was obvious Chris Gardner was no longer one of Manhattan's most eligible bachelors. And this woman by his side was the reason why.

Chris Gardner was a man in love.

Amy wondered if Carrie understood what she was up against. Because she would be willing to bet her one and only pair of Jimmy Choo heels—snagged on eBay for a ridiculously low price—there were a whole lot of other women just like Lauren, who'd jump at the chance to have a go at Chris.

Girlfriend, or no girlfriend.

The fact Carrie lived in Cleveland would make this even easier to happen.

If there was one thing Amy had learned about living in New York, it was every man, or in this case, every woman for themselves.

She glanced over at Chris to see he was studying her, a wary expression on his face. Taking this as her cue to leave, she flashed another big smile at him and Carrie. "I don't want to take up any more of your time. And I really should move on. There are a lot of people I wish to talk to before the dinner starts. I also need to check out what table I've been assigned."

She smiled at Carrie. "I wish you luck on your award, Carrie."

After giving a nod to both of them she began to back away. "It was so nice to meet the both of you."

She turned, to disappear as swiftly as she had arrived.

Chris watched Amy walk away.

Damn...

He was furious.

He couldn't believe how tempted he was to run after this woman, this Amy... and ask her what the hell she was trying to do. Instead, he made the effort to calm down, his only concern now for Carrie. Even though he had whispered reassuringly in her ear that Amy was probably just another one of the hundreds of harmless bloggers in the city looking for another story, the worried expression hadn't left her face.

He made their excuses to everyone, and taking Carrie's hand, he began searching for a quiet corner of the room.

You can imagine how hard this was. The best he could manage had both of them pressed up against the wall in the far corner of the lobby, almost, but not quite, hidden behind a grouping of ornamental ferns.

Unconcerned about what people might think, he framed her face in his hands, his eyes holding hers.

"Carrie, listen to me. I don't know who this Amy is or what her motive was. Or if she's a friend of Lauren's. I only know she has upset you. Tell me, what did she say to you?"

She shook her head. She didn't want to talk about it. She wanted to block the whole conversation out of her mind.

She wanted to forget about Lauren, once and for all. Because, for some reason, she kept coming back to haunt her, planting even more doubt in her mind. The mention of her name alone was enough to bring back the memory of the angry and threatening tone of her voice during the phone call they had shared.

And now to find out Lauren's father and Chris were involved in many of the same business dealings?

This wasn't good. Not good at all. It was a grim reminder Lauren was never going to go away.

She gazed up into Chris's face. His concern was so obvious, she wanted to assure him. "It's okay. She talked mostly about the article you were featured in. And how successful you've become." She reached up to stroke his cheek. "I'm so proud of you."

He studied her for the longest time before he leaned in to give her a kiss. His hands drifting down to hold hers, he smiled at her. "Just promise me you'll always tell me if you're worried about something, okay? No matter what it is. So, we can talk about it."

She started to nod, but then she hesitated, searching his face before she spoke. "I really am thankful you're here with me tonight."

Far back in the corner of his mind, a warning flashed. She hadn't given him the answer he wanted. Making a mental note they needed to talk about this later, he moved to press a kiss to her cheek. A smile touched his lips when she tilted her head to have his mouth meet hers instead.

He groaned against her mouth. "Ah, princess, you're making me crazy. This dinner can't be over soon enough."

He took her hand. "Come on, let's go find our table. Then I'll rustle up something to drink. I don't know about you, but I could use a glass of wine right now."

CHAPTER 20

Chester was in his office, studying game clips from last season's games.

The sound of Sophie's voice broke his concentration.

"Chester, can you come here for a minute?"

He gave a long sigh. Then after hitting the pause button on the computer, he leaned back in his chair, massaging his forehead with his fingers.

He finally stood, and after raising his hands over his head in a long stretch, he left his office.

Yes, he was stalling. This was because he was pretty sure whatever the reason for Sophie's summons, it was only going to involve more work for him.

Work that, as far as he was concerned, was probably unnecessary.

He found her sitting on the floor in front of the closet by the front door. She was surrounded by piles of boxes, clothing, boots and shoes. When she sensed his presence, she peered up at him, her forehead furrowed in a deep frown.

"Look at all of this stuff." She waved her hand at everything around her. "Can you believe this all came out of this tiny closet? You can't possibly have a need for most of it. I want you to go through it right

now. Then we'll pack up everything you don't need and give it away."
She shook her head. "Honestly, Chester? You are a real pack rat."

Lowering himself to the floor next to her, he pulled her up against
him, his arms going around her. He nuzzled his way under her hair
and placed a trail of soft kisses up her neck and behind her ear. He felt
her shiver against him before she suddenly stilled, leaning away from
him. "Stop it. What are you doing? Come on, you need to listen to me.
We've got to get all of this cleaned up, because we don't have a lot of
time."

"*Shh ...*" He pulled her back, this time holding her more tightly
against him. His hands resting on her stomach, he began moving them
in a gentle massaging motion. When she began to relax against him,
he leaned in to whisper in her ear.

"What don't we have enough time for, angel?"

Her only response was to rest her head back against his shoulder,
offering her mouth for the kiss he willingly gave her. She closed her
eyes as she let herself get swept up in the kiss.

*He always does this to you. He only has to touch you and you forget
about everything but him.*

Like now.

There was also the fact she really didn't know what her answer
was. She wasn't sure why she was doing what she did. If anything, she
was a bit concerned about her behavior… this obsession to get everything all sorted and in order. She slowly shook her head against his
shoulder.

He sighed. "Angel, you don't need to do any of this. *My god*, you've
swept through every inch of the place, tossing away almost everything
we own, I'm afraid when you finally get done, we'll both be down to
one change of clothing and a pair of shoes. If even that. Trust me,
everything is fine just the way it is."

She turned to him and he was dismayed to see the hint of tears in
her eyes. "Chester, I don't want these babies coming in here, thinking
we live like a bunch of gypsies. I want everything to be perfect."

She twisted around even more and gazing right into his face, she
began to cry. "Chester, I'm scared."

He was completely dumbfounded. Where was all of this coming from? Up until now, she had been the positive and stronger of them during this pregnancy. She had him convinced having a baby, or should he say two babies, was going to be a piece of cake.

And now he was ready to take on the job. More than ready.

It was his turn to step it up and be the strong one, the one to hold them together. Any worries he had been holding inside? Well, it was time to push them right out of his mind.

He framed her face in his hands. "Sweetheart, listen to me. The babies aren't going to care about what's going on in the closets. Or if everything isn't in the right order. The only thing they're going to care about is you and me being here for them. And how much we want and love them."

She was watching him intently, hanging on his every word. He smiled, smoothing the hair back from her face. "You have no reason to be scared, because I'll be with you every baby step of the way. From the minute these little ones decide they are ready to enter this world, to when we finally bring them home for good. I'm sure it will be a challenge at times, but together, we'll make it through."

He rested his forehead against hers. "*Ah, angel* … think of how lucky we are. We're going to be a family. You're going to be a wonderful mom. And I'm going to give it my all to be the best dad I can be." He suddenly looked worried. "I have a feeling this will be quite a learning experience."

This finally brought a smile from her. "Oh, Chester, I know you'll be a great father. I'm not worried about you at all."

He pressed a kiss to the top of her head, holding her even tighter. "And I'm not worried about you, either." He smiled down at her. "Over the past few days, every time I think about the babies, I get so excited. I can't wait until we finally get to hold them in our arms."

She leaned her head back against him, her eyes locking with his. Her words were a whisper. "I love you so much. And I'm so sorry. I don't know why I'm acting so crazy."

His answer was to give her another kiss before he stood, pulling her up with him. And before she could give him the please-don't-pick-me-up-because-all-the-weight-I've-gained-could-very-well-kill-you-speech, he scooped her up into his arms.

How many times had she warned him about this? He was pretty sure it had to be at least a dozen times. But at this point in her pregnancy he had come to ignore her protests.

As he carried her down the hall to their bedroom, he planted a kiss in her hair. "It's almost ten, way too late to be cleaning out closets. Let's get you into bed so you can get some sleep. I have a few things to finish up on the computer and then I'll come join you."

Chester put everything back in the closet. Back in his office, he glanced over at his computer. Did it really matter if he didn't watch the videos right now? No, it didn't. The only thing that mattered was Sophie. The videos and everything else could damn well wait.

His phone rang just as he finished signing off his computer. It was Alex. Leaning back against his desk, he was smiling as he answered the call. "Hey, what's up?"

Alex's voice was as cheerful as always "Nothing much. I hope I didn't call too late. I'm checking in to see how you guys are doing." He chuckled. "Let he rephrase that. I'm really only interested in finding out how Sophie is. And this is because Lisa wasn't going to let me rest until I did. So, how is she?"

Chester sighed, dragging his hand through his hair. "She's been like a tornado, going through the condo like we're expecting a visit from royalty or something. She has to be totally exhausted, but only gets all worked up when I try to stop her."

He could hear Alex telling this to Lisa, with Lisa giving him an answer before he came back on the phone.

"Lisa says she nesting, whatever the hell that means." Again, Chester could hear Lisa talking before Alex spoke into the phone again.

"Lisa wants to talk to you."

After a series of rustling noises and what sounded like a loud crash, Lisa was on the phone. "Chester? Hi. Sorry about that noise.

Alex was trying to be funny and tossed me the phone. It was the worst possible throw ever. It's a good thing he plays first base, because with his aim he'd never make it as a pitcher. Or, God help us, an outfielder."

"Don't I know it." Chester chuckled. "Now tell me, what's this about nesting? Is this another one of those pregnancy myths everyone has been so eager to share with us? Both the good and the bad? Whether we want to hear them, or not?"

"Yep, nesting … like birds, I guess. Supposedly, there's this old wives' tale that claims when the birth is near, a woman gets the urge to ready the home for the new baby. Going through the house like a whirlwind, she starts cleaning and organizing everything."

She laughed. "So, this could mean your little one is about to make an appearance very soon. A lot of people don't believe nesting is a real thing, but I can still remember how out of control I was right before I had Chloe. I practically tore the house apart."

She laughed again. "So, get ready. And now, I'm going to give you back to Alex. He's still pouting about my pitcher remark. Honestly, the man isn't happy unless he thinks he excels at everything."

He was about to comment, but she had more to add. "And Chester? Tell Sophie, Chloe is going crazy with waiting. She's so excited. Every time we go shopping she wants to buy something for the baby. We're betting on a girl over here. So, make sure you call us as soon as something happens. And give my love to Sophie."

Chester chuckled. "I guess you could say all bets are on, because we still don't know. We want to be surprised. And tell Chloe to hold on to that excitement because in a couple of years we'll be counting on her to babysit for us. And Lisa? Thanks for calling. I'll be sure to tell Sophie what you said."

After he ended the call, he stayed where he was, staring down at his phone and thinking about what Lisa told him.

So, it was going to be soon, huh?

Wow …

He wasn't sure if he wanted to tell Sophie about this nesting thing. It might put her right over the edge.

He had to think about this.

And they thought it was going to be a girl, did they?

Hmm ... could be, could be two.

As he turned out the light in his office, he was smiling.

With a great deal of effort, Sophie pushed herself into a sitting position on the bed. She looked over at the clock on the nightstand.

Glowing a bright red in the dark, the time read twelve-sixteen.

Seriously?

She thought for sure it would be much closer to morning.

She threw her head back to stare up at the ceiling. She wanted to scream. But when she glanced over at a sleeping Chester, she knew this probably wouldn't be a good idea. She was pretty sure it would send him flying right off the bed and out the door. She was more than aware of the worried look creeping back into his eyes over the past couple of days.

She sighed.

It's just not fair.

Giving a loud sigh, she began fluffing up her pillows. Then she punched them down before she settled on her side, arranging the pillows comfortably under her head.

With another sigh, she closed her eyes.

This lasted about two minutes.

She sighed a third time, this sigh much longer and more vocal than the previous two. After she managed to flip onto her other side, a move far from easy for a person who was nine months pregnant, let alone carrying twins, she made quite a production of propping a pillow against her stomach.

Once again, she closed her eyes.

When this didn't work, she flipped back onto her other side before finally rolling onto her back.

Frustrated, she stared up at the ceiling again. If she had to describe how she was feeling right now, she'd have to say she felt like a beached whale. Or a balloon, filled with way too much air and about to pop.

Or maybe a better description would be to compare herself to that pink bunny in the commercials on TV. She couldn't remember what they were advertising. Batteries, maybe? The commercial claimed the bunny never stopped. It just kept going, never running out of power.

Yes, this is what she was. A big, fat, hyped up version of that bunny. Both her mind and body racing a mile a minute. All worked up about what needed to get done before the babies made their appearance.

But the similarity to the bunny ends there. Because you're really close to running out of power, batteries or no batteries.

At her appointment yesterday, the doctor told her she could go into labor any day now. This had sent her right into a state of panic. Because she wasn't ready. And it looked like, at the rate she was going, she never would be.

She propped herself up on her elbows and glanced over at Chester again. He still hadn't moved. He'd flung the sheets off in his sleep and since he only slept in his boxers, the body she had come to love was on glorious display.

What were the words your Aunt Louise used when referring to him? Ah, yes ... she said he had a magnificent physique.

Well, there was no doubt about it, her aunt was right on the mark with this. Her gaze slowly traveling over him, Sophie knew she would never tire of reminding herself this man, this beautiful man, was all hers.

A heat began to build inside of her, spreading like wildfire. And now the only thing she could think about was how much she wanted him to make love to her.

She couldn't believe how much she craved this.

But with the way she had been pestering him lately, about every little thing, he deserved to have a night of undisturbed sleep. So, after one more really, *really* loud and resigned sigh, she closed her eyes.

Again, it just wasn't fair.

An arm came around her, pulling her close.

Startled, she opened her eyes to see Chester's face mere inches from hers, his mouth turned up in a slight smile. "So, tell me ... what's going on in your mind that would merit such a thorough inspection?"

He pressed a soft kiss to her mouth." More importantly, what was it you were looking for? Tell me, so I can help you out if need be."

She stared up at him, her eyes wide.

She was thankful, because of the total darkness, he couldn't see she was blushing. You'd think by now she'd be over this shyness with him when it came to things like this. But she wasn't. He had a way of making her become so flustered, falling apart in every possible way.

Like now.

She reached up to caress his cheek. "I thought you were asleep."

He chuckled. "How could I sleep with those big sighs coming from you, one right after the other?"

His gaze remained steady. "So, what's going on? What's wrong?"

She closed her eyes, shaking her head. "*Oh god*, I'm just so uncomfortable. And even though I'm so tired, I can't sleep. I feel like there is so much pressure, like I am ready to explode." Opening her eyes, she started to say something, then stopped.

He smoothed the hair back from her face, waiting.

She finally reached up to frame his face in her hands, her whisper brushing over his mouth. "Make love to me. Please? I need you to do this ... I need you."

His gaze holding hers, at first, he didn't say anything. She could only hold her breath, watching as a flicker of desire began to build in his eyes.

His answer finally came in the kisses he began pressing in a leisurely trail along her jaw. "What about the babies? Or you? I don't want to hurt you or the babies."

She had already begun to sink into that state of anticipation he always managed to stir deep inside, her body no longer hers to control. She moved closer to him, barely able to shake her head in response. "The doctor said it would be okay. I asked."

When she felt his lips curve into a smile at this, she blushed, once again grateful for the darkness.

"Chester, I'm serious. He said it might even bring on the delivery. I want to have these babies soon. Before I go completely insane. You don't want a crazy wife, do you?"

Chester's answer was delayed because he was too busy easing off the jersey she was wearing, to finally pull it over her head.

She watched as he tossed it to the end of the bed.

His mouth came back to travel over hers, teasing her in a whisper. "I'll love you no matter if you're crazy or whatever." His lips suddenly slowed and he pulled back to look at her, his mouth turned up in a smile. "You do realize what you're asking, is what got you into this state in the first place, don't you?"

His hands were now moving over her in slow, sensuous strokes. And this would be absolutely everywhere. She was finding it hard to think, let alone answer him. Straining to get even closer, again let there be a reminder this was not an easy move in the pregnant state she was in, her answer came out in a long sigh.

"I know …"

He placed a slow, hot kiss to the pulse now beating wildly at the base of her neck. "And if I do this for you, you're going to owe me in return. You're also aware of this, aren't you?"

The smile was still in his voice. How he was able to tease her at a time like this, she had no idea. God, she couldn't even think. She only knew whatever he asked of her, she was going to agree.

She pulled his face closer, her mouth searching for his. "Yes, I'll do whatever it is you want. Please stop talking and make love to me. Now, *please …*"

So, this was exactly what he did

After all, when your wife is about to have a baby any minute and this is what she wants you to do, you certainly can't disappoint her, can you?

Chester was awake.

Sophie was not. Immediately falling into a deep sleep after they made love, she was now tucked against him, her breathing soft and even.

He pressed a kiss in her hair before his gaze was drawn to the floor to ceiling windows spanning one wall of the room. He saw it had started to snow. This brought back the memory of the first time they had come together. The day before Valentine's Day. It had been snowing then, too.

Valentine's Eve, he had called it. He promised her, from then on, it would be their own special holiday in celebration of Valentine's Day.

He smiled. Who would have thought, not even a year later, they would have reached this point in their lives, married and almost about to become parents?

Sophie stirred against him, giving a soft little sigh. He almost considered waking her up to let her know it was snowing. Reluctantly, he decided against this, knowing how desperately she needed her sleep.

Pressing another kiss in her hair and pulling the quilt more securely around them, he closed his eyes.

"Chester!"

He felt like he just fell sleep when this cry from Sophie jerked him awake.

He sat straight up in a panic, shooting a quick glance around the bed to see she wasn't there. When she cried out again and he realized this was coming from the bathroom, he dove off the bed to go sprinting in that direction. There he found her, standing in the middle of the room, a horrified look on her face.

His hand running through his hair, he stared wildly at her. "Angel, what's wrong?"

Her hands cradling her stomach, her eyes were wide. "*Oh my god, Chester, my water just broke.*"

For an instant, neither of them moved as they stared open-mouthed at one another. Then they were both grinning. Making his way over to her, he framed her face in his hands and pressed a soft kiss to her forehead.

"So, it looks like this is finally it, sweetheart. Remember what I told you. I'll be with you every step of the way. And everything is going to be just fine."

She nodded as she leaned against him.

He gave her another kiss, this one to the top of her head before he pulled back to look into her eyes.

"Let me call down and have them bring the SUV around while you get ready. I'll be right back to help you."

He was smiling. "Come on, it's time to bring these babies into the world so we can bring them home."

CHAPTER 21

Every single second my love for you grows.
~ Unknown

Carrie and Chris were both laughing when they came, almost running, out of The Seasons Hotel.

He reached for her hand to pull her with him towards the first available taxi he saw. He was moving so fast, she could hardly keep up with him.

Her award plaque clutched to her chest, she slid into the back seat. Once he was settled next to her, she leaned back against him and gazed up into his face.

She was still laughing.

"I don't think we're very good at making a smooth exit. At least I'm not." She shook her head. "If you hadn't caught me, I know I would've made a very undignified tumble down those stairs. And it wouldn't have been good, because there were an awful lot of them."

She made a face. "Not the best way to be remembered."

He shook his head. "*God,* for a minute there, I thought I was going to lose you." His gaze swept over her. "Are you sure you're all right?"

"I'm fine." She glanced down at her shoes before she looked back up at him. "I'm going to blame it on these shoes. I tried to tell Sophie I wasn't coordinated enough to wear shoes like these. But she insisted I buy them. Everyone should have a watch-out-here-I-come pair of shoes like these, she said. And that's exactly what I almost did, but not in the way she meant it, I'm afraid."

She laughed. "I guess they did make the outfit, even as dangerous as they are."

Chris pulled her up against him, his lips finding the sensitive place behind her ear. "Don't ever give up the shoes. They're so damn sexy and on you. Let's just say I can visualize so many different things with you wearing them."

His whisper sending a volley of shivers through her, she arched her neck towards him, which he saw as an invitation for more. His head dipped down and his mouth changing course, he claimed hers in a long, passionate kiss.

Her fingers lost their grip on the plaque, which for some reason, she was still clutching in her hand. This sent it sliding off her lap, heading right down to the floor of the taxi.

She let out a cry as she tried to grab it, bringing an abrupt halt to Chris's kiss. As he pulled back from her in surprise, he saw he had pushed her down onto the seat until she was almost reclining underneath him.

He quickly scrambled to sit back on the seat, pulling her up with him. The look on his face was almost comical in its horror. "*Damn ...* what am I doing? God, I'm so sorry, princess. I'm afraid I got a little carried away."

She started to giggle, shaking her head. "Believe me, I wasn't trying to stop you. The plaque slipped out of my hand and since its glass, I was afraid if it hit the floor, it might break. I'm planning on displaying it in my office, so it would be nice if it was all in one piece."

He shook his head as he settled her next to him. "Thank God for that, because I think it provided a much-needed interruption. I have no intention of making love to you for the first time in the back of a taxi. Remember your promise? We're going to continue right from where we left off. And this would be at home."

After she reached up to place a quick kiss to the corner of his mouth, he took the plaque from her.

Even though he had seen it during the awards dinner, he read the inscription aloud.

Upcoming Designer of the Year,
Midwest Region
This award is presented to Carrie Mazzori
For her excellence in the field of Interior Design

He smiled over at her. "I can't make out the rest of the fine print in this dim lighting, but I don't really need to. It's all good, sweetheart. I know I told you this at the dinner, but I'm so damn proud of you."

She leaned her head back against his shoulder. "It is all good, isn't it? *Everything …*"

He tightened his hold on her.

"Yes … yes, it is."

The taxi pulled up in front of Chris's brownstone.

Once they were inside, he took the plaque from her and set it on the hall table. After he helped her off with her coat and hung it in the closet, he turned to find she was watching him.

He moved closer, the intensity of his gaze making her feel unexpectedly shy. She reached up to run her hands down the lapels of his jacket, her gaze focused on his shirtfront.

"I want to thank you again for going with me tonight. You made it the perfect evening. I don't even mind we left before the band started to play, even though I had hoped to share a dance with you."

The huskiness of her voice had him ready to move even closer. Instead, he smiled, and taking her hand, he led her down the hall to his bedroom. After he took his phone out of his pocket, he motioned for her to wait as he searched through his music play list.

A smile on his face, he slipped the phone back in his pocket just as music began to fill the room.

He dropped the phone on the bed and held out his hand. "May I have this dance?"

She went right into his arms, relaxing against him as he led her in a slow dance around the room, softly singing along with the words to the song.

Well, to be truthful, he only sang some of the words, randomly here and there, as he wasn't exactly sure what they were.

He only knew the song was everything he wanted to say.

When she smiled up at him, he shrugged. "I'm sorry, I'm not sure of all of the words, merely a handful. But I do know they're a perfect fit for this moment. Just listen, princess ..."

Lady in red,
Dancing with me,
Cheek to cheek.

There's nobody else,
Just you and me.
And it's where I want to be,
Always want to be.

Lady in red,
I'll never forget,
The way you look tonight.

He smiled as he stepped back to twirl her around for one last spin. "See? Just like I said. Perfect."

To his complete surprise, she came right at him, the force of her embrace sending him staggering backwards. Her arms wrapping around his neck, her mouth claimed his in a kiss.

As you can imagine, this immediately sent any thoughts of future dancing, or anything else for that matter, flying out of his head.

Finally ...

A groan coming from deep within, he began moving them towards the bed. His mouth still in possession of hers, he began searching through the layers of her dress for a zipper. Or buttons. Or any other method he could think to remove it. But he found none of these.

Frustrated, he pulled back, while still keeping his hold on her. "Baby, you've got to help me out here. How the hell do you get out of this dress? I don't want to rip it."

She almost started to giggle. But when she saw the look of desperation on his face, she guided his hand to the zipper hidden on the one side of the dress.

They fell back onto the bed. Her frenzied movements matching his, her fingers fumbled with the buttons down the front of his shirt, to finally pull it loose from the waistband of his trousers.

This was when a loud ringing pierced the silence.

Chris didn't even flinch. At least not until Carrie stiffened, and giving a sharp gasp, she pushed away from him. She scrambled off the bed and after glancing wildly around the room, she looked over at him.

"My phone ... where's my phone?" Met with his bewildered expression, and before he even had the chance to open his mouth, she went running out of the room and down the hall, leaving him half sitting on the bed to stare after her.

What the hell? Now what?

She came careening back into the room, wearing only one shoe and her dress hanging halfway off her shoulder. He wasn't quite sure if she was crying or laughing as she waved her phone at him. "Oh my God, the babies are going to be here soon. Chester just called from the hospital and said the doctors predicted it should happen in about 8 hours."

She suddenly stilled, her eyes searching his face. "Chris, I need to go home. I promised I would be there. No matter what."

Chris ran his hand slowly over his face, shaking his head. With a very long and deep sigh, he pushed himself off the bed and made his way over to her. After he gently pulled her dress back up over her shoulder, he pulled her into his arms, resting his cheek in her hair. The tone of his voice was resigned. "Okay, I'll start checking flights. We'll get you out on the first one we can."

She pulled back to gaze up at him, a distressed look on her face. "Oh Chris, I'm so sorry. *So, so sorry.* But I have to go. I don't want to, well, be with you and then have to run and catch a flight. This isn't the way I want it to be for us, in a rush. Not the first time. I'm really sorry."

He planted a kiss in her hair. "I understand."

And yes, he really did understand. While at the same time, he didn't. He wanted to remind her she'd made him a promise they would have this time together, but knew this wouldn't be fair. He knew how excited she was about the babies.

Hell, he could still remember how he had rushed to be at the hospital when Emily had Connor.

He sighed. "We'll get you on the first flight we can."

When she didn't answer, only remaining silent in his arms, he gazed down at her. "Carrie?"

Carrie was having a hard time, intoxicated by the feeling of being in his arms. He still hadn't buttoned up his shirt and she was now resting against his bare chest.

She ached for more. A shiver of need racing through her, she brushed her lips against his bare skin.

He stilled, giving a sharp intake of breath. "Carrie?"

Weakly pushing away from him, she shook her head. "I'm sorry, it's just that … *oh my god* … you feel so good."

He groaned into her hair. "Princess, you're killing me." He watched as she slowly buttoned up his shirt before she lifted her face to his. "I'm sorry. I …"

He stopped her with a kiss, the hint of a smile on his lips. In fact, he was still smiling as he picked up his phone. "It's okay, princess. We'll work it out. You go ahead and start packing while I see what I can find."

He wasn't worried.

Again, he could wait.

. . .

It was when Chris informed Carrie there were no available flights until eight in morning at the earliest, she informed him she was going to rent a car and make the drive herself.

Again, she wanted to be there before the babies were born.

Remember? She had made a promise.

This turned out to be the beginning of their first argument.

He, of course, didn't think this was a good idea.

So, he put his foot down, or at least went through the motion of doing so. He told her he would be much happier if she took the next available flight instead.

This, in turn, had her even more determined. She told him she was more than confident she could do this and he had no reason to worry.

And his response to this?

With so little sleep over the past three days, he didn't feel she was in the best condition to drive for over seven hours. By herself and through the night.

My god, she had to realize he would worry the whole time she was gone.

She came back with the fact she really didn't have a choice. Did she need to remind him again that she promised Chester and Sophie she would be there for the birth? And she couldn't break that promise? This was her brother and his wife, for heaven's sake.

Chris closed his eyes …

She promised, huh? But what about her promise to you?

After a long and tense filled silence, he realized he was acting like a child. Carrie certainly had nothing to do with the timing of Chester and Sophie's babies arrival.. And if they did have to wait a little longer to be together? Well, so be it.

After all, as far as he was concerned, they had a lifetime ahead of them to be together. This certainly wasn't a make-or-break it moment.

What he did know, he didn't want to spend what time they did have arguing about something like this.

As he watched her, kneeling on the floor and refusing to meet his gaze as she haphazardly began throwing items into her suitcase, he finally spoke. "I think I have a better plan. I'll go with you. This way, you won't have to make the trip alone. We'll take my car and I'll do the driving. Please just humor me on this and say yes, princess."

Chris waited. Then he cleared his throat. "Well?"

She settled back on her heels to gaze over at him. "But what about you? I don't want you to jeopardize your work just for me."

He smiled at her. "Carrie, you're far more important to me than my job. Or anything else. It's only … well, it would drive me crazy, sending you off alone and in the middle of the night. Call me old fashioned, if you want, but this is the way I feel."

He shrugged. "I haven't taken any time off in I don't know how long. So, I'm due. And if you let me, I'll stay with you for a day or two. So, how about it?"

Leaving her place on the floor, she came over to lean against him, a relieved sigh coming from her when he wrapped his arms around her. "If you're sure, then my answer is a yes. I'd love to have you make the trip with me. And I'd love it even more if you'd stay with me for a little while."

He pulled her closer, pressing a kiss in her hair. "Try and stop me." A wicked gleam in his eyes. "Maybe then we'll finally be able to finish up what we started, huh?"

Her answer was to give him another kiss. This one so much more than a promise and making him wish he could stop time. If only for a little bit. Enough to see where this kiss would take them.

After she returned to her packing, she glanced over to see he was standing where she had left him, a bemused smile on his face.

"Chris?

He blinked. Then running his hand through his hair, he gave her one of those crooked smiles.

"Yeah, I guess I need to start packing, huh?"

CHAPTER 22

In another part of the city, Amy Porter sat back in her chair and took a sip of her tea, dismayed to find it was cold. She glanced over at the clock on her desk to see it was almost two o'clock in the morning.

She groaned, massaging her forehead with her fingertips.

It hadn't been her intention to stay up this late working on her latest post, but she liked to get them written and posted as quickly after the event as she could. While everything was still fresh in her mind.

She read it over one last time.

Hey, it's Amy!

This past week was a busy week for me at work. Which means I had to pass up on a number of the invitations I received. But I made sure to make it to the American Board of Realtors Awards dinner.

When my ride pulled up to the entrance of The Seasons Hotel, I could actually feel the excitement in the air. The flash of jewels, designer dresses and expensive cars were a hint everyone who's who in the world of Manhattan real estate was in attendance.

It's a well-known fact an event at The Seasons is always one of perfection, down to the smallest detail. And this one was no different. The theme chosen for the evening was Live the American Dream. The choice of a red, white and blue color scheme was most noticeable in the magnificent centerpieces on each table. These consisted of a tall blue glass vase overflowing with white and red roses, ivy and baby's breath. At each place setting, the favor was a crystal paperweight, engraved with the words, Live the American Dream. Of course, the food was amazing. The dessert, a crème de brûlée with a chocolate garnish in the shape of a house? It was to die for.There were so many people I recognized at this event. But the one person I was most interested in, as I know you are, too, was Chris Gardner. And I don't quite know how to break this to you, but he's a taken man, ladies. He was actually attending the event as the guest of Carrie Mazzori, an interior designer from Cleveland, Ohio.

Yes, you read right. She calls Cleveland her home and was nominated for the Upcoming Designer of the Year for her region. An award I'm happy to report she won. I say this because I couldn't help but like her. Both she and Chris seem like such genuine people.

Since I was seated at the table right next to them, I was able to observe them throughout the evening. And from what I saw, it's obvious they're deeply in love. If a man looked at me the way Chris looks at Carrie, I don't think I'd ask for anything more.

Maybe someday, you say? I hope so.

Well, I've had a long day and even a longer one planned for tomorrow. If only my real job didn't have to get in the way all of the time.

Have a great week. And remember to always keep your eyes open and your ears ready to listen while you're out and about this city of ours. Because anything can happen. Maybe even change your life.

Amy

After she uploaded the few photos she'd taken, her favorite where she captured the bemused expression on Carrie's face as Chris appeared to be whispering in her ear, she hit send. Once she checked to see everything had posted as it should, she began getting ready for bed.

She was brushing her teeth when she heard the 'ding' alerting her someone had messaged her about the post.

She grinned.

Wow, already? Talk about a dedicated follower.

Then she frowned, filled with this awful feeling whoever sent the message was the last person she wanted to hear from?

She checked her computer.

Her intuition had been right. It was from Lauren.

Damn ...

She knew she should ignore the message. Maybe wait until tomorrow. Or not read it at all.

She sighed. It was going to drive her crazy if she didn't read it. Cringing, she opened the message.

> *Amy, I'm sure you're exaggerating*
> *about Chris and this designer from*
> *Cleveland. Don't be surprised if, in*
> *the near future, you find out*
> *they're not the perfect couple you*
> *thought they were. Chris has a*
> *bright future in front of him,*
> *but only with the right woman.*
> *And Carrie isn't that woman. Trust*
> *me, I know what I'm talking*
> *about.*

Amy read the message one more time before she turned off her computer. She was suddenly very worried. And very angry.

She crawled into bed, her mind still racing.

After she had left Carrie and Chris, she wondered if she might have come on a little too strong with the warning she gave Carrie. But, after this message from Lauren, she was feeling a lot better about what she'd told her.

Not that you think Lauren would do something drastic. She wouldn't go that far, would she?

Her intuition had been right. Lauren was not a friend… to anyone. From now on, the less contact she had with her, the better.

She groaned and pulling the comforter up over her head, she closed her eyes. She needed to get some sleep.

There was nothing to worry about. Chris and Carrie would be fine.

This was her last thought before she fell into an exhausted sleep.

After Lauren sent her message off to Amy, she sat at her desk, glaring at her laptop. Then she slammed the top down and went storming into the bathroom. As she brushed her teeth, she tried to avoid her reflection in the mirror. She didn't need to be reminded of the frown lines becoming more and more pronounced as she grew older.

She couldn't believe the newest development between Chris and this Cleveland woman. And now it turns out she's an interior designer? This wasn't good.

She was also somewhat attractive. If you like that type.

But what was with the red dress she was wearing? A simple well-cut black dress would've been more suitable. Obviously, by her choice of such a bright color, she was a woman who craved attention.

She set her alarm and got into bed. After punching down her pillow, giving it a few hard smacks in her frustration, she laid down and closed her eyes.

She had a feeling it was going to be a long time before she fell asleep.

It was also beginning to look like she needed a more aggressive plan of action.

CHAPTER 23

Sophie's hands drifted down to cradle her stomach. Momentarily taken aback when she didn't feel the familiar baby bump she'd been living with for the past nine months, she jerked her hands away.

Then she smiled.

She was exhausted, yet at the same time, so wide awake.

She leaned back into the pillows of the hospital bed, her gaze drifting over to Chester, who was slowly walking around the room, a sleeping baby tucked in each arm. He was singing.

"Hush little babies, don't say a word,
Daddy's gonna buy you a mockingbird.
And if that mockingbird won't sing,
Daddy's gonna..."

He paused, a smile coming to his face, before he continued to sing.

"Daddy's gonna get you a World Series ring."

He glanced over at Sophie to see she was watching him. She was smiling, but it was a shaky smile. He studied her more closely to see she had her lips pressed tightly together to keep them from trembling.

Uh oh ... not good. You know what this means.

He slowly lowered each baby into the crib, arranging them close together. After he gazed down at them for a few moments, he gently tucked the blankets more securely around them before he made his way over to sit on the bed next to Sophie.

He kicked off his shoes. "Angel, can you move over?"

When he was settled next to her, he put his arm around her and rested his cheek to the top of her head. "Have I told you lately how much I love you? Because I do ... so, so much."

Her only response was to nod her head against him. He knew this was because she was crying. And she didn't want him to know.

So, he decided he was going to act completely clueless and let her cry.

As far as he was concerned, she could do whatever she wanted.

After watching her give birth to their two beautiful baby boys, a time during which he could only stand by feeling so completely helpless, he was in total awe of her strength and determination.

He couldn't even imagine what she was thinking right now. Or how she was feeling. Besides being completely exhausted, she had to have so many different emotions swirling around inside of her.

There was also the fact the nurse had pulled him aside to tell him not to worry. If Sophie cried a lot or became overly emotional, it was the hormones talking, she told him. This would go away with time.

He only knew, right now, he'd do anything for her. To think he'd thought of her being so small and fragile, and look what she pulled off.

His fingers running lightly through her hair, he felt her give a long, shaky sigh against him.

He smiled right before he began to sing, his lips moving softly in her hair.

"Hush little angel, don't you cry,
Chester's gonna buy you a mockingbird.
And if that mockingbird won't sing,
Chester's gonna buy you two diamond rings ..."

He reached into the back pocket of his jeans and pulled out his wallet. Her tears coming to a stop, Sophie watched as he took something from the wallet before he stuffed it back into his pocket. He reached for her right hand and after he put two diamond eternity rings on her ring finger, he adjusted them until they locked together.

He pressed his fingers to her lips. *"Shh* ... don't even say it. I know how you feel about me giving you gifts, but I will never stop giving you diamonds. These rings represent the beautiful babies you just brought into the world. It is only right I give these to you, if only to show how much I love and admire you right now. You're amazing, angel."

New tears forming, she studied the rings on her finger before she reached up to give him a kiss. "Oh Chester, thank- you. But I couldn't have done it without you."

She smiled. "After all, you did have a very important part in making this happen."

He chuckled, shaking his head. "My part seems to have been way too enjoyable and easy. And definitely, so little compared to what you had to go through."

His expression suddenly turned serious. "And this is why I've come to the decision two children are more than enough for us. There's no need for you to go through this again."

She leaned back to look into his eyes and noting the determined expression on his face, she tried not to smile. *"Hmm...* I see. No more, huh? What happened to the baseball team you had planned?"

She shook her head, still trying to hide her smile. "It seems so unfair."

When he merely shook his head, she settled more comfortably against him. "Chester, it wasn't that bad. And look what we've been given in return." They both gazed over at the two babies, still sleeping side by side in the crib, before Sophie reached for his hand. She gave a long sigh. "It's really so unbelievable."

It was her turn to be serious. "Of course, I'm not talking about doing this right away. I think we should see how we do with these two before we start on another one."

Chester chuckled. "And who knows? It could turn out to be another double delivery." His eyes lit up. "Or maybe even triplets."

At the horrified look on Sophie's face, he began to laugh as he gathered her even closer. "Oh angel, how I love teasing you. And I agree. We'll wait and see how it goes with these two. But I have a feeling we'll do just fine."

There was a soft knock on the door before a nurse came bustling into the room. She smiled when she saw the two sleeping babies. "Well, it looks like you two already have this parenting thing figured out. No worries."

She was confused when Sophie and Chester looked at each other and burst out laughing. Once they explained, she smiled. "I have a feeling you'll do a great job. You'll become sleep deprived, but that will pass by in a blur. I seriously believe this is nature's way of helping you through the first few months of your baby's life."

She handed them the papers she was holding. "But before you take these little cuties home with you, you need to fill out the information on these pages. I'll come by later to pick them up."

After she did a quick check on the babies and left the room, Sophie looked down at the papers. "They want the names. Are we still going with the two names we picked?"

Chester nodded. "Yes, Trevor Paul and Hudson James. Unless you've changed you mind?"

Sophie shook her head. "No, Trevor Paul and Hudson James it is."

She glanced over at the two in question before she turned to Chester, a worried expression forming on her face. "*Oh my God...* Chester, what have we done?"

He pulled her against him right before she started to cry again.

Yep. Emotions were running pretty high right now.

Having a baby will do that to you.

But having two?

Figure on doubling everything.

Chester was standing by the window. Holding one of the babies in his arms, he watched as the door to the room opened slightly. Carrie peeked into the room, a hesitant smile on her face.

He grinned. It was a grin that lit up his whole face, bringing her to grin right back at him. After he motioned for her to enter, he walked over to Sophie, who was holding the other baby.

After she was finally able to tear her gaze away from the sleeping bundle tucked against her, Sophie gazed up at him.

He smiled at her. "It looks like Aunt Carrie is here. Like she promised she would be."

Sophie glanced over just as Carrie turned to hold out her hand to someone in the hall. She was grinning as she brought Chris into the room with her.

This brought an even bigger smile from Chester. He leaned down to whisper in Sophie's ear.

"Ah … it also looks like Trevor and Hudson may not be the only new members to join our family."

CHAPTER 24

Hannah Michaels was excited.

Not even the brisk wind blowing off the lake, forcing her to tuck her face even deeper into the turned-up collar of her coat, was enough to ruin this good mood she was in. Keeping a tight grip on her shopping bag, packed with gifts, she hurried across the parking lot to the entrance of the hospital.

Once inside, she smiled at everyone she passed on her way to the elevator.

She had a lot to smile about. Two reasons, as a matter of fact. She was about to see her brand new nephews, Trevor Paul and Hudson James, for the first time. How Sophie and Chester had been able to keep the information they were having twins a secret, was beyond her.

Once she was in the elevator, she pushed the button for the fifth floor. As the doors began to close, a hand came between them, forcing them open with a jerk. She watched as a man slipped into the elevator with her.

When he looked over at her, his expression turned to one of surprise. A big smile coming over his face, he quickly whipped off the cowboy hat he was wearing and nodded. Almost as if he knew her

"Well, hi there." His voice was deep and if she wasn't mistaken, hinted at an Australian accent.

Maybe this explained the hat?

At her hesitant smile, he immediately looked embarrassed. After he gave her another smile, a much smaller one this time, he shrugged. "Sorry."

When he saw the button was pressed for the fifth floor, he sent her a quick glance, almost as if he planned to say something, Instead, he put his hat back on and moved to the other side of the elevator. After he jammed his hands in the front pockets of his jeans, he bowed his head and stared down at the floor.

She was confused. Had they met before? She didn't think so. Even though by the way he'd greeted her, it was as if they had.

But, come on … she was pretty sure she'd remember meeting someone like him.

In a heartbeat. How could you not? Even without the hat, he would be the kind of man you'd find hard to forget.

Since he now appeared to be deep in thought about whatever went on in the mind of a cowboy, she had the perfect opportunity to study him.

He was tall, very tall. At least a foot taller than she was. He was also very attractive. Let's be honest here… he was way more than what could be considered attractive. As her sister Sophie would say, he was what you would call a drop-dead-gorgeous-hunk-of-a-man.

His hair, cut in a slightly longer and layered style, was a deep, reddish-brown, a shade she'd describe as a deep mahogany. His eyes were also brown, like pools of a warm brandy, and framed by the longest eyelashes she'd ever seen on a man.

Seriously? You'd kill for eyelashes like his.

He also had that slightly rough and unshaven look going on. Almost as if he'd just returned from a long day of riding his horse, rounding up cattle, or whatever other activities your everyday, average cowboy would be involved in.

Umm … yeah, your imagination is really kicking in now. Next thing you know, you'll be looking for a horse out in the parking lot.

And even with the bulky sweater and down vest he wore, it was obvious he worked out on a regular basis. She had a feeling she wouldn't be at all disappointed at what was hidden beneath his attire.

But what she liked most about him, was the way his eyes crinkled at the corners when he smiled. An indication this was something he did quite often.

Yes, from what she could see, he was pretty darn near perfect.

Cowboy hat and all.

He cleared his throat.

She blinked, meeting his gaze.

A tentative smile on his face, he raised an eyebrow.

When she realized he'd caught her staring at him, it was her turn to be embarrassed. She stared down at her shopping bag, a blush rising in her face.

You should be thankful he couldn't know what you were thinking.

After all, she certainly didn't want him to get the impression she was interested in him. Because honestly? She wasn't.

She was merely curious. She was an artist, so this is what she did. She observed everyone and everything, always on the look-out for any new material she could use for her illustrations.

Ha ... this isn't the only reason you were staring at him. *Admit it, you're definitely attracted to him.*

In fact, she was actually starting to imagine what it would be like to have him as a boyfriend. She smiled just thinking about this.

However, to even have a chance of this happening, she needed to take the plunge and start up a conversation.

But, for some reason, she couldn't.

Besides the fact she had always been shy when it came to meeting someone new, especially when that someone was as hot as this cowboy, it was as if she'd suddenly forgotten how to talk.

The silence seemed to go on forever before the elevator finally came to a stop, the doors sliding open to the fifth floor. When he gestured for her to go ahead of him, she put her head down and practically sprinted past him out into the hallway. There she continued her fast pace, following the path of pink and blue footprints painted on the floor leading to the maternity ward.

As soon as she came to the glassed-in nursery for the newborns, her encounter on the elevator was almost, but not quite, forgotten. She scanned the rows of babies, searching for the cribs labeled with the name Mazzori.

She finally found them in the front row and right in the center. Her not even one-day-old nephews were sharing the same crib, curled up next to each other and sound asleep.

She set her shopping bag on the floor and leaned closer to the glass to get a better look.

She grinned. *They were beautiful.*

As far as she was concerned, they were by far, the most handsome babies in the room. She didn't even have to look around to know this.

Unable to tear her gaze away, she watched as one of the babies gave a huge yawn. When the yawn ended, he moved his head even closer to his brother, who scrunched up his face at the close contact.

She laughed.

Sean Young had watched the woman, who he knew as Hannah, go diving past him and out of the elevator before she set off in a fast trot down the hall. Since they were heading in the same direction, he followed behind, but at a much slower pace.

The last thing he wanted, was for her to think he was stalking her or something.

Uh, uh ... no way.

He didn't want to even go there. After the fiasco he went through with Amanda, he couldn't afford any additional publicity in his life, bad or good. He'd learned very quickly his choice of career frowned upon such things. Especially when it came to the fans.

When he'd first entered the elevator and saw Hannah, he'd been surprised.

Well, this wasn't completely true, because he'd actually hoped he'd run into her. Since she was Sophie's sister, he knew she would be stopping by the hospital to see Sophie and the babies.

But what were the odds they'd both arrive at the same time?

Then to share the same elevator?

You're not a big believer in fate, but this encounter seems more than a coincidence. It certainly couldn't be luck, considering the way your life has gone lately.

But as it turned out, these two things didn't really matter. Because it was obvious she had no idea who he was. Or even remotely remembered him.

But, wait a minute ... why do you even care? You have no interest in a relationship at this time. Remember? Isn't this what you've been telling yourself?

Yes, that's right.

His plan was to enjoy this new single life he'd been thrown into. Being left at the altar tended to change a guy's perspective on women in general.

Hell, he'd been made to look like a complete fool. So, he'd be damned if he was going to take the chance of something like that happening again.

But he didn't want to start thinking about that episode of his life, because he'd only get riled up. He was here to see his friend and congratulate him on the new additions to his family.

This was a time to celebrate, not a time to be feeling sorry for himself.

He'd now reached the maternity ward and lo and behold, there was Hannah. Against his better judgement, he slowly sauntered closer to where she was standing, observing the babies.

He smiled.

She had her face practically pressed up against the glass, something a little kid would do.

He moved to stand next to her, just in time to watch the antics of the two babies in the crib.

He grinned, suddenly feeling very happy to be sharing this with her.

So, when she started to laugh, he did, too.

Hannah turned to see the laugh had come from the man who'd shared the elevator with her. He cleared his throat before he spoke, his gaze fixed on the babies. "It looks like they're off to a good start, doesn't it?"

Was he speaking to her?

She shot a quick glance around them, to see there was no one else even remotely close by.

So, this had to mean his comment was aimed at her. A nervousness beginning to build inside of her, she nodded before she quickly turned her attention back to the babies.

And now she was even more confused.

Was he following her?

And if he was, why?

They stood in silence, their attention riveted to the sleeping babies.

She waited for him to leave.

But he didn't.

In fact, she could actually feel his gaze on her, his eyes studying her. This, for some reason, sent this deep shiver running through her, all the way from her head to her toes and back again. Bringing her to press her hand against the window to steady herself.

Now she was starting to worry. But at the same time, she was gripped with this sudden excitement.

This is your chance. You need to say something. Anything. Just start talking. Ask him why he's here. For all you know, he may be married and one of the babies in the nursery belongs to him.

She frowned at this sobering thought. Then, feeling extremely brave, she glanced up at him.

A bad move.

He was gazing down at her. And from what she could see, he looked like he was trying to hide a smile.

Oh no ... the smile is probably because of you. No doubt, he thinks you're a fool. Say something.

"So, is one of these yours?" She blurted this out, waving her hand toward the filled to capacity nursery.

He gave her a startled look, Then he began to laugh. Really laugh. A laugh that had her grinning, even though the brief thought flashed through her mind he might be laughing at her.

He stopped laughing enough to speak. *"Lord, no ..."* These two words came out in a long drawl, his accent even more pronounced. Then he shook his head. "Not that I don't like kids. Or babies. Come on, who doesn't love babies? Or kids, for that matter? But I'm not sure if I'm ready for that stage of my life yet."

Here he paused to gaze at her, a baffled expression spreading across his face. "At least I don't think I am."

He shook his head, very decisively. "Nope, right now I need to stay focused on my career. Only after I get everything in that department under control, can I even start thinking along those lines." He smiled. "You know ... marriage, kids, mini-van, turning into my father ..."

He laughed at this, evidently pleased with this attempt at humor.

Even though Hannah heard every word he said, she was having a hard time getting past the sound of his voice. Deep, with a sort of husky or rough tone, the more she heard it?

The more she liked it.

She found it quite sexy. She liked to think of it as sort of an easy, rugged, cowboy kind of voice.

What? Sexy? Easy rugged? As he would say, Lord, no ...

Jamming her hands in her pockets, if only to ground herself, she glanced up at him again. "I'm sorry. I thought you might be one of the fathers. And it's okay if you aren't ready yet. I'm sure one of these days you will be."

He gazed down at her, his expression unreadable. Then he smiled. "I believe you're right."

They smiled at each other before an awkwardness came between them, their attention swinging back to the babies. This was followed by another stretch of silence.

Finally, even though this wasn't something she'd normally do, she reached over to put her hand on his arm. This was only to get his attention, mind you. "I need to ask … have we met before? For some reason, I feel like I should know you."

He looked down at her hand before he shot a glance over at her, a funny expression on his face.

Immediately thinking he was uncomfortable with her touch, she, jerked her hand back. "I'm so sorry. I didn't mean … "

He cleared his throat before he smiled at her. "I, uh … I mean it's okay. Trust me, it is. I don't mind, really I don't. And in answer to your question, you don't really know me. But I know Chester. I'm on the team with him."

He hesitated. "As a matter of fact, I was at his wedding. At the time, I'd just joined the team for practice in Arizona and he was kind enough to invite me, since I was sort of lost."

At the look of concern on her face, he quickly shook his head. "Not lost in that I didn't know where I was going, of course. Just feeling new to everything. New country, new people and all."

He nervously adjusted his hat. "When I saw you that night, I asked who you were. They told me you were Sophie's sister and that your name is Hannah. But, I never got to talk to you. Or introduce myself."

A sudden smile lit up his face. "So, maybe now is a good time to do this?"

Without even asking, he reached for her hand, holding it a firm grip. He gave her a big smile, the genuineness of it making her heart skip a beat. "Hello, Hannah. It's great to finally meet you. I'm Sean Young. Something I probably should've told you right from the beginning."

A stricken look came over his face. "Not that you should know who I am. Or, I think I'm some kind of a big deal or something. No, I think it's only fair, if I know who you are, you should know who I am, too."

He shoved his hands in his vest pockets, giving a nervous laugh. "But now I don't seem to be making much sense, do I? Again, I'm sorry. I think it's because of you."

Now he was completely embarrassed. "Oh geeez … here I go again. What I mean is, I'm just so pumped I'm finally talking to you. But, as you can see, I'm not really good at choosing the right words when I'm around a beautiful woman."

Hannah was in shock. Her mouth falling open, she could only stare at him.

Did you hear right? How is this possible?

This man, this extremely handsome man, sexy accent and all, had asked about her. And you make him nervous. So much so, he can't even talk straight. All of this because he thinks you're beautiful.

You ... Hannah Michaels. Your everyday, average twenty-five-year-old woman.

Why?

Why you?

And believe it or not, she came right out and asked him. "May I ask why? Why you wanted to know who I am, I mean."

Then realizing she probably shouldn't have asked this, she shook her head. "Again, I'm sorry. You don't have to answer. I'll understand."

He gave her another big smile. "Don't be sorry. And I don't mind answering you. I guess, well ... I guess it was because you seemed like someone I'd like to get to know better."

The bewildered expression on her face made him wonder if he'd come on a little too strong; He was treading in unfamiliar territory, the women here so different from what he was used to back home.

So, he was quick to reassure her. "You know, as a friend."

The expression on her face went from hopeful, to one of disappointment, in zero seconds flat.

A friend?

Ah ... you should've known this was too good to be true.

Suddenly feeling both irritated and depressed at the same time, she gazed up at him for a few moments before she picked up her shopping bag. She shrugged. "Sure, if you like. Because who doesn't want new friends?"

Giving him a bright smile, she began backing away. "I'm sorry, I really should get going. Sophie and Chester are probably wondering where I am. It was nice meeting you."

She turned to quickly walk away, not an easy thing to do. She couldn't believe how hard it was to not look back, to see if he was watching her.

This was exactly what Sean was doing.

In fact, he followed her progress all the way down the hall, until she finally disappeared around the corner. And even then, he continued to stare in that direction.

He rubbed the back of his neck, his brow furrowed in thought.

What the hell?

He didn't get it. He thought he'd made it pretty clear he'd like to get to know her better. Then she just turns around and walks away?

He let out a frustrated groan, and removing his hat, he ran his hand through his hair. Evidently, this was some kind of a sign. An omen he needed to forget about women for good.

Because look what happened. It didn't matter who the woman was, he always wound up striking out.

Shoving his hat on his head, he turned on his heel and headed back to the elevator. He'd come back later. After he saw the shopping bag Hannah was carrying, he realized he probably should've brought a gift. He'd go pick up something now.

He jammed his hat down even harder on his head, mumbling to himself as he punched the button for the elevator. Alone this time, he rode it back down to the first floor.

He shook his head. He was so confused *Was it something you said?*

He honestly didn't have a clue.

Much later, Hannah was waiting for the elevator. She'd been at the hospital much longer than she'd intended.

Not that this was a bad thing. She'd been able to hold both Trevor and Hudson. And neither one had cried the entire time they were in her arms. So, she was feeling pretty good about this.

She just didn't understand what happened to him. You know, Sean, the guy from the elevator. Chester's teammate. Every time someone had come into Sophie and Chester's hospital room, she'd eagerly looked over at the door, expecting it to be him.

But it wasn't. Which didn't make sense. Did he change his mind and leave after they talked? Was it something she said?

Think about it... you certainly hadn't acted all that positively to his suggestion the two of you should be friends.

But, and she knew this was silly because she really didn't know anything about him, she wanted more than his friendship. There was something about the way he looked at her, that made her want to get closer.

Much closer. If only to find out more about him.

Well, it looks like that isn't going to happen, does it?

Because, what are the chances she'd run into him again?

Not good. At least she hadn't embarrassed herself by asking Chester a lot of questions about him. How stupid would that have been?

Really stupid.

She entered the elevator. After she punched the button to the main floor, she leaned against the elevator wall and closed her eyes, a frustrated sigh escaping her. She never got it right. And she was beginning to think after this, it was pretty obvious, she never would.

So, it was a somber Hannah who left the hospital. Wrapped up in her thoughts and her face once again tucked into the collar of her coat against the frigid wind, she didn't even notice someone waving to her as she opened her car door.

If she had, her mood would've improved dramatically.

Sean had just pulled into the hospital parking lot, when he saw Hannah get into her car.

Buy by the time he got out of his car, waving and yelling like crazy to get her attention, she had already begun to drive away.

It didn't help he had to go diving back into his moving car to put on the brakes. In his excitement, he'd jumped out of the car without putting it in park.

Thank God, you realized this before the car took off and plowed into something. You never would've heard the end of it, had this happened.

Yeah, it was bad enough he'd already had a few near misses with this driving on the right side of the road thing they had going on here in the states.

So now, he could only watch as Hannah's car disappeared from view.

Darn ...

He'd hoped, against all odds, she might still be at the hospital. And if she was, his plan had been to ask if she'd be interested in maybe getting a pizza. Or a hamburger. Or whatever she preferred. He didn't care.

You know, just an outing with a friend type of thing.

After all, he didn't want to push it. Not with her.

Because for some reason, ever since he first saw her at Chester's wedding, whenever he started thinking about his future?

She was always in it.

CHAPTER 25

"Hey, you have to let me know when we need to turn."

When Chris didn't receive a response to this, he glanced over at Carrie.

Her head resting against the back of the seat, her eyes were closed. There was a smile on her face.

He could certainly understand how she was feeling right now. It had been a long night and an even longer day all rolled into one. A time filled with so many mixed emotions, all rolled into one. He hoped everyone he'd met during the time they spent with Chester, Sophie and the babies at the hospital, would forgive him if he didn't remember their names.

He and Carrie had gone to lunch with Kevin and Abby. Alex, another one of the guys on the baseball team had joined them, along with his wife, Lisa.

He'd also met Carrie's Aunt Evelyn. He was feeling pretty confident he'd given her all the right answers to the volley of questions she'd thrown at him. Very seriously she went about this, actually pulling him aside and away from Carrie. He'd say it was a sure bet she now knew more about him than his own parents did.

He'd met so many people over the past twelve hours, his mind was now overflowing to the point nothing was making sense to him anymore.

Except for Carrie, that is.

He smiled over at her again.

It felt so good to finally be alone with her, even if it was only in his car.

After he brought his car to a stop for a red light, he reached over to take her hand. "Sweetheart, you need to help me out here. I'm not all too sure where we're going. I know you're exhausted. I am, too. But you can sleep all you want once we get to your place."

Her lashes slowly fluttering open, she turned her head to smile at him. "I wasn't sleeping, I was thinking. About how amazing it all is. How these two, brand new and perfect little people, have come into our lives. And now we're going to have the chance to watch them grow up, each with their own unique and different personalities."

She grinned at him. "And two boys. Oh my gosh, Sophie and Chester are going to have their hands full. Look how Connor kept us on our toes and we only had him for about twenty-four hours. Just imagine that, times two."

She began to laugh. "I'll bet you anything, Chester is already wondering how soon he'll be able to take them to the ballpark."

The light turned green. When they started to move again, her hand still in his, Chris cast a curious glance over at her. "What about you? Can you picture yourself in their place? I mean, as a parent? A mom?"

She gave this some serious thought before, a smile flashing across her face, she shrugged. "Honestly? Before today, I guess I never thought that much about it. But seeing those beautiful little babies and all of the love on Chez and Sophie's faces, I almost felt jealous. Wondering if I'd ever be lucky enough to experience having a child of my own."

She shook her head. "I didn't think this could be possible, but I feel like Chez and Sophie are more in love with each other now, than they were before the babies."

She glanced over at Chris, a tentative smile on her face. "I don't know, maybe I just imagined this?"

He almost didn't answer, his imagination having taken over as he envisioned having a child with her. This hit him so hard, he almost swerved the car off the road.

After he gained back control of both the car and his thoughts, in that order, he reclaimed her hand, giving it a gentle squeeze. "Sorry, I took my eyes off the road for a second. And, no, I don't think it's your imagination. I remember thinking they were very much in love when I met them at the wedding. And now, they've suddenly become this family of four, with even more love to go around."

He grinned. "I don't know how they will be feeling, say, fifteen years from now. Two teenage boys starting to drive at the same time? Or going out with girls?"

He shook his head. "I can't even imagine what this would be like." He shot her a quick smile "Not that I was wild and crazy when I was a teenager. Playing baseball and trying to keep up with Kevin kept me so busy I didn't have time to get into trouble."

Carrie laughed. "I have a feeling you weren't as perfect as you're making yourself out to be. Just as I know Chez will have his hands full keeping these little guys in line. I wonder if they'll play baseball, too?"

She suddenly pulled her hand from his and leaned forward to peer out the window. "Oh my gosh, we missed my street. We need to turn around at this next stop sign, so we can go back."

After he put the car in park and turned off the ignition, he grinned over at her. "We made it."

She smiled back at him. "Yes, finally. I can't wait to show you my little house, my pride and joy. If you saw it when I first bought it, you would've thought I was crazy." She laughed. "I have to admit, there were times I would've agreed. But now, with all the planning and renovations finally finished, I love it."

Before he opened his door, he leaned over to give her a kiss. "If you love it, I'll love it, too."

Chris set their suitcases next to the stairs going to the second floor. After a series of long and very mournful meows. Jingles came right up to him, weaving around and against his legs. This was her way of letting both him and Carrie know, after being left on her own for so long, she was in desperate need of some human companionship.

Someone stopping by twice a day to feed her certainly hadn't been enough.

As Carrie began to turn on the lights, Chris picked up the cat and sat down on the steps, taking softly to her as he ran his hand through her fur. He glanced over at Carrie, who was watching them, a smile on her face.

He smiled. "So, this is Jingles. I don't know much about cats, but she seems to have made herself comfortable here on my lap. I hope this means she approves? And she won't mind if I'm here to spend time with you?"

He held her gaze.

His eyes were searching hers with an intensity that sent her heart into high gear, almost beating out of control. She knew what he was asking. For it seemed whenever they'd found any time alone, something or someone managed to interfere, keeping them apart. And now he was wondering if Jingles could be the next in line to do this.

She smiled. "It looks like she'll be fine. "

With a loud purr, almost as if she knew they were talking about her, Jingles jumped off Chris's lap to go leaping up onto one of the chairs by the fireplace. Once settled, she peered at them through narrowed eyes.

No doubt she was wondering why they were both showing such an interest in what she was doing.

Carrie glanced over to see Chris was making his way over to her. Their eyes meeting, the message in his was clear. It was of a man who knew what he wanted and his patience had about reached its limit.

Nervously running her hand through her hair, she gave him a tentative smile. "So, are you hungry?"

These words no sooner out of her mouth, she sidestepped him to almost sprint the short distance to the kitchen. She yanked open the freezer door and pulled out the first covered container she could get her hands on. When she finally turned around, it was to find Chris was right behind her

She gave a breathy laugh, almost shoving the container right at him "My Aunt Evelyn made this clam chowder. You met her at the hospital, remember? She's an amazing cook."

He opened his mouth to say something to this, but he didn't have a chance. She'd already begun to ramble on, barely taking a breath between words.

"Unfortunately, I can't claim the same. Being an amazing cook, that is. I wish I'd taken her up on her offer to teach me, but you know how that goes. When you're young, you don't have time for things like that. So now I'm pretty clueless when it comes to being in the kitchen."

She shrugged, careful to avoid his eyes. "Unless it's something you can make in the microwave. I'm pretty good at that. Like popcorn. I've got that down to a science." Her eyes lighting up, she grinned up at him. "I can make some, if you'd like."

Here she finally stopped to take a breath. He didn't want popcorn. And he didn't want soup. Which meant she needed to stop talking.

But it was suddenly all too much. Her kitchen felt so small with him standing so close, that darn come-hither smile on his face aimed right at her.

It's not fair. He only has to give you that smile and you're putty in his hands. You can't fight it, even if you were to try.

She dropped her gaze to the container in her hands.

Her behavior wasn't making any sense. Especially since she hadn't been able to stop thinking about what almost happened less than twenty-four hours ago. When they returned to his apartment after the awards dinner and, unfortunately, only minutes before the call came from Chester about the babies.

She glanced up at him and their eyes meeting, it was obvious by the gleam in his, he was re-living this same memory, ready to continue from where they'd left off.

If you remember, you did promise him this.

She swallowed, her words, almost tripping over each other. "You're probably in the mood for something more than soup. Let me see what else I can find. In the meantime, we can start heating this up. It won't take long."

She began tugging at the lid and losing her grip, the container went flying out of her hands to almost hit him in the process. He made a grab for it, but it slipped out of his reach and went sliding across the counter to hit the floor with a loud bang. This sent Jingles flying off the chair and through the air with a series of loud meows before she went tearing up the stairs.

Miraculously, through all of this, the lid of the container remained intact.

Carrie watched Chris pick it up off the floor and put it back into the freezer. When he turned to her, she shrugged, giving him a weak smile.

He gently pulled her against him. "Carrie, it's only me. Remember me? Chris? What's wrong? Why are you so nervous?"

She buried her face in his chest, helplessly shaking her head.

His head dipped down until his mouth found hers, his lips teasing hers with feather-like kisses. At the same time, he slipped his hands under her sweater, his fingers moving in a slow trail over her bare skin. Everything he did, he did it slowly, almost reverently, waiting to see how she responded. Every move, every touch, every kiss. With the state she'd worked herself into, he didn't want her to feel he was pressuring her.

His words were a whisper against her cheek. "You are in complete control here. I won't do anything you don't want me to, okay?"

He felt a tremor run through her at his words before she nodded. Pressing even closer to him, she gave a soft sigh. "I know you won't. I don't know what's wrong with me. I really don't. I guess it's a combination of everything all at once.

The babies … the award …" She closed her eyes. "And you … *Oh my god … mostly you.*"

He pressed a kiss in her hair. "I know, it's been one hell of a last few days, hasn't it?"

She lifted her head to gaze up at him. A hell of a last few days? It was more like heaven, she wanted to tell him, this place they'd fallen in together. Instead, she reached up to wind her arms around his neck. "I haven't even thanked you yet for coming home with me. I'm so glad you did. And I'm so happy you're here with me now."

He shook his head, remembering how she'd so adamantly insisted she was going to make the drive from New York to Cleveland alone. Nothing he could say was going to change her mind. Little did she know, there wasn't even the slightest chance he was going to agree to this.

No, it just wasn't going to happen.

He moved to settle her even closer, smiling when he felt her begin to relax against him.

He shook his head again. "There's no way I was going to let you make the drive by yourself." He pressed another kiss in her hair, "And, there's no place I'd rather be than with you right now."

He now had her pressed against the counter, the heat radiating from him, bringing her to sigh against him. Everything about him was just so intoxicating. The feel of him so solid, so strong, so overwhelmingly masculine. The familiar scent of his cologne… of him. All this, coming at her all at once, made it hard for her to even think.

She closed her eyes as he began to speak. Lulled by the deep, calming tone of his voice, she soaked up the promises coming through in his words. "Even though I'm sure your Aunt Evelyn is a wonderful cook, I'm not hungry right now. At least not for clam chowder. Or any other kind of food. Certainly not when it looks like I have you all to myself."

He glanced around the room, his gaze falling on the chair, recently vacated by Jingles. "Even Jingles has recognized we need this time alone and has decided to respect our privacy."

Before she could even turn to check this out, he cupped the back of her head in his hand to bring her mouth to his. The kiss he gave her was slow and sweet, a kiss that just about stole any hesitancy she might have left at this point. He did this very thoroughly, as though he intended to savor every moment.

His lips going on to press a soft kiss to her eyelids, his whispers were a brush of warm breath against her face. "Tonight, you're finally all mine. No interruptions … No excuses … No thinking." He dropped a soft kiss to her jaw. "Or talking …" He pressed a trail of slow, hot kisses down her neck. "Or anything else your gorgeous mind might be dreaming up right now." His mouth came back to hover over hers. "Tonight, it will only be the two of us and from here on, I want your undivided attention. As I promise you'll have mine."

His voice slipped to a husky whisper. "I want to make love to you. Over and over and over … or until you tell me to stop." His next words came out in a long groan. "*God*, Carrie, I've been dreaming of this ever since the very first moment I saw you."

Oh my …

With this onslaught of kisses and whispered promises coming at her almost faster than she could handle, she was surprised she was even still standing. She was melting, suddenly very grateful for the support of the counter.

She opened her eyes, swept up in the heat of his gaze, unable to look away. Never before had a man looked at her like this. Or brought her to this state, this quiet hunger building inside of her, making her desperate for the promises he made.

Whatever he asked of her, she would give him.

She was the first to move. Her lips slowly curving into a smile, her fingers moved to the top button of his shirt. She slowly began to ease it through the buttonhole. "So, tell me, what exactly happens in these dreams you have about me?"

For a few seconds, he remained silent, his gaze fixed on her face. Then the corners of his mouth lifted in a slight smile. "*Hmm* … you really want to know, huh?"

She nodded, her hands stilling against his shirt as she gazed up at him, waiting for his answer.

Momentarily becoming lost in her eyes, he had to clear his throat, before he was able to speak. "Well, let me start out by saying, in every single dream, your body is pressed up against mine and you're gazing at me the exact same way you are right now. The look in your eyes telling me there's no other place you'd rather be than here with me. And your beautiful mouth ... your lips are parted, ready for my kiss. Like they are now." He pressed a soft kiss to her mouth as proof of this.

A smile flashing across his face, he glanced down to where her fingers had now moved down to the second button.

"And this button thing you've got going on right now? Definitely an added plus. Something that hasn't happened in any of my dreams. Maybe because I didn't get into a lot of the little details. But I like it, so please don't stop."

His eyes scanned the room before they settled on her face, another smile hovering at the corner of his lips. "But I'm afraid we're missing a key element here, the one thing always making an appearance in each and every one of my dreams. And this would be a bed."

She nodded, gently untangling herself from his arms. He waited, watching as she moved around the room to turn out the lights.

When she returned, he reached out to pull her back into his arms. But she shook her head and reaching for his hand, together, they climbed the steps to the second floor. She brought him into her bedroom, where she turned on the lamp on the dresser, a soft glow filling the room.

She turned to him and wrapping her arms around herself, her smile was shy. "This is my bedroom, but I also like to think of it as my retreat, a place to come whenever I want to get away from it all. This house originally had three-bedrooms, but I decided to combine two of the bedrooms into a master suite."

She shrugged. "Everyone told me it was a bad idea when it came to resale purposes, but since I can't imagine ever wanting to leave, well ..."

At the sight of him, hands shoved in the pockets of his jeans and a patient smile on his face, her words came to an abrupt halt.

She dragged her hands back through her hair, closing her eyes. She was doing it again. Running on with all of this information she knew he wasn't interested in.

At least not right now, he wasn't.

"I'm sorry ... so, so, sorry. I know the last thing you probably want to hear right now is all about the décor of my bedroom. It's just that I ... well, I don't want you to think ..."

She gave a frustrated sigh. "I seriously don't know what my problem is."

He was at her side in an instant, his hands framing her face. After he studied her for a few moments, he smiled. "It's okay. We have all the time in the world." At this observation, a flash of concern crossed his face. "At least I think we do. So, let me take a look here."

And though she was right about how this was the absolute last thing he wanted to do at this time, he casually strolled around the room, taking it all in.

He decided it wasn't what you would call a frilly bedroom, but at the same time, the decor definitely hinted it was a woman who occupied the space. The bottom third of the walls were done in a white wainscoting, the wall above painted a calming shade of periwinkle. The window treatments and bedding were a periwinkle, soft yellow and spring green garden design on white. The traditional trellis design, of the huge area rug anchoring the bed, complimented these color choices.

The style of furniture was French Country, the finish a soft white. In one corner, two chairs were grouped around a table to form an intimate sitting area. They were upholstered in a striped polished cotton of the same colors found in the window treatments and bedding. There was an ornate crystal chandelier hanging from the center of the raised ceiling and a set of French doors leading out to a small balcony.

He gave a very quick glance into the adjoining spa-like bathroom, the large expanse of white marble accented with touches of the same colors used in the bedroom.

His very, *very* brief inspection complete, probably the quickest he'd ever done when doing an appraisal, Chris made his way over to where Carrie was standing, watching him.

She smiled. "So? What do you think?"

His smile was bemused. What did he think?

Yes … what exactly was he thinking?

Well, if he were to be truthful, he'd have to say he couldn't remember a damn thing he saw. No, thinking was something he was absolutely incapable of at the moment. At least not about the interior design of the room. Or what the re-sale value of her house would be.

No, Carrie was what filled his mind. How much he wanted to hold her in his arms. Kiss her. Touch her. How he wanted to be able to look into her beautiful eyes and whisper his words of love to her. Words he was becoming so weary of holding inside.

In fact, his mind had already taken them over to the bed, so he could love her the way he had been dreaming about for far too long.

So, this was exactly what he did.

In one swift move, he swept her up in his arms. Gently tossing her on the bed, he kicked off his shoes and settled next to her. She was laughing, the astonished expression on her face bringing a chuckle from him. "Caught you by surprise, didn't I, baby? Let this be a lesson to you. You need to be ready for anything when you're with me."

His hand smoothing her hair back from her face, he leaned in to give her a kiss. "In answer to what I think about this room? You made the right move converting it into a large master suite. If you ever did put this house on the market, this room alone would sell it for you."

He kissed her again, longer and slower this time, a thrill running through him when she reached up to tangle her fingers in his hair, pulling his head down to prolong the kiss.

His fingers went on to lightly trace the curve of her cheek before trailing down over her jaw. "But I really don't want to talk about decorating and selling houses right now. I'd rather continue our conversation of a few minutes ago. The one about my dreams and the part you played in them. Like now, when I threw you on the bed, your response was quite different from what I envisioned in my dreams."

He watched her mouth twitch as she tried to suppress a smile. She reached over to resume her work on his shirt buttons, slowly undoing the second and then the third button before she finally spoke. "Please do continue. I'm listening."

His mouth came to hover over hers. "*Ah ... but first ...*" His kiss sent a slow heat flowing through her, this deep ache that had been building inside of her since they first met, this desperate need for him, now completely consuming her. This made it hard for her to concentrate on what she was doing, the buttons slipping through her fingers as she eagerly returned the kiss.

He smiled down at her flushed cheeks. "Let me just say, you always reacted very passionately, practically tearing my clothes off in your haste to get closer to me."

After leaving a trail of kisses down her throat, ending with a slow, hot kiss to where he could feel her pulse beating as if in a race, his mouth teased hers with his whisper "As you can see, I have a very vivid imagination. Especially when it comes to you."

Under his close scrutiny, she continued to unbutton the remaining buttons going down his shirt, pausing to give him a kiss between each one. When her hands drifted down to his belt buckle, he groaned, his hand stopping her.

"Oh no you don't, it's my turn. It's only fair we take turns." After he shrugged out of his shirt, his mouth swooped back to cover hers while he began the serious task of removing the rest of their clothing. He worked slowly, following each move with a kiss, each kiss becoming longer and more heated between each article of clothing he sent flying off the bed.

With his hands and his lips everywhere, for Carrie, the simple act of breathing was almost impossible. She couldn't think. She couldn't speak. She kept trying to pull him closer, her hands reaching out in an attempt to help him, if only to make him move faster.

But this wasn't what he'd planned. He wanted this first time with her to be something they would always remember. And even though he was having a much harder time than he'd anticipated, he was still making every effort to take it slow. Afraid if he didn't, he'd explode into a frenzy of need, taking her like there was no tomorrow.

It wasn't helping everywhere he touched her, his fingers coming into contact with the softness and warmth of her skin, she gave these little, soft lingering sighs. This alone was enough to drive him crazy, urging him on.

Their clothing finally scattered all about them, he moved to gaze down into her face. The huskiness of his voice betrayed the emotion he was feeling. "This is where I have to tell you all of my dreams would fade away. I wasn't even able to imagine going beyond this point with you. It just never seemed possible."

He bowed his head for a moment. When he looked up, the hunger in his gaze sent her heart hammering even harder in her chest. He dipped his head to rest his forehead against hers. "I think I was afraid if I did finish the dream, everything else would come to an end. And you'd be lost to me."

His whisper was as soft as the kiss he gave her. "But now, here we are."

"Yes, I'm here …" And, believe it or not, this was all she had to say.

She would have liked to say so much more, but now completely surrounded by him, the only thing on her mind was how much she wanted this with him. Though they hadn't yet come together, she knew this was the beginning of something she'd want again and again.

Just like he'd promised. And she'd never tell him to stop.

You want to make his dreams become everything he'd imagined them to be.

Her hands going up to clasp behind his neck, she pulled him down against her. At the contact, he buried his face in her hair, letting out a low growl that seemed to travel from deep within his soul and right into hers.

"*God, Carrie* … I wanted to take this slow, but I don't think … I don't know how much longer I can hold …"

Her mouth finding his, her hands pulled him even closer.

"Then don't."

CHAPTER 26

It was that peaceful hour just before dawn, the skies bordering between the darkness of night and the early morning light.

Carrie was drifting in a world somewhere between sleep and wakefulness. Her eyes closed, and in this dreamlike state, she was vaguely aware of what sounded like sleet bouncing off the windows. She gave a long, contented sigh as she burrowed deeper under the warmth of the quilt.

She brushed up against something. More like someone. Someone decidedly male.

This was more than enough to shock all of her senses into becoming completely awake.

Chris ...

Her lashes fluttering open, she fell right into his eyes. A place she knew, without a moment's hesitation, would be her home from this moment on.

The sound of sleet hitting the windows was what woke Chris. Now lazily basking in the aftermath of the night, both his mind and his body were still humming with the memory of all he and Carrie had shared. How they'd loved each other until, completely spent, they finally fell asleep in each other's arms.

When he'd opened his eyes to find her next to him, his first thought was he'd been caught up in another dream. For the longest time, he hadn't moved. Then ever so cautiously, he'd inched closer, his eyes searching her face, almost devouring her with his gaze.

Her hands tucked under her face and her cheeks flushed with sleep, her lips were parted almost as though she was waiting for his kiss. Tempted to do just that, but reluctant to wake her, he settled with running his fingers lightly through the silky strands of her hair, spread across the pillow in total disarray. He smiled when her lips curved in a small smile in response to even this simple touch.

She was, without a doubt, the most beautiful woman he'd ever known.

She was gorgeous.

And she's yours.

Almost holding his breath, he watched as she began to stir. She gave a big sigh as she burrowed under the quilt, moving closer. When her leg brushed up against him, she froze, her eyes suddenly looking right into his.

And he knew ...

She would always be a part of everything he was.

This knowledge tucked inside of him, he gave her a slow smile as he reached over to gently stroke her cheek with his fingertips. His voice was gruff with sleep.

"Hey ..."

Definitely a sexy voice, she'd have to say.

He looked perfect. Even with his hair all crazy, sticking out in every direction and his face, rough and in need of a shave. This, along with the memory of their night together, still so fresh in her mind, she felt herself growing light-headed, suddenly swept up in another rush of desire.

Let's face it, she didn't have a chance.

Her heart caught up in her throat, she moved even closer to give him a soft, lingering kiss.

"Hey ..."

He pulled her into the curve of his arm, exhaling a long, contented sigh. His lips went on to move in her hair. *"Mmmm ... this is how I'd like to wake up every morning for the rest of my life. With you beside me, I wouldn't need anything more."*

As these words came out of his mouth, he realized he'd never meant anything more than what he just said. It was true. She really was all he'd ever need. And all he'd ever want. With her by his side, he'd be able to face the world and everything that was handed to him.

Unfortunately, his comment was met with silence.

For him, this was a bit worrisome, sending him off into a whole new train of thought, one he didn't even want to consider. This being what his life would be without her. No, this was enough to scare the hell out of him.

So hopefully, her silence was only because she was trying to come up with the right words?

But if this was the case, she was certainly taking her time. Enough to make him extremely nervous. Because one really shouldn't have to think about something like this, should they?

He knew he didn't.

He cleared his throat. "I believe this is one of those times when it's your turn to jump in with a response. Maybe say something like, wow, that would be great. Or, yes, I'm feeling the same way. Whatever you feel most comfortable with. But hey, you take your time. I can wait. Because I'm not planning on going anywhere just yet."

She stirred against him to press a kiss to his shoulder.

"I love you."

These three little words coming from her were so soft, he almost missed them. In fact, he wanted to be sure he'd heard right. Moving to face her, he tenderly smoothed the hair back from her face, his eyes searching hers.

"Say it again. I want to hear you say it again."

She smiled. A smile that reached all the way into her eyes.

"I. Love. You. Only. You."

She took a deep breath, her eyes suddenly so bright in the dimness of the room. "I want you to know I've never said these words before to anyone. And this is because I've never felt this way about anyone before. But now I know what it's like to love someone with everything I have. And to want someone as much as I want you."

She shrugged, her smile shy before she reached up to lightly run her fingers through his hair. "I'm pretty sure my heart has been yours from the very first moment we met. It will always be yours."

It had taken every ounce of courage she had to say this. And now she could only hold her breath, almost afraid of what he might say in return. Or, an even worse possibility, what he wouldn't say.

So many times, in past relationships, she'd made the mistake of jumping in too quickly to let her feelings be known. And, just as many times, she'd set herself up for disappointment.

He was silent. The way he was gazing at her, his answer shining in his eyes everything she wanted to believe, her only hope was this time it was for real... he was for real.

She closed her eyes.

Oh god, please make it real.

"Carrie, open your eyes."

She did as he asked, watching as his mouth slowly curved into a smile. "I love you, too, baby. I've known this from this very first second I looked into your eyes." Here he stopped to shake his head. "Spilling that drink on you was the best thing I've ever done, because look where it brought me ... here with you. And there's no place I'd rather be. So, I'll take you up on the offer of your heart in an instant. But only if you promise to hold on to mine in return."

Her eyes slowly began to fill with tears before she closed them, shaking her head. To say he was concerned was putting it mildly. He framed the side of her face in his hand. "What is it? Tell me."

She opened her eyes, her voice barely a whisper. "I don't want you to say it if you don't mean it."

Between her tears and uncertainty, coming at him all at once, he wasn't quite sure of what to say, his response coming out in a stutter. "But, I ... you just ... I ..."

At the panic in his voice, she uttered a shaky laugh before she put her hand over his mouth. "I'm so sorry. I shouldn't have said that. But you have to understand, I never do very well at this kind of thing. It seems like every relationship I've been in, has always ended badly."

Now she was off and running, unable to stop the words flying out of her mouth even if she tried. It was suddenly so important she let him know this. She knew it was a big gamble to throw it at him and all at once. But with him, more than anyone else, she needed to be sure.

She took a big gulping breath. "If what we have turns out not to be the real thing, I don't think I could take it. I really don't. I think back to all of those months after we met, when I didn't know if I was ever going to see you again. And I remember how miserable I was. And now, after what we just shared, if everything were to fall apart, it would be so much worse. I don't even want to think of what this would do to me."

She searched his face, her eyes pleading with him to understand. "When it comes to you, I so want to believe it will be different."

He framed her face in his hands, his thumbs wiping away the tears. He slowly shook his head.

She was beginning to feel desperate. "I'm sorry … I …"

The rest of her words never had a chance. Instead they were swallowed up in his kiss. A kiss that went on and on and on, with each of them falling back into the kiss where the other left off.

For Carrie, it was like the first kiss they shared back on that February night. The kiss she'd initiated after he came to her rescue.

A kiss, that for her, opened a whole new world.

For Chris, this was so much better than that first kiss they shared. It was certainly better than the kiss he'd tucked away in his memory all through the months that followed, the nagging fear he'd never see her again always hovering in the back of his mind.

Yes, this was definitely better.

They were where they were meant to be.

CHAPTER 27

This time when Carrie opened her eyes, it was to a room filled with the late morning sunshine.

She glanced over at the space next to her on the bed

It was empty.

The aroma of freshly brewed coffee was what finally brought her out of bed. She pulled on a pair of flannel pajama pants and a tee shirt. After she gathered her hair up in a loose ponytail, she went running down the stairs, only to come to a halt when she came to the last step.

Who was Chris talking to?

She peeked around the corner to see he was in the kitchen, in the midst of buttering a piece of toast.

Jingles was next to him, lounging on the floor, as she went about the serious task of grooming herself.

She watched Chris smile down at the cat. "Well, what do you know, it appears you're finally happy now you've had something to eat? I hope you'll remember I'm the one who spent a good ten minutes rifling through every drawer and cabinet in this kitchen in search of your food. If only so you wouldn't go meowing your way upstairs to wake Carrie."

He grinned as Jingles came over to rub against his leg. "*Ah* ... so you are thankful, huh? I hope this means I can count on you to return the favor and be just as nice to me in the future."

Here he paused to give her a very serious look, pointing the knife at her for emphasis. "Just so you're aware, I'm planning on spending a lot more time with Carrie. A whole lot of time. Which means it would be nice if we could all be friends."

He abruptly tilted his head, to remain completely still for a few moments.

Then he chuckled.

He set the knife down on the counter and bent closer to Jingles, his voice an exaggerated whisper. "You're not going to believe this, but I'm pretty sure Carrie is hiding right around the corner and on the stairs as I speak, listening in on our conversation. Pretty silly, huh? I'm rather curious to know what she thinks about what I just told you. How about you?"

He leaned back against the counter and crossing his arms, a big smile spread across his face as he watched Carrie slowly slip around the corner. His gaze never leaving hers, he waited for her to walk right into his arms.

He let out a long, contented sigh. This was followed by a deep chuckle rumbling in her ear. "Busted, huh? Believe me, you've got such a hold on me, I can sense when you're anywhere nearby. I'm drawn to you like a magnet."

He pushed away from her and his gaze roaming over her face, he let out a long sigh. "*God*, baby, even in the morning, you're so damn gorgeous. I'd be more than happy to make breakfast every morning if it meant I could share it with you."

There was a teasing smile on her face. "You better be careful about the promises you make, because I might just take you up on them. I've already told you I'm not all that good of a cook."

At first, he didn't respond. This was because he was too busy pulling at the tie holding her ponytail, to then watch as her hair tumbled down over her shoulders. Burying his hands in the shining waves, he lifted her face to his. "So beautiful. Everything about you is so damn perfect."

His gaze held hers. "My offer will always stand. I could care less if you can't cook. Or sew. Or anything else. The only thing I care about is that you're mine."

After he gave her a kiss, he studied her for a few moments, a faint smile touching his lips "I love you, princess. I don't think you have any idea how much."

Her fingers going up to link behind his neck, she gazed up at him. She shook her head. "Oh, I think you're so wrong about that. Because I'm pretty sure I love you just as much, if not even more."

This called for another kiss before he drew away from her. "Come on, you must be hungry. I know I'm starving. Then you can tell me what plans you've already cooked up for the rest of the day. I'm game for whatever you've decided."

After Carrie popped the last dish in the dishwasher and turned it on, she gave a satisfied glance around the clean kitchen. She could hear the sound of water running, which meant Chris was still in the shower.

They had made tentative plans for the day. Before they dropped in to see Chester and Sophie at the hospital again, they planned to stop somewhere to buy gifts for the babies.

She also wanted to show him her office.

And the rest of the day?

Carrie didn't care what they did. As long as they spent it together.

She folded the dishtowel and draping it over the edge of the sink, she gazed out the window. The bright morning sunshine of earlier was now a thing of the past and it had started to rain again. Or sleet. Whatever it was, it was beginning to look like it was going to be another cold and wet November day. But this was what could be expected in Cleveland this time of year.

She sighed.

Bad weather aside, she should be happy. And she was. She was unbelievably happy. This love she felt for Chris was like nothing she'd ever experienced before. And for the very first time ever, she was feeling optimistic enough to believe this time, what they had together, was a love meant to last a lifetime.

But at the same time, there was this feeling of impending doom hanging over her.

So, what's the problem?

They were both trying to avoid what they didn't want to talk about, and this was Chris's imminent return to New York. Of course, he had to go back. He had a job, a very good job. A job he was building into a very successful career. That he'd dropped everything to come with her to Cleveland was a huge sacrifice on his part.

And as much as she'd like, she couldn't go back to New York with him. The last time she had opened her laptop, it showed her schedule for the next several days packed with even more meetings and consultations.

This reminded her, she really needed to give Marion a raise. A big raise. A large part of the reason business was so good, was due to her great organizational skills, something Carrie had struggled with from the beginning. But now it felt like they were working too hard, putting in too many hours. A person needed to have a good balance between work and personal time.

No ... your career shouldn't be your top priority in life. Right?

A wry smile touched her lips.

Are you the same person, who, only a short time ago, convinced yourself, your career was enough?

But then, along came Chris ...

And now your priorities have changed. You want a plan. A forever, until death do us part, plan. And you want this with him.

She smiled, remembering the pact they made in February, the night of Abby and Kevin's wedding. The pact that began with the promise of their first dance. They had vowed, if neither had married within three years, they'd marry each other, big wedding and all.

At the time the chances of this happening seemed more hopeful than possible.

But now?

Even with the time remaining now down to a little over two years, this seemed like a long time to wait.

But she was getting ahead of herself. And for all she knew, Chris may have completely forgotten this pact.

One more quick glance around the kitchen and she headed for the stairs. The sound of water running had stopped. This meant Chris was finished with his shower and would soon be out of the bathroom.

She needed to search through her closet to find something to wear.

Chris swiped his hand across the fogged-up bathroom mirror. Unfortunately, the refection that greeted him was a very somber one, indeed.

Absentmindedly picking up the hairdryer and turning it on, he began drying his hair.

His thoughts were all over the place. Used to being in control of any situation, for the first time in his life, he felt like he had absolutely no say over what was going to happen next. As you can imagine, for him, this was very confusing.

Carrie had shaken up the very foundation he stood upon. And the funny thing about this? He was fine with it, more than fine.

So, things are good, right?

Well, maybe …

His plan was to leave for New York first thing tomorrow morning. Already things were beginning to pile up at the office, the numerous messages and emails he'd received a confirmation of this. He certainly couldn't expect his assistant to keep carrying the brunt of the load.

But with Carrie now back in his life, the only thing that felt right was spending all his time with her. And if he were to be honest, he was almost afraid to let her out of his sight. He'd already learned his lesson about what could happen if he did.

You'll only be a quick hour and a half flight away. Or, as you've now learned, a mere seven-hour drive.

Yes, he was more than aware of this. But he was also at the point in his life, this wasn't an option. He didn't want what he had with Carrie to turn into one of those relationships that involved commuting back and forth, only to see each other on weekends. Week after week, month after month, the time they spent together coming second to their careers.

Nope, his mind was made up. He knew what he wanted.

From now on, Carrie would always come first. His career, or anything else in his life? These would now be a distant second.

He wanted to be able to drop in on her during the day, wherever she was. If only just to say hi and give her a kiss to let her know she was always in his thoughts.

And *my god* … he couldn't even begin to explain how much he wanted to share all of his nights with her. Nights that continued into the early morning hours. If only to be able to hold her in his arms.

He wanted the reassurance that after he finally closed his eyes at night and until the morning when he opened them, she'd be there. So, he could tell her how much he loved her, with a passion he now realized he'd been saving for only her.

You're not asking for much, are you?

He turned off the hairdryer to look into the mirror, his determined face staring right back at him.

Yep, it looked like he had his work cut out for him.

He needed to come up with a plan.

A really good plan.

Carrie walked out of her closet, a change of clothes draped over her arm.

Almost at the same moment, Chris came out of the bathroom, his only attire a towel slung loosely around his hips. Running his hand through his hair and deep in thought, at first, he didn't even notice she was in the room.

It was only after her sharp intake of breath, he looked over at her, a smile lighting up his face.

Considering the night they had shared, that Carrie became so flustered at seeing him like this, didn't make sense. But then again, she certainly wasn't used to having such a beautiful man coming out of her bathroom. In the middle of the day ... and attired only in what appeared to be one of her skimpier-sized towels.

And yes, to her?

He was beautiful.

Absolutely and perfectly beautiful, in every way possible.

She came to an abrupt stop, clutching the clothes she was carrying to her chest. "Oh, I'm sorry. I didn't know. I mean ... what I mean is, I wanted to pick out something to wear before I took a shower and I thought you'd still be in the bathroom." She started to slowly back out of the room. "But I can wait. You go ahead and ..."

For some reason, this made his smile become even bigger. Before she could even take another step, he was next to her. Taking the clothing she was carrying and tossing them on the chair, he pulled her into his arms, the fresh scent of soap, shaving lotion and shampoo coming at her all at once. She burrowed her face in his chest, intoxicated by it all.

He managed to lead them, almost in a dance, until they were both on the bed. With him gazing down at her, the grin still on his face. "So, I think I could get used to this, having you around in the mornings."

He glanced over at the clock on the nightstand. "Or should I say, in the afternoon. And the evening. Or most definitely, all through the night. What do you think?"

He leaned in to place a soft kiss to her mouth, his voice a husky whisper against her lips. "But in the future, how about we time it a little better?" Plan on meeting up in the shower? At the same time?"

His hand drifting under her tee shirt, his touch sent a tremor racing through her. At her soft moan, his mouth captured hers in another kiss. She could feel his smile against her lips when she clasped her hands together behind his neck, surrendering to the kiss.

"*Hmm ...* I ... whatever you want. You smell so good. And you feel so, *so* wonderful. So, please … please kiss me again." Her voice coming out even huskier than usual, it traveled through him like a fast-moving storm, striking every nerve.

And now he was the one who was lost, completely caught up in her spell. But not so much that he wasn't able to do as she asked him.

Along with so much more.

Curled up next to Chris, her head resting on his shoulder, Carrie's eyes were closed. She felt like she was floating, still trying to come down to earth after the love they'd shared between them.

Chris shifted beneath her. His fingers brushing through her hair, his voice rumbled through her, deep and contented. "I think we've got something special here, princess. Something really, really good."

When she remained silent, he lifted his head to peer down at her.

"Carrie?"

Refusing to meet his gaze, her voice was muffled against his chest. "But what's going to happen now? We both know you have to go back to New York and I have to stay here. But I don't want to be one of those couples caught up in a long-distance relationship. Especially with you. I'm so afraid we'll eventually drift apart. Or lose each other again."

Seeking reassurance, her hand moved across his chest, searching for his. He linked their fingers, bringing them to his mouth for a kiss.

Her words had completely thrown him. Because this was exactly what he had been thinking only a short time ago. So, now he was the one who was silent.

He finally rolled onto his side, taking her with him. Face to face, she waited for what felt like the longest time, bordering on forever, before he spoke.

"Carrie, you're like the final piece in the puzzle of my life. The one I've been searching for, the one to make me complete. And now that I've found you, everything is the way it should be. You've given me hope for the future, as long as it's with you. So, there's no way we're going to lose each other. I won't let this happen."

He brushed the hair back from her face, the look in his eyes so tender it took a real effort on her part not to cry.

He saw this. "Don't cry, princess. We'll figure it out. Maybe not right away, but we will. I have faith in us and even more faith in you. You only need to hold on tight and trust me."

His gaze holding hers, he waited.

She nodded. "I love you. I love you so much." Then she smiled as she began tracing his lips with her fingertip. It was a very mischievous smile. "And now, I really need to take a shower."

Her eyes going wide, her frown was dramatic. "It's too bad you already took yours because…" She left the sentence hanging before she gave a slight shrug, her eyes never leaving his.

He, of course, quickly caught on to what she was suggesting. He rolled away from her and pushing himself off the bed, he pulled her up against him. He smiled down at her.

"I've heard it said, one can never be too clean."

CHAPTER 28

Chris laid his phone on the desk and leaned back in the chair. After spending the last twenty minutes on the phone with Carrie, his smile was bittersweet.

He could see her so clearly in his mind. But even with this and hearing her voice, it wasn't enough.

God, you miss her.

Five days and counting… then she would be with him. At this thought, another smile flashed across his face. Just like Carrie, it appeared he was also keeping track of the days.

This a reminder he needed to check on the plans he'd made for the weekend, he logged into his computer. He wanted to make sure everything was ready to go so it would be a birthday celebration she would always remember.

And the beginning of a whole new chapter in her life. Her life with you. All of her weekends, her days and her nights.

He pushed away from the desk and walked over to gaze out the window. The clear blue skies and the bright sunshine reminded him of the last day he shared with Carrie in Cleveland.

Then again, everything reminded him of her. He closed his eyes.

Lady in red …

He gazed around the room, wondering what the hell he was doing. This was what neither of them wanted, him here in Manhattan and her in Cleveland. Spending time with their memories, instead of each other.

And this was all for what? A prime office location in the biggest city in the world? A full staff of people dependent on his leadership for their livelihood?

Ah ... don't forget the constant reminder your reputation of being the best at what you do, could so easily be trumped by the competition.

But none of this seemed important anymore.

He shook his head, a wry smile on his face. He must be flat-out crazy. Most people would kill for what he had.

Yep, you're crazy, all right.

Crazy for Carrie.

His phone rang.

With a sigh, he walked over to pick it up. But he had a smile on his face. It seemed lately, it was always there.

And again, this would be all because of Carrie

Carrie stared at her phone, a dreamy expression on her face. After ending the call with Chris, she was so tempted to book a flight and fly to New York. Swept away with the possibility of this even happening, she closed her eyes, imaging Chris opening the door to find her standing on his front steps. He would take her in his arms, kiss her like there was no tomorrow and after that? Well, she was pretty sure they'd find something to do.

You'd definitely wear your red shoes.

She sighed. There was no time for dreaming. She needed to get back to work. She laid out her newest design plan on the large conference table in her office. When her phone rang, she almost let the call switch over to Marion, but with the good mood she was in, she decided to answer it herself.

This was a move that would turn out to be her first mistake.

"Carrie Mazzori here. May I help you?"

Her greeting was met with silence. About to delete the call, she saw the number had a New York area code.

Now, this is when her intuition kicked in, screaming out a warning to end the call. So, you'd think she'd listen and hang up, right?

But she didn't.

This would be her second mistake.

Instead, she spoke louder this time. "Hello?"

"Carrie?"

She almost dropped the phone. It was a voice she'd hoped to never hear again in her lifetime.

Lauren ...

Her heart hammering in her chest, she slowly sank down into her chair. She swallowed. "Yes … yes, this is Carrie."

Hang up. Now. Whatever she has to say, it's not going to be good.

But for some reason, it was as if she'd suddenly become paralyzed, unable to lift her finger to hit the end button.

And, yes … this was her third mistake. Probably her worst so far.

"This is Lauren Fisher. I've heard you're a friend of Chris Gardner."

A friend?

Even though she was tempted to tell her differently, Carrie remained silent.

"Hello? Are you still there?"

Carrie shook her head, clearing her throat. "Yes, I'm here."

Lauren voice was very businesslike, almost as if she was about to offer Carrie a deal. This, Carrie was soon to find out, was exactly what she had in mind.

"I don't know if you're aware of this, but Scott Fisher is my father. It's because of him, Chris is now where he's at in his career. But this could change very quickly if my father were to find out Chris isn't the man he thought he was."

Carrie closed her eyes. She wanted to tell her to stop talking. Or tell her she wasn't going to listen. Anything to make her go away.

Closing her eyes, she desperately sent a plea up to God. If only to ask him, maybe plead with him, to please, *please* stop Lauren from saying what she was so sure she was going to say next.

But evidently, God was busy. Or he decided he wasn't going to help her out with this one.

A sick feeling slowly building in her stomach, she could only listen.

"I always get what I want. And Chris is on the top of my want list." Lauren laughed, an arrogant laugh. "Come on, you have to agree Chris and I are a perfect match. Add in my family's business ties and the support of my father and there's no limit to what Chris can achieve."

Here she paused. Maybe for effect?

If so, it worked.

"So … I'm suggesting you drop out of the picture. Completely. And if you don't? Well, let's just say once I talk to my father, Chris's future won't be so bright anymore. And, I wonder… would you really still want him if this were to happen? Something tells me you wouldn't."

This was when Carrie finally found her voice. Granted it was shaky and a voice that probably didn't sound very convincing, but it was the best she could do. "I can't believe you'd actually do something like this. If only to fulfill your wish list. You can't possibly love Chris, if you do. And, you're wrong. I'll stand by him no matter what happens, career or no career. He's more important to me than anything."

Again, Lauren laughed. "You are so naïve. This is the way most marriages come about when big money or business mergers are involved. Trust me, I know Chris wants it all. He made this perfectly clear during the time we were together."

Trust her?

This was the last thing Carrie knew she should do, anger coming through in her voice. "I can't believe we're even discussing this. Chris needs to know what you're implying. I'm sure he'd be shocked."

Lauren laughed again. "Shocked? I seriously doubt this. But, you go right ahead and tell him. And if you do, I'll definitely have that talk with my father. If it comes down to which one of us he should believe, Chris or me? I'm sure I don't have to tell you who'll win that contest."

This was followed by a long silence.

Her head down on her hand and her eyes closed, Carrie didn't know what to say.

So ... she hit end.

For the longest time, she stared at her computer, almost hypnotized by the screen saver bouncing around. She felt numb, only one word echoing in her mind.

Why?

She didn't understand. How could someone think it was okay to do something like this?

Her phone rang again, but this time, she let Marion pick up the call. Instead, she reached over to turn on her computer. After typing out a name, she hit search. Within seconds her screen was completely filled.

It appeared there was a lot of information available about Scott Fisher.

It was completely dark when Carrie finally left her office to start her drive home.

Her original plan had been to stop in to see the babies tonight. Chester had left her a message they were all now home and she was welcome to come over anytime. He'd also hinted they could probably use her help.

She wasn't sure if ... no, she *knew* she couldn't to do this. Chester and Sophie had been asking a lot of questions about her and Chris. After Lauren's call, and what she learned from her search on the computer, she felt like she no longer had the right answers.

Or, for that matter, any answers.

Her mind was filled with sales numbers, forecasts and mergers. Along with what she now knew was a very long list of the successful and wealthy people in the New York real estate business.

All of them, it seemed, with ties to Scott Fisher.

When she finally walked into her house and turned on the lights, the first thing she saw was the sweater Chris had left behind, draped over the arm of the sofa. She picked it up and closing her eyes, she held it up to her face, breathing in the scent of his cologne, of him.

When she had let him know he'd left the sweater behind, he'd laughed. He confessed he had done this on purpose, his way of leaving a small part of him with her until they could be together again.

He'd gone on to tease her, telling her since it was his favorite sweater, this was a guarantee he'd be back.

She sank down on the sofa and burying her face in the sweater, she began to cry.

She cried for the longest time.

With only Jingles to comfort her.

Later that same evening, Chris unlocked the door of his apartment. He flicked a switch, flooding the hallway with light.

He gave a big sigh of relief.

Home sweet home.

After he flipped through the mail, he changed into his sweats.

It had been a long day, to finally end after a late dinner with one of his most demanding clients … a dinner he thought would never end. Now he only wanted to relax. Maybe watch a little TV before he finally called it a night.

He was about to connect his phone to the charger when he saw he'd missed a call from Carrie about forty-five minutes ago. Throwing himself down on the sofa, he was smiling as he hit her number.

"Chris …"

The sound of her voice when she answered was enough to make him forget all about the day he had.

"Hey princess, what's up? Miss me?"

In the silence that followed, he immediately sensed something wasn't right.

Uh oh …

He tried again. "Hey, is something wrong? With you? Or the babies? I know they were coming home today."

Carrie finally spoke, her voice sounding strained. "No, the babies are home and they're fine. I … I was supposed to go there tonight, but I couldn't. I … how was your dinner with your client?"

Her eyes closed, she was leaning against the kitchen counter. She was stalling, searching for something to say.

Anything …

If only to avoid giving him the real reason she'd called.

He sighed. "Baby, right now my dinner isn't what's important, you are. I can tell by your voice you're upset about something. Whatever the problem, together, we can work it out."

At his words, she clutched the phone even harder against her ear, trying so desperately not to cry.

No, this isn't something we can fix. Because for him, you're the problem

She took a deep, gulping breath, her words pouring out. "I have to cancel for the weekend. I'm sorry, but I don't think we should do this. I've been thinking… and, well, you and I… I don't think it's a good idea. Not only for this weekend but for the long term. You have your life in New York and I have my life here. And after going over our options, I really don't see any way of compromising enough to make it work."

While she was telling him this, he had risen to his feet in disbelief, stunned by her words. Dragging his hand through his hair, he tried to think. There was only thing running through his mind, and this was he never should have left her.

His job, his apartment, everything. None of these mattered if he didn't have her.

What the hell were you thinking? You should have figured it out by now. When you leave, something always goes wrong.

"Chris?"

He rubbed the back of his neck. He wasn't sure he could get his brain to work with his mouth. So he could answer her without sounding like a complete idiot.

He cleared his throat. "Carrie, where is all of this coming from? It's not making any sense."

When he didn't receive an answer, he began pacing back and forth. He glanced down at his watch. "I'm going to book a flight. We need to talk in person. Because I'm having a really hard time trying to figure out why you suddenly feel this way."

Carrie pushed away from the counter

No, no, no ... you can't allow him to do this. You won't be able to stand your ground if he does.

Her voice was barely audible. "No, I don't want you to come here. It won't do any good, because there's really nothing more to say. One day you'll look back and thank me, I know you will."

The tears now flowing down her face, she could hardly talk. "I've got to go. Again, I'm sorry. So, so, sorry."

Chris was frustrated. And angry. It was bad enough she was telling him this over the phone, but now she didn't even want to discuss it?

There's really nothing more to say? And one day you'll thank me?

He didn't think so.

But before he had a chance to tell her this, he realized she had ended the call.

He stared down at his phone in shock.

What the hell just happened here?

He gazed around the room, his eyes drawn to the painting hanging above the mantle. The painting he purchased from The Gallery East... Early Evening in Spring. He had been looking forward to seeing the expression on Carrie's face when she saw it hanging in the same place once occupied by his big screen TV.

It was his way of showing her he knew what he wanted in life now. No more changing channels for him.

This is when it hit him. It didn't matter anymore.

Not one damn bit.

CHAPTER 29

There's really no shortcut to forgetting someone.
You just have to endure missing them every day.
Until you don't anymore.
~ Anonymous

The skies were just starting to show a hint of dawn when Carrie unlocked the door to her office the next morning.

After a sleepless night, crying until she didn't think it was possible to shed another tear, she came to the decision the only cure would be to completely immerse herself in her work.

The work she'd neglected while living the fairy tale life she'd let herself get caught up in with Chris. This would be the only way she'd eventually be able to forget about him.

Yeah, right. Like there's even a chance this is going to happen.

Almost angrily brushing at the sudden tears, she turned on her computer. She needed to get to work. She needed to move on.

Chris had also spent a very long and restless night. It was finally at four in the morning, when he saw the reflection of his exhausted and

276

haggard face in the bathroom mirror, he knew he had to do something.

Anything, he didn't care what it was. He only knew he couldn't leave things the way they were.

His mood had been fluctuating between despair and anger. And the only way he'd be able to rid himself of this raw and empty feeling inside of him was to confront Carrie, face to face.

You need a reason. A really good, logical and honest reason to understand. Maybe it still won't be enough, but you need to at least give it a shot.

Within seconds he was in his office and on his computer looking up flights to Cleveland. A half hour later, he was in a taxi on his way to the airport.

She had told him there was nothing to be done, but he felt differently.

He wanted only one thing. And this was for Carrie to look into his eyes and tell him she meant everything she'd said to him over the phone.

And she didn't love him after all.

Only then would he believe it was over.

After an uneventful flight, and a long wait in line for a car rental, Chris finally pulled into a parking space in front of Carrie's office.

And now, in the reception area, he was only a few feet away from her door.

He was nervous, more nervous than he could ever remember. He felt as though his life was on the line.

Which he would be quick to tell you, it was.

It wasn't helping that Marion, Carrie's new assistant, had greeted him with a look that could only be described as very hostile.

He gave her a tentative smile. "Hi, Marion. Is Carrie in her office?"

She hesitated, as though she wasn't quite sure she wanted to give him this information.

She finally gave a curt nod. "Yes, she's been holed up in there all morning. I think she came in really early, because she was already here when I arrived. She told me she was not to be disturbed, no exceptions."

She gave him an accusing look. "She appears to be very upset about something. Do you happen to know why?"

Cautiously moving towards Carrie's office, his hand now resting on the doorknob, his expression was unreadable. "I guess you could say this is why I'm here. And even though she asked to be left alone, I'm going to take my chances."

He shot her a quick smile. "Don't worry, I'll take the blame if she gets mad."

After struggling her way through the morning, Carrie was now staring blindly out her office window. She blinked, slowly gazing around her office. She was wasting her time. She had no interest in paint samples or fabric swatches.

Not with the mood she was in.

Nothing looked right.

Nothing *was* right.

She needed a distraction. Maybe this would be a good time to visit Sophie and Chester. Surely spending time with the babies would make her feel better. Or at least take her mind off this mess she'd made with her life.

She opened her desk drawer and pulled out her purse. As she came to her feet, she heard Marion talking to someone in the reception area. It was someone with a voice she'd recognize anywhere, anytime.

Her hand going to her throat, she froze.

She could only watch as Chris walked into her office.

Chris looked over to see Carrie standing by her desk.

The look of longing that flashed across her face when she saw him, was the first thing he noticed.

This gave him hope. Unfortunately, he was to find this was short-lived.

For a few moments they eyed each other, Chris warily, Carrie in shock.

When she realized she was shaking, she sank down into her chair and closed her eyes. Everything she wanted to say, she couldn't, the words frozen in her throat.

Chris was the first to speak, the tone of his voice a combination of pain and anger. "You told me not to come, but I knew I'd never be able to live with myself if I didn't. So, after a very long night, I booked the first flight I could find. And here I am."

She only shook her head.

He made his way across the room and placing his hands, palms down, on her desk, he leaned in close. "Carrie, I want you to look at me. So, you can tell me what the hell is going on. And just to forewarn you, I'm not planning on leaving until we resolve this."

Her head jerked up, an angry expression flooding her face. "Forewarn me? Until we resolve this? Is this what I am to you? Just another business deal you want to finalize? Well, I'm sorry, but this isn't going to happen. Maybe you'd be better off finding a woman who's better suited for that kind of life. A woman who idolizes you for the success you've become and puts you on a pedestal. Because you're not going to get this from me."

When he stepped back, a look of such total shock on his face, she wanted to crawl across the desk, throw her arms around him and tell him she didn't mean it like that.

No, no, no ... She had no idea why the words came out the way they had.

Because it wasn't what she'd intended to say. Or what she believed. *God, no ...*

She'd only wanted to let him know she wasn't the right woman to be a part of the life he deserved.

Because you have nothing to offer him in return...

He searched her face, desperately trying to find something there, anything ... to let him know why she said what she had. But in his confused state, he was only able to see her anger.

He bowed his head and closing his eyes, his voice was weary. "Carrie, I didn't come here to argue. This is the absolute last thing I want to do. I just need to understand. I want you to explain to me, why you came to the decision it's over between us." He swallowed. "I thought … well, what I mean is, I was so sure what we have is something meant to last a lifetime."

He gazed up at her, so much emotion in his eyes, she quickly had to look away.

He groaned. "Carrie, please … I want you to look at me and tell me you meant everything you said on the phone. And then …" He paused, his next words rough with emotion. "Then I want you to look right in my eyes and tell me you don't love me anymore. If you can do this, then I'll leave."

The silence between them seemed to go on forever. He waited, watching. She didn't move, her head bowed and her hands in her lap.

He cleared his throat. "Carrie?"

Still avoiding his gaze, she finally spoke. "You should leave."

He dragged his hand through his hair, his voice resigned. "Okay. I'm at a loss here. I guess you were right, there really was no reason for me to make the trip. Because it's clear you're not going to tell me what's really going on."

When this was met with silence, he gave a frustrated sigh. "I'm going to leave. I don't know where the hell I'm going to go quite yet, but if you decide you want to talk, you know how to reach me, anytime. Because, God help me, no matter how you feel about me right now, I still love you. I'll always love you. And this is never going to change."

As he turned to walk out of the room, it took everything he had to not look back, if only to say something more. Because there had to be some magical words he could say to make her change her mind.

There had to be, right?

He shook his head.

With the state they'd both worked themselves into, it might be better for him to leave. God knows, the last thing he wanted to do, was say something he shouldn't. At this point, he didn't trust himself not to do that.

Obviously, he should've listened to her. Nothing had been solved. And now, any hope had been drained from him, leaving him so damned tired. So much so, he couldn't even think straight.

You tried. It's all up to her now. You can only hope.

He turned to leave.

In the state he was in, he failed to pay attention to where he was going.

Only seconds after Chris arrived, Sam Bridges also pulled into the parking lot. Since the last time he saw Carrie was when they were in New York, he decided it was about time he stopped by her office to check on her.

He was almost embarrassed he'd waited until now, but hey, give him a break. Striking out with two women, who also happened to be sisters, and this all taking place on the same night? This was enough to make any man want to keep a low profile for a while.

Talk about a blow to your ego.

He wanted to congratulate Carrie on the award she won. He also missed the almost daily conversations and the laughter they shared.

So, when he walked into the reception area of her building, the last thing he expected to hear was the sound of angry voices coming from her office.

With Carrie's one of them.

He and Marion tried to pretend they couldn't hear what was being said in Carrie's office. But they could. In fact, they were able to hear almost every word.

Just as Sam was wondering if he should come back another time, Marion picked up her purse and slipping into her coat, she gave him a weak smile. "Can you tell Carrie I went to lunch? You're more than welcome to wait here for her if you'd like."

With that, she was out the door and gone.

Now Sam didn't know what to do.

His concern for Carrie finally winning over, his intention was to casually enter her office and announce his presence.

But he never made it. Instead, he collided with Chris as he came charging out the door. Reaching out to steady the both of them, Sam immediately recognized him as the guy who'd taken off after Carrie at the gallery preview.

Oh, geeez ... this can't possibly be good.

He made light of his next words. "*Whoa ...* sorry. But hey, what's your hurry?"

"Sam ..." This came from Carrie, who came over to join them.

Slowly dragging his hand through his hair, Chris glanced from her to Sam and this was when, for him, everything began to make sense. Evidently this Sam meant more to Carrie than she'd let on.

His laugh was harsh, his words addressed to Carrie. "Ah... so, this is Sam. Now I'm beginning to understand." His gaze going once more to Sam, he shook his head. "I guess this is my clue to leave."

Sam and Carrie watched him leave.

Finally gazing up at Sam, a look of anguish on her face, Carrie shook her head. "I didn't want to do this, I didn't. But I had to, Sam. I had no choice."

Even though he didn't understand what she was trying to tell him, he did the only thing he could.

He held her in his arms as she cried.

Unfortunately, Chris was able to see all of this from his rental car. And this more than confirmed what he now suspected.

He started up the car and after he drove it out of the parking lot, he headed for the freeway. He had told Carrie he didn't know what he was going to do, but now his choice was obvious.

He was going to drive back to New York.

He'd already done it once.

One more time should about do it for him.

Carrie stared down at the cup of coffee she was cradling in her hands.

It was cold.

Marion had brought it to her when she returned from her lunch break and now it was cold.

But this was okay. She really didn't want coffee. She'd really only been using it to warm her hands. Ever since Chris had walked out of her office, she hadn't been able to get warm.

When he left, it appeared he'd taken the life right out of her.

What she wanted, more than anything, was to go home.

Where she could crawl into bed, hide under the covers and go to sleep for as long as it took to erase everything going so terribly wrong in her life right now.

This way, when she finally woke up, everything would be back to how it had been before.

"Do you want me to heat up your coffee? It has to be cold."

She gazed over at Sam. That he was still here, made her want to start crying all over again. She wanted to tell him, he didn't have to stay, she'd be fine on her own, but she didn't have the energy to do this.

Nor was she okay.

She really hadn't told Sam much. Only that she'd decided a relationship between her and Chris would be too hard, their careers demanding too much of them to make it work. So, it would be better to end it now before things became more complicated.

And now, thinking about this, she was almost beginning to believe she had done the right thing by sending Chris away.

Almost ... but not quite.

She hadn't told Sam about the call she received from Lauren. She was still debating whether she should tell him what Lauren had threatened. Not that she didn't think he wouldn't believe her. No, it was only because she didn't think he'd understand how much Lauren scared her.

Managing a faint smile, she shook her head at his offer to heat up her coffee.

Sam gave a long sigh and leaning forward in his seat, for a few moments, he gazed seriously at her. Definitely not a look she was used to seeing from him.

"Carrie, why is it I feel like you're not telling me everything?"

She started to shake her head again, but then the words just came out. "She called me again yesterday. Lauren… you know, the woman who told me she was Chris's fiancée."

Sam leaned back in his chair, his expression almost triumphant. Finally, they were getting somewhere. "*Ah, ha* … I knew she was somehow involved in this. Why did she call you?"

She told him everything Lauren had said, all of her threats. When she finished, Sam was shaking his head.

"Carrie … Carrie … Carrie … Haven't you learned anything from what happened last time? If you ask me, this Lauren sounds like she's definitely got a screw loose. Chris doesn't want her. He wants you. And as far as needing her father's help? I have a feeling he doesn't need help from anyone."

He smiled, slowly shaking his head. "*My god*, Carrie… he got on a plane to come here so he could tell you how much he loves you. No man does something like this unless he's in love. Trust me, this is from a man's point of view."

She studied him for a few seconds before she answered him. But it wasn't in regards to his comment. "What happened between you and Livy? I could've sworn there was some serious chemistry going on with the two of you. Instead, she's back with Zack. I don't get it."

Taken by surprise, for the longest time he was silent. Just when she began to think he wasn't going to respond at all, he shrugged

"Evidently it was the wrong kind of chemistry. Because it's obvious there's still something between her and this Zack. And to be honest, I really don't know how I feel. I only know she keeps popping up in my mind. And this keeps happening more than I'd like to admit."

He shrugged again. "So, in answer to your question, I don't have a damn clue."

Carrie was grinning.

Something he knew he had reason to be happy about, since he hadn't seen this from her since he'd arrived.

He grinned back at her. "I'm a real piece of work, aren't I?"

She laughed. Another good sign. "Oh Sam, I'm so grateful to have you as a friend. And Livy? Let's just say she can be very stubborn at times."

When he gave her a look of mock surprise at her comment, she grinned again. "She's always been like this. But she'll figure it out. I have a feeling you stirred up feelings she doesn't know how to handle. And by going back with Zack, she's playing it safe. Just be patient, ok?"

Sam nodded as he tried not to look too pleased with what she said. He cleared his throat. "Okay. Duly noted. But enough about me... you're the one we need to talk about. Do you want to know what I think?"

At her nod, he continued. "I think you should take a day or two to give both of you time to cool down. Then you get on a plane and make that trip to New York. I know you said the plan was for this to take place on Wednesday, but don't wait until then. Take a chance and surprise him. I guarantee you he'll be thrilled."

She didn't respond, her attention on the marker she held in her hand, nervously capping and uncapping it. When he reached over to place his hand over hers to stop this, she gazed up at him, a worried look on her face. "But what if he isn't? And what about Lauren?"

He shook his head. "Don't even think like that. Need I have to remind you again, he came here to tell you how much he loves you? And Lauren? I have a feeling she's full of a lot of empty threats. I bet her father doesn't have a clue of what she did and if he did, he'd be mad as all get out. As successful as he is, he certainly isn't going to take the chance of muddying his reputation over something like this."

He stood and after giving a long stretch, he motioned to her. "Come on, I'm going to take you out to lunch. Then you're going to take the rest of the day off, maybe get some sleep."

He smiled. "You've got a big weekend coming up."

CHAPTER 30

It had been two days since Chris made the trip to Cleveland, and just about everyone in the office had made it a point to stay out of his way.

He knew his mood was nasty, but to be honest?

He didn't give a damn.

He left his desk again to wander over to the window. He was pretty sure this was his tenth trip so far this morning. And, as he'd done each time before, he stared down at the city, not really paying any attention to what was out there. After a few minutes of this, he wandered back to his desk.

He couldn't seem to sit still. It was as though both his mind and his body were on alert, waiting for something to happen.

Yeah, like anything good is going to happen. It's been over forty-eight hours and you still haven't heard from Carrie. Which probably means you never will.

He glanced over to where his phone was on his desk. Then, jamming his hands in his trouser pockets, he gazed over towards the window again.

He'd be damned if he was going to check again to see if she'd called.

He sat at his desk, wearily pulling a pad of paper in front of him. For a few minutes, he stared at it. Because honestly? Everything seemed so fruitless, not even worth the effort. Finally, he reached for his pen. His plan was to write down a list of what he should be doing. Maybe this would galvanize him to actually get something done.

He was hard at this when he heard someone clear their throat.

He glanced up to see he had a visitor.

It was Emily.

Emily had come into the city to meet friends for lunch and an afternoon of shopping.

She was worried about Chris. A few days ago, he'd left a voice message to let her know he would be out of town for a couple of days. Thinking he'd surely be back by now, she called him this morning.

But he hadn't answered. Nor had he responded to her voice message.

This was *so* not like him. He always got back to her, even if it was only just a quick text to say hi. So, she'd know he was all right.

She was also curious as to whether he knew he was the subject of a blog written by some woman in Manhattan. Advised by a friend to check it out, both she and John now realized Connor hadn't been exaggerating about what he told them about Carrie.

And even though John told her not to get involved, she was determined to find out what was going on.

And what better way to do this, than stop by to see him in person.

One look at Chris, and Emily wanted to take out her phone and call John, if only to tell him she'd been right.

Because something was definitely wrong. She was used to seeing Chris always so perfectly groomed, but the Chris now in front of her was a sorry sight.

She dove right in, not even taking the time to say hi. *"Hmm ... who are you? And what have you done with my brother?"*

He remained stone faced.

So, she dug deeper. "What's going on? You didn't return my call and now I find you looking like you haven't shaved or put a comb to your hair in days. For heaven's sake, look at how wrinkled your suit and shirt are. I hope to God, you haven't been sleeping in them."

He gave her a long look before he answered, his voice dry. "Well, it's good to see you, too."

After he rubbed his hand over his chin, he glanced down at his shirt, making a feeble attempt to smooth out the wrinkles. "Yeah, I know I'm not looking my best. And no, I didn't sleep in my clothes. *Geeeez* ... give me some credit here."

He abruptly gave a frustrated sigh, throwing his pen down on the desk. "And tell me, does it really matter? No, it sure as hell doesn't. In fact, nothing matters anymore."

Now Emily was even more concerned.

This was definitely not the Chris she knew. But she thought she had a pretty good idea what put him in this mood. Or, should she say, *who* put him in this mood.

Which meant it was time to bring out the evidence. Reaching into her purse for the copy she'd made of the blog post about him and Carrie, she pushed it across the desk to him.

"Who is Carrie Mazzori and why haven't you told me about her? The only information I have so far is what I read in the blog post you're now holding, along with what John and I learned from Connor."

She laughed. "I must say, we found Connor's comments to be very interesting. He told us he really liked Carrie, she's very pretty, but, and here's the kicker, you aren't having a baby just yet."

Chris glanced up at her, an actual smile appearing on his face as he shook his head. Then, he frowned, his attention going back to the paper in front of him.

After giving it a quick scan, he pushed it back across the desk to her.

He shrugged. "Unfortunately, none of what is written here holds true anymore. At least not as far as Carrie is concerned."

Emily held his gaze. "Do you want to tell me about it?"

He shook his head. "No, because talking about it isn't going to do any good. Carrie has already made it quite clear she doesn't want to be with me anymore. I even flew to Cleveland, hoping we could talk about it and she'd change her mind. But that turned out to be a mistake."

A vision of Sam holding Carrie in his arms popping into his mind, he closed his eyes. "A huge mistake, I'm afraid."

He pushed away from his desk and walked over to look out the window. In his mind, he noted this would be number eleven.

He gave a short laugh. It appeared this was another way Carrie had gotten to him. He was starting to count everything. If only to hold on to the hope, if he kept count, there was a better chance of a future between them.

Which made absolutely no sense whatsoever.

So not only are you frustrated, angry and clueless, it also appears you are now on the verge of becoming completely crazy.

His back to Emily, he remained silent.

Concerned, she finally came to stand next to him. "I'm sorry. Maybe …"

He turned to her, his expression almost threatening. "There is no maybe. It's all up to her now. I told her if she changes her mind, she knows how to reach me. "He shook his head. "But I'm not counting on it."

Emily sighed. "Oh Chris, you haven't changed a bit from when we were kids. You're still so stubborn. And a little advice here? You don't try to make a deal with the person you love. Or give them an ultimatum. If you really want her, you have to fight for her, the heck with your pride."

When he remained silent, she glanced at her watch before she gave another sigh. "I've got to get going. I'm meeting friends for lunch and shopping. But I'll stop by your place later and bring dinner. I'll text John and tell him to pick me up there. He's here in meetings all day and we're going to take in a show later."

She reached up to give him a kiss on the cheek and in typical

Emily fashion, he heard her give one more dramatic sigh on her way out of his office.

It was dark when Chris finally shrugged into his coat, ready to call it a day. As he was about to turn out the lights, he hesitated, and making his way over to the window, he took in one more look at the city.

For a few minutes he gazed out at what appeared to be the lights of a billion windows.

He remembered Carrie telling him, when she'd checked into the hotel, she wondered if he could be in one of the buildings she could see from her hotel room. And how she'd waved, just in case.

A slow smile on his face, he lifted his hand and gave a tentative wave.

Silly, yeah. He knew this.

But he was hoping for a miracle.

Little did Chris know, he would've had better luck had he looked up at the sky. Because one of those planes, circling among the stars as it waited to land, was carrying all he could ever want.

For at that very same moment, Carrie was gazing down at the amazing light show that was Manhattan at night. As she became caught up in the oohs and aahs from the rest of the passengers on her flight, she couldn't help but feel optimistic.

Like Chris, she was also hoping for a miracle.

CHAPTER 31

It's easy to fall in love, but sometimes
it's hard to find someone who will catch you.
~ Anonymous

Emily set the bag down on the counter.

"I think I may have ordered too much. But, look at it this way, you'll have dinner for tomorrow, too. We have salad, bread, chicken parmesan, pasta and oh, good … they remembered I asked for extra sauce."

Chris glanced over to where she was pulling the take-out containers out of the bag and setting them on the counter.

"That's great." He nodded as he continued to work at opening a bottle of wine, throwing every bit of concentration he could into the job.

This was because he was trying not to think about the last time he'd opened a bottle of wine.

It had been the last night he spent with Carrie before he returned to New York.

They had been sitting on her bed, a pizza between them. After he'd finally managed to open the wine, he glanced over to see Carrie was watching him, the look on her face enough to have him forget about everything but her. The next thing he knew, the pizza and wine were on the floor and she was in his arms.

He stopped to smile at the memory of this before he gave an almost angry pull at the cork, a grunt of satisfaction coming from him when it finally popped out of the bottle.

After he poured out the wine and gave Emily one of the glasses, he proposed a toast.

"Here's to good times, celebrating Thanksgiving with family."

As soon as these words came out of his mouth, he groaned, shaking his head.

How will this even have a chance of happening? This was supposed to be your time with Carrie. You're weekend together to celebrate her birthday.

Choosing to ignore his dramatics, Emily set her wine glass on the counter and handed him a plate piled high with food. "Here, eat."

After she filled a plate for herself, she picked up her fork. "I really shouldn't be eating this, since John and I are going out to dinner after the show, but I'm starving. And I did only have a salad for lunch."

Chris smiled, shaking his head. "You don't have to make excuses to me. Just eat."

After a few moments of silence, Emily turned to him. "So, will you still be coming for dinner on Thanksgiving? Connor will be so disappointed if you don't. He keeps asking me if you and... uh, well, I mean... if you'll be there. He has a new game he wants to play with you. I swear, he'd play games twenty-four-seven if we let him."

She set her fork down, frowning over at Chris. "I hope this doesn't mean he's going to become a gambler."

Chris laughed. "Hey, I like games. And I'm not a gambler."

She gave him a sly look. "Yes, that's true. But maybe it's about time you should start. And I don't mean with games or your business. I'm talking about your personal life here. It's good to take chances every once in a while."

He wiped his mouth with his napkin before he gave her a long look. "I really don't think I need any more lectures from..."

The rest of his answer was cut off by the sound of the doorbell.

Emily started to stand, but he stopped her. "I'll answer it, you go ahead and eat. It's probably John."

He went sprinting down the stairs and opened the door. "It looks like you're just in—"

His words came to an abrupt halt.

It wasn't John standing in front of him.

It was Carrie.

"Hi."

This one word coming out in a husky whisper, Carrie swallowed.

Her heart feeling like it was beating a million beats a minute, she anxiously searched Chris's face, waiting for him to answer. When he only stared at her, she gave him a hesitant smile.

The smile is what finally moved Chris to action. His hand keeping a tight grip on the door, he closed his eyes.

Are you hallucinating? You must be.

He opened his eyes to see, no, she was still there. She was real.

She smiled again, a more nervous smile this time. "I thought… well, I thought I'd come a day early. I hope this is okay?"

He ran his hand slowly through his hair. It was shaking.

This sent such a flood of emotion rushing through her, she had to close her eyes. Blinking furiously, she willed herself not to cry.

"Carrie …" This came from him in a long sigh as he began to move closer. "I …"

"Chris, whoever you're talking to, either invite them in or tell them you have to go. Your dinner is getting cold. And I don't have much time before I have to leave for the show."

Carrie glanced up the stairs, to where this voice was coming from. A woman was leaning over the railing, peering down at them.

A woman with long, blonde hair.

In a panic, Carrie began backing away, her hand going to her mouth.

Oh, god … no, no. This can't be happening.

She sent Chris an anguished look and after grabbing the handle of her suitcase, she turned to go running down the steps, the suitcase bouncing behind her on each step.

Chris was in an even more of a state shock.

Again? She's running away from you again?

Galvanized into action, he started after her, only to realize he wasn't wearing shoes. He turned to go flying down the hall to his bedroom, where he pulled on the first shoes he could find. Sprinting back down the hall, he went charging out the door.

Confused, Emily watched all of this from the railing before she finally called out to him. "Chris, what are you doing? You aren't even wearing a coat. Chris?"

He didn't hear her.

He was already gone.

Chris went running down the steps. Shooting a glance in each direction, he finally saw Carrie. She was almost running, dragging her suitcase over the uneven sidewalk behind her. And he'd be willing to bet she didn't have a clue of where she was going.

Her only goal to get away from you, it seems.

So, he was smiling as he took off after her. Because, running away or not, it really was a miracle.

She was here.

And even better?

She was here to see him.

Carrie had absolutely no idea where she was going, only that she needed to get as far away as she could. Evidently, it had been a really, *really* stupid idea to surprise him like this.

Why did you even listen to Sam? He's a man, remember? Just because he was right once, doesn't mean he knows what he's talking about.

Chris's voice came from behind her. "Carrie, come on ... please stop. Because you're not going to lose me. If I have to, I'll follow you all the way to wherever it is you think you're going."

She slowed her run to a walk, confused by the tone of his voice. It almost sounded like he was smiling.

This immediately made her angry. There certainly wasn't anything to be smiling about right now.

She tossed her answer over her shoulder. "Just go away. Evidently, I made a mistake by coming here. Go back to whatever you were doing. I'll be fine."

He chuckled. Now granted, he knew this probably wasn't a good time to see the humor in what was happening, but truthfully? He was just so damn happy she was here. He was also pretty sure he knew why she'd taken off in such a hurry.

You'll eventually have to get to the bottom of this. But for now? You need her to turn around and listen to you

He was now right behind her, something she was trying to ignore. But it was when he chuckled, she whirled around to face him, her voice angry. "I have no idea why you think this is so funny."

He flashed that crooked smile, setting her heart fluttering. And, even in the dark, she could see the teasing gleam in his eyes.

He crossed his arms over his chest, a thoughtful look on his face. "I'm sorry. I guess I'm a little confused. Tell me, what do you have against my sister? Because I'm pretty sure she's probably wondering why I ran off on her. Especially after she was kind enough to bring me dinner. Since John had to come into the city for meetings, they're taking in a show. He's picking her up in about twenty minutes."

He shook his head, "It's a shame. Because I think if you met her, the two of you would hit it off."

He watched as it took Carrie a few seconds to let this sink in.

She groaned, closing her eyes.

"Oh, no ..."

Then her lashes flew open, an expression of such hope on her face, he moved closer.

"So?" Even though the temptation to pull her into his arms was almost too much to resist, he waited.

Her voice came out in a whisper. "I thought ... I guess I thought it was someone else." When he raised an eyebrow, his look challenging, she briefly closed her eyes. "I thought it was Lauren. She ... your sister, when she said she was leaving for the show, well, I thought ... I'm so sorry. I'm so, so sorry."

He let out a long, drawn out sigh. "Trust, princess. It all comes down to trust. Haven't I told you this? So many times, I believe. You *need* to trust me."

Her bottom lip starting to quiver, she nodded. Now only inches away, he reached out to press his fingers to her lips, shaking his head. "Don't you dare cry. Because if you do, I might start crying right along with you."

She nodded again, sending a couple of those forbidden tears slipping down her cheeks. He gathered her in his arms, his voice rough with emotion. "*Ah ...* now look what you've done. This means in order to save face, I have to kiss you."

And he did. He kissed her thoroughly, hanging on to the kiss for as long as he could. Long enough to make him feel he was whole again. Finally dragging his mouth from hers, he gazed into her eyes. "I hope to god this is the last time I ever have to chase you down the sidewalks of Manhattan."

A big sigh coming from him, he shook his head. "But something tells me it probably won't be."

He rested his forehead against hers. "I'm think its time I take some drastic measures to keep this from happening again." Pulling her closer, he pressed a kiss in her hair. "*God, Carrie ...* I can't even begin to tell you how glad I am, you're here. I've been going crazy, thinking I might have lost you for good this time."

He gave her another kiss, this time to her mouth. Now that he had her in his arms, he wanted to keep kissing her. And kissing her ...

Forever ...

She buried her face in his shoulder before she lifted her head to search his face. "I know, I know. I'm sorry, I'm so, so sorry. I need to explain ... to tell you ... "

He pressed another kiss to her mouth. "Later ... you can tell me later. Right now, the only thing I want, is for you to look into my eyes and tell me how much you love me."

She did better than this.

Not only did she say what he wanted to hear, over and over, she gave him a kiss that left no doubt in his mind she meant every single one of those words.

He grabbed the handle of her suitcase and moved to take her arm, but she stopped him. She was grinning.

He grinned right back at her. "What?"

She gave a pointed look down at his feet, He glanced down to see he was wearing two different shoes. He burst out laughing. "See, how crazy in love I am with you? I can't even dress myself anymore."

His arm around her, they began their walk back to his apartment.

"Come on, I want you to meet Emily. It also might interest you to know you've already received a glowing review from Connor. In Emily and John's eyes, this is a very good start."

He smiled down at her. "Evidently, you've worked your magic on him, too."

They both watched Emily run down the sidewalk to where John was waiting in his car. After Chris closed the door, he took Carrie's hand. "Come on, we need to talk."

As he started up the steps, she pulled him back. When he saw the anxious expression on her face, he moved to take her into his arms.

He smiled as he gazed down at her. "Don't look so worried, princess. I only want to talk about what happened. If it was because of me or something I did. Whatever it was, this way we can make sure it doesn't happen again."

Her face burrowed in his chest, everything about him so achingly familiar, Lauren's threats now seemed so unimportant, almost bordering on ridiculous. She was feeling foolish to have even believed her.

How could she have believed this wonderful man she'd fallen so deeply in love with, was the person Lauren claimed him to be?

And now, the need to be with him suddenly felt as necessary as her next breath. She didn't want to talk. She wanted to show him how much she'd missed him, how much she loved him. If only to make amends for what she had done.

Her heart pounding hard in her chest, she pressed a trail of kisses along his jaw, to end at his mouth. "Not now. I want you to love me instead. Please? Then we can talk."

He made one last feeble attempt to convince her of what they really needed to be doing, what they should be talking about. But with her touch and with the way she was gazing up at him, desire shimmering in her eyes, he completely forgot what he intended to say.

When she reached up to press her fingers against his mouth, shaking her head, his resolve completely shattered. He groaned her name, his mouth coming down on hers in a mind-boggling kiss.

Let's face it, he needed her. Just as much as she needed him. He wanted to love her. To get lost in her. For this would be the only way he'd be able to erase these past few days forever out of his mind.

He grabbed her hand and they all but ran down the hall to his bedroom, Their fingers working at each other's clothing, leaving it scattered behind them as they made their way to the bed.

They came together in a frenzy of passion unlike they'd shared up until now, their desire for each other the only thing that mattered. He gave and he took. And she responded in the same, matching him, kiss for kiss.

His hands slowing, his mouth hovered over hers. "Open your eyes, baby."

Her lashes fluttered open and their eyes locked, the look in his, raw with emotion. "Tell me you're mine. That you'll always be mine."

"I'm yours … always."

Trust … it's a beautiful thing.

They were in the kitchen, eating the leftovers from the take-out food Emily had brought earlier. With the trauma of the past few days now in the past, suddenly, they were both starving.

Chris reached over to tuck a strand of Carrie's hair behind her ear. His fingertips going on to trace her jaw, he leaned in to give her another kiss. He couldn't seem to stop touching her, kissing her. She filled his senses, her smile alone enough to make him want to promise her everything.

After he finished what remained of his wine, he glanced over to see she was studying him, a hint of a smile on her lips.

He linked his fingers with hers. "What are you thinking about, beautiful?"

"How much I love you." She slowly shook her head, a sadness filling her face. "How I didn't trust you enough to believe you."

He brought her hand to his mouth, his lips brushing over her fingers. He shook his head. "All I care about right now is that you're here."

He hesitated. "Though I'd really like to know what happened."

When she opened her mouth to answer, only to close it again, he brushed his fingers down her cheek in a caress. "We need to talk about it, Carrie. I promise it won't change anything we have now."

She didn't answer. Instead, she began clearing the dishes and containers off of the counter. She was suddenly reluctant to tell him about Lauren's call. If anything, she was starting to feel sorry for her. Her threats seemed like such a desperate act, with no real win to be gained in the end.

They silently went about cleaning up the kitchen before he reached for her hand. "Come back to bed with me. I need to hold you, if only to know you're mine."

It was when she in his arms, his heart beating so close to hers, she finally told him about the phone call from Lauren and what she'd threatened.

When she finished, he was silent.

This was because, honestly? He didn't know what to say. Or even what to think. That Lauren would go after Carrie like this, and for a second time? It just didn't seem real. It was like something you'd expect to see in a movie. Or on the news, happening to someone else.

She shifted until she could see his face, her voice soft, almost apologetic. "It was Sam who convinced me I should show up early and surprise you. He told me I needed to tell you what Lauren did."

He closed his eyes at the mention of Sam, bringing her to sigh. "Oh, Chris … Sam is my friend. There's nothing between us and there never has been." Her eyes held his. "You are the only man I'll ever love."

He pressed a kiss to her forehead before he slowly nodded. "*Ah, yes* … Sam. When I saw him, I think I went a little crazy. But at the time, I wasn't thinking straight. I couldn't believe I was finally standing in front of you and you wouldn't talk to me. I couldn't even get you to look at me. So, I was looking for someone to blame and unfortunately, he turned out to be the one."

He shook his head.

She sighed. "I gave you every reason to think the way you did. But at the time I had let myself believe Lauren was right. I didn't fit into your kind of life. So, I needed to convince you the same. But it was so hard when you came to my office, I…" Her voice becoming choked, she closed her eyes.

He pulled her closer, pressing a kiss to the top of her head. "Princess, you *are* my life. My job and everything that goes with it, would mean nothing if I didn't have you."

He suddenly grinned. "So, this means you really do idolize me. And in your eyes, I more than deserve to be up on that pedestal Lauren was talking about"

She groaned. "*Oh, no* … you're never going to let me forget that, are you? But that's okay. If I do have to do those two things, I will."

She grinned. "You're lucky I love you so much."

He smiled, "I love you, too."

After a short silence, he ran his hand through his hair, exhaling a long breath. "But now we need to decide what to do about Lauren. I don't even know where to start. I seriously doubt she'll carry through on her threats, but it's your call, baby. What do you think?"

She shook her head. "Unless she does something to hurt you, I don't think we should do anything." She hesitated. "I almost feel sorry for her. God knows, if I were her, I'd fight for you, too."

He moved to face her. He was smiling. "You would, would you? Tell me, how would you go about this?"

She pressed a kiss to his jaw. "Well, I'd start out by kissing you until the only thing you'd be able to think about would be me."

"*Hmm* … really? That's way too easy, since I think about you all of the time as it is. But these kisses … would they start out like this?" He began pressing a trail of kisses up her neck and along her jaw before he stopped to smile down at her. "Or would it be more like this?"

The kiss he gave her was exactly, if not better than, what she'd meant.

So, since he was so good at it, she let him take over.

CHAPTER 32

Carrie set her phone down on her desk.

Her chin propped on her hand, she gazed dreamily out her office window.

It was the last day of November. The sky was a brilliant blue and even though it was cold, the sun made it seem much warmer than it was.

She couldn't even tell you how many times she'd talked to Chris since she had returned from New York two days ago. She only knew it was a lot. And each and every time she heard the sound of his voice, it still wasn't enough. She wanted more.

She wanted to be able to see him.

She wanted to be with him.

The long Thanksgiving weekend they spent together had passed in a whirlwind of activity. Except for Wednesday. This was the one day they never left his apartment, spending a leisurely and quiet day together. They had watched old movies on the TV in Chris's bedroom and ordered take-out for dinner.

And, yes … Carrie had noticed the painting, Early Evening in Spring, was hanging over the fireplace where the big screen TV used to be. The same painting she had hoped to buy for him.

She liked to think he'd purchased the painting because of what she'd said, but didn't ask. That he purchased it at all, was enough.

Chris had been able to secure the keys to an apartment on the route of the Macy's annual Thanksgiving Day parade. Belonging to a friend who'd gone out of town for the long holiday weekend, this sixth-floor apartment was the perfect spot to view the parade. Emily, John and Connor had joined them and after the festivities were over, they had all gone back to their house for dinner.

On Friday, brunch had been followed by a day of sight-seeing and Christmas shopping. That evening they'd stayed in, enjoying the left-overs Emily had sent home with them from the Thanksgiving dinner she'd prepared.

On Saturday, after a morning and afternoon of more shopping and sight-seeing, Chris had made reservations for both dinner and a show. He had surprised her at dinner with a gorgeous necklace, a beautiful amethyst pendant hanging from a delicate sterling silver chain. He told her he knew it wasn't her birthstone, but he had to buy it because the color of the amethyst reminded him of her eyes.

He had also given her a huge bouquet of flowers, made up of every variety and color of flower you could imagine. And after the show, he'd arranged for a horse drawn carriage ride, even going as far to convince the driver he should take them back to his apartment.

After a leisurely brunch on Sunday, they'd spent a lazy afternoon together before she had to leave. And even though she told him it wasn't necessary, he insisted on going with her to the airport. This turned out to be a good thing, since her flight was delayed and they were able to spend a few more hours together.

And now?

She was back home in Cleveland, alone.

And she missed Chris … she couldn't believe how much, she missed him.

She gazed around her office. This was silly. She certainly wasn't getting any work done. Surely there was something she could do on such a beautiful day… something productive.

She knew the perfect thing. She had finally chosen the color for her front door. Cardinal Red. And today would be the perfect day to paint.

After all, this was Cleveland, always unpredictable when it came to the weather. Tomorrow it could very well be snowing and painting the door would have to wait until spring.

Since she was already planning to hang a fresh evergreen wreath on the door, wouldn't it look a lot better if the door was a bright Cardinal Red?

Filled with a sudden sense of purpose, she decided to call it a day. She turned off her computer, put on her coat and closed the door to her office behind her.

Marion looked up from her typing to smile at her. "You're leaving?"

"Yes, and I want you to take the rest of the afternoon off, too. It's too beautiful of a day to be working. Whatever needs to be done can wait until tomorrow."

Marion's smile got even bigger as she quickly began clearing her desk. "Oh, Carrie, I'd love that. If I leave right now, I'll be just in time to pick up the kids from school. They'll be so excited. Do you have something special planned?"

Carrie turned to give her a smile. "I'm going to go home and paint my front door a cheerful shade of Cardinal Red. Enjoy your time with the kids. I'll see you tomorrow morning."

When Carrie pulled into her driveway, there was a car parked there.

A very familiar car. A car with New York license plates.

There was also someone on her front porch. And from what she could see, they were just about finished painting her front door.

It was a shade of red that looked suspiciously like Cardinal Red.

And, yes. This person also looked familiar.

Very, *very* familiar.

Her stomach immediately starting to do somersaults, she got out of her car. A smile on her face, one she couldn't have erased even if she tried, she swiftly made her way to the front porch.

Without even turning around, Chris dipped his paintbrush into the paint can and brushed one last stroke over the door. It was only after he stepped back to admire his handiwork, he spoke.

"Hmm … should you be here? Didn't you tell me, about a half hour ago, you have so much work to do?"

She was still smiling. In fact, she was now smiling so hard, she was almost on the verge of tears. She had to swallow before she could speak. "I did. But then I decided it was too nice of a day to stay cooped up inside of my office. My plan was to come home and paint my front door before the weather turned cold for good."

A look of comprehension came over her face. "You were already here when we were on the phone, weren't you?"

He turned to set the paintbrush next to the paint can. After he put the lid back on the can and wiped his hands on a rag, he looked over at her.

He nodded. "Yes, I was. I found the last couple of days didn't feel right. You here, and me in New York? It just wasn't working. Not when this is where I want to be. With you."

The tenderness in the look he sent her held her captive. Still at the bottom of the steps, she gazed up at him, her heart in her eyes.

Her voice came out all shaky. "I love you. I love you so much."

"I love you, too." And there it was, that crooked smile of his, coming right at her. A huskiness in his voice, he held out his hand. "Come here …"

She did. To go right into his arms for his kiss.

She rested her head on his shoulder, giving a soft sigh. "Thank you for painting the door. It's perfect." She pulled away from him. "When did you get here?"

He pulled her back. He couldn't believe how good it felt to hold her against him. When he'd made the decision yesterday to make the drive here, if only to tell her what he was planning, he'd wondered if he was doing the right thing. But now, with her in his arms, he knew he was.

It was exactly right.

She grounded him, made him feel all was right in his world.

In *their* world.

He smiled down at her. "I've actually been here since right before noon. I had made plans to meet Sam for lunch."

She scrunched up her face, puzzled. "Sam? You went to lunch with Sam?"

He chuckled. "Yes, princess … Sam. I wanted to talk to him, get an idea of how things operate here. And if he might be interested in a partnership of some kind. I'd do the buying and selling, he'd oversee the renovating."

Here he stopped to grin at her. "Maybe even get you in on it, using your design skills. With the three of us working together, we could take the world by a storm." He chuckled again. "Well, at least this part of the world."

Carrie was having a hard time trying to understand exactly what he was telling her. She gazed up at him, searching his face. "But how …?"

He took pity on her and framing her face in his hands, he told her what he knew she was so afraid to ask. "Carrie, I quit my job. I don't want to live that kind of life anymore. And I found someone to rent my apartment. Right now, I guess you might say I'm both homeless and jobless."

When he saw the telltale trembling of her bottom lip, he pressed a soft kiss to her mouth. He was smiling. "So, I was wondering … do you happen to know of a place I can stay? I'd be willing to do any odd jobs. Maybe even cook. And I'm …"

With a shaky cry, she threw her arms around his neck. "Please, *please* tell me you mean this. Because I so want to believe this is really going to happen."

His mouth curved into a smile. *"Hmm* … here we go again with the trust issue. Let me think, what do I have to do, to make you realize how serious I am about this?" He tilted his head to study her. Then he abruptly released his hold on her and stepped away.

"I'll tell you what, let's put all of this paint stuff back in the garage and then we'll go inside and talk about it."

As he turned to gather up the painting supplies, he spoke over his shoulder. "Oh … and I stopped in to see your brother. And Sophie and the little guys, too. They're all doing fine. I told them we'd come over soon to give them a break. I hope this is okay with you?"

She nodded. She was totally confused now. He went to see Chester, too?

First Sam and then Chester?

Nothing was making sense. But with him now down the steps and headed for the garage, she could only tag along with him.

She listened as he told her how easy it had been for him to get into her garage. This concerned him, he said. It made him think they needed to remedy this soon. Put a better lock on the door or something.

He then went on to tell her his drive to Cleveland had been pretty uneventful since he had left so early in the morning. And even though he'd been able to fit quite a few of his things in his car, he still needed to go back to pack up the rest. Maybe she could go with him?

Still trying to take in what he'd said about Sam, his job and his apartment, she realized he was looking at her, waiting for a response. She nodded, not even all that sure what she was nodding about. But honestly? With all of this new information running around in her mind, she couldn't seem to think at all.

It was when they were finally in the house and their coats were hung on the hook in the kitchen, Chris watched Jingles jump off the sofa to greet Carrie. It hadn't escaped his notice the cat had been curled up in, of all things, the sweater he'd left behind. His favorite sweater, if you remember.

He shook his head at this, casually leaning against the island counter. "So … do you notice anything different?"

She had. About a second before he'd asked.

The painting, Early Evening in Spring, was now hanging above her fireplace. When she turned to him, he shrugged. "I had a feeling it would look better here than over my fireplace, or should I say my new tenant's fireplace. What do you think? Do you like it?"

She nodded. She needed to stop doing this... this nodding. But now she was afraid if she were even to open her mouth, she'd start to cry.

He was slowly making his way over to her, still talking. One might say it was almost as though he was nervous.

This was because … in a way, he was.

He cleared his throat. "Yeah, it's been sort of a busy last few days for me. Turning my accounts over to the guy who's taking my place, writing up the contract for the rental of my apartment, my meeting with Sam and making sure I had Chester's approval."

"Not that it would have stopped me if Chester hadn't given his blessing." He was studying her very closely. She could see a smile tugging at the corner of his mouth.

Her hands slowly going to her mouth, Carrie became perfectly still. She watched, mesmerized, as he moved even closer.

Slowly shaking his head, he chuckled. "He did agree with me, the pact you and I made didn't make much sense. Three years seems too long of a time to wait when you know what you want."

A thoughtful look came over his face, the smile still lurking at the corner of his mouth. "Well, I guess it would be down to just a little over two years now, wouldn't it?"

Carrie still hadn't moved.

He tilted his head, the smile still lingering there. "Aren't you at all interested to know what else Chester and I talked about?"

She had closed her eyes. She was shaking, her voice coming out in a whisper. "Chris, please …"

"You'll need to open your eyes, princess."

She did as he asked, to find him down on one knee in front of her. In his hand, was a small jewelers box holding a ring.

An engagement ring. And for Carrie, it was the most beautiful ring she had ever seen.

He didn't even have the chance to say the carefully thought out and planned words he'd practiced while in front of his bathroom mirror. Sinking down on her knees, she threw her arms around him.

She was crying. She was laughing. Then she was crying again. All of this was happening while she kept pressing kisses to his face between saying *yes, yes, yes...*

Over and over and over she kept doing this.

It was when he was finally able to put the ring on her shaking finger, she gazed up at him. Her voice was trembling. "Say it again … *Please* … Say the words, so I can know they're for real."

He ran his fingertips in a soft caress down her cheek. "*Ah, Carrie* … it looks like I have my work cut out for me, convincing you what we have is meant to last a lifetime." He smiled. "But this is okay, because I'm sure I'll be able to come up with plenty of ways to show you how real this all is."

She was still gazing up at him, waiting. And as every time before, he became lost in her eyes. It was only after he took a deep breath, he was finally able to say the words she wanted to hear.

"So … Carrie Mazzori, will you marry me?"

And again, she said yes.

CHAPTER 33

Big, fluffy snowflakes were beginning to drift down from the sky as Chris put the last box in his car.

After he slammed the trunk shut, he gazed up at the swirling flakes. "It looks like we finished loading everything just in time."

He glanced over at Carrie, who was watching him, a concerned look on her face. "Are you okay?"

He came over to wrap his arms around her, pressing a kiss to the top of her head.

"Princess, I've never been better. I enjoyed living here and all the perks that came with it, but now I have something I love so much more. And, this is you."

He smiled down at her. "I think of this as the start of a whole new life. *Our* real life. The life I was meant to be living all along."

She lifted her face for a kiss. "I promise you'll never regret it." Her eyes lighting up, she grinned. "Maybe I'll even learn to cook. I'll get my Aunt Evelyn to teach me."

He threw his head back, a big laugh coming from him. "Wow, I know this is a big commitment. But do you know what? I won't hold it against you if you don't."

A thoughtful look came over his face. "*Hmm* ... but if you could learn how to make clam chowder like she does, it might bring you up a notch in my eyes."

Now it was her turn to laugh. "It's a deal."

He gave her another kiss before he opened the door of the passenger side of the car. "Come on, jump in so we can be on our way. I promised Emily we'd get there for dinner as early as we could."

He closed her door and came around to slip into the driver's sea. He was still talking. "The way she's acting, you'd think we're never going to see each other again. It's not like we're going to be living somewhere in the middle of nowhere and miles away. If anything, it looks like we'll be coming here quite often on business."

He grinned. "Sam's been showing me all of these properties he's been eyeing and they all happen to be located somewhere in New York. Some of them look quite promising."

He shook his head. "I have to admit, when it comes to enthusiasm, he's on it, one hundred percent."

Carrie was thinking about what he said about Sam. Especially about his sudden preoccupation with New York. "*Hmm* ... I wonder if Sam's interest in these properties has anything to do with Livy?"

A sudden eagerness lit up her face. "Oh my gosh, I bet it does. Do you think this might be a way to get him and Livy together?"

He looked over at her, shaking his head. "Carrie ..."

She shook her head right back at him. "I'm sorry, but if you had seen the two of them together, you'd agree with me. It really was like fireworks. The good and the bad. This leads me to believe they're *very* attracted to each other."

Her expression changed, a dreamy smile touching her lips. "Though it was nothing like how it was with us. I still get that amazing *wow* feeling when I think back to the first time I saw you."

She was giving him that look, the love shining in her eyes sending him to a place that made him forget everything but her.

He reached over to cup her cheek in his hand.

"Princess, when you look at me like you are right now, I'll go along with anything you want."

He brushed his mouth over hers.

"Anything … even playing matchmaker, if need be."

And then he kissed her, a slow, sweet kiss.

After all, there was really no rush.

O ne of the first things Carrie did when they got back to Cleveland, was to ask her Aunt Evelyn for her clam chowder recipe. She found out it wasn't all that hard to make.

And Chris? He loved it. But even more so, because Carrie made it for him.

So, here is the recipe.

Aunt Evelyn's Clam Chowder:

Ingredients:

- 6 slices bacon, chopped
- 3 cans (6.25 oz each) minced clams
- 1 cup finely chopped onion
- 1 cup thinly sliced celery
- 2 cups cubed potatoes
- 1 cup shredded carrots
- 1 cup chicken or vegetable stock
- 3/4 cup butter
- 3/4 cup flour
- 1-quart half and half
- 2 tablespoons red wine vinegar
- 1-1/2 teaspoons salt
- Fresh ground pepper, to taste
- Chopped parsley and croutons for garnish, if desired

Preparation:

- In a large skillet, sauté bacon until just crisp; remove bacon with a slotted spoon and set aside
- Drain juice from clams into large skillet used to cook bacon. Set clams aside.
- Add onions, celery, potatoes, carrots and chicken or vegetable stock to skillet with clam juice.

- Cover and cook over medium heat until vegetables are tender.
- Meanwhile, in a large, heavy-duty saucepan, melt butter over medium heat. Whisk in flour until smooth.
- Whisk in half and half, stirring constantly until mixture is smooth and starts to thicken.
- Stir in bacon and vegetable mixture from the skillet. Heat through, but do not bring to a boil.
- Stir in clams just before serving, cooking only until clams are heated (they will toughen if cooked too long)
- Stir in red wine vinegar, add salt and pepper to taste.
- Serve, garnished with parsley and croutons, if desired.

6 -8 servings

ABOUT THE AUTHOR

L. B. Joyce lives in Chagrin Falls, Ohio. A freelance artist by day, with designing Christmas ornaments her specialty, she's also a writer by night. She loves getting lost in a good book, has redecorated almost every room in her house more times than she'd like to admit, loves baking up a storm in her kitchen, hates housework with a passion and will drive just about anywhere because of her fear of flying.

To keep up with the news about the the first 8 books of the series, Twelve Months, Twelve Love Stories - *A Million Decembers, For the Love of July, February's Angel, Promise Me November, An Unexpected June, A January to Remember, September's Moonlight Serenade, and Goodbye Heartbreak, Hello May* - along with the new series, Holidays in White Oaks Valley - *A Grand Slam Kind of Christmas* - check out the website/blog at: lbjoyceauthor.com

Or Facebook: https://www.facebook.com/AuthorLBJoyce

Or send an email: lbjoyce12@gmail.com

And, if you have a chance, check out the latest L. B. Bear Christmas Ornament designs and just about everything you ever wanted to know about Christmas at: www.facebook.com/LBGlitterGirl

This novel's song inspiration ~
The Lady in Red by Chris de Burgh

Cover by Soxsational Cover Art